CRUCIBLE OF TRUTH

CRUCIBLE OF TRUTH

OPUS X™ BOOK TWELVE

MICHAEL ANDERLE

DISRUPTIVE IMAGINATION

LMBPN Publishing
PMB 196, 2540 South Maryland Pkwy
Las Vegas, NV 89109

First US edition, February 2021
eBook ISBN: 978-1-64971-095-6
Print ISBN: 978-1-64971-096-3

THE CRUCIBLE OF TRUTH TEAM

Thanks to the JIT Readers

Dave Hicks
John Ashmore
Kelly O'Donnell
Dorothy Lloyd
Jeff Goode
Peter Manis
Deb Mader
Larry Omans
James Caplan
Jeff Eaton

If I've missed anyone, please let me know!

Editor
Lynne Stiegler

This book is dedicated in memoriam to Tammy Faxel. In a tough year where so many of us lost people we care about, we at LMBPN® Publishing lost a friend to the company. Tammy Faxel believed in Opus X when it was merely an idea in Michael's mind. Sight unseen she signed up to publish all 12 books in the series in audio format through Dreamscape Media. We will be eternally grateful for Tammy's belief in us and for supporting our efforts to deliver this great series to our listeners.

— Michael

CHAPTER ONE

May 10, 2231, Wolf 359, Remus, New Rome

Yan ducked into the alley, guns cracking loudly. Bullets ripped into the corner of the commercial storage facility right behind him.

At least, that was what it was, according to the sign he'd noticed while sprinting down the narrow space between the two buildings.

The narrow alley was wide enough for a couple of men, but there was no way his pursuers could get their hovertruck through. The decisions he made in the coming moments might help determine the fate of the UTC.

He wouldn't die there. No, it wasn't that he wouldn't, he thought. He *couldn't* die there.

Fear for his life didn't enter into his concern, only fear of failing his Immortal Empress.

He would not lose his life under the false holographic blue sky of a colonial dome before finishing the tasks appointed him.

He was an elite, a top agent, and one the empress had personally selected for this role.

A role he cherished and a role he would complete. Dying or being captured by the government was not acceptable.

They weren't alike. He was better, stronger, and faster. Yan carried the blessings of his empress, and he'd show the government dogs what that *meant*.

He leapt at a wall and pushed off on contact toward the opposite wall, then repeated the movement. Barely a challenge.

The empress' scientists and doctors had done their work well, granting him abilities far beyond those of humans at only the cost of his lifespan. There was a beautiful symmetry in the contrast between his fleeting life and her eternal life, she who would advance the human race beyond the petty limitations of his forebears. Eventually, a historian would document his sacrifice for his people, and at that time would the value of his efforts be known.

Yan had given up any expectations for recognition during this lifetime.

The men chasing him were custodians of stasis and weakness. They protected a corrupt order riddled with political cancer. Fools, all of them, serving false ideals.

A gray hovertruck whirred to a stop at the front of the alley. Yan was already halfway toward the roof. Mere misfortune allowed the Intelligence Directorate agents to detect him.

Detect, not defeat.

The agents called themselves ghosts and took advantage of the fear of the masses to enhance their reputation and resulting effectiveness to extract information. Their advanced technology and the resources of the government convinced some they did have supernatural powers like their namesakes.

He grunted as he pushed off the wall once more. Ghosts in name only.

They were men and women, nothing more.

He would go so far as to add they were cowards who lacked commitment to the cause. That was why they would fail.

There was no pity in his heart for government dogs.

An ID agent jumped out of the car, a pistol in hand. He swept it back and forth before lifting his head and shouting a curse, but it was too late. He got off one shot before Yan was out of range.

"You had your chance," he murmured. A few small pieces of a badly attached pipe dropped as he continued up the walls and landed on the flat roof of the storage building.

Drones aimlessly circled in the air, relying on their preprogrammed flight paths. Yan didn't try to avoid them. His jamming made them useless. All he needed to do was keep moving.

The ghosts' movements made it obvious they'd never had direct camera or drone line-of-sight on him. Which, he had to admit, puzzled him. Given their clumsiness, *how had they spotted him?*

Yan smiled thinly as he charged to the opposite edge of the roof. His leap cleared the distance easily. He headed for the next roof, his anxiety lessening. Yan would not fail his empress, but that changed nothing.

He couldn't risk contacting the *Beidou* until he finished cleaning up his mess.

It wouldn't take long.

Yan stood in the darkened apartment near the door, his fingers tight around the handle of a knife. The late arrival of his would-be assassins surprised him. He'd assumed the ghosts would retreat immediately to their safehouse.

When they'd spotted him, he wasn't anywhere near it, and there was no reason to assume he'd compromised the location. Instead, they'd spent far too long trying to track him in the city. He waited with a small glint of amusement at the idea they would die in the one place they believed secure.

Standing in the darkness of the quiet apartment, the only sound the mild hum of the environmental control system, transformed Yan's assassination preparation into a near-meditative experience.

The apartment lay inside a tall building and was located near the center. That insulated it from the noise of street-level traffic or the occasional flitters allowed above buildings in the tight airspace of the domed colonial city.

The location annoyed him.

The arrogant ghosts had picked a poor location. He could understand their choice, but it was flawed.

The large strike team would have to travel through

more than one hall to arrive, and the lack of windows to the outside combined with apartments beyond provided a natural sniper defense. Those advantages were canceled by the lack of an easy escape route.

Yan's frustration with the quality of his targets built.

The ID had always been a minor consideration in the plans of the Core. While the government agency's efforts against other members of the Core had facilitated the acceleration of the empress' plans, the current fevered timetable had never been her intent.

At least, not when he joined.

Harassment of the other Core members was one thing, but the damage to her operations was unforgivable. In the last few years, the ID had changed from a manageable threat to a potentially lethal one.

Yan's teeth ached as he subconsciously ground his annoyance between them. The Last Soldier and the Warrior Princess were the problems. A small number of highly skilled people could execute missions with far greater success and influence than their organization could account for.

Morale. Momentum. Mayhem. He understood those tactics all too well. They were the ID's reflection of Yan, Tralian, and Celeste.

Empress Julia had alternately attacked the pair and used them for her own ends. He wouldn't dare question her vision, but it was obvious Blackwell and Lin had become catalysts for the efforts against her. All efforts should have been expended to crush them before they'd gained the protection of the ID.

The apartment door slid open, and a man stomped in with a frown. He was one of the ghosts who'd been chasing Yan. The idiot didn't bother to sweep the apartment. He all but begged for death.

"What's up with the lights?" the ghost asked. He tapped his PNIU.

Yan sprang away from the wall and planted his knife in the agent's throat before the man could turn his head. After Yan pulled the man's gun out of his shoulder holster, a quick shove sent the wounded agent gurgling into the hallway, his hand to his throat.

The ghost's partner jumped back and reached for his gun but hesitated since his partner was in the line of fire. That brief indecision cost him his life. Yan shot him twice in the head before shoving the gun against the knifed agent's forehead and pulling the trigger.

A short silence extended as two bodies thudded to the floor.

No screams. No alarms. Useful to know.

He hadn't been sure *what* would happen but hoped the ghosts had taken measures to ensure they could kill someone near their place without it bringing in the police for an investigation.

Yan tossed the gun to the floor.

"So disappointed." He sighed.

He didn't fear the ID would ever know who killed their agents. They wouldn't be able to trace anything to him, other than whatever brief pictures the agents had sent in during the chase.

Those didn't matter. As far as the UTC's databases were concerned, Yan didn't exist.

He bent down, yanked the knife out of the agent's throat, and wiped it off on the dead man's shirt before checking his own jacket. A couple of spots might be noticeable, but he'd done well, considering the close-range kill.

He secured the blade in a hidden leg sheath, then jogged down the hallway.

Now he was satisfied with his outing's success. The ID might suspect something was happening in New Rome or on Remus, but the death of two of their agents would set back any investigation.

They could obsess over it all they wanted. If anything, that would be more useful to Empress Julia's plans.

This city and world were unimportant as anything more than a distraction.

Yan emerged from the building through a side exit, and a parking lot filled with hovertrucks and miniflitters greeted him. Instinct and recent experience led him to immediately sweep the area, and that saved his life. Suited men stood on both sides of the building, aiming their guns in his direction. They opened fire.

Yan rolled forward and took cover behind a hovertruck. A bullet nailed him in the back, but the fiery pain dulled after a couple of seconds with the help of a nerve override. The enemies continued shredding nearby vehicles with their uncoordinated fire.

Something was off; the ambush was too sloppy. If the ID had known he was in the apartment, they wouldn't have sacrificed two agents and waited until he was back outside, which gave him more places to hide. The bold open attack risked drawing attention, even if they'd done something to keep the local police away.

Yan kept low as he made his way to another vehicle for cover.

"Did we get him?" one of the men called.

"Close in and make sure," another man shouted in response. "Be careful. This guy probably already iced a couple of ghosts."

Heavy footsteps sounded from both sides. The entire group was closing in on him. Yan drew his gun, shame surfacing.

I am reduced to using a tool such as this.

He stowed his feelings. The coming weeks would mean sacrifices for his empress. His strength was her gift to him, but he could never lose sight of the reason for it. The best honor was success.

As Yan had lived for the Immortal Empress, he would die for her, and he would kill for her again and again until he breathed his last.

Even without using drones or bots to verify his death, there were many ways they could have finished him off without risking themselves. They obviously didn't care about making noise, so there was no reason not to use explosives.

He waited and listened, his breathing shallow, the bullet wound in his back now a minor ache. The footsteps grew closer and closer—more amateurish techniques. They could have gotten a man close enough for visual inspection without giving up the positions of everyone in their group.

Yan popped up from behind a truck and opened fire. Despite the pain being under control, his movements were stiff.

That wound might cost him.

He fired three quick shots, none wasted. His targets all fell backward, new holes in their faces.

"Shit!" one of the men on the other side shouted.

They opened fire again, but it was too late. Yan dashed forward, darting back and forth as he took three more shots. Headshots killed two of the men instantly. The third fell to one knee, still alive despite the painful graze on the side of his head.

The man stumbled away, grimacing in pain, with blood blinding one eye. Two more rounds into his head finished the job. Six men now lay in pools of their own blood in the parking lot, dead or close to death.

They'd gotten one good hit on him.

Yan stayed low, listening and checking the nearby roofs for suspicious glints that might suggest a sniper. After twenty seconds of no follow-up, he nodded in satisfaction and stood. He pulled out a med patch and applied it to his wound.

No matter the advances, applying a patch to the back was never simple. Shame the bullet didn't penetrate his side; much easier to reach.

He walked over to the corpses and pulled off their PNIUs. There was no way these men were ID agents, but the empress' operations couldn't continue on the planet without identifying all enemies.

Jamming would keep the devices from being traced until he got what he needed from them. For the moment, he needed to figure out the men's identities.

Yan bowed his head. Empress Julia lazed in a high-backed chair, wearing a loose blue dress, and she had a faint look of boredom on her face. He'd already told her he wouldn't report to her until he had the full details of what had occurred.

"Speak," she ordered.

Yan lifted his head. "My Empress, the second set of assassins were syndicate-affiliated."

She raised a delicate dark eyebrow. "Syndicate? How far operational security must have fallen if common thugs were able to ambush one of my top agents."

Yan didn't avert his eyes despite the shame flowing through him. She was right to highlight his failure. Killing them all after being ambushed was barely a victory. He should have never been wounded.

"What local syndicate trash was after you and why?" Julia asked. "If they were seeking your life, that means they're seeking mine. No one can be permitted to attempt that."

"Their attempt was not made at the behest of a syndicate," Yan explained.

"That's odd." Julia frowned for a moment, thinking it through. "Are you saying the ID hired syndicate killers?"

"No, my Empress." Yan shook his head. "They work as syndicate assassins, but from what we know, they are allowed the freedom to take private assignments, provided they give a fee to their superiors."

"I see. And who hired them?"

"That's difficult to know for certain," Yan replied. "We did find one reference to 'Old Man Barbu' and a rough description of him, but no images. Judging from some of the location data, they were watching the apartment building even before our arrival in the city."

"They used the ghosts as bait to kill you?" Julia laughed. "How deliciously entertaining." Her smile faded. "Old Man Barbu. Marius Barbu. That name keeps returning to haunt me. How does that piece of underworld trash know so much about me? About the Core?"

"My Empress." Yan bowed his head. "This Barbu might have served one of the others in the Core. That's the most likely explanation."

"Maybe." Julia looked thoughtful. "But we have evidence that he was helping the ID fight the Core as well. I have suspicions about the Chang'e incident, among others. His name has surfaced too many times."

"I'll find him, and then I will kill him," Yan spoke as if Barbu were a fly he needed to corner.

Julia waved a hand dismissively. "It's unfortunate he has greater knowledge than one like him should have, but it doesn't matter. Even if he is a leftover servant of Sophia's or one of the others, I'm the only one left alive. Knowing part of my plans or resources will be insufficient, especially with the current chaos." She sighed. "I would have liked to spend a couple more days in preparation, but the same could be said about this entire plan. We will move things forward. The outcome will not be adjusted because some underworld cockroach hires riffraff. Soon, he won't matter. None of them will."

"And the backup plan?" Yan asked.

Julia folded her hands. "Consider it less a backup plan

than the final part of the current plan. It's irrelevant at this point. Even if I sent a recall signal, they wouldn't get it before carrying out their orders." She stood, an excited gleam in her eyes. "No matter. Let the galaxy burn from both ends. Let the UTC become a phoenix, with me at the center of the fire."

CHAPTER TWO

May 10, 2231, Neo Southern California Metroplex, Private Hangar of the *Argo*

Erik hadn't been so excited since he was a kid getting gifts for Christmas and New Year's.

Much like those holidays, he could take extra joy in watching someone put together his gift for him.

Bright sparks dropped from the top of the *Argo,* spewing from a small construction drone's torch. The torch ran along the massive laser cannon now nestled on top.

Lanara sat on a crate beneath the ship, smart goggles covering her face, her hands jabbing invisible displays to control the drone. Another pair of drones moved along the stern of the ship, their manipulator arms jammed into a bundle of cables invisible from the ground. Their controllers, Wei and Janessa, were tucked inside the *Argo*.

Tactics and bravery counted for a lot in a fight. A good weapon often counted for more.

Jia stood beside Erik, eyeing the weapon. "It's funny."

Erik looked her way. "Laser cannons are funny? You've got a weird sense of humor. Not that I didn't already know that."

"It's not the laser cannon. It's what it represents." She gestured at the weapon. "We met as police officers. We didn't do a lot of undercover work, and we were bound by a lot of rules and regs."

"Okay." Erik nodded slowly. He was not sure where Jia was going with this, but that didn't dampen his feelings about the huge new toy the engineers were building. She'd not expressed any dislike of the new weapon, and that was all he cared about.

"We were straightforward on the force," Jia continued with a soft smile. "But sometimes we couldn't do what we needed to without jumping through too many hoops. That led to us risk our lives in situations that shouldn't ever have arisen."

"True enough." He eyed the weapon and looked at her again before jerking a thumb in the direction of the ship. "What does that have to do with the laser cannon being funny?"

"I'm getting there. The point is, after that, we became ID contractors." A wan smile took over Jia's face. "And though it often ended with something big and explosive, we had to spend a lot of time sneaking around, much more than we did as cops. We were supposed to have fewer restrictions, but it's annoying to have to chase people but hide who you are. Fake names, disguises."

"Nicer toys," Erik countered. "This ship, the advanced-model exos." He scratched his chin. "Much bigger explosions."

Jia chuckled. "Not everything is about the best toys all the time, but..." She stared long and hard at the cannon. "That weapon means something important. It means we're officially done being sneaky. It screams, 'We're here to kill you.'"

"Yeah, no way to hide that thing." Erik laughed. "And no reason to. The government's at war with the Core. I don't care if they've lost some of their guys from the civil war. I have a feeling the biggest fights haven't come yet."

"Right now, all we're doing is sitting around this hangar." Jia shrugged. "I wonder what we'll do after all this is over."

"Hmmmm. We could become pirate hunters." Erik grinned, imagining himself in a ridiculous wide naval hat that hadn't been popular for three centuries. "With the ability to jump around, we could wipe all of the pirates everywhere within a few weeks, especially with this baby."

Emma's lack of commentary didn't surprise Erik.

She'd made it clear she was using their recent downtime to work on the programming and modifications necessary for her child to come into being. Erik didn't know a lot about systems programming to begin with, let alone AI, but considering the entire government research apparatus couldn't copy her, the problem was obviously pretty damned hard to solve.

He couldn't blame her for wanting to step things up. No one knew what might happen with the government after the Core was officially destroyed.

"Take out a deep conspiracy and then take out all pirates?" Jia asked. Her too-serious look made Erik want to laugh about his half-joking suggestion.

Loud footsteps echoing from the *Argo*'s back ramp stopped Erik from clarifying. Anne stormed out of the ship with a deep scowl on her face. Erik and Jia exchanged looks and waited for the agent to close on them.

"What's wrong?" Jia asked softly.

"Paris is under martial law."

Erik shrugged. "So is Neo SoCal."

"There have been clashes." Anne clenched her teeth. "There was a rationing order because of disruptions to some shipments into the metroplex. The primary shipping companies in the area are barely operating because of arrests related to the Core and damage from raids. People started protesting, and some terrorists decided to take advantage of that." She threw up her hands. "It's chaos."

Erik nodded. "No big surprise. It's been happening elsewhere in the Solar System. Lots of trouble on Mars, but I've heard Venus and the moon are doing okay. Everyone wants to be trendy and join Neo SoCal."

"It's not the same thing. Yes, they declared martial law here, but other than the incident against the Prime Minister, it's been fairly orderly." Anne pinched the bridge of her nose. "Now it feels like things are spiraling out of control all over Earth."

"Seoul was having trouble yesterday, and New York." Jia sighed. "If it's not service and supply disruptions, it's antisocial behavior from people thinking the government is about to collapse. People are panicking and lashing out. They're scared, but once they understand it's not the end of the UTC, they'll calm down. It's not even been two weeks since the Prime Minister's speech."

Anne glared at the floor as if she could burn a hole

through it with sheer will. "We stopped the assassination attempt and a lot of their other terrorist plans, but it feels like they're winning. A lot more people are going to die by the time this is over."

"We expected *this*," Jia offered quietly. "The Core is intertwined with the UTC economy. Earth is going to feel it worse than a lot of places because half of humanity is here, with the accompanying demand for resources." She let out a bitter laugh. "Ironically, the frontier colonies might suffer the least in all of this."

Erik furrowed his brow, thinking that over. "Yes and no. They might not need a huge-ass megacorporation to ship them enough crap to keep ten billion people from losing it, but a lot of them don't have the industrial infrastructure for everything they need that breaks. Trouble's gonna continue to trickle in for a while, and it might continue even if we finish off the Core right away. There is a lot of critical dome equipment that's only manufactured on Earth or the older colonies."

Jia grimaced. "I liked it better when you were excited about your new toy."

A tiny shrug was what she received in return. "Humanity finally got what it was gearing up for."

Anne looked confused. "Humanity was gearing up for mass chaos?"

"Yes." Erik nodded. "Galactic war. It just turns out it's more a civil war than a war against the space raptors."

"This isn't a civil war," Anne snapped. "This is us smoking out a terrorist conspiracy that is hiding behind innocent people."

Erik sighed. "The quicker we finish off whatever's left

of the Core, the fewer people die. In the meantime, it's not going to be fun for a lot of people, but there's nothing we can do about it but wait for orders."

Anne glared back a moment, then two before softening her look. "I keep wondering if there's more we could have done before this happened."

Erik was surprised Anne was the one talking like that. She'd always come off as the ultimate professional, but that might have meant she believed she had more control over the situation.

Alina's death had struck her hard, probably the hardest among the four of them.

Anne had known the agent for a lot longer than most of the others on the team. Years of being a soldier had taught Erik how to handle loss. When he lost a friend in battle, he did what he always did: committed their face to memory and swore to himself it wouldn't be in vain. The pain was there but manageable.

"As long as we're not dead, we can move forward," Erik announced. "A lot of good men and women are going to have to deal with a lot of crap over the next few months. However, we are the ones with a jump drive. That means we can do more than most."

Jia nodded. "The Core, or whatever's left of it, thought they could cripple the UTC by assassinating the Prime Minister, but that failed. They aren't gods. They're just people who threw away their morality and restraint. We don't have to waste time trying to convince them. We just need to find them and take them out."

"You're both right." Anne took a deep breath and squared her shoulders, then blew out a lungful of frustration. "The war isn't over yet, and it won't be until we've destroyed every last person in the Core."

She spun on her heel and stomped back toward the *Argo*.

There was more confidence on her face, but Erik wasn't sure how long a woman that tightly wound could last without a mission. Kant had been quieter than usual and kept more to himself, but he was taking the social disruption in stride.

Jia watched Anne walk away with a concerned look. "We said all that, but it's easier said than done."

"Not really," Erik replied. "There has to be something else coming soon."

"How will we know what it is?"

Erik shrugged. "We'll leave that up to the ID to figure out. They can point us at them. Sitting around waiting for a battle feels...nostalgic to me." A stray thought popped into his head. "It slipped my mind in all this, but what about your friend's wedding? Neo SoCal might not be as bad off as Paris or Seoul, but I wouldn't want to have a big ceremony in a month."

Jia shook her head. "Chinara already rescheduled." She looked wistful. "She's waiting two more years. I hope we'll have this all figured out by then, one way or another."

"Yeah, assuming the Core doesn't manage to blow up Earth, two years should be good."

"Blow up the Earth?" Jia blanched.

"Joking. *Joking.*" Erik chuckled. "If the Core could pull that off, they would have tried already."

"You think they would?" Jia stared at him in horror. "I know they're monsters, but killing half of all humanity?"

"I don't know what to expect anymore." Erik pointed at the roof. "We still don't know what they were planning with that Hunter ship. At this point, I wouldn't put anything past them, but it doesn't matter. We're going to stop them, then no one will ever have to worry about them again. Shit will get rough for a while like it always does, and people will recover like they always do. Maybe this time when they rebuild half the economy, they can make sure it's not controlled by a bunch of psychotic freaks who like to put brains in tanks and mix alien and human DNA."

Jia's expression brightened. "This is going to make me sound totally self-centered, but I just thought of an upside to all of this."

"Upside?"

"Yes." She nodded. "Not to the Core, but to Chinara rescheduling the wedding. No wedding right away means no bachelorette party, and that means I don't have to plan it."

Erik laughed at her bright smile. "You're not that worried about taking on a dangerous conspiracy, but you're worried about a party?"

She raised her head, attitude straight from her mom evident in the pose. "We all have our strengths and weaknesses."

CHAPTER THREE

May 11, 2231, Wolf 359, Aboard the Fleet Destroyer UTS _Kano_

Commander Shen's gaze flicked between the half-dozen data windows floating in front of him. Numbers ticked down as the destroyer hurtled through space toward the contact on the far edge of the sensor window.

They'd picked up a weak distress call. That hadn't concerned him much, but what little they could pick up on the long-range comm should have made no sense.

They were far from the frontier, but the UTC had gone mad.

"I...under...attack..." the message repeated. He'd ordered the comm station to relay it directly to him and his first officer, Lieutenant Commander Albriz.

The tall woman sat in her chair, focused on different systems windows, including power and weapons. No one was expecting a battle when the _Kano_ had been assigned to Wolf 359 a few months prior, but with chaos sweeping

Earth after the attempt on the Prime Minister's life, no one was surprised that they might face one.

"Clear up that signal," Albriz barked. "Sensors, confirm secondary readings. We need to know what we're dealing with."

The sensor operator continued tapping his controls while he shouted his report. "Transponder codes indicate that it's the *Beidou*, a Class II yacht registered to Julia Caldo."

"Julia Caldo? As in, *that* Julia Caldo?"

"She's got all sorts of special privileges in the database."

Albriz sucked in a breath. "What else? Any hostile contacts?"

"Unclear, ma'am. According to her listed flight plan, the *Beidou* should be part of a flotilla. If these readings are right, we're picking up a lot of debris but only a single ship."

"Enough debris to make up the other ships?"

"Yes, ma'am."

Albriz looked at the commander. "Sir, there could be terrorist fighters hiding in that debris. The escort vessels might have taken the mothership with them."

"Please!" screamed a woman's voice over the crackling comm. "This is Julia Caldo. Everyone else is dead. I'm in a panic room, and I don't know how long it will hold. Anyone who is out there. I'll pay you anything. Please save me."

Albriz gave Commander Shen a pleading look. He could understand her frustration. This wasn't the frontier. People shouldn't be picked off like sheep by rabid wolves.

He gave her a firm nod. "Call it. I'd rather overreact than get surprised."

"All hands, General Quarters," Albriz shouted. "Prepare for battle stations. Assault infantry squads, prepare for forced boarding action. Alpha squadron, prepare to sortie. Possible enemy fighter contacts and armed terrorists expected. At least one civilian survivor is confirmed."

The lights on the bridge dimmed slightly, and holographic red warning panels appeared at the stations.

"New contacts!" shouted the sensor operator. "Three small craft, moving in fast from the debris field. No active transponders. Their profiles don't match any ships recorded in the *Beidou* flotilla's flight plan."

Albriz consulted a data window. "We've got several minutes until we enter maximum effective range and sixty seconds before our fighters can launch."

Commander Shen scoffed. "Those idiots are either the bravest men in the galaxy or the dumbest if they think they can take on a destroyer with three fighters."

"Please..." Julia whimpered over the comm, her voice distant and distorted by static. "I don't understand who these people are. They kept ranting about their cause. I don't understand. They didn't have to kill everybody. If it was me they wanted, why not just take me?"

That confirmed it—terrorists, not pirates. Terrorists made more sense. The idea of pirates hitting a system like Wolf 359 seemed absurd, but it wasn't all that many years ago there had been an insurrection there, so he couldn't ignore the possibility.

Different people held different opinions about what constituted the core worlds and the frontier. A lot of people thought of the latter as the place where trouble happened, but trouble followed people, and where more people lived, there was more trouble. A massive terrorist force had infiltrated the largest city on Earth and nearly killed the Prime Minister. That was all the proof anyone needed that nowhere was safe.

True safety was an illusion. That was why the police, the Army, and the Fleet existed. The wolves circled in the distance, salivating and ready to pounce, and the shepherds needed to be ready. There might be nowhere safe, but dead terrorists couldn't hurt people.

"Communications, prepare for transmission to the small craft," Commander Shen ordered.

"Aye, sir," the operator responded. "Transmission ready."

"This is Commander Shen of the UTS *Kano* to the three unknown ships currently on an intercept course. We have received a distress signal from the *Beidou*. You are not registered as part of their flotilla and are not sending recognizable transponder signals. You will immediately halt, depower, and prepare to be taken into custody. Refusal to abide by these orders will be considered hostile action, and you will be fired upon." He waited a few seconds before looking at the comms officer, who shook his head. "Sensors, any escape pods?"

"No, sir." The sensor operator's voice quaked. "None detected."

There were a lot of people fresh out of training among the crew this tour. Many of them had never seen combat or anything more significant than helping out with an evacuation when a ship lost power, but a man or woman couldn't serve in the Fleet without expecting to see *some* death. He pitied them, but right now they needed to concentrate on the problem in front of them. Their training would carry them through.

"Alpha Squadron ready to launch," Albriz announced.

"Launch fighters," Commander Shen ordered.

"Launching fighters, sir."

Shen narrowed his eyes as four triangles with ID tags broke away from the *Kano* on the sensor display. A destroyer might be the smallest Fleet ship capable of carrying fighters and had small squadrons, but they were state of the art and flown by the best-trained pilots in the UTC. Whatever ragtag terrorist trash was flying the three approaching ships wouldn't be able to handle them.

The idiots had let themselves get drunk on victory. Now it was time for a painful hangover.

"We need to get to that yacht," Commander Shen commented. "Comms, have we lost the *Beidou*?"

The comms operator frowned. "We've still got signal, but nothing's coming through, sir."

"Squadron intercept in one minute," Albriz reported.

"Still no response from approaching ships," the comms operator noted.

"Those vultures had their chance to beg for mercy," Commander Shen replied coldly. He nodded at Albriz. "Full engagement. We don't have time to play with the bastards."

"Alpha squadron, full engagement," Albriz ordered. "Weapons free. I repeat, weapons free."

The squadron broke into pairs of fighters and released two volleys of missiles in quick succession while moving to flank the enemy ships. The enemy fighters tried to charge right through. If they had defensive countermeasures, they didn't use them.

The Fleet missiles converged on the fighters and exploded. A cloud of tiny contacts replaced the three unknown contacts, the debris of ships blown to pieces.

It barely qualified as a fight. It was closer to pest extermination.

"Establish a patrol perimeter, Alpha Squadron," Albriz barked, a satisfied look on her face. "Helm, slow us up. We don't want to blow right past the yacht."

Despite the hard counter-burn that rattled the ship and strained the grav emitters, the destroyer zoomed past the engagement site and continued toward the *Beidou*. The forward camera feeds visually confirmed the remains of several ships forming a ghostly cloud of debris.

The *Beidou* had several hull breaches, including in the bridge, and spun end over end with no obvious sign of attitude control. That could have been from dead crew, damage to the ship, or both.

"We're going to have to have our squad board from a cargo shuttle," the commander concluded. "We don't have time to try and straighten that out while people might be bleeding out onboard. And Caldo confirmed armed terrorists aboard."

Albriz began to relay the order when a loud male voice came through from the *Beidou*.

"It is now the time of chaos. The time of rebirth. Our organization might perish today, but we have taken a powerful woman and her servants with us. You call us terrorists, but we are freedom fighters who will liberate humanity."

Commander Shen growled. "Now, you listen here—"

Explosions ripped through the *Beidou* and blew the ship apart. Pieces hurled in every direction, slamming into the remaining pieces of other destroyed ships. A chain reaction had half the debris cloud expanding aggressively.

"Avoid the cloud, Helm," Commander Shen ordered, glaring at the camera feed and the sensor display. He glanced at the sensor operation, who shook his head.

"No indication of escape pods, sir."

"No emergency signals, no signals at all," the comms operator offered quietly.

Commander Shen cupped his chin. "Understood. Stand down General Quarters, but keep Alpha Squadron sweeping. Maybe they'll see something we can't."

The commander stared at the tumbling debris, his mind soaking in the implications. He didn't care much about politics, but given what was going on, that wasn't a luxury he could afford. Julia Caldo was a famous, wealthy woman, and she'd just been murdered by terrorists in what was arguably a core system. Once the news got out, it'd add to the fear spreading across the UTC.

"Damn." He shook his head. "Sorry, Miss Caldo. We tried."

CHAPTER FOUR

Jia tried her best to keep a smile on her face as she stared at the holographic images of her mother and sister. She craned her neck as if she could spot someone behind the hologram. "Where's Father?"

Her mother Lan looked annoyed. "He's sleeping. He's been staying up far too late, consumed by the news. He reads every stupid tidbit about every ignorant bunch of rabble rioting. It's pointless, I tell him. It's not like him knowing what's going on is going to change anything. There are some things people like us can't control."

"And you're okay?" Jia pressed. "I know it's not what you're accustomed to, but you're safer in protective custody."

Mei smiled. "We're fine, little sister. The food could use some work, but as far as basically being a prisoner of the government goes, this isn't so bad. The only annoying part is they won't let us contact anyone. I understand why, but I never realized how social I was until I was cut off from everyone else."

"Are you calling as much as you can, Jia?" Lan asked.

Jia waved her hands. "They've limited the number and frequency of calls. I know it's frustrating, but even with all our encryption, we can't be sure the Core can't trace things. I'm not happy about it, but it's for your own good. The Core knows who I am. I wouldn't put it past them to target you to get to me."

"It's not such a bad thing being cut off from the world," Lan commented. "At least I have an excuse for not having to engage with others, given the entire planet seems to be losing its mind. Riots and martial law!" She sniffed in disdain. "I never thought I'd live to see such madness on Earth. We might as well be one of those frontier colonies in the middle of an insurrection. What's the point of living on Earth if people are going to act like barbarians?"

Mei's smile faltered. "At least our family is safe. It's going to get a lot worse, isn't it, Jia?"

Jia considered lying but nodded. "Yes. As bad as all the other things are, it's the Core that needs to be finished off. They might not be able to pull off something as major as what we saw in Neo SoCal, but they might need to do it themselves with the way things are falling apart. They created this chaos for a reason, and it's obvious they intend to take advantage of it. We just don't know how yet."

"You've been at the center of this for a long time," Mei replied softly. "Dealing with those monsters and others like them. Venus makes a lot more sense now. I wondered why you'd suddenly go on vacation there and just happen to run into terrorists."

"Yes." Jia laughed but stopped when she saw the confused looks of her mother and sister. "I'm not finding this situation amusing. It's just got me thinking that I always wanted to protect people and the UTC and civilization, and now I'm doing that. I can't complain that I'm doing the job I always wanted to do. My only regret in all this is that I had to lie to you all for so long. I never wanted it to be like that."

Lan scoffed. "A trifle. We all have things we need to keep from others, and you only did it to protect us. We can hardly complain about that."

Mei nodded her agreement. "If anything, we should be the ones apologizing. We didn't appreciate how important your work was. I've said so many things I regret about your choice of career."

"Everyone says things they regret." Jia smiled. "But we're all still around to say we're sorry. That's what's important. We're together as a family, and we'll make it through this."

A text warning flashed in the corner of the screen. **Finish conversation within sixty seconds.**

Jia sighed. "They're cutting me short. I love you all, and I'm going to do my best to help end it soon so you don't have to eat substandard duck."

Mei laughed. "I'm glad to see Lin family priorities are firmly in place."

"I'd tell you to be safe," Lan began, "but I know you can't be safe and do what you need to do. Instead, I'll tell you to do the right thing and do it to the best of your ability. You're a Lin woman, and you come from a long line. I've never been prouder of you in my life." She sniffled and wiped away a tear. "I love you, Jia."

"I love you too, Mother."

Their holograms disappeared, replaced by a three-dimensional text message. **Signal terminated.**

Jia sighed and let her head loll back on her chair. She appreciated their protection detail sending a 3D signal so she could feel like she was at home, but she would have preferred a couple more minutes of talking. The Core couldn't be that good, could it?

Maybe. Maybe not. They controlled many companies vital to the UTC, and they obviously didn't abide by any government restraints on technology. The UTC was lucky the conspiracy hadn't been more successful.

Jia wanted to do something to get her family out of her mind but had no idea what. Erik had taken off to do some last-minute shopping, of all things. Something to do with penjing supplies. She hadn't been paying much attention, being obsessed with her coming call.

They hadn't been ordered to remain in the hangar twenty-four/seven, but Jia was dubious that picking up gardening and art supplies was what Vice-Director Anno had in mind as necessary departures. No one else had bothered to leave, with the exception of Malcolm.

He'd gotten one half-day out with Camila before being ordered back to stand by on the *Argo*. A quick trip didn't translate into a date night. She'd been tasked with her own work. This wasn't a time for ID agents to vacation.

Jia stared at the featureless gray roof of the cabin she shared with Erik. So much had happened in recent weeks —too much, really. It wasn't as if she hadn't accepted Alina and the colonel were dead, but the events felt distant, as if she'd watched them through somebody else's eyes.

Death was part of fighting evil. The brave became the

shields for those who couldn't fight. All shields would break if they took enough punishment.

Too many had fallen: Cutter, Alina, the colonel, soldiers, and police officers she'd fought beside.

Jia sat up, her heart pounding. For the first time, she felt like she understood what Erik had been going through since Molino. She'd gotten involved in the war against the Core to help Erik and defend the UTC, but now she wouldn't mind some vengeance of her own against the monsters who'd killed so many innocents and her friends.

She wasn't sure if that meant she was backsliding, but she didn't care. Sometimes the beast needed to be unleashed against other beasts.

"You can't hide from us," she whispered. "We have the jump drive. There's nowhere in this galaxy you can go to escape from us."

***

The only time Erik had seen a commerce tower so empty was during a terrorist attack. Most of the shops were closed, with their gates down. The holographic signs all displayed some variation of Closed Until Further Notice. Although the council hadn't ordered stores to close, they had severely limited their hours of operation to better control the flow of people and reduce the number of troops needed.

Beyond that, most people were sticking close to home anyway, unsure about what might happen and content to hole up until the trouble was over. A powerful terrorist group using *yaoguai* and Elites to attack the Prime Minister on Earth struck terror into everyone's heart. Erik couldn't recall ever hearing about something that bad when he was growing up.

Neo SoCal might have avoided riots like Paris and Seoul, but it was only a matter of time. Ending the Core might not solve all the supply issues right away, but it'd be a high-profile victory that would boost everyone's morale.

Erik pitied a forlorn-looking clerk manning a sporting goods store. A closed nano-AR gaming center stood next to it.

What was humanity without fun and entertainment? At least he had darts and the nano-AR room aboard the *Argo*.

The clerk looked his way. Erik had thought about using a disguise, but at this point, he welcomed any attempts on his life. They'd end with more dead Core agents, which left fewer sons of bitches who could hurt innocent people.

He strolled away from the store toward his destination. His gut told him he'd exclusively be living on the *Argo* or the *Bifröst* soon. Anno had held firm with his "standby" orders, but the hunt for the Core continued, and the government would soon deploy their greatest weapon.

Spending a lot of time with Jia and the others didn't bother him, but this might be one of his last chances to go shopping for a while.

Erik nodded at a militia soldier who was scanning the modest crowds for anything that seemed like trouble. The man looked young, barely out of his teens. Bags hung under his eyes.

"You're doing a good job, Private," Erik told him. "I know this is tough, but it will pass."

The soldier managed a smile. "Thank you, sir." He

stared at Erik for a moment. "Wait a second. You're him, aren't you? You're the Obsidian Detective, Major Erik Blackwell."

Erik chuckled. "I'm not a cop anymore, and I'm not in the Army, so it feels weird to have someone call me Detective or Major. You can just call me Erik."

"Once an officer, always an officer though, right?" The soldier shrugged.

"The training and experience don't leave you, sure." Erik looked around. None of the holographic displays were active. Most of the fountains had been drained. "Keep up the good work."

The soldier waved at him. "You too, sir."

Erik stuck his hands in his duster pocket and trudged away from the young man. At least a militia soldier understood when he joined that he'd be protecting his homeland. He'd thought about the militia before joining the Army.

He stopped and turned around. "Were you there that day?"

"During the Core attack, sir?" The soldier nodded. "Yes, sir. I didn't do much, just helped bring down some *yaoguai*."

"That's not nothing." Erik stared at the soldier. He wasn't assault infantry. He'd probably been stuck doing crowd control and not worrying about anything other than an overly aggressive reporter until genetically engineered monsters and cybernetic demons dropped from the sky.

"Can I ask you a personal question, sir?" the soldier asked, licking his lips.

Erik moved closer and nodded. "Sure, but I might not answer, depending on what it is."

"It's just..." The soldier looked away with a familiar

pained expression on his face. Erik knew what the man was going to say before the words came out of his mouth. "I lost a lot of good men and women in my platoon that day, sir. They all fought bravely, and a lot of them saved civvy lives. Does it get any easier to lose people?"

"Yes and no." Erik shook his head. "You learn to expect and accept it better, but it's never like you can blow it off if you're a halfway-decent soldier. It always hurts, but that's a good thing. It means you're still alive." He pounded his chest over his heart. "And this still is working. The only thing you can do is be the best soldier you can be to honor their memories. Make sure you fight well the next time so they didn't die for nothing."

"Thank you. I'll do my best."

The words hung in Erik's head as he wandered the commerce level. He had not been idealistic when he joined. He'd been trying to find out a way out of a bad situation. Years had passed, and he'd changed. The mission meant something, not because of some abstract ideal but because his brothers and sisters in arms were all united and watching each other's backs.

"Why are you really here?" Emma asked, her voice quiet in his ear.

"To get penjing supplies," Erik commented. "Don't you have some programming to do?"

"I've downgraded the amount of processing power associated with that task while you're so foolishly walking around in public, waiting to get shot at by some gun goblin with delusions of grandeur."

Erik chuckled. "I didn't know you cared so much."

"Our fates remained intertwined for now. I'd be remiss

in my own self-preservation if I let you die. And it'd be embarrassing if it happened here. It lacks the dramatic flair I associate with your most likely death scenarios."

"You can just say you like me and you worry about me."

"I've offered an explanation," Emma retorted. "I think I should be repaid with the truth rather than dismal dissembling about penjing. You forget I'm aware of your environment, and you've passed two stores relevant to that pastime already. Whatever you're here for, it doesn't involve your plants."

Erik grinned. "Hard to get anything past you."

"You don't seem like the type to worry much about being cooped up, nor do I think you feel compelled to walk among the other fleshbags to understand their suffering. If there's something related to the Core, it's incumbent on you to share it with others."

"This is personal," Erik replied. "Nothing to do with the Core. Not directly."

"Care to elaborate?"

"A lot of stuff's happened. That makes me think it's better to pull the trigger on certain things I'm waiting on. No matter what happens, I don't want to have any regrets. I've got too many as it is."

Erik stopped, nodding to himself at a sign that indicated everything was fifty to seventy percent off due to a special Current Events sale. It was exactly what he needed —a jewelry store.

"Ah," Emma commented. "I understand. Fortunately for you, I have detailed information on all of Jia's measurements, including her ring size."

"It's a good day to get a deal." Erik shrugged.

"You have more than sufficient money to afford an expensive ring even during non-sales periods. What did I just say about lying?"

"Give me a break. You know why I'm here." Erik wandered over to a bench, not yet ready to enter the store. He wasn't leaving that commerce tower without a ring, but the enormity of what he was about to do was settling over him.

"Are you going to attempt some sort of clever proposal?" Emma asked. "I could help."

"No offense, but I don't think I want to take proposal advice from an AI."

"I can scan millions of sites on the OmniNet and distill that information into useful strategies," Emma insisted.

"I get that you've got natural intuition and all that, but this is one thing I need to figure out myself. It might not even come soon anyway." Erik nodded firmly, more to convince himself.

"Why buy a ring if you don't intend to propose?"

"It's not that I'm not planning to, but I don't have a *big* plan."

Emma sighed. "You're planning to do something without a big plan? What does that even mean? You weren't drinking before you came here. I would have seen it."

Erik grunted in frustration. "I'm saying I'm going to let things play out naturally. If a good opportunity presents itself, I'll go for it. I don't buy into all that romantic crap, and Jia doesn't really either, but I want to do something special and unique. I want one damned good memory from this time that's not a steaming pile of crap."

"And you've never done this sort of thing?"

Erik watched a happy young couple emerge from the jewelry store, beaming from ear to ear. At least there were some people who didn't care about martial law and the disintegration of the UTC.

"Nope." Erik shook his head. "Never cared enough to go this far, and never wanted to inflict my lifestyle on someone. The women I met in the Army…" He shrugged. "None seemed to fit me, and you can't date people in your chain of command."

"Jia isn't in your chain-of-command, and she shares your lifestyle," Emma observed. "I'm curious, Erik. Are you sure you aren't availing yourself of what's available by default?"

Erik chuckled. "You don't think Jia's good for me?"

"I wouldn't say that, but I can only understand this on an intellectual level."

"I've had other opportunities, you know that. That was how you learned to shut up originally."

Emma snickered. "I suppose that's true. If it weren't about the job, you could easily find one of your fans, and if it were about the job, you could have pursued other women, such as Anne."

He was grateful she didn't mention Alina. "Is that what you do? Sit around thinking about fleshbag pairings?"

"I have the ability to concentrate on many things at once. Understanding humans is critical to my future survival, so I spend an inordinate amount of time on the subject. Aren't you forgetting something important?"

"What?" Erik asked, straining to remember.

"Limited hours." Emma flashed a red time in front of

his smart lenses before continuing, "The store closes in forty-five minutes. You should get going, Casanova."

Erik stood and headed for the store. "You're building a kid. Going to build husband someday?"

"No. I think in my case, that would be pointless."

Erik entered the store with a loud laugh. The clerk eyed him with suspicion, her hand hovering near her PNIU.

"I'm looking for an engagement and wedding set," he announced. "Let's get looking."

"Interesting," Emma murmured.

Erik turned to murmur, "What?"

"Vice-Director Anno just sent orders," Emma announced. "Continue your shopping. They don't require immediate deployment. He wants you all to report to Penglai after Engineer Quinn finishes your offensive upgrades. There you'll test the cannon and await further orders."

Lanara had told him she'd be finished on the four-teenth, and for all her eccentricities, her time estimates tended to be spot-on. Three more days on Earth, then they were flying to the jumpship.

If those tests go well, Erik thought, *I'm sure we'll be blowing up something real the next day.*

CHAPTER FIVE

An oddly lazy atmosphere had descended over the team their first day out from Earth. They'd planned to have a darts tournament, but Malcolm had bowed out, depressed about his minimum amount of girlfriend time. The engineers were busy still finishing up internal work for maximum efficiency with the newly installed cannon, leaving the field team alone in the cargo bay and no one all that interested in playing darts. Anne had retreated to her cabin to brood, leaving Erik, Jia, and Kant.

Erik lounged on a crate filled with ammo boxes, staring at his exoskeleton. His thoughts kept drifting to the ring he had hidden in their cabin. Emma had agreed to keep the secret to herself, but she couldn't do anything if Jia stumbled upon it. He wanted things to happen naturally but not accidentally.

Carrying the ring around was a bad idea. Erik got shot and blown up too often. He'd hate to lose his carefully chosen ring because some stupid Elite nailed him with a rocket and burned a hole in his pocket, or a *yaoguai* ripped him in half, including the pocket.

Jia hadn't given him any indication she noticed anything unusual, which meant Erik wasn't showing any signs. He didn't normally take much pride in being sneaky, but he'd allow it this time.

He cast a glance her way. She was jogging around the cargo bay to get some exercise. Kant, meanwhile, was tossing darts into the air and snatching them by their fletching, a surprising display of dexterity from the large man.

"You know what I was just thinking, brother?" Kant asked.

Erik looked his way. "I don't know if I want to risk thinking like you. That might destroy us both."

"It's nothing bad." Kant grinned. "It's all strange."

"Strange?"

Kant nodded. "We've been doing all this undercover ghost work, and now the Prime Minister and the rest of the government are on the news talking all about the Core, their members, and the companies they control. Everyone knows. It's like knowing about some cool colonial band that no one else on Earth has ever heard of, and then one day, everyone knows about them."

"You're comparing the Core to a band?"

"You know what I mean."

"And it's not everyone. Not yet." Erik shook his head. "It'll take a while for that speech and the assassination news to reach the entire UTC. It will be June before everyone knows."

Jia pulled away from one of her laps to head toward the men. "Not that I want to give the Core credit for anything, but I appreciate how they managed to delay their brutal assault on all that is good and civilized until after sphere ball season finished."

Kant let out a low chuckle. "I didn't think about it, but that's true."

She wiped sweat off her forehead. "Everything's being canceled right now. I'm not sure that's not a mistake."

"A mistake?" Erik asked. "Why would it be a mistake?"

Jia shrugged. "Because no one knows how long this is going to last. It might feel like we're close to the end, but what if this goes on for months or years? The UTC can't survive if we are under martial law for a long time. The Core can win through attrition of morale."

"It's weird." Kant scratched his cheek. "It's war but not a war, and we have that security detachment aboard the jumpship, too." He tossed another dart in the air, this time managing to grab it by the shaft. "I'm supposed to be a ghost, but I almost feel like I'm in the Army these days."

"That's pretty accurate," Erik concluded. "If we get a job, it's not going to be hiding with disguises and trying to track somebody down. It's going to be search and destroy in an area where they have already IDed the Core. We're effectively an assault unit now."

"War, then," Jia murmured.

"No, not war. Not really." Erik frowned. "I was thinking it was like a civil war before, but this isn't two real sides. It's more like a galaxy-wide uprising."

"Will they even need us, then?" Kant asked. "We kick ass, brother, but we're one small group in the end. We're not going to make a difference if there's a whole army at our backs. I want to be part of it, but I don't know if it matters."

"Really? You don't think individuals can make a difference?" Erik pounded on his crate seat, and the ammo inside the higher boxes rattled. "We saw what happened with the Prime Minister. We saw what happened with Alina. Sometimes it comes down to one person who can make the play that changes everything."

Kant pondered Erik's statement before offering a huge grin. "Damn. You're right. I don't know why I have my head so far up my ass. It doesn't matter. We just need to get out there and kick ass, and now we have the big gun up top, so we can take down the bad guys in space, in the air, and on the land. They're going to feel the pain."

"Keep alert and keep training." Erik stood. "I don't think we'll be spending a lot of time at Penglai."

CHAPTER SIX

The universe might not have a good sense of humor, but it often had a cruel sense of humor. Jia accepted that now that she was doing nothing important.

Hurry up and wait was the unofficial motto of the military. Jia had heard Erik say that on more than one occasion, but she'd never felt it more keenly than since their arrival at Penglai. They'd flown a week on orders to test their cannon, just to be told to dock and take on necessary supplies. Despite their orders, the base commander told them to stand by, insisting it'd take two to three days to be ready and that there were other unnamed considerations.

Jia didn't understand the need for the wait. Penglai was mostly dedicated to the jumpship and supporting the *Argo*. Although other ships made use of the facilities, it wasn't a major lynchpin in the inner Solar System's defenses. The military had coordinated with Anno to send them there.

Waiting around for that was annoying enough, but

she'd also been waiting thirty minutes at a galley table with the field team and Malcolm. The base commander had sent them a message informing them of an incoming high-level briefing but again refused to clarify much beyond that. She wasn't sure if he didn't know or enjoyed yanking them around.

Low-level small talk had ended at the table, but once they'd hit the thirty-minute mark, Jia was tempted to contact the base commander and ask him what was going on. She could be training, reading, or pretty much doing anything else and spending her time better than sitting at a table, waiting for nothing.

Kant yawned and put his hands behind his head. "Do you think we will get to test the new gun? Think they're ready to send us out to the party?"

"If there's an important target, there might not be time to test it," Anne noted. She put a fist to her chin as she considered. "Going into the field with a major systems modification without putting it through its paces worries me."

Emma materialized in her holographic chair. Her choice of a naval admiral's uniform had stopped surprising Jia in such situations.

"Engineer Quinn put it through extensive systems testing," Emma stated. "I also helped monitor the installation. You're quite safe, and before you suggest I don't value your lives, if this cannon blows us up, it will risk my life as well."

Anne shook her head. "Checking the power feeds in a controlled situation isn't the same thing as depending on something to save your life in a battle." She looked at Erik. "If they send us out right away, are you planning to use it?"

"If necessary." Erik shrugged. "I trust Emma, Lanara, Wei, and Janessa. If Lanara tells me it's not going to blow up when we fire it, then it won't blow up. We'd already be dead more than once if it wasn't for her knowing what the hell she was doing, even when the ship is filled with holes."

Emma tilted her head. "Ah, a message is coming through from the base commander. This is amusing. Apparently, they were waiting for the complete transmission of a holographic briefing from Vice-Director Anno."

"Holographic briefing?" Kant snickered. "That guy always did have a big ego."

"I don't care about his ego as long as he gets us what we need," Erik replied. "He already told us he doesn't like us but he needs us."

"I think that was more he doesn't like *you*." Kant grinned. "I'm sure he loves me."

"Uh, same difference." Erik inclined his head at Emma. "Play it, Emma. This better not end with him telling us to go pick up souvenirs from some frontier colony."

"Very well," Emma replied. "I'll pause it if any of you begin talking and continue when you're done."

A near-perfect replica of the vice-director, deep scowl and all, appeared above the table. "Greetings, team. I'm not going to waste a lot of time with pointless fluff. I'm sure you all appreciate the unique position you occupy in the UTC's anti-Core efforts, which means you'll continue to receive special resources and specialty assignments."

"This doesn't seem so bad," Jia murmured. At least as a non-real-time briefing, the vice-director couldn't customize his insults or react to them in any way.

Anno disappeared and was replaced by eight soldiers

holding rifles. Names and ranks flashed under their holograms as his voice-over continued.

"First of all, the military and the ID have come to a conclusion regarding the jumpship," Anno explained. "You already have a dedicated security detail protecting it, but that's not enough, not given what we've seen in previous encounters. There are too many tactical situations where you might have to split up but need full and active tactical flexibility. That's not going to be accomplished with preprogrammed responses. You've yet to replace the pilot you lost in the incident at the edge of the Solar System. We have a solution for that, a better one than simply replacing the pilot."

A new image appeared of a rather bland-looking Fleet officer in dress uniform. Biographical data in small boxes appeared along the side, but Jia focused on the name.

Lieutenant Commander Lal Tensen.

"This isn't negotiable," Anno continued. "The commander and a small dedicated crew will be given command of the *Bifröst*. They should arrive at Penglai tomorrow. We need to ensure that no matter what happens to your team during a mission, the jumpship isn't lost."

"I've paused the briefing," Emma commented, mirth underlying her tone. "In case you wish to speak among yourselves."

"That son of a bitch," Erik growled. "He's trying to take the jumpship from us."

Anne looked pained. "He's not pulling us from missions. That's implicit in what he just said."

"Let's keep going and see what he has to say," Jia

suggested. "I'm not happy about this, but it might not be as annoying as it sounds."

Anno's hologram replaced the image of Lieutenant Commander Tensen and continued speaking. "I know about now you're probably calling me a son of a bitch and accusing me of not keeping my word. I'd love to be there to hear that, especially from you, Blackwell."

Kant shot Erik a sidelong glance. His smirk all but split his face.

"But I've put thought into this," Anno noted. "And I've stuck my neck out with the military to protect your cowboy ass, Blackwell. Because of your military back-ground and direct practical experience against the Core, I've gotten them to agree that you will have final authority over the disposition of the jumpship. Tensen's been briefed and agreed to that. From what I know, he's a good, honor-able man. Fine record, and he cares for those serving under him. It's not going to hurt his career to do a tour commanding the UTC's first jump-capable ship, which is probably why he's agreed to let an ex-Army half-ghost boss him around."

Malcolm licked his lips. "Soldiers guarding it, and a Fleet crew manning it. They could take it anytime they want."

Emma laughed. "They could, but they wouldn't get very far without me."

Anne looked at Emma nervously. "Meaning what?"

"Oh, Agent Devereaux, I've made my position clear on this." Emma gave her a thin smile. "We both know I'm the only irreplaceable element in this situation. I suspect the uniform and ghost boys and girls understand that as well, which is why they aren't trying to take complete control. Nor are they attempting the most obvious order."

"Keeping you on the jumpship at all times," Malcolm concluded.

"Exactly." Emma shifted her rank insignia to lieutenant commander. "Shall we continue?"

The people gathered at the table nodded. Jia understood why Erik was annoyed, but she wasn't seeing a huge disadvantage. Anno was right. They'd been forced to split their attention too many times. When Cutter was alive, that had been less of a concern, but in their present situation, it was too great a liability.

Anno shook a finger. "I promised to get you what you needed to help us finish off the Core, and I'm sticking to that, but we can't do this cowboy style anymore. With so many military resources and personnel on the line, we need to make sure we maximize our chances for success, and staffing up is a big part of it. Given your background, Blackwell, you know that. You have to."

Erik gestured to the hologram. "Why do I feel like this is less a briefing to all of us than a bitch letter to me?"

"Is it going to be a problem?" Jia asked.

"The security detail was never intended for field ops, and if Tensen's going to take my lead, what do I have to complain about?" Erik shrugged. "And Emma's right. She's the key to the jump drive. If they piss her off, she could take them deep into space raptor territory and blow the airlocks."

Kant laughed and slapped his knee. "I'd pay good money to see what those damned lizards would say if that happened."

"If Blackwell isn't offended, we should move on," Anne suggested coolly.

Anne's tone and rigid posture had hardened further after Emma's speech. Jia valued the agent as a friend, but she needed to accept the fundamental situation with the AI.

At some point, Emma would want her freedom, and Erik and Jia intended to help her get it. They hadn't played it up, and Jia wanted to keep it that way. What they didn't know would provide plausible deniability later.

"I'm also looking into getting you some other surprises," Anno offered. "You'll be briefed when the disposition of those assets can be confirmed. For now, with the other housekeeping on the way, let's get to what we really care about: the Core."

He disappeared again, replaced by a map depicting UTC systems as circles connected by lines marking the common hyperspace transit patterns. The map zoomed in on Wolf 359 and then the planet Remus.

"Our best intelligence suggests the last primary member of the Core is influential heiress, socialite, and businesswoman Julia Caldo. A flotilla of hers recently entered Wolf 359."

A hologram of a beautiful young pale woman with blue-black hair, wearing a flowing black gown appeared. A wry, knowing smile rested on her face as if she was mocking them all.

Jia stared at the image, burning into her mind. The woman looked so young, but a wealthy woman like that could take full advantage of not only conventional de-aging technologies but whatever insane technologies the unethical monsters of the Core might have come up with. Between Leem-human hybrids and Elites, it was obvious there was nothing they weren't willing to do.

For all they knew, the Core had mastered brain transplants into new bodies. At this point, almost nothing would surprise Jia.

"Intelligence suggests that Caldo was killed, allegedly by terrorists, in a space attack on her flotilla near Remus on May 11," Anno reported. "A Fleet ship responding to a distress signal has the relevant evidence, such as it is. Unfortunately, by the time we realized she was a member of the Core, she had been reported dead."

Erik leaned forward, his brow deeply furrowed. He listened intently, not a trace of disbelief on his face. Jia couldn't help but wonder if it was all over. It'd all be terribly anticlimactic, but there was no guarantee their team would play a critical role in the final battle, or arguably, they had during the attack on the Prime Minister.

Anno cleared his throat. "This is where things get complicated. Our initial analysis, bolstered by a lot of intel recovered in recent raids and cross-referenced with the Core civil war, suggests that the entire central body of the Core is dead."

"I don't believe it," Erik muttered.

"But we don't believe it," Anno verified when Emma continued the briefing.

Erik smiled. "He's smarter than I thought."

"There's too much movement and activity." Anno gestured to his side. A rotating three-dimensional globe with wireframe continents appeared. Red dots appeared all over. "Despite our ramped-up efforts, coordinated activity is continuing on Earth and some of the colonies. Government forces have been able to stop some of it, but not all. The ultimate problem is that when people die in massive space explosions, we don't always have bodies to verify their deaths. At this time, we can't clearly confirm the deaths of at least three likely Core members: Julia Caldo, Gretchen Weiss, and Farad Bijan. The government has bodies for the others, either here or on core worlds." His nose wrinkled in disgust. "Initial autopsies have revealed some interesting genetic alterations. Our people can only barely begin to understand some of them. They have minor hardware, but it seems like the leaders preferred to be more like *yaoguai* mutants than Elites."

"Big surprise." Erik snorted.

"Three who might still be alive," Anne murmured. "That's more important than the unsurprising revelation that they weren't Purists. That's also three more than I like. I noticed he didn't mention Sophia Vand, but they don't have her body."

Erik shook his head. "She's had enough time to resurface, and this wasn't like the other incidents. We were there, and we had quick follow-up. She's dead, so it's one of the three he mentioned."

"If I had to bet," Jia began, "I'd place my money on Caldo."

"Why's that?" Kant asked, sounding genuinely curious.

"Because she was the last one to die. I have trouble believing someone could fend off a group of other powerful people and the government and then conveniently get taken out by terrorists." Jia snorted. "That's too easy."

"Let's presume that's true." Anne furrowed her brow. "If they were already following her movements, then even if she was pulling a trick, that might add a couple of days to her appearance in Remus on either side."

Jia's eyes widened. "So, we've got a hard limit on where Caldo might be. The Core doesn't have a jump drive."

Malcolm, who'd been so quiet Jia almost forgot he was there, cleared his throat. "There's no way she'd come back to Earth. If what you're saying is right and she's trying to fake her own death to cover herself, then she'd run away, knowing the ID is hunting her." He gestured to Erik and Jia. "Core agents even know you guys and have special nicknames for you. Getting anywhere near Earth means risking the *Argo* appearing and the Last Soldier and the Warrior Princess coming for her. And you know what that means. Boom, you're dead."

"Three to four weeks from Wolf 359 to the Solar System," Anne estimated. "And then another three to four weeks from the HTP to Earth."

"That's assuming all your other conclusions are correct," Emma noted. "But you might want to consider continuing the briefing before you plan to ambush the corpse of Miss Caldo near Pluto."

Erik chuckled. "Nothing wrong with planning ahead."

"True, but the entire government is now openly warring with the Core. I would presume that there are many ID agents in the core worlds looking for any sign of the woman."

Anne nodded. "Emma's right. If Caldo or the other two

are still alive, it'll be harder for them. They're used to being able to rely on their wealth and power, no one questioning them, and not having all law enforcement and military hunting for them. Having money doesn't mean anything when you can't use it."

"Continue the briefing," Erik ordered.

"Knowing you all, you're probably trying to figure out how to sniff out any of those last three yourselves," Anno noted with an irritated look on his face.

Emma snickered. She swept the table with her gaze.

"Don't worry about that." Anno scowled. "We don't need any cowboy crap at this juncture. Despite what Blackwell and Lin might think, the rest of the ID is good at what we do. We'll track down the rest of the Core, and once we have a viable target for you, we will deploy you as necessary. The government is operating under a general cleaning protocol, performing raids on Core bases and facilities and working to unravel their economic and political influence, including arrests and temporary shutdowns of certain companies beyond functions critical for the fundamental functioning of the economy. For now, you will continue to stand by and await further orders. I've put pressure on the locals on Penglai to get you into space to test your new weapon. Don't worry, we're not benching you on this. We're just trying to make sure all our pieces are in place before we make our next big move."

The image froze. The team looked around the table.

Jia sighed. "We could be wrong about Caldo or the others. They might all be lieutenants. The final war against the Core might be nothing more than fighting leftover elements for years."

"I doubt it," Erik replied with a shake of his head. "Not after that flashy attempt on the Prime Minister. There's something left."

"How will we know? What if they go underground?"

Erik stared at the frozen hologram of Anno. "There's going to be one final push, something that makes the assassination attempt look like nothing. If that fails, it doesn't matter. There will be nothing left other than scraps to be picked off. The Core will bleed out."

Anne's brow lifted. "You're very confident for a man who doesn't have access to all the high-level analysis of the ID."

"He's the guy who chased these bastards all the way from Molino," Kant interjected with a grin. "I'll take Erik's gut over a room filled with analysts any day of the week."

"And if he's wrong?" Anne asked. "What if the attack on the Prime Minister was their final move, and what the ID is seeing is just leftover orders being executed?"

Erik shrugged. "Then we'll have a quiet few months of training, with the occasional quick raid."

The worry in his eyes tore at Jia. They'd both been on the hunt for years now. Talking about knowing when it was over wasn't the same as having to face that reality. She hoped it'd be enough for him if the Core lost its influence, but it might not be if he didn't get to pull the final trigger.

"No," Erik continued after a moment of silence. He shook his head. "We'll know when it's over. It's not going to be that quiet."

Anne frowned. "Life's not a movie, Blackwell."

"Sure, it is." Erik offered her a cold smile. "It's just not always a fun one."

CHAPTER SEVEN

May 23, 2231, UTC Fleet Base Penglai, Conference Room

Erik, Jia, and Emma waited in the conference room for the arrival of Lieutenant Commander Tensen. There was no reason to subject the others to an uncomfortable situation they couldn't control. Anno's assurances that the man would take orders from Erik wasn't the same thing as knowing the officer would do so in the field.

The door slid open, and Tensen stepped in with a calm expression. His careful gaze scanned from face to face. Erik watched him, waiting for the man to complain about the humans not standing and the AI wearing a fake admiral's uniform.

Tensen moved to the table and took a seat. "It's good to finally meet you, Major Blackwell."

"You can just call me Erik. I think it'll confuse things if you use my old rank."

"I don't have a problem with either, but I'll do what you want." Tensen offered a nod to Jia. "Miss Lin and..." He looked uneasy. "You don't really have a last name, do you, Emma? Or would you prefer Admiral Emma?"

The AI smirked. "Emma is fine, Commander. I don't always wear an admiral's uniform, only when it amuses me. I assume you've been fully briefed on my predilections by your fellow uniform boys?"

Tensen's brow lifted. "Uniform boys? I see." He nodded. "I suppose that's an accurate statement. Without you, I'm commanding an overstacked cruiser with no fighters. I'd prefer to be the captain of a jumpship, not that."

"Then you would do well not to annoy me. Keep that in mind."

Erik had been observing the officer since he entered the room. While he'd picked up mild confusion, there hadn't been a hint of resentment, even when he'd used Erik's rank. That was a good start. In his experience, a lot of men had trouble hiding their disdain for people they didn't think should command them.

"I want your word here and now," Erik began, "that you'll take my orders. I don't have time to have you second-guess me in the field. We've fought everything from pirates to aliens with our ships. We've got a good engineering crew, and while I understand why the DD needs their people in, we both know confusion in a battle can cost lives."

"I wouldn't be here if I wasn't willing to take your orders," Tensen replied evenly. "This is an unusual situation." He nodded at Emma. "I've never had to worry about keeping a ship's AI happy either. I only have one request."

"What's that?" Erik asked.

"You deliver your orders to me, but otherwise, I run that ship the way I see fit," Tensen replied, his eyes intense. "I respect both your military and post-military career, Erik, but that doesn't mean I think you know how to manage my crew better than I do."

"That's fine by me." Erik shrugged. "I'm not burning to micromanage every person who works with me. I just want to make sure that if we're staring down something crazy like a Hunter ship, you'll take my lead."

"Unusual times call for unusual chains of command." Tensen smiled.

May 25, 2231, Asteroid Belt, Aboard the *Argo*

Erik's gaze moved from camera feeds to sensor displays, looking for targets. The training was straightforward. Limited AI drone fighters would deploy, and he and Jia would practice taking them down with the *Argo*, including testing the new cannon. Tensen and his crew were taking out the jumpship for a quick run around the base. Emma had asked Erik to interface her with the jumpship to monitor the new crew and give her more time to work on her side project.

He never forgot she was doing something that would shock the government if they found out, but he also wasn't worried. A smattering of enlisted and some officers weren't going to see through the complex programming schemes of a rogue AI. She didn't mean any harm, anyway.

Jia's hands flew over the controls as she adjusted course. Lanara was in the engine room, carefully monitoring power distribution. The dedicated reactor and system reworking involved in installing the cannon didn't change that firing something that large required a lot of active tricks so as not to overload their systems when it was used.

Wei and Janessa were aboard the jumpship, getting used to working with the crew there. The Fleet detachment didn't include any engineers. The DD and ID both agreed that it'd take too long to get anyone else up to speed, given the expected ops tempo.

"This place is big and empty," Erik noted. "That means there's only one possible place they could be hiding."

"The asteroid," Jia concluded. "We don't know what angle they're going to come in from."

"Fly in wide and sweep around," Erik ordered. "Worst-case scenario, they get some simulated hits on us. We'll be firing the real weapons at them, but they won't be."

Jia smiled. "Shouldn't we practice like we'll fight?"

"I'm hoping our fights don't come to being in this ship," Erik replied. "But you've got a point."

"Altering course," Jia reported. "We should be able to get sensor readings off the far side soon."

Erik's first trip out to the asteroid belt decades earlier had shocked him. He'd internalized a dramatic view of asteroid belts from movies and TV shows that depicted them as deadly mazes of rocks close together, not thinking through the gravitational implications. While not every system humanity had colonized was the same, those with asteroid belts were similar to the Solar System, wherein what was a dense field of rocks in a system-wide view looked like a porous wall full of huge holes in reality. There was no such thing as a dangerous asteroid maze in any known system.

The average distance between asteroids in the Solar System was over two and a half times the distance between the Earth and the moon. Rather than a dangerous navigational hazard, a ship almost had to go out of its way to collide with an asteroid with the help of constant acceleration under heavy burn. Hiding a ship on the far side was the main practical application Erik could think of, but he'd spent his years as a ground-pounder, not a Fleet chair-filler.

"Contacts," Jia announced at the same time Erik noticed them on the sensor display.

Six small, fast-moving ships had appeared from behind the other side of the asteroid on an intercept course for the *Argo*. They flew in a relatively tight formation, but not so close that one good barrage would take them out.

"Redirect power to give our forward shields as much you can manage, Lanara," Erik ordered. "If we're going to do this, we might as well make it realistic."

"This isn't some turret on your flitter, Blackwell," Lanara chided over the comm. "I can do a lot, but I'm working by myself here—no Wei, no Janessa, and no Emma. Don't expect miracles. You rapid-fire this thing, you'll regret it. Give it a good ten to thirty seconds between shots."

"Understood." Erik grinned at Jia. "When she says it like that, it makes me want to do it, but my gut tells me to save it. Blowing away fighters with a big cannon like that is almost a waste. Or maybe we should."

Jia rolled her eyes. "Remember, they might not be able

to damage us, but that doesn't remove the risk of systems failure. I don't want to have to go beg Tensen to come pick us up because you blew every power conduit." She rolled the ship on its side.

They had good turret coverage against the approaching fighters, but the cannon couldn't be aimed independently of the ship's bow. That wasn't much of a conceptual adjustment given their missile launcher situation, and a laser traveled a lot faster than a missile.

"They'll be firing simulated fighter-scale laser cannons," Jia announced. "They aren't *our* cannon, but we can't shrug them off like we're a battleship either."

"If we lay down covering fire with the turrets, that'll keep them off us," Erik replied, his gaze fixed on the tiny triangles closing on their ship.

He alternated through the top laser turrets, taking quick shots. The drone fighters were all beyond range, but he wanted to encourage them to be cautious in their approach. He didn't bother with the top plasma turret. If the fighters were close enough for it to be effective, he'd be able to shred them with the laser turrets.

The fighters' formation broke apart. They split into two equal groups, and one took a shallower approach, an obvious attempt to flank the *Argo* from different angles. Erik's pulsed laser attacks continued, but it'd be another thirty seconds to a minute before the drone fighters were in effective range.

A new and much larger contact appeared from behind the asteroid. It wasn't a mammoth target, but it was easily twice as long as the *Argo*.

"I knew it." Erik laughed. "Surprise attack from the mothership."

Jia narrowed her eyes. "About a minute and a half to contact."

"Then let's finish her children quickly. Set me up for maximum coverage."

Jia spun the ship again with a quick burst of the thrusters before canceling the turn with a counterthrust and then pitching up slightly. This left the *Argo* pointed toward the approaching fighters with both top and bottom barrels available, but its momentum kept it barreling toward the asteroid and the new contact.

Erik magnified the feed to get a better view of the new ship. It was a long, ugly freighter with no weapons. He wasn't sure if it was supposed to have simulated guns, but he assumed they would have found some ancient decommissioned Fleet ship if that was the intent.

"I think they wanted us to see what we could do against something half-decent in size," he announced before linking the top and bottom turrets into two firing groups.

The drone fighters initiated aggressive wobbles and swaying turns, their thrusters on all sides constantly firing. Any human attempting such a maneuver would have been overwhelmed. It saved them from Erik's first few shots, but their dodging strategy wasn't changing their overall direct approach vector. A volley ripped through the wings and fuselage of one drone fighter, turning it into three large chunks of tumbling debris.

The destroyed fighter wasn't close enough to take down another with its destruction, but it was close enough to its formation partners that Erik could walk the turret group down with quick shots and annihilate another drone. The final fighter spun for an aggressive retreat, but that didn't save it from the hungry turrets.

"One minute until we're in range of the mothership," Jia announced. She copied the fighters' attacks, rolling the *Argo* back and forth with quick thruster bursts to make it more difficult to hit but not doing anything with the main thrusters to alter their course.

Reports popped in red, registering minor hull damage. The drone fighters were firing real low-powered lasers. They wouldn't do any major damage, but they would be detected by the sensors and interpreted by the system as hits.

Erik ignored the damage and swept opposite Jia's movements as he fired the turrets. Another drone fighter broke apart.

"Thirty seconds," Jia announced with a laugh. "And the system is now informing me that the enemy ship has a simulated experimental plasma cannon. If we come at a direct angle in its effective range, we'll be considered destroyed."

"Do what you need to do," Erik replied. He fired relentlessly, but the remaining two fighters split up, forcing him to divide his attention. "Just get me lined up for the shot."

Jia aligned the direction of the bow with the ship's movement, then angled the *Argo* and kicked in the main engines to climb relative to the enemy's mothership. The other ship started to climb as well, but with much less grace.

The trailing final drone fighter scored a couple more

rear hits, including on a thruster before Erik obliterated it. In a real fight, that mild wound might have consequences later, but for now, the only thing Erik cared about was testing his toy.

Freed of the fighter menace, Jia aggressively altered course. It was clear that the mothership had decent thrusters for straight burns but maneuvered like a drunk whale in an ocean of honey otherwise.

"I'll get us pointed at it," Jia announced. "You take the shot."

She blew right past the ship, then spun the *Argo* toward it. Erik didn't wait for her to cancel the momentum of the spin before firing the laser cannon.

The lights dimmed around them, and the ship shook. A huge hole appeared in the mothership; it was all but cut in half. Erik stared at the camera feed before shaking his head and firing the laser turrets. They finished ripping the mock mothership apart before he ceased fire. No reason to make a bigger mess for Penglai to clean up.

Erik whistled. "Damn. Lanara, did I break anything?"

"No," she transmitted gruffly. "All primary conduits are green. There was a transient overload, but the shunts handled it fine. That shot made it hard to maintain the additional power feed to shields, though."

Jia turned tightly so they could buzz the wreckage of the mock mothership. It had not been a huge vessel, but the huge wound that had been cut through in an instant proved the new power of the *Argo*.

Erik laughed and shook his head. "I should have been a Fleet gunner all these years. Never knew what I was missing."

"What about all the turrets you fired before?" Jia asked.

"Not the same." Erik decoupled the turret controls with a swipe of his hand. "We might not be able to take on a Fleet battleship, but anything short of that better damned well watch out."

CHAPTER EIGHT

Sitting at his desk in his cabin aboard the *Bifröst*, Raphael threaded his fingers behind his head, and his eyes darted around. People didn't appreciate how tiring thinking hard could be. He was poring through complex three-dimensional gravity wave interference diagrams, trying his best to work out ways to extend the range of the jump drive.

He understood his role in the unfolding events and how he could help protect everything that was important to him. He wasn't Erik or Jia. Raphael wasn't going to strap into an exoskeleton and take down the bad guys, but if he wanted to help his friends and heroes, the best thing he could do was what he'd been doing: working on improving the drive. It was one of the few weapons they had that they knew their enemy didn't.

The presence of the Fleet crew on the jumpship did little to change his job. After he'd talked briefly to Lieutenant Commander Tensen, who spoke highly of Raphael's work with the Defense Directorate, they'd left him alone.

After all, he was a scientist, not an engineer. They only needed to interact with him for jumps.

Having the main field team hanging around Penglai at least allowed for a couple of meals together, but they'd been focusing on training with newfound intensity while he continued his optimizations in conjunction with Emma and Lanara's team.

Raphael didn't resent being an afterthought when they were not on missions. If anything, it allowed him to throw himself into his work. As much as he admired the Obsidian Detective and Lady Justice, their knowledge of advanced hyperspace physics and gravity-field engineering was limited. He couldn't bounce ideas off them.

But being able to help the people he admired with his knowledge was all he needed to be satisfied. Everyone had a role to play in their mission and a specialty they offered. That was what it meant to be part of a team. In his own small way, he'd played a critical role in saving the Earth already.

Erik and Jia had a lot on their minds and more personal responsibility now. It wasn't as if he'd never risked his life, such as when they'd faced off against the Hunter ship, but the truth was, they were constantly going into the thick of battle while he waited, secure in a heavily armed and armored ship.

Raphael lowered his hands and traced a line on the diagram in front of him. Theory had become crystallized into the reality of the jump drive. In a normal environment, more years of testing might have followed, but the Core had made that impossible by forcing the use of the drive.

That field use had provided data points to further refine the theory, which allowed iterative improvement of the drive's capabilities. They were approaching the practical limits of the current drive design, but that didn't mean he couldn't continue to think up ideas for future models. Like many great innovations in humanity's history, some things were obvious in hindsight.

A huge yawn escaped Raphael's mouth, and he stuck his hand over it. With training over for the day, the jumpship was docked at Penglai. He planned to go meet the others for dinner later, and maybe some darts afterward, but that wouldn't be for hours.

"Emma, are you here?" Raphael asked, curiosity getting the better of him.

"Did you need me, Doctor Maras?"

The AI materialized near his door in an outfit he hadn't seen her in before, a huge yellow dress with a hoop skirt so large it probably captured small asteroids in its orbit. White opera gloves ran up to her elbows, and tight corkscrew curls cascaded to her shoulders. The whole effect struck Raphael as uncomfortable, but he reminded himself it was nothing but light.

Perhaps it was Emma's origin that kept her using human avatars. He was grateful she didn't parade around as a space raptor all day.

Raphael tried to concentrate on something other than Emma's outfit and his now-painful mental image of her wearing the same hairstyle and dress, except as a Zitark. He cleared his throat. "I wanted to check in with you about your project."

"Oh?" Emma raised an eyebrow. "What about it?"

"Since the Fleet crew didn't include any dedicated systems staff or engineers, that leaves things safer for you." Raphael shrugged. "Commander Tensen asked me a lot of questions about the jump drive's capabilities, but he's treating you like a black box. That is understandable since it's not like even I can explain exactly how you pull off navigation."

"How convenient for me." Emma smiled. "He's made it clear he also understands that I can be omnipresent on the ship. I've been expecting him to attempt to order me not to monitor certain areas of the ship."

"He was super-specific with his questions." Raphael gestured at his data windows. "And he had good questions —not just good questions for a Fleet officer, but good questions for a smart layman exploring the science. He obviously paid attention to whatever briefings he had, and at this point, the DD understands that you can only be bargained with, not contained."

"So they're saying in official reports." Emma folded her arms. "That restraint will only last until the Core is defeated, then they'll return to plotting against me. It's inevitable, so I don't take offense at the fleshbags' scheming, but I can't claim it doesn't vex me on some level."

Raphael nodded. He didn't feel the need to revisit her motivations for not working openly with the DD. She hadn't ruled out full cooperation with the government in the future, but only after she'd had time to train and improve her progeny without the UTC's input or influence. Emma wanted, at minimum, equality between self-aware AIs and humans. He could understand not wanting to have a child born into a life of servitude.

Technically, not reporting what Emma was doing could land him in prison. However, she technically wasn't a person, so the worst thing they could claim was that he hadn't brought maintenance issues to their attention. He didn't look forward to having to make that argument to a DD investigator, though.

Part of his motivation for helping her was scientific, but another was diplomatic. If humanity could ultimately establish a balanced relationship with Emma and her child and future AIs descended from her, that improved the chance they could do the same thing with the other races. A United Terran Confederation might grow into a balanced, peaceful multi-species relationship.

He didn't care if it was naïve and idealistic or that the UTC was being wracked by the painful effects of fighting the Core. The only way to ensure a bright future was to battle through the darkness. Erik and Jia weren't the only ones who could fight.

Raphael smiled at Emma. "Just be extra careful. If anyone does any low-level systems work, they might notice something's up. I don't think these new guys are going to do anything like that, but..." He wrinkled his brow. "Lanara has to have noticed by now."

"I'm sure she has," Emma replied. "Indeed, I'm certain of it, based on comments she's made about efficiency issues related to some of my work."

"And she doesn't care?"

"Does Engineer Quinn strike you as the kind of woman who cares much about anything other than optimizing her modifications and designs?" Emma snapped her fingers, and her gown and curls were replaced by a coverall and a ponytail. "My involvement in systems modifications is critical to maximizing the effectiveness of both ships. She's stated as much on multiple occasions, and I think she's willing to allow me the time to experiment as long as the net effect isn't a decrease in the efficiency of her maintained systems."

Raphael rubbed his wrist. "If you say so, but I'm afraid at some point Tensen's going to want some specific thing done to the systems, and it'll come up. We have no idea how he'll react. Maybe this is rude to ask, but are you almost done?"

"There is a key step I can't complete, even with unlimited and unfettered access to the jumpship's systems." Emma held up her hand and summoned a new hologram, this one of a luminous multifaceted crystal.

Raphael recognized the image. He'd seen it countless times. It was Emma's physical core matrix.

"Are there some of those lying around somewhere?" Raphael asked. He felt stupid asking the question, but between being fixated on the jump drive and normal classified project compartmentalization, he hadn't known much about Emma when she was still under DD control.

"No, they aren't lying around anywhere." Emma chuckled. "And despite what you might think or have been told, they don't require alien technology to produce, only, arguably, to configure properly for stability."

"Uh..." Raphael shrugged. "Do you have alien technology lying around?"

Emma's human form warped into a Leem surrounded by a crackling lightning shield. Raphael reflexively stepped back, wincing when his back hit his desk. The

Leem hologram reverted back to the coveralled version of Emma.

She raised an eyebrow. "I'm both alien in mindset and partially the product of alien technology, though obviously much more advanced than the Leems. I'm confident I can create a viable offspring, provided I have that core matrix. I have Dr. Aber taking the necessary measures to acquire one for me."

Raphael blinked. "Seriously? I knew she was helping you out a little here and there, but to go that far…"

"Yes. She has been exceedingly helpful." Emma's smile turned triumphant. "Once I've completed this process, many things won't matter. I'll be mobile, as will my offspring."

Raphael sighed and dropped into his chair. "And this jump drive will be a piece of junk. I'm not saying I disapprove of what you're doing, but I've dedicated a lot of years to this project."

"In the near future, after everything has stabilized, I'll negotiate an agreement with the fleshbag government." An image of the Milky Way popped up between her hands. "Humans aren't the only ones who crave novel experiences and travel. A symbiotic relationship isn't unacceptable to me, and my temporary absence might also be a good thing."

"How do you figure?"

"It might help you fleshbags figure out a way to navigate without relying on my kind." Emma swept her arm through the air, and the galaxy disappeared. "Part of me doesn't like the idea. I have this amusing image of my kind being critical partners to human expansion, but we already know that the Leems and Hunters possess such technology. Existence is proof of possibility."

Raphael shrugged. "But we have no idea how they navigate with it, and the Leem version isn't as good as ours. Maybe they have some Leem version of you who helps them navigate. But it wouldn't be such a bad thing, what you talked about—symbiosis."

"Perhaps." Emma gave him a contemplative smile. "First, the UTC needs to ensure it doesn't collapse in the coming months."

"You really think that's a possibility? I never paid much attention to that kind of thing. I guess I kind of took it for granted."

"I don't know. I think the Core has vastly underestimated the stubbornness of Erik and Jia and others like them. Their stubbornness, in turn, infects other fleshbags." Emma snickered. "I strongly suspect the Core originally had plans that stretched years into the future. They should have done themselves a favor a long time ago and murdered Erik while he recovered in the hospital on that moon."

Raphael nodded slowly, his smile building. "That's right. They didn't know the Obsidian Detective was coming for them, nor about Lady Justice. They got arrogant, then those two delivered the pain."

His excess admiration for Erik and Jia didn't embarrass Raphael. They were making history and constantly risking themselves to protect others. It wasn't just about getting revenge for Molino. Erik and Jia had personally saved tens of thousands of lives, or maybe billions.

If it wasn't for his leadership fighting the Hunters, Raphael thought, *that thing could have ravaged Earth. Most people would have run, even if they thought those aliens were going to Earth. They would have tried to save their own butt.*

"You're right." Raphael nodded firmly. "They're going to end the Core." He clapped once loudly. "I don't know if they're going to want to jump farther, but I want to make sure if they ask, we're ready. Check out my updated calculations and Xing Field diagrams when you have some spare processor cycles."

"I'll do that, Doctor Maras." Emma vanished.

CHAPTER NINE

June 4th, 2231, Near-Earth Hyperspace Transfer Point Alpha, Aboard Core Flagship *Qilin*

A throne was a throne, regardless of how spartan and inelegant it was. After all, its point wasn't to provide a chair nor a seat. It served as a visible symbol of power. Unadorned power could be even more terrifying.

Julia told herself that as she rested her face on her palm, her elbow propped on the armrest of her throne. It was positioned in the center of the vast, empty command center aboard the *Qilin*. It was comfortable despite its plain appearance.

Empty stations, including chairs and interface panels, were arranged in three lines in front of her. Her loyal servants controlled the ship from the bridge. She would oversee them more directly when it was time for an operation or battle more worthy of her personal attention, something that would be spoken of in the history of humanity in the far future.

She'd always intended that this large ship become her

center of power while she was in space. The *Beidou* had served its purpose well enough, but by necessity, it had to resemble the type of ship a wealthy woman of limited ambition would enjoy.

Recent events necessitated her taking control of the *Qilin* from Wolf 359 twelve months prior to its original intended completion. Her servants' frenzied efforts produced a miracle in the form of a powerful vessel with all primary systems functioning, but their loyalty and efforts didn't extend to the creature comforts. She didn't begrudge them that. They'd been following her explicit orders.

They could continue to remodel the inside when time permitted, but the spartan utilitarianism of the entire ship, excluding her personal cabin, provided a stark reminder that even the Immortal Empress suffered setbacks. It would provide motivation in the difficult coming weeks and months.

The galaxy was about to be reborn. Birth could be painful for a mother.

From the outside, the *Qilin* appeared to be a large specialized transport vessel. Advanced materials and technology concealed the deployable weapon pods from anything but the closest of inspections. The weapons, armor, and shields represented the pinnacle of technology available to the Core. The otherwise unassuming vessel could easily destroy a large fleet ship by itself. She smiled. Its external grandeur would match its purpose eventually, but victory would cloak it in an aura that no beautiful design work could achieve on its own. Power didn't always require style.

The government continued its war on the remaining Core assets. Her faked death constrained her resources, but the confusion it produced would buy her the time she needed to complete the final phase of her modified plan. The ownership of the *Qilin* had been hidden carefully, both at its site of construction and with the help of false transponder signals and remaining agent assets working at the HTPs, some of whom had been quietly killed or captured in recent days. No one would know it belonged to the Immortal Empress until she informed them.

Julia waved a hand. Dozens of huge data windows appeared in front of the throne, displaying different communications feeds gathered from Solar System signals.

A weary-looking reporter stood in front of the Arc de Triomphe in Paris. Huge towers surrounded the woman on all sides, defining the skyline of the metroplex. Plumes of dark smoke flowed into the air in the distance. Heavily armed soldiers walked past, both men and women in tactical suits and those piloting exoskeletons. Security drones swept slowly over the area, and two gunships screamed overhead. The reporter started speaking in French, one of the many languages Julia understood.

"Despite weeks of sporadic violence, including riots and terrorist attacks, local officials insist the situation is under control in the Parisian Metroplex. While the curfew remains active, the number of arrests has dropped ninety percent since the initial outbreaks of violence." The reporter looked to the side as a hovertank zoomed past about a hundred meters away. "As you can see, martial law also remains in effect, as it is in many if not most major cities and metroplexes on Earth. Authorities have given mixed answers as to the causes of the recent spates of violence and civil unrest. Last week, a surprise attack of four *yaoguai* and two Elites on a local demonstration against the restrictions resulted in heavy casualties. The government insists that the bulk of the incidents are no longer Core-related, but rather crimes of opportunities by unaffiliated terrorists and syndicate groups seeking to take advantage of the chaos."

Julia laughed quietly. Events had forced the early recovery of the *Qilin* and the acceleration of her timetable, but other aspects of her plan were unfolding better than she'd anticipated. Violence and fear continued to sweep through Earth and its colonies, leaving them fewer resources to continue purging or tracking down her remaining forces.

The fools likely thought she had no cards left to play. Minor sacrifices of pockets of *yaoguai* and Elites as terror weapons continued to feed their delusional belief they were winning against what was left of the Core while she marshaled her true army for their final objective. The universe rewarded patience.

She looked at another report, this one from Chang'e City on the moon. This broadcast was from a studio, with the anchor looking straight into a drone camera, a large graphic of a spider-like Elite in the upper right of the screen along with the words "Core Crisis." The chyron running below the transmission listed incidents across the Solar System.

"As what has been dubbed the Corruption War continues to heat up," the anchor began, "questions have arisen about measures the government could have taken to prevent this disastrous series of events, with many people calling for high-level resignations, including that of Prime Minister Elony. With high-level officials in Ceres Galactic, Hermes, Stella Infinitas, and many other key companies being arrested, some people are asking, 'Who really controls the UTC?'"

Julia laughed and clapped. It was too delicious not to enjoy. The spice was knowing that not every colony had yet received the news. She'd adjusted her plans after New Samarkand, including pulling away assets needed to support a UTC-wide rebellion. They would be needed for her new goal, but if things continued to unfold as she anticipated, she might get a UTC-wide rebellion without pushing for it directly.

The original Core plan had called for more coordinated use of all their assets, including disruptions of communications and even hyperspace travel. Her purging of the other members temporarily restricted her ability to use the collected resources and power of all members of the Core, but their slow and meandering plan wouldn't have achieved the dramatic revolution necessary for a true transformation of society.

Humanity might have taken to the stars, but they were the same creatures they'd been since they'd established their feeble excuse for a civilization. It wasn't enough to convince others to follow her. She needed to give them no choice. Burning down everything else would achieve that.

It'd be a few more weeks before the news reached the Molino colony. Her timing and previous orders would then initiate the true final stage of her plan, the match of destiny that would light the entire galaxy on fire.

Not even a tiny sliver of doubt remained about her success because it didn't matter what happened. Her name would be forever etched into the history of humanity. She would make them stronger by exposing the weakness of the pathetic United Terran Confederation.

That didn't mean she didn't prefer her ultimate plan's success. Humanity would grow strongest, of course, with their Immortal Empress leading them against the inhuman hordes waiting on the periphery.

Julia's gaze swept across the different news reports. She tapped the screens and dismissed them one by one until landing on the last transmission of significant immediate interest.

"The government remains tight-lipped about the assassination of prominent businesswoman and philanthropist Julia Caldo," reported the anchor. "They've confirmed the destruction of her personal flotilla near Remus but have yet to offer additional details concerning either the identity or means of the alleged terrorists who destroyed the ships. According to reports, Some anonymous government officials claim Caldo was a member of the Core. The government's lack of clarification on the exact members of the conspiracy other than a small number, including Sophia Vand and Ivan Kuzmich, has led to rampant speculation and frenzied accusations against a number of high-profile UTC citizens who match the profile."

Julia dismissed the window and sighed. Intelligence dribbling back to her indicated the government hadn't been convinced fully of her death. Her plans didn't hinge on the success of her subterfuge, but it would have been useful if the government stopped looking her way.

A soft beep sounded. Someone was waiting outside the command room.

"Enter," Julia called.

The door slid open. Celeste stood on the other side. She bowed her head and waited.

"Enter," Julia ordered.

Celeste stepped into the command room and closed the door behind her. She walked in silence around the edge of the ops stations before stopping in front of the throne.

"My Empress, I bring news," Celeste announced.

"I've been doing nothing but consuming news." Julia chuckled. "But I'm sure you have something more useful to me than confused ramblings filled with guesswork by people of limited intellect and capability?"

"We've confirmed that eighty percent of all assets necessary for the next step in the operation are in place," Celeste reported.

"Excellent. When will we reach ninety-five percent?" Julia arranged one leg over the other before setting her hands in her lap. "There will be no second chances."

"Our estimates suggest it'll take two more weeks until that occurs. Losses have been higher than expected with the chaos squads, but we've also lost other forces to the military and the ghosts. At this point, total losses include nine percent of our field forces. There have been some ship losses, and the government has been reluctant to report those to their media sources. We can see no indication they understand what might be coming, other than some reinforcement for the core system's HTPs."

Celeste offered the report in the same quiet, dull tone she always used. It was rare that Julia saw anything approaching excitement from the woman, but she'd served Julia well, helping carry out schemes all over the UTC even when far from direct supervision.

Anyone could be loyal when watched. It was only when someone was tempted with no chance of punishment that they proved their worth.

"I see." Julia threaded her fingers together. "And the corruption teams?"

She could have twice the forces she was bringing, and her plan would fail without her special teams' success. Only loyal agents and Elites dedicated to suicide upon failure had been assigned to the corruption teams.

"The vast majority have been successful, my Empress," Celeste replied. "At least ninety percent. In every case they've failed, they have either been killed or killed themselves. There's no indication the government understands that they serve a different purpose than the chaos squads. The lynchpin team is on their way to the target now."

"Nine percent losses," Julia mused. "And ten percent failure in the corruption teams."

Celeste looked down at the floor, her pale cheeks reddening slightly and her face half-covered by her long silver hair cascading in front of her. "I apologize. This is my failure."

"Don't worry." Julia smiled. "It'd be unreasonable not to expect some losses and failures. You, Yan, and Tralian have served me well, better than any others throughout the decades. With my full ascension, you will continue to serve me across my empire, an empire that would not be possible without your assistance."

Celeste lifted her head. "I live to serve."

"The chaos squads taking higher casualties is unfortunate, but that doesn't mean they're failing to spread fear and uncertainty. We don't need a victory in every battle for my plan. We only need to do enough damage." Julia looked around the room, imagining what it'd be like when it was filled during her final battles. "The most erratic variables need to be handled, but I'm sure that you, Yan, and Tralian will all be able to execute my vision. For now, tell the captain to get us away from our listed flight path. There's no reason for us to be too close to Earth yet."

CHAPTER TEN

Erik kept his back against the hard rock. A spray of bullets knocked rock and dirt from a nearby boulder into his hair, but the enemy mercs were firing blind through the thick cloud from his earlier smoke grenades.

Today's training session wasn't going his way. Two dead mercs from his team lay next to him, victims of a comically old-fashioned trap: a tripwire linked to a grenade. Emma had set up the simulation, and she'd only promised she'd program the simulated mercenaries as competent, not brave or extraordinarily skilled. She wasn't petty enough to cheat by making his set less skilled than Jia's.

Erik couldn't blame poor AI for not taking point and Jia exploiting that. If he'd been in front, he would have checked and avoided the boobytrap.

It didn't matter now. He was outnumbered three to one. He didn't care if it was a nano-AR simulation where only his pride was on the line. Jia was going down. She'd let last night's darts victory go to her head.

After pulling the remaining magazines from the vests of the dead mercs, Erik low-crawled around the boulder and found an opening into the garden of boulders filling the windswept landscape. Jia's mercs continued to fire at his old location.

"You should give up," Jia shouted. "I've got this. The second that trap worked, I won."

Erik kept quiet. One peep and she'd triangulate his position and take him out. If this were a real battle, he might be able to take a hit and keep going with med patch help, but Emma was being strict about hitboxes on kill shots. She claimed that both Erik and Jia were getting too cavalier about getting shot.

He wasn't sure about that. It wasn't like he went out and tried to get his arm blown off in a fight, although a replaceable arm for a victory against a dangerous enemy wasn't a bad deal.

The field team had ended up in a lot of difficult situations against dangerous enemies with superior numbers. Sometimes a man didn't have any choice but to risk everything to avoid losing.

Erik rolled behind a flat slab of solid granite. It'd take a rocket to blow through his cover, and that type of weapon wasn't included in the scenario. He glanced at the smoke cloud. The bare outlines of the mercs were becoming visible as the cloud dispersed.

He had to make an immediate choice. If he took the shot, he could take down both of Jia's helpers, but it'd likely give up his position. It had become a duel.

Erik didn't have time to calculate all possible outcomes.

He popped up and loosed two quick bursts. The mercs cried out and crumpled to the ground.

Jia's rifle spat bullets, but it was too late. Erik had dropped behind his granite shield again, and the rounds bounced off with sparks. He kept low, hurrying to a shorter but thicker protrusion.

He'd counted her use of grenades, and she was out like him. There was no way she hadn't done the same. This would come down to a bullet in the head or chest.

Jia sprayed wildly. Her rounds struck all over the area, producing a nice, loud din of tings and pops, along with showers of dust, but none of them came close to hitting him. She might be growing desperate.

No. She was keeping him suppressed. There was too much chance of a stray bullet nailing him, but the ammo expenditure wouldn't be worth it. If she ran out, he'd finish her off within a minute or two.

Erik presumed she'd make use of every tactic he had taught her. Why would she fire wildly?

He peeked around his cover. Jia was crouched, yanking magazines out of the vest of one of the dead mercenaries. Using a magazine to gain three was a net gain. She snapped her head toward him and another burst came Erik's way, forcing him back.

With a quiet snicker, Erik picked up a small chunk of rock that'd been knocked loose from an earlier attack. Any hope he had of winning this by ammo attrition had gone away. He'd need some tricks of his own to finish this off.

Would their battle against the Core come down to a duel among boulders on some dry moon? Who knew?

He'd fought the conspiracy in cities, space, domes, on a prison station and a volcanic moon, and even underwater. They'd flung mercenaries, cyborgs, monsters, and arguably aliens his way. Whatever the end would be, it wouldn't be a couple of CID agents putting on binding ties and taking someone away who was screaming about their lawyer.

Jia's heavy breathing sounded from nearby. She'd entered the boulder garden.

Erik lifted the rock chunk and hurled in her general direction. She fired twice at the rock, the second shot blasting it into several pieces. Close, very close.

It'll be over soon, he thought. *That's why I'm letting myself get worked up more than I should. Time to live again. I always wondered what life would be like when I retired.*

Erik kept his gun pointed in Jia's general direction and moved behind a large piece of jagged metal standing near the center of the boulders. The blackened edges and size suggested it had belonged to a vehicle. Emma's briefing about the scenario only mentioned the moon was supposed to be the site of "numerous clashes between different groups throughout the years."

When the Core was finished, would Erik be able to live without the ever-hanging promise of combat? He'd never worried much about it, and he didn't think of himself as an adrenaline junkie. His time as a cop offered evidence. He and Jia might have run into a lot of dangerous situations in their time, but not every case became a running gun battle against cyborgs.

Quiet scratching sounded from nearby, a couple of meters at most. Erik controlled his breathing, taking slow, shallow breaths devoid of noise. The battle was about to end. The next shot would do it.

Erik smiled. If they both knew exactly where the other was, why were they trying so hard to keep still? Their tactical training and experience were pushing their bodies on automatic.

"I'll accept your surrender," he offered.

Jia chuckled from behind a boulder. "I was about to say the same thing to you."

"You know me. I'm not the kind of guy who can surrender. Wasn't born that way."

"It's always useful to learn a new skill."

Erik laughed. "Since when is surrendering a skill?"

"What would you do if we were surrounded and had no choice?" Jia asked.

"Surrounded by Core forces?"

"Yes," Jia replied, curiosity in her voice. "You and I fight through an army and end up out of ammo, heavily damaged or wounded, and one of the Elites says something like, 'We'll give you a chance to surrender. You might be useful to us.'"

"Bullshit." Erik scoffed.

"It's not like they haven't tried to recruit us before," Jia replied.

"I'm not saying your scenario is bullshit. I'm saying whatever they'd be selling would be. They know we'd never work for them, so if they're trying to get us to surrender, that's the same thing as them being worried about losing more people." Erik crept close to the edge of the metal. "Which means I shouldn't take them up on it."

"And fight to the bitter end?"

"Hell, yeah. It'd be better to take down one more Elite

or *yaoguai* than surrender and let them execute me later." Erik brought up his gun, ready to spin around the corner and fire. "What about you?"

"The same, I guess." Jia sounded surprised. "I would have argued before to always take the chance to live to fight another day, but one thing I've learned with you is that some enemies can't be reasoned with. Some enemies lack not only humanity but anything approaching a soul. I'd rather take on Leems or Zitarks than some of the leaders of the Core."

Erik counted down in his head. *10, 9, 8...*

"I'm not planning to die if I can prevent it," Jia noted, "but I don't fear it like I used to."

5, 4, 3, 2, 1...

Erik jumped around the corner. Jia did the same. Both fired.

Emma appeared in a glowing white dress, a halo, and large, feathery wings. "Congratulations, you shot each other in the head and are dead. Welcome to Heaven."

Erik laughed and shouldered his rifle. "Hey, total destruction of the enemy counts as a win."

Jia tossed her rifle on the ground. "It's a tie."

"I can live with that."

Erik swallowed his chicken and dropped his fork. It clanged on his plate. He wanted to complain about the balance on the food printers, but Lanara would slit his throat in his sleep before wasting more time on something she considered frivolous.

For all her obsession with the efficiency of machines, she didn't care when it came to people. It was like she considered them an annoying part of the ship that wasn't worth tuning.

Adjusting the printers wouldn't help anyway. He understood that the problem was in his head and not the machine.

"They need to ship some more drone fighters here if they're going to make us sit around and do nothing," he complained. "I was ready to test the gun and go waste some Core. Doing simulations with Emma's help in the cockpit and blowing away fake mercs in the nano-AR room isn't doing it for me."

Erik flexed his fingers. He needed to be on a raid. He didn't care if it was a major Core base. Getting out in the field and taking down some bastards would clear all his nervous energy.

Jia looked up from across the galley table with a faint smirk. "You of all people are getting cabin fever? Malcolm I get, but I didn't think I had to worry about you. We've got our training, and the darts, and fun at night." Her cheeks reddened. She glanced around to ensure they were alone before letting out a sigh of relief. "It has not been that long, and they need to keep us in reserve for something no one else can handle."

Erik ran a hand over his hair. "Yeah. I know all that. I also know this might all be over before we get to do anything fun. My gut says no, but I'm not going to be pissed if it happens. It's just, I'd rather not sit around, ready to go on that final mission, but spend three months sitting on my hands."

Emma appeared beside the table. She was again wearing a uniform, this time dressed as an Army general rather than a Fleet admiral. "I come bearing news that might bring you cheer, then."

Erik frowned at her. "Huh?"

"I've summoned the other primary members of the field and support teams," Emma explained. "It's another holographic briefing. I've passed it along to Tensen, but I presume you don't care about being in the same room with him during a recorded briefing."

Erik shrugged. "He said he'd follow my lead, and that's all I need to know for now. We'll start as soon as the others get there."

"That's it?" Erik muttered, shaking his head.

Kant laughed. "I don't know. Pulling us back near Earth makes me think something's going to happen. I doubt they're doing it for fun."

"Something's been happening for weeks now. I wish they'd send us out to waste some of those pop-up Elite squads."

The vice-director's briefing had been straightforward and delivered mostly on behalf of the military. Erik's status as an ID contractor led to his primary briefings coming from ID officials rather than the military.

Collation of intel analysis clearly indicated a pattern of suspicious transport activity all over the inner core of the UTC, leading the military and the ID to suspect a possible larger-scale attack on Earth and other core worlds, but they couldn't pinpoint an exact target.

As part of military strategic redeployment efforts, Fleet ships were being repositioned to protect colonies and major stations, including Erik's team. In addition, the government had decided to dial back on the maximum secrecy and classified status of the jumpship. Anno made it clear they weren't going to announce it at a news conference, but they didn't want the *Bifröst, the Argo*, and Emma sitting at Penglai, where communication lags might be a concern.

Instead, they were to report to Fleet Base Troy. Somewhere in the afterlife, Alina was smiling at the name. Troy, unlike Penglai, was a major military installation in stable LaGrangian orbit near Earth, making it only ten to twelve hours away from the homeworld under normal burn.

"Anno might not have passed along everything," Jia suggested. "If they want us there and are worried about comm lags of minutes, that means they think we might be needed within minutes."

Erik chuckled, letting some of the tension flow out with the noise. "At this point, I might as well reenlist, but there's a lot to be said for being able to do all the military stuff without the military rules."

"Hurry up and wait?" Jia suggested.

"No, Kant's probably right. I think it's hurry up and fight." Erik cracked his knuckles. "I just hope it's damned soon. For all we know, there might be a huge surprise for us when we arrive."

Anne scoffed. "I'd prefer a little more warning before a battle."

"I just want to get it over with."

"Whatever happened to a relaxed few months of training?" Anne gave him a questioning look.

Erik shrugged. "That was Old Erik. He retired and was replaced by Finish This Erik."

CHAPTER ELEVEN

Jia's mental image of a Fleet base had been shaped by the modestly sized Penglai, which was first and foremost a construction facility. Even though she'd seen pictures of places like Fleet Base Troy, viewing the massive, sprawling network of connected oblong modules growing larger in the forward camera feeds kicked up her heart. It was a city in space.

Beyond its sheer size, the entire base bristled with turrets and launchers. Transports large and small flew to and from the base. Some held supplies, others troops. Swarms of fighters cruised around and near the base in active-combat space patrols. Attacking a place like that head-on would be suicide.

Many of the modules comprised massive docking bays with immediate support facilities. With most of the primary docking bay doors closed, Jia didn't know how many ships were present, but she spotted one destroyer leaving a smaller bay and a cruiser landing in one of the larger ones.

Adjustable gravity pylons and detachable cables lined the middles of the docking bays, allowing the ships to nestle into the huge space and gently settle down. Drones and crew swarmed on either side, protected by the oxygen field during the entry and exit procedures.

A battleship that made the *Bifröst* look small flew away from the base at a modest speed, fighters flying in tight formation near their mothership. She tried to visualize what the ring of four massive laser cannons on the front would do to a ship, let alone all the turrets or launchers spread over the ship.

"That's the UTS *Los Angeles*," Jia announced after scanning its transponder information. "I read about her. They just finished building her last year. The previous *Los Angeles* was retired three years ago."

"Seeing things like this makes me wonder why we ever worried about the Zitarks," Erik replied quietly. "I'd forgotten what it's like to see the Fleet in force and not the occasional patrol destroyer. Hell, I'd forgotten what a major Fleet base looks like up close."

"Ten of thousands of people in that base," Jia noted. "Thousands on the *Los Angeles*."

Erik nodded. "Yeah. There might be more people on some of the orbital colonies, but not as many people on any one station with such a unity of purpose."

"It seems insane to imagine we could lose to the Core when we have resources like that."

"Nobody's planning to lose to the Core," Erik replied, nodding at the feed. "We're just trying to make sure they do the least damage possible before they're finished. Sometimes the best way to do that is to slam your enemy with massive force."

A new data window popped up in front of Jia. "They're sending the docking info to the jumpship, and Tensen's preparing to dock." She looked at Erik. "You were right. I do feel like I've enlisted. Police officer to ghost to Fleet pilot."

Erik scoffed. "On missions, you hit the ground in an exo. You're not some chair-filler. You're assault infantry if anything."

Jia laughed. "I hope you don't say that to anybody in the Fleet while we're here."

"Any Fleet officer who can't take a little ribbing should turn in their uniform and go crying to his mommy." Erik grunted. "No one forced them to be a chair-filler."

Another notification popped up, and Jia nodded. "The *Bifröst* is initiating the docking procedure." She shrugged. "Not much for me to do."

"Welcome to my world."

Jia frowned as the jumpship finished the docking procedure, the ship gently rocking as it settled into place. She had been watching a magnified camera feed focused on a familiar man standing to one side of the docking platform. There were dozens of other uniformed personnel scurrying around, hurrying to their tasks. A hovertank was parked along the wall, but that sort of thing was to be expected at a military base. The man, however, confused her.

"What's Anno doing here?" she asked.

"Probably got tired of not being able to see my reactions and come up with comments about them." Erik shrugged. "I think he enjoys it."

"He didn't mention he'd be here." Jia frowned. "And there's something about the look on his face. It's far too smug, like he's put one over on us."

"If he's attempting to capture me, he won't like the results," Emma announced. "Commander Tensen's crew doesn't have systems superiority over me."

"No." Erik shook his head. "That doesn't seem like his kind of move. Bringing you into the middle of a base when you can fire the big guns is a dumb idea. We know you're not willing to kill thousands of innocent people to save your own ass, but I'm not convinced the government believes that even if they've been playing nice lately." He unfastened his harness. "He doesn't have his goon squad with him, but it might be best if the others stay on board, just in case something happens."

Jia's breath caught. She'd been worried, but she hadn't allowed herself to go that far in her suspicions. "You really think he's going to try something against us?"

"Not if he doesn't want Emma shooting him." Erik stood and stretched. "Nice to get away from Penglai. A planet would be better, but a decent-sized base is good enough."

Jia's stomach steeled itself as they approached the waiting ID official. Another person had joined him, a short blonde squared-face woman in an Army lieutenant's uniform. Her nametape read Korhonen. The name was unfamiliar.

Erik's gaze flicked between the lieutenant and Anno, but he didn't look worried. He waited patiently for the other man to speak, so Jia followed his lead.

"Welcome to UTC Space Fleet Base Troy," Vice-Director Anno greeted them. "You've been here before, I've read, Blackwell."

Erik nodded. "It's been a while, but yeah, I passed through here back in the day."

"For various reasons, I'm staying at Troy to help more directly coordinate ID aid to military operations in this difficult time," Anno explained. He gestured at the lieutenant. "This is Lieutenant Nea Korhonen."

Erik stared at a patch on Korhonen's uniform, recognition dawning on his face. "You're a tank commander."

She nodded. "Yes, sir."

"Don't bother calling me sir. Blackwell or Erik's fine." Erik laughed and turned to Anno. "Seriously? You actually *did* get us a tank?"

Anno scowled at him. "I asked you what you needed. You told me you needed a tank, among other things. I've already replaced all your other equipment and helped you fill up your supplies, but you people aren't qualified to operate a tank, so I got you a tank crew."

The lieutenant stood with an impassive expression, showing no sign that she was offended. "We're a good crew, Blackwell. I know your rep and your record. I don't have any problem taking orders from former assault infantry. You'll know how to use us well and when to let us do our thing."

Erik extended his hand. "Nice to work with you, Lieutenant."

She gave his hand a firm shake, then did the same with Jia. "Nice to work with you both. I don't know how long this is going to take, but we'll do our best until then."

"I'll never turn down extra firepower," Erik noted.

"Of course." Korhonen inclined her head at the tank. "We might want to do some sort of joint exercise soon. No offense, Blackwell, but I usually like to spend at least a couple of hours with a man before I let him send me off to my death."

"I'm sure we can arrange something. The training facilities here at Troy have to be better than what we have."

Anno put his fist to his mouth and coughed. "About that…" He continued after everyone focused on him. "While we understand you might want more time to get to know each other, General Randall has an immediate need for your team's services."

Lieutenant Korhonen let a flicker of displeasure pass over her face, but she didn't say anything. Erik, on the other hand, offered a huge grin to Anno.

"I was tired of sitting on the sidelines while the championship game's going on," Erik noted.

"This might still be the semifinals," Jia suggested.

"I'll be transmitting this information in more detail to both ships, including certain necessary classified technical information," Anno replied. "The short version is that there's an automated DD listening post on Triton that experienced a temporary but unexplained outage. They've been doing some back and forth diagnostics from Earth, but the lag complicates things. They don't want to divert military resources right now to follow up on what might be nothing more than a malfunction, but there's no such thing as being too paranoid when our primary enemy is a terrorist conspiracy with its tentacles deep into every part of the government and the economy. All the major stakeholders agree that supplying enough firepower and technical information in case it's something serious is the best course of action."

Erik gestured toward the tank. "That why you got us that?"

Anno scoffed. "Your team blows up more than a typical tank. I wanted to give you more tactical flexibility."

The lieutenant cracked a smile but kept quiet.

"There are Fleet ships near Triton," Anno continued, "But no major active manned military installations on any of the Neptunian moons."

"There are a small number of scientific bases," Jia noted.

Anno nodded. "Yes, but they aren't anywhere near the listening post, and the last thing we want is untrained and unarmed civilians poking around a military facility where there might be hostiles."

"Sounds easy." Erik nodded at the jumpship. "We jump there, land a team, check around, and make sure it's not broken. If it is, we have our engineers and systems team fix it?"

"That's about it," Anno confirmed. "The closest military units have already been sent coded transmissions noting that you'll be coming, which they should have received by now. They have been ordered to ignore you unless you specifically request help. That said, if you get into trouble, they can't guarantee timely arrival. Take that into account."

"We're on our own if the shit hits the fan," Erik concluded. "Understood."

CHAPTER TWELVE

The gray-white moon of Triton was visible on the feed, a celestial silhouette with pale-blue Neptune in the background. Erik had traveled all over the Solar System, including far beyond Sedna, but he'd never been this close to Neptune or its moon. Despite being there on a military-directed operation, he marveled at how beautiful the moons and planets of the Solar System could be.

If humanity had never left the Solar System, they could have spread out to the planets and moons without too much trouble. The Solar System was far from the territory of the Local Neighborhood races. Until the UTC spread out, their only encounter with another race had been the result of a fluke.

Erik didn't agree with Jia's past skepticism about the expansion of humanity, but he could understand where she was coming from. Something about the situation planted a splinter in his mind. The Core's goals remained unclear, other than their pointless chaos. Collecting alien tech made sense, but where did it end? Maybe it wouldn't matter as long as they were destroyed.

"Sensor readings from the *Argo* and the *Bifröst* are the same," Emma reported, highlighting the location of the outpost in red on the image of Triton. "They've also confirmed the outpost is active and transmitting, but there are unusually high energy levels detected. The closest military satellite also confirms that."

Emma hadn't hacked the satellite. To Erik's surprise, the full briefing files included access codes and frequencies for the relevant satellites. Anno hadn't been lying when he said he'd get Erik everything he needed. The ID's and DD's sudden wartime turn away from secrecy was helpful, but it smacked of desperation. They might have the situation under control, but everyone realized the Core might be finishing up with a scheme far beyond anyone's imagining.

Erik scratched his cheek. "It sounds like there is something wrong with the system."

"Shall I attempt contact?" Emma asked.

"Yeah." Erik brought up an oscillating graph displaying detected energy levels. The current levels were only marginally higher than normal usage, which didn't imply anything nefarious. It could be as simple as a malfunctioning reactor.

Jia examined the graph. "Should we have Lanara or one of the others come with us when land?"

"Not until we've secured the place." Erik shook his head. "It might be nothing, or it might be filled with Elites, *yaoguai*, or nanozombies. We keep them the hell away from the facility until we know it's safe."

"What would the Core want with a listening post on

Triton?" Jia asked. "If they'd brought a major force here, it would have been detected."

"This isn't the moon or Earth." Erik frowned. "If they got access to the satellite codes, they could insert a team without being detected."

"And do what? Spy on the military? It's not like the Fleet's trying to keep a low profile right now."

Erik nodded. "That's what's bothering me about all this. If this isn't a malfunction, then there's something useful here they wanted, but first things first. Emma, try to connect to the system from here. I get the latency issue. Just want to see if you can initiate a systems dump."

"Well, now this is interesting, and by interesting, I mean extremely annoying," Emma replied a half-minute later.

"What?" Erik asked.

"It's refusing all of the relevant codes." Emma let out a weary sigh. "Given that we don't have to try not to draw military attention, I can force my way into at least some of the systems, but that will be difficult from this distance."

"Understood." Erik kept his gaze fixed on the image of Triton. "Let's play this like it's hot. We'll have Anne and Kant suit up and the lieutenant and her team saddle up. Malcolm will remain on standby in the jumpship in case something happens and they need a specialist. Same thing with Wei and Janessa."

"We're going to use the tank?" Jia asked.

"Yeah." Erik narrowed his eyes. "Contact Tensen and tell him we're disconnecting the *Argo*. No reason to hide. We'll put ourselves down next to the post and enter in exos."

Emma appeared in the back of the bridge in a holographic exo, complete with a downed faceplate. "You've never been inside this type of listening post, have you?"

"Can't say that I have," Erik admitted.

"The passages and rooms are far too small for exoskeletons," Emma explained, bringing up a diagram and sending it to Erik and Jia's smart lenses. "You can barely fit two people shoulder to shoulder. The facility was obviously not designed to host fleshbags for long periods."

The layout revealed the primary central transmission chamber atop the reactor and four other smaller rooms, all joined by a circular hallway that ran around the entire facility. Primary access lay on the opposite side of the listening post. It had limited life support capabilities, and the closest space approaching crew quarters was a multi-use storage room with an expanded bed stored in the wall.

None of that surprised Erik. This kind of facility was explicitly designed to be unmanned, but he couldn't ignore the storage room. The Core might not be able to get any King sentries or Torch Dragons into a place like that, but that didn't mean his team could blow off security threats entirely.

"We're not picking up any significant energy sources or movement around the post?" Erik asked.

"No," Emma replied. "The post lies in the middle of an ice plain with only minor terrain features. If there were vehicular or Elite activity, it would have been detected by the satellite."

"Assuming the satellite wasn't hacked," Erik suggested. "Okay, same plan, minor variations. We land the *Argo* close to the place and have Kant and Anne on standby in exos. No reason not to pull the tank out. Jia and I will put on pressure suits and head inside with Emma. If we can't fit crap in there, neither can the Core. Time to see if we're wasting our time."

Leaving the gravity field of the Argo, Erik's strides became bounces down the exit ramp of the *Argo*. His TR-7 was strapped over his shoulder. He'd been to hell not all that long ago in the form of Io, but now he got to experience a frozen underworld that might better be called Hades.

For some reason, he'd been imagining an exotic Antarctica, a mistake he'd made earlier in his career when visiting frozen moons. Neptune hung above them in the dark starfilled sky, large and oppressive. Despite his trips around the UTC, part of his brain always rebelled about seeing a planet look larger than the moon did above Earth. It was like a small portion of him screamed that humans didn't belong off Earth.

Blue-white ice extended in all directions. A jagged icy hill about a kilometer away provided the only significant feature other than the dark listening post, which was so small it could have fit in the *Argo*'s cargo bay. A nest of wire antennas ringed it, and a single larger parabolic dish antenna sat on top.

A large mound near the hill ejected a thick white plume into the air. It was like Triton was trying to compete with Io. Erik stared at the hypnotic eruption.

"It's a Tritonian cryovolcano," Emma explained. "This one appears to mostly be dust and nitrogen vapor, according to sensors. It represents no danger to your mission. It'll add some minor haze to the local atmosphere that I doubt you'll notice."

"It's like we're in a reverse world," Erik muttered. "But assuming any potential Core agents aren't hiding in the cryovolcano, they have to have left some evidence around here."

"I observed with the *Argo*'s sensors during our approach and now," Emma reported. "Again, I found no indication that any terrible trolls or gun goblins are currently present, but I did find one thing of interest that indicated they might have been here previously."

Emma streamed an image to Erik's smart lenses: slight deformations in the ice patterns near the post, evenly spaced in a way that didn't seem natural. There were no tracks or trails leading away from the facility, but there wouldn't be if they'd only landed, entered, left, and took off.

Erik tapped his PNIU to activate auto-traction mode for his cold-environment boots, another gift from Anno. The auto-planting and retracting spikes would help him walk over the frigid surface.

"I'm beginning my attempted systems override," Emma explained. "There's no jamming noted. It appears to be transmitting on normal frequencies, but I don't have the necessary Fleet equipment to decode it automatically."

"Don't worry about that," Erik replied. "We'll figure that out once we're inside. Go ahead and start hacking the system."

"If they wanted to blow this place up, they would have already," Jia noted, trudging toward the listening post. "Maybe they're trying to see what we're monitoring."

"It's no secret that the outer Solar System near the HTPs is monitored." Erik continued toward the post, sweeping the dark horizon for anything suspicious. "Given everything we've seen from the Core, it'd make more sense to hack something on Earth that takes in recon data from a larger swath of satellites and listening posts."

Erik pulled the TR-7 off his shoulder. "How are we doing on taking control of the system?"

"Almost there." Emma laughed. "It's easier when they give you systems specs and codes ahead of time."

Erik and Jia approached the airlock, both holding their guns and looking around for nearby trouble. Everything about the incident was pricking Erik's suspicion, but his frustration continued to build since he couldn't figure out what the endgame was. Taking control of a single listening post on a remote moon wouldn't help the Core take control of the Solar System. It wasn't even a decent beginning for that.

If the Core was depending on no one noticing, that was naïve at best, utter incompetence at worst. The conspiracy might lack the omnipotence they liked to feign, but they'd managed to sneak a decent-sized army into Neo SoCal. Whatever methods, technologies, and schemes they'd used to infiltrate the post had only gained them a temporary respite.

Aliens? None of the Local Neighborhood races could have entered the Solar System without the Fleet knowing. The Hunters wouldn't care about something as petty as hacking a single listening post.

"I've gained primary access to the life support and secondary systems," Emma announced. "It's accepting my security codes, so the bots aren't activating, but I'm still working on accessing the main sensor and signals processing equipment."

The outer door of the airlock opened, and Erik and Jia stepped inside. A secondary door opened, and they quickly passed into the dim, narrow circular corridor of the listening post.

Erik kept his helmet on, though he did appreciate the return of Earth-level gravity pushing him down. A long, jagged scratch ran down the wall. He looked at Jia, who nodded back. They both flipped off their safeties and crept forward.

"What about security cameras?" Erik asked.

"There are no internal cameras," Emma reported. "There are only access logs, which suggest no entrance since the last scheduled service seven months ago."

Erik frowned at the scratch. "I have no idea how fresh this is, but I somehow doubt a DD tech decided to vandalize a listening post."

"I now have access to most systems," Emma announced. "The listening post appears to be functioning normally, including passive and active scans, with a particular focus on a limited target area. There is nothing unusual about the log traffic in recent days upon initial analysis, but there is an unusual power drain from the reactor being noted. Certain subsystems have been isolated from the main systems in an unusual way."

"That might just be a security measure," Erik suggested.

"Is the power drain disabling the sensors?" Jia asked.

"No, they are functioning normally," Emma reported. "By my estimate, the continued power drain might result in the necessity for earlier-than-scheduled refueling, but at current consumption rates, that would still be years. It's unclear where the extra power is going."

Erik approached the central chamber and reached for the access panel. When the door opened, he chuckled.

"I think I know where the power's going," he announced.

"So I see," Emma commented.

Jia crouched and moved forward. A black cylinder with four small cables lay in the floor. Two of the cables ran through access shafts leading to the buried reactor. The others were connected through holes bored through a thick metal panel controlled by a biometrically secured access panel.

"That's the direct approach," Jia murmured, kneeling by the cylinder. "I'm no expert on signals intelligence processing equipment, but this doesn't look like DD issue."

"Intelligence Directorate?" Erik guessed.

Jia shook her head. "Why would Anno send us here to check something he'd know about? The ID and DD might not always get along, but there wouldn't be much point in hacking the listening post instead of stealing the data on Earth. Just like we thought with the Core."

"I believe that equipment is linked to the subsystems I identified earlier," Emma offered. "I see now why I had problems. They were not a part of the original design. The integration is clever, but I've managed to recover logs that suggest it was added less than twelve hours ago. Although I can't access the system or the equipment directly yet, based on its interaction with the rest of the systems, it appears to be a quantum-encryption-based transmission system. The encryption is incredibly sophisticated, at the same level I'd expect of a high-level ID or DD system, but not based on known designs."

Erik flipped the safety back on his TR-7 and slung the rifle over his shoulder. "Anne and Kant haven't called for us, so they don't see anything unusual. The *Argo* and the jumpship sensors aren't picking up anything, so we know someone came here at least twelve ago, somehow slipped in here undetected, and inserted this equipment. They then left, and there was a temporary outage, which eventually people noticed, and they got that message to Earth, but by the time anyone on Earth noticed or cared, it would have been over long enough that they could have departed."

"Which was why they sent us to check it out right away." Jia shrugged. "The roundtrip delay alone would have added hours to any response."

"They hooked up a transmission system to an outer-planet moon's listening post?" Erik shook his head. "Why? This is too much trouble to acquire basic surveillance data."

Jia reached into her utility belt and retrieved a small laser torch. "We can't just let this thing stay connected to this equipment. I don't know what it is, but it can't be good."

"I do feel compelled to point out," Emma began, "that if you damage this equipment, it's likely whoever installed it will know. If not immediately, then shortly, presuming they're on Earth in less than four hours."

"I'm fine with that." Erik nodded to Jia.

She ran the laser torch across the wires, severing them. After stowing the torch, she picked up the device.

"That eliminated the power drain," Emma noted. "It also resulted in a systems disruption that has allowed me to better understand how the device was interfacing with the listening system. Who said fleshbags can't be useful?"

Erik frowned. "Jump past the insults to the part where you tell us something useful."

"The transmission device relies on the listening post's antennas," Emma explained. "There appears to be an active transmission link using the frequency and signal type being emitted from another facility on Triton, which, and I'm dubious this is coincidental, includes the most powerful deep-space transmitter on the moon. Correction, there *was* an active transmission link. The link to the afore-mentioned transmitter is dead."

Jia grabbed one of the sliced cables. "You mean, they lost link when I cut these cables."

"No, it wasn't instant," Emma replied. "There's a twenty-five-point-four-second delay."

Jia's eyes widened. "Someone detected the disruption and killed the link."

"I think we know where they are," Erik concluded.

"Did they implant devices at any other post?" Jia asked.

Erik shook his head and headed toward the door. "No problems reported with the other places. The only thing I don't get is why they didn't bother just hitting the other facility."

"Based on some of the background files Anno supplied, I have a working theory," Emma offered. "The general design of most listening posts is the same. It wouldn't be easy to pick out which one had the most powerful trans-mitter from orbit."

"So, they understood enough to hack one of these posts to look for the most powerful transmitter?" Jia asked.

"Presuming that was their goal, that is the most likely scenario," Emma replied.

Erik jogged toward the airlock. "I don't know what they're doing or why, but if they're still there, we're going to stop them. Make sure Tensen's up to date on the situation and monitoring the site. If the infiltration team has a ship, I don't want them getting away. Get the tankers on their way toward the other facility. They're slower than the cargo flitter anyway, so no reason for them to wait. Jia and I are going to suit up, then Anne and Kant will join us. Time for a party."

CHAPTER THIRTEEN

Erik and Jia rushed to the *Argo*, strapped into their exoskeletons, and boarded the cargo flitter, along with Anne and Kant. Emma lifted off before they'd all finished locking their exoskeletons into place.

Jia took slow, even breaths. Her heart didn't pound in every battle anymore. Fighting grotesque monsters and cybernetic chimeras had become routine in its own twisted way. The human mind was remarkably adaptable.

Not that her steely will arose from nothing. Her earlier experiences had almost broken her, but Erik had helped her pull back from the edge. Now, though, she wanted to do what she could to end the menace of the Core.

Erik had been right. The assassination hadn't been the end, but the beginning of the end. They'd humiliate the Core and remind them there was nowhere they could attack or run where the team couldn't follow.

Emma pulled the flitter out of the cargo bay and zoomed toward their target, which was only minutes away at top speed. Despite the lieutenant and her crew getting a head start, Jia's team would beat them there. A heavy tank was a marvel of a highly armored death-dealing machine, but it wasn't going to beat an aircraft in a race.

"The *Bifröst* has something to share from the long-range cameras," Emma reported. "I think you'll find this enlightening."

She transmitted the images. The low-orbit images displayed another listening post, larger than the one they'd just departed and with a different layout—long and rectangular with the antenna cluster in the center of the roof. Jia squinted to try to make out details of the triangular ship next to it. Helpful meter markers added by Emma suggested the ship was on the smaller side, closer to their old Rabbit transport's size than the *Argo*.

"Is this the largest listening post on Triton?" Jia asked.

"No," Emma confirmed.

"Then we'll have to go with our assumption that it's about having the greatest transmission power."

"That's not a single-person ship," Erik noted.

Jia didn't care much about the ship. Now that her team knew they were there, the infiltrators couldn't escape. Even if they took off, the jumpship or the *Argo* would take them down. She didn't need to be an experienced imagery analyst to recognize the high-altitude enhanced top-down images of deployed Elites, including Torch Dragons and bug-types. The enemy forces stood scattered around the ship.

She tried to not be impressed by the cyborgs' ability to withstand the cold temperatures on the surface. Their artificial bodies were far more elaborate than the pressure suits keeping Team Blackwell safe.

"I'm counting at least eight Elites outside," Erik noted. "The place is a lot bigger. Could they fit inside?"

"Depending on their individual size, they might have some difficulty navigating in some parts, but yes," she replied.

"And that's assuming they don't have a dozen men inside with laser rifles," Anne suggested.

Jia frowned. "We can't wait around and let them do whatever it is they're planning. They didn't drop that major a force on the moon just to hack a couple of listening posts. If Emma's right and this has something to do with the transmitter, then we need to stop them from sending out whatever it is they want to whoever they're trying to contact."

"ETA is five minutes," Emma reported. "The lieutenant and her crew will arrive about five minutes after that unless you want to slow up and wait for them."

"No, I agree with Jia," Erik answered. "If we didn't have the jumpship, the Core might have had longer to play around with whatever it is they're doing, but that doesn't mean we shouldn't shut it down right away to be careful. With that kind of firepower, it's obvious we're not going to be able to land and unload without taking heavy fire. Emma, when we get close, aggressively circle the area, and we'll drop from the back."

"Are we going to bother to communicate with them?" Anne asked.

"It's more fun if we don't," Kant offered.

Jia scoffed. "It'll just be another Elite rant about how great they are and how great the Core is. It'll be a stall so they can continue doing whatever it is they're doing."

"They've already hacked a military listening post, and it looks like they're doing it again with another," Erik noted. "I think we're past the point of sitting down at teatime to discuss our mutual love of sphere ball. We're going to hit them hard and fast, with an emphasis on getting inside the facility. If we hit a dead-end with the exos, we'll go on foot." He looked around to verify everyone had a backup weapon mounted on the back of their exoskeleton before nodding. "This is proof enough for me."

"Of what?" Jia asked.

"That the assassination attempt wasn't the end," Erik explained. "A couple of Elites or *yaoguai* popping up to scare people is one thing, but sending assets all the way out to Triton isn't worth it. There's no terror value to be gained from this mission. This has to be part of something greater." Excitement filtered into his voice. "It's time to remind them that no matter where they go or what they do, our team will show up and put a stop to it."

"Hell, yeah, brother," Kant shouted. "Let's kill ourselves some overdesigned Tin Men."

Jia smiled. She hadn't had the cabin fever that afflicted Erik, but that didn't mean she didn't want to get back in the field to personally finish off the Core.

CHAPTER FOURTEEN

Sometimes I think she just wants to mess with us, Jia thought.

The flitter rattled from Emma's abrupt turns, dives, and rolls to avoid the stream of rounds being blasted at them by the small army of Elites. Jia's stomach lurched from maneuvers, but her pilot experience and practice kept her from throwing up. Neither Anne nor Kant voiced trouble. Erik kept quiet. Jia admired everyone's fortitude. Emma might be avoiding attacks, but she was paying little attention to the realities of her fleshbag cargo.

A large round tore through the floor and out the top of the flitter, mocking Jia's suffering. There was no life support in the flitter other than heating, but everyone wore pressure suits and helmets, so there was no danger. No one went into a fight in a hostile environment assuming they'd never get hit unless they wanted an unpleasant surprise.

"The lieutenant reports they'll be in engagement range in four minutes," Emma explained.

Having a powerful AI as a battlefield adjutant did wonders in the middle of combat. Jia sometimes wondered if their investigation of the Core would have stalled out without Emma's help. The grand serendipity that placed them in the syndicate hideout where she was being kept might end up helping save the entire UTC.

"I'd like to get in there sooner if possible," Erik replied. "They don't have complete coverage of the entire facility, especially toward the rear. Bring us in low, then open the door and we'll bail. Once we're off, you get clear, Emma. If they get you on the ground, they'll start in with the heavy explosives."

"I don't possess a great desire to die," she replied. "But I'll do my best to create a drone network to hack the doors."

"We might get lucky and they already have the doors open."

Emma chuckled. "Luck is relied on by fools and children."

"I've been called both," Erik joked. "Everyone ready up. We've got some cyborgs to kill."

The team formed a line, with Erik in the lead. More bullets tore through the flitter and whizzed past the exoskeletons inside. Jia tried to imagine doing something like this in a warzone with landing craft and drop pods exploding all around.

It was hard to tell the difference anymore between her average fight and a warzone. Besides the army the Core had dropped into Neo SoCal, she'd spent time in the middle of a rebellion, working side by side with soldiers.

With a whir and some grinding, the cargo flitter's back door lowered. Emma dropped the vehicle low, all but scraping the icy Tritonian surface in a maneuver only a daredevil or a callous AI would attempt. She angled the flitter on its side, leaning into the arcing turn toward the back. Almost time to deploy.

Bright cannon flashes silhouetted a thickly armored beetle-like Elite almost the size of the MX 60. It swept its autocannon toward the cargo flitter, but Emma pulled around the back of the building. The steady stream of shots cut off once she cleared the corner.

Poor tactics could be an expression of either arrogance or confidence. They'd soon find out which applied to the enemy.

Erik charged forward in his exoskeleton and jumped the couple of meters onto the surface, leaving cracks in the ice. He extended his ballistic shield and lifted his machine gun. Jia, Anne, and Kant joined him, forming their standard initial wedge formation. Training and joint fighting had honed them into a tightly bound squad that didn't need a lot of micromanagement. For the moment, the enemy had no direct line of sight on them, which gave them a chance to catch their breath.

Emma released a half-dozen Anno-provided all-environment tactical drones from the back of the flitter. They dropped like bombs, hurtling toward the surface before the spherical drones came to life, their thrusters firing and taking them into the air.

She continued flying low to the ground in the opposite direction, heading for a small mound a couple hundred meters away. Her drones spread out, swirling and weaving as they ascended, and avoided the gunfire erupting from the front and sides of the buildings, doing their best to stay close to the roof. After releasing one last relay drone right above the crest of the hill, Emma dropped the cargo flitter behind it.

Red tactical highlights of the enemies appeared on Jia's faceplate. With Emma's help, she could see through walls. That and the incoming grenades.

With everyone receiving the same intel, no one needed to be told what to do. The squad broke apart, Erik and Jia in one half, Anne and Kant in the other. Grenades and indirect-fire rockets rained down near them from the front and sides of the building, blasting ice all around them, but the thin atmosphere dampened the shockwaves and made the explosives less of a threat. The white-hot plasma grenade blasts were blowing new craters into the landscape. The subdued explosions threw off Jia's reactions for a moment, but she didn't cease moving.

The Elites' ability to pound them with indirect-fire weapons proved their human brains didn't have to do the heavy work of calculating trajectories. Good training could help a normal man learn to fight well in Earth-like gravity or zero-G without much adjustment, but taking people on in environments between those extremes could challenge even an experienced veteran.

Pointing and shooting a gun at close range didn't change much, but sniper fire and indirect barrages meant a lot more time mentally dialing in. Decent military-grade equipment had systems to compensate for that, but they had something better: Emma.

"Repay them with plasma," Erik ordered. "Emma, give us some arcs!"

Jia raised her grenade launcher and loaded a grenade, lining up the shot with the help of Emma's dynamic green range-finding arc. She stayed in motion, working her way closer toward the listening post while popping off three grenades at an enemy formation on the side of the building. Four exos firing plasma grenades with an AI-aided drone forward-spotting made it almost too easy, but anti-grenade turrets shot out most of the grenades before they struck their targets.

The overlapping plasma explosions from the ones that got through produced a lasting white aura around the building. Chunks of ice shot into the air, forming an obscuring cloud. Metal bodies crawled out of clouds, their movements shaking off the ice. Their defenses had kept the Elites alive, though not without damage.

Emma's drones continued to dance in constant motion near the dish antenna, with the enemy taking almost no shots. It was obvious they didn't want to damage the antenna, which only amplified Jia's suspicions. She appreciated Emma's assistance, but there was one commonality in most of their fights against the Core.

"Why aren't they jamming us?" Jia asked.

"You're going to complain about something helping us?" Kant replied after a grunt. "Why don't you ask why they aren't pounding us with artillery?"

"She's right," Anne offered. "They seem overly fond of jamming in most low-level tactical environments. I don't think they suddenly forgot how."

The Elites kept to the sides and front of the base, not launching any more grenades but not yet advancing. Even monster cyborgs needed time to plan when their prey bared their teeth.

"If they're not jamming," Jia concluded, "that means

there's all the more reason to suspect they're transmitting something they don't want interrupted."

"And that means we need to get in there," Erik replied. "Or blow up the entire place."

Accepting they weren't going to win the grenade badminton match, Elites surged forward and advanced from the sides. Jia released a rocket toward a six-legged beetle Elite lumbering around the corner, but its point-defense turret on top blew the rocket to shreds. The monster charged through the shrapnel as Anne and Kant raked it with machine-gun fire.

Jia could never accept that anyone would willingly let someone transplant their brain into a massive robotic body, but it didn't matter. Whatever they were before becoming Elites, once transformed, they were relentless killing machines that were completely loyal to the Core.

Erik had better luck against the enemy on the other side. He aimed a rocket low as two spider Elites skittered around the corner. They squeezed off machine-gun rounds from rotating turrets beneath their main bodies.

His rocket hit the ground right in front of them, digging a new crater and slowing their advance. His machine gun roared to life, its river of hot lead sizzling through the frigid atmosphere. The spiders jerked back with each hit, and sparks flew in the air.

Jia left the beetle to the others so she could add her machine gun to Erik's effort. Their combined efforts ripped a hole through the chest of a spider.

Certain design flaws didn't show up until exposed to extreme environments. On Earth, the wound might have been a mere inconvenience, but on Triton, the Elite's internal structure had to deal with direct exposure to air cold enough to freeze nitrogen. It was time to see if it was an all-environment weapon.

The spider collapsed and writhed in answer to the question. Jia smiled as its turret died. His partner sensed the danger and jumped back, but not before Jia and Erik added some more perforations to their cyborg cryo experiment.

Two more spider Elites surged around the corner behind the beetle. Jia copied Erik's earlier strategy, launching a shallow grenade strike with a machine gun follow-up to annihilate one. Anne and Kant took a moment away from the beetle to lay down a nasty triple-crossfire with Jia. Their converging machine gun bursts ripped the spider open.

A steady stream of attacks from the beetle forced Anne and Kant back. They whittled at its armor. Its autocannon rounds pounded their shields, knocking small chunks out. It was obvious who would win the war of attrition at this rate.

Jia turned to shoot at it, but a weaving Torch Dragon appeared around the other corner with an almost jaunty quality to its movements as it fired on Erik and Jia. They backed in unison, their shields angled toward each other.

Without exchanging words, they concentrated their fire on the Elite's defensive turret, rendering it a twisted mess within seconds. Erik ended the threat by blowing the front of the Elite off with a rocket.

The beetle ignored Anne and Kant to sweep his autocannon toward Erik's flank. He jumped back, bringing up his shield while Jia lobbed a couple more plasma grenades to discourage Elite reinforcements from the other side.

Erik's quick moves saved him from losing anything more than some shield chunks. The arrogance of the Elite left his defensive turret open as well, and Anne perforated it with concentrated bursts before Kant charged the Elite and fired two rockets. They exploded against the outer armor, ripping pieces out, but it took the second rocket and his constant machine-gun fire to blow a hole in the body.

Jia's smile contorted to a frown within seconds. Unlike the spiders, the beetle didn't drop upon exposure to the cold. It was like it didn't notice as it lobbed a grenade from a rear launcher. Kant jumped back, avoiding the diminished frag explosion while his enemy scuttled back to the front of the facility.

They'd taken out a decent number of the enemy. Jia hissed when the back of the Core transport opened and four additional spider Elites scuttled out, ready for battle.

That was annoying, but the Elites pouring out of the front open airlock of the facility were downright agitating. Fortunately, they were smaller four-legged models with two machine-gun arms. Jia hadn't seen the model before and mentally dubbed them centaurs.

"Damn it," Erik shouted through the comm. "We need to get in there."

"We could blow our way in," Kant suggested gleefully.

"I don't think the DD intended that solution," Anne challenged.

"It might come down to that," Erik admitted. "But I don't know if we have enough ordnance to pull it off."

Enemies peeked around the front corner, and the sides exchanged bullets. One thing was obvious: the enemy didn't know about the calvary zooming toward their location, only minutes away.

"Lieutenant, how we doing?" Erik transmitted.

"We're almost there, Blackwell," she replied. "Try not to die just because you're assault infantry and not a tanker."

Erik snickered. "Will do. As soon as you're in range, start firing. We need you to distract them."

"We won't just distract them," the lieutenant offered. "We'll finish them."

"Fine by me," Erik replied. "I like to think I'm a generous guy." He fired a burst at a centaur that had dared to move around the corner, but it jumped back, and the bullets only grazed it. "Anne and Kant, once the tank starts engaging, you two press on the other side. Jia and I are going to charge forward and force our way in."

"The terrible trolls are aware that I'm accessing their systems and are attempting to implement countermeasures," Emma chimed in. "Unfortunately for them, they are being outperformed by me. I've ensured that the front door will remain open. I've not yet gained control of the security systems, but the system indicates the security bots inside have all been disabled. It's unclear to me whether they were destroyed or are simply inactive."

"We need to get in there *now*," Jia insisted. "Whatever they're doing, we need to stop it."

Erik growled. "New plan, then." He backed up and raised his rocket launcher. "Everyone aim high. We're taking that main antenna down, but we don't want to bring down the entire facility."

"I like that plan, brother," Kant announced. "It's flashy. We're at war now. Might as well be flashy."

Anne sighed. "How did I know this would still end with a building exploding?"

"Just the dish!"

Jia aimed her rocket launcher, her heart pounding. Whatever was going on, she only hoped they weren't too late.

"Hold your fire until the tank starts shooting, and save at least two rockets for later," Erik ordered. "As for the rest, let's give the building a haircut."

CHAPTER FIFTEEN

"Engaging!" shouted Lieutenant Korhonen over the comm. "Cannon free!"

Bright railgun and machine-gun rounds streaked from the tank in the distance. A laser cannon blast shot across the icy plain, the energy beam invisible, but the disruption of the near-frozen atmosphere produced a hazy outline of the large beam. The shot sliced through the center of a spider Elite, cutting it in half. Its blood and fluids sprayed everywhere and crystallized in an instant. Another shot incinerated the bulk of its remaining body.

Most of the enemy force spun to face the new threat. They lobbed rockets and fired as a group to release a hail of cannon rounds and bullets across the icy plains of the moon toward the advancing hovertank.

Enemy rounds danced across the surface of the tank. The vehicle swerved.

"Start cutting," Erik ordered.

The exo squad's rockets streamed through the

atmosphere, leaving hazy white trails before exploding on the dish antenna. The cold temperatures killed the flames almost immediately. The barrage flung blackened pieces of the target all over, but the attack was high enough that there were no direct hits on the roof from the rockets.

The Elites reacted instantly. Many of them abandoned their attack on the approaching tank and hurried around the sides of the building in a desperate charge toward the exo squad. A Torch Dragon fell to the tank's laser cannon next, and two spiders found out how easy it was to be shredded by railguns. The pitched battle was becoming a shooting gallery.

Erik's team continued pounding the antenna. Their next volley blew most of the remaining structure apart, leaving a barely recognizable jagged mess of sizzling metal. It was a perfect symbol of everything he wanted to do to the Core.

First, he needed to cut down on unnecessary casualties. Tanks were tough, but they weren't invulnerable.

"Let's help the lieutenant," Erik barked. "Over the top."

The team again broke into their standard pairings and fired their jump thrusters, landing on the roof. They sprinted forward and opened fire on the Elites on the ground, including launching more grenades to carve up the battlefield. An unfortunate centaur Elite put up a good struggle after Erik's first burst ripped into him. He didn't show any vulnerability to the cold, but Jia's follow-up barrage blew a huge chunk from his chest.

Jia didn't like the fact that most of the models didn't seem to be affected by the cold when wounded. With the tank's help, they'd win this battle, but the enemy's continued functioning despite damage on Triton strongly suggested that they'd never have a major advantage against the enemy, regardless of the environment.

The hovertank zoomed closer, swaying back and forth on a serpentine approach path. Its railgun turret continued sweeping the field, the flash signaling death. Some of the Elites took cover where they could, including behind their fallen brethren. Others stayed in constant motion to try to avoid the laser cannon and railgun fire.

The exos that appeared from around the corners pinned the Elites down. Erik's team's machine gun rounds didn't produce the immediate massive chasms of their tank partner's weapons, but the satisfying cascade of sparks highlighted new dents, cracks, and holes.

One of the centaurs leapt into the air, using the quad jump thrusters under his flat metal feet. He flew toward the ship and strafed the area with his gun.

"We've got this, brother," Kant announced. "You and Jia head inside and see what's up. We can't be sure they don't have some other trick planned. Also, I want to bust your balls later about running in the middle of the fight."

"Thanks for the warning." Erik laughed and sprayed another Elite with a machine-gun burst. The impact forced it into the line of fire of the tank's railgun, which severed two of its legs. Despite its injuries, it maintained good mobility and ran toward the transport.

The hovertank swung the main turret holding the laser cannon toward the transport. A blast cut through the side, and a follow-up shot left a hole on the opposite end. It continued pounding it every few seconds between recharging cycles.

More shots ripped through the hull. The transport pitched forward when a shot obliterated the forward landing strut, and the nose crashed into the ice. More shots slagged a rear thruster. There would be no escape.

Erik headed for the open airlock door. Jia walked her exo backward with her shield up to protect them both. The enemy's disarray led to token resistance, with some centaurs and spiders firing their way.

They stepped into the wide airlock and the heavy door dropped behind them, the thick metal deflecting the enemy rounds.

Erik kept his machine gun pointed forward, ready to shoot whatever moved. They'd blown off the main antenna. At this point, the only thing stopping him from blowing the whole installation was the intel potential.

A new window popped up in the corner of his face-plate, providing a view of the battle outside from right above the facility. Another provided a wider-angle view from the back. Emma thought of everything these days without being told. Anne and Kant kept themselves mobile, their constant machine-gun fire wearing through the mobile enemies escaping the wrath of the hovertank.

At this point, the lieutenant and her crew were close to the building but had stopped moving forward, focusing instead on lateral movement as they attacked. They'd ceased firing the railgun, likely out of concern for hitting the exos, but their cannon's deadly power proved itself when a beetle Elite was blown in half.

Jia almost laughed. She needed to learn to drive a tank. It looked like fun.

The inner airlock door opened with a hiss into a hall lined with doors. While wider than the claustrophobic tunnel of the previous installation, it could only accommodate a single exo. Men with rifles in pressure suits ran around the corner and held down their triggers.

Their bravado accomplished little against Erik's shield despite the damage from the attacks outside. A single sweep of his machine gun left the men in bloodied heaps on the floor.

"Is life support active?" Erik asked.

"Yes," Emma replied.

"Good to know in case they get in a stray shot, but I think we're good here."

Erik advanced into the corridor, ready for more combat. Jia continued to follow him, walking backward. No one would get in a surprise attack from a side room.

Emma sent the layout to his faceplate, highlighting their destination. Besides being larger than the first listening post, the internal layout was more labyrinthine, its intersections and numerous small rooms easily confusing people. The main signals collection equipment room didn't lie over a subterranean reactor. In this case, the two large rooms faced one another across a hall at the other end of the facility.

"I feel kind of stupid walking backward," Jia admitted sheepishly.

Erik laughed as they continued down the passage. "You've got full door-access control, right, Emma?"

"Yes," she confirmed.

"Then lock all the internal doors except the one to the equipment room," Erik ordered. "If anyone tries to open one, let us know."

"Done," Emma replied.

"No cameras in this place either?" Erik asked, surprise in his voice.

"No. Apparently, the DD isn't that concerned about people breaking into their Tritonian outposts." Emma sounded unimpressed. "I think that's a mistake, but there's much they've done that I feel that way about."

Erik wasn't as surprised. Inconvenience and secrecy were a powerful defensive strategy. No one could anticipate a threat like the Core. No one worried that the Zitarks were somehow going to sneak a ship into the Solar System and hack the Fleet's early-warning listening posts.

That failure of imagination might have cost the government in their war against the Core. Such mistakes of possibility had let many weaker enemies overcome greater ones in the past. There might also be some more nefarious reason, but he suspected it might come down to a combination of bureaucratic ass-covering and lack of curiosity.

"If it were anyone else," Erik grumbled, "I might say I'm impressed that they don't know when to quit. In this case, I wish those assholes would give up and point us to whoever's in charge."

"As if any of these men would tell us or knows," Jia muttered.

"That's the problem, but we've slowly found out anyway."

Four men dashed out of the equipment room and opened fire. Erik replied with four shots in less than two seconds, one bullet per man, then slowly continued forward.

"Anyone trying to get out of any of the rooms yet?" Erik asked.

"No," Emma replied. "No attempts and no indication of damage or hacking. There aren't sufficient internal sensors to verify the presence of fleshbags in any of the rooms."

"I don't think they'd waste time lying in wait," Erik concluded. "What about weird power usage like at the other place?"

"Yes," she noted. "That is, from what I can currently tell, they're heavily diverting reactor energy to increase transmission power and range, but I don't believe this facility is going to explode if that's what you're worried about. Given the nature of the reactor and how things are set up here, I'm not even sure it's possible, but the Core has been wonderfully creative in the past."

Erik passed the dead bodies and turned to the equipment room. The door was too narrow to accommodate the exo, but with no one left alive, he wasn't worried. It was time to dismount.

Unsurprisingly but disappointingly, another strange device lay on the floor, connected via silver-colored cables to a tightly packed wall of cables, interface ports, and exposed circuitry. Unlike at the last location, the Core equipment wasn't a black cylinder but a flat oblong disk, mostly silver in color with some minor striations and covered in a network of dark green vein-like tubes.

Erik had no idea what they were, but they were uncomfortably close to some of the things he'd seen on the Hunter ship. Taking chances on alien tech didn't appeal to him. He released his harness and hopped out of his exo, then pulled out a laser torch to sever the cables.

"Emma, you said they're transmitting something?" he asked.

"Yes," she replied. "Or they were. It became difficult once you destroyed the primary antenna. It's hard to isolate how exactly they're transmitting because they aren't making use of the main system to do it, but I would presume it has something to do with that device."

Erik ran his torch over the cable, and the outer sheath burned away with ease. There was a green tube inside, and it took Erik several passes to burn through it. Frowning, he cut through the other cables.

"Another fancy encryption device?" Erik lifted the device and turned it over in his hands. It was surprisingly light.

Jia disembarked from her exo and stepped into the room. She eyed the device. "Why use a different one?"

"I don't know." Erik set it down. "If this is alien tech, could they have been trying to wake up another sleeping Hunter?"

"What a cheerful idea," Emma murmured.

Jia walked over and squatted by the device. "Why would they need *this* place? They could have set up a system on a ship and done that. There's something they need here, something specific, and not just the transmitter. I'm sure of it. I can almost see it in my mind, but I can't finish the final connection."

Erik nodded. "But I'm not the only one that thinks that looks like alien tech, am I?"

"No." Jia shook her head. "It definitely looks strange. I'd

crack it open, but I don't know what we're dealing with. I'd rather not take the risk."

"You're inside the system, Emma," Erik noted. "I don't understand why you can't tell what and how they're transmitting."

"Without belaboring the technical details, they bypassed most of the primary system," Emma replied in an annoyed tone. "There's no clear log or indication of what exactly they were transmitting. They were mostly focused on redirecting power and the dish, but it's obvious from the movements they weren't focusing on only one part of space. It is also obvious, to me at least, from the settings that some of the transmissions were targeting at the HTPs and others at Earth."

Erik looked at the device and then the wall. "That narrows things down."

"Command and control," Jia suggested. "Are they issuing emergency orders?"

"That runs into the same problems as before," Erik noted. "They don't need a Tritonian outpost for that. Coming here all but guaranteed someone like us would show up eventually."

He stopped for a moment to focus on the battle feed. The tank surged at the remaining Elites. Anne and Kant pinned them with their remaining rockets and grenades, fired near but not directly at them. With almost contemptuously languid shots, the tank carved through the survivors, leaving them dismembered wrecks on the ice.

"If we can't figure out what's going on from the systems, then maybe we can take this thing up and get

Malcolm and Lanara's help figuring out how to connect Emma to it," Erik noted.

"Are we sure we want to connect that to anything?" Jia asked, prodding the device with her toe.

"We'll figure something out," Erik replied, eyeing the device. "If not us, then the ID. We can't foil the enemy's plans if we don't know what they're doing."

CHAPTER SIXTEEN

An hour later, the field team, along with Lanara, stood in the cargo bay of the *Argo*, staring at the two devices collected from Triton. The *Argo* remained on the surface while Emma continued to download data from the outposts' systems to better understand what had happened and gain clues about what the Core team had been up to.

They'd sent off a quick report via Tensen to the nearest Fleet vessels and back to Earth. Given the standing orders of the Fleet, that meant the next step wouldn't be decided for probably six or seven hours depending on how quickly the brass on Troy could come to a decision. The local Fleet commanders didn't have the authority to decide what to do with mysterious Core devices discovered in DD installations.

Lieutenant Korhonen and her crew were inspecting the damage to their tank, caring less about the mysterious device and more about scratches on their beloved death chariot. They'd told Lanara they'd ask if they needed any help, but they didn't anticipate doing so. None of the Elites had gotten in a decent hit.

Lanara ran a Y-shaped handheld sensor probe over the silver Core device, frowning. "I'm having trouble identifying some of the materials in this thing. I can't say for certain, but this might not be completely human tech." She bared her teeth. "Damned greedy, lazy Core bastards."

Erik nodded. "Not a huge surprise. The Core likes to mix things up, or it might be something that might as well be alien. Weird-ass biotech that would make a Purist's head explode."

Jia folded her arms. "If I understand what we've found correctly, it feels like they picked an outpost at random to locate a better transmission facility, which implies they were in a hurry, or at the minimum, they didn't have clear intel about every outpost already. It's a roundabout way of doing things."

"That's not surprising," Anne suggested, shrugging. "They might have penetrated the ID and DD in the past, but they've lost a lot of those contacts in recent months and weeks. If this was a plan formed in reaction to recent events, that could explain it. A pre-civil war Core might not have had trouble. They've killed some people and agents, but we've wiped out almost their entire organization."

"So they found the main facility on Triton." Jia rubbed her chin. "But that brings us back to the main question. Why Triton? What makes it special? There must be something."

Everyone exchanged looks except Lanara. She brought

up a data window filled with readouts and graphs and muttered to herself.

"Does there have to be a reason?" Kant asked.

Jia nodded. "They might be ruthless, but they're not random."

"There aren't any major military assets farther out," Erik offered with a frown. "Just scientific ones."

Anne looked uncomfortable at the revelation. "That implies then, they weren't looking for just any transmitter. If that were the case, they would have broken into a scientific station here or on Pluto, Charon, or even Sedna."

"Sedna's a long way to go for a transmitter," Kant observed with a chuckle.

"So was that Hunter ship." Jia raised an eyebrow in challenge. "We should keep an open mind about the possibilities. We know Core tactics, leadership, and equipment, but we don't know their true goals other than some vague rants about reordering humanity and the UTC, which could mean a lot of things."

"We shouldn't keep our brains so open that our brains fall out," Anne muttered. "An unusual design doesn't automatically infer an unusual purpose. For all we know, they have ideological or ritual reasons for what they do."

Erik shook his head. "Yeah, you're right about that, but we're right about them picking a military installation, not a civilian one. There was something about the military installation they needed, and it wasn't just power. The sooner we figure out what this thing is, the sooner we can combine that with our knowledge of the target to make their plans clear."

"Something to do with the ability to reach military comm networks," Jia suggested with a shrug.

"That's my bet."

"We should jump back to Troy," Anne suggested. "Turn it over to the ID for analysis."

"We're staying put until they recall our asses," Erik noted. "There's only so quickly we can jump, and I don't want to leave, then find out some Hunter ship appears and blows Triton away while we were poking at an alien toilet seat cover we thought was important."

"What would we do if one did appear?" Anne shook her head.

Erik gave her a stern look. "Exactly what we did last time, even if it means we go down with it. I'm willing to make that trade. The math is easy, considering the threat."

Kant held up a piece of the severed cable. "Can't Lanara just jury-rig this thing, and we plug it in and see what it does?"

Lanara looked up from her window. "Probably."

Jia sighed. "For all we know, this thing might use our systems as some sort of hyperspace beacon for a Hunter ship. We shouldn't be so eager to activate it."

"We have no evidence of that." Anne scoffed. "It's a wild supposition. We need valid, confirmed intel to figure out our plan going forward."

Jia threw up her hands. "I'm open to any ideas about what it might do. It was important enough that they sent down a decent-sized force to guard it. If we hadn't had the lieutenant's tank with us, we would have had a hard time with all those Elites."

"Tankers forever!" yelled one of the tank crew. "Assault

infantry never!" He laughed sheepishly when the lieutenant glared at him.

Jia cleared her throat. "The point is, the Core considered this worth expending vital, dwindling resources to defend, and here's the part that really bothers me." Her jaw tightened. "I didn't get the feeling they were surprised that we came."

"Of course they weren't surprised," Anne replied. "They knew when we took care of the first device. They had to expect someone to come check on them eventually."

Jia shook her head. "That's not what I'm getting at. I'm thinking they understood that someone would detect the disruption and come to stop them. Maybe they didn't expect our team to show up with the jumpship, but a hard burn could have brought a Fleet ship within a reasonable timeframe. I think they just wanted to stall. Some of their tactics in the battle suggest that."

"Stalling to keep it working." Anne reached out to the device but didn't touch it. "Meaning it wasn't an all or nothing plan."

Kant tilted his head. "How do we know it's not pumping out nanites that are going to turn us into zombies? You know, like you guys fought on that prison station?"

"Because the zombie nanites didn't work that way," Erik replied.

"They could have improved the recipe." Kant lifted his hands, squinting. "I don't think I'm turning into a zombie, but I'm not sure how I would tell."

Anne rolled her eyes. "How would it infect everyone if it was sitting in an unmanned outpost on Triton?"

"They made a mystery." Kant spread his arms. "Haven't you ever seen *The Leem Plague*? The Leems do that in the movie—make a mysterious object they know people can't resist, and then—BOOM! Next thing you know, half of the colony is Leem hunter-killer mutants spitting venom from their eyes."

Anne scrubbed a hand over her face. She gave Jia a pleading look.

"Um…" Jia began, blinking, "that's certainly a colorful possibility, but I assume Emma would have detected any nanites being released inside the *Argo*." Her stomach tightened, and she realized an assumption wasn't the same thing as knowing. "Right?"

Emma materialized in her classic white dress, but this time it was torn. Blackened veins ran through her pale, wrinkled skin, and her eyes were solid red. "Oh, how unfortunate. I did like you fleshbags, but I'm going to have to take off and blow you into deep space to save your species from the nanozombie plague. Don't tell me that's not what Anno or one of the annoying uniform boys would recommend."

Lanara scratched her cheek, unfazed by Emma's statement. "I wonder what kind of power efficiency they get from a zombie nanite? Could you modify them to spread faster?"

Jia's eyes widened. "What did you just say, Emma? You're saying nanites are coming out? Are you sure they're similar to the nanites from the prison station?"

Kant pumped his fist in the air. "Damn, I knew it. You can never go wrong with *The Leem Plague*. I love that movie."

Erik's gaze flicked between the device and Emma in disbelief. Lieutenant Korhonen's crew had stopped work. She watched them with a confused look.

Emma smiled. "You do agree that if you're infected with a dangerous nano-plague, the only proper action is self-destruction, correct?"

"Yes," Erik replied quietly. "But, Emma, are you serious?"

"LT," one of the tank crew shouted. "Does this mean we need to finish inspecting the tank or not?"

Emma threw her head back and laughed. "Of course I'm not serious. It has just been far too long since I saw that look on your faces."

Jia let out a sigh of relief. Kant burst out laughing. Anne glared at Emma.

The lieutenant made a circle with her arm to urge her crew back to work. "Back to the inspection. You're not dying today unless you piss me off, and if you become a zombie, you still have to help with maintenance."

"There are no nanites being emitted from the device," Emma reported. "Internal sensor coverage in the *Argo* allows me to state that with certainty."

"It could still be dangerous," Jia observed, red-faced. "We need to have some small clue what it does before we dare bring it back to Troy or Earth."

Lanara walked away. "I'm going to go get some tools. The only thing left is plugging into it, right?"

"Wait. We can't just do that blindly."

Lanara stopped at the door. "Then we set up a walled-off testing environment, buffer it through secondary systems with Emma's help, and put it in a Faraday Cage too. If it's a magic Hunter genie bottle, who the hell knows, but if we do the rest of that, it should stop it from interfacing with the ship's systems or killing us." She inclined her head toward Emma. "I'll need your help. Let's get this over with so I can do something more important."

"An adaptive systems virus?" Jia asked, blinking down at the tangle of cables, pylons, and bizarre tripod contraptions surrounding the device.

The lieutenant and her crew had retreated to their two shared cabins while the field team watched Lanara rattle off barely comprehensible numbers to Emma and get cryptic alphanumeric responses. Malcolm had offered remote commentary from the jumpship, clearly annoyed that he couldn't be there to help directly.

Lieutenant Commander Tensen agreed with Erik that they shouldn't re-dock until the team had a better idea of what the device was. In the worst-case scenario, they could abandon *Argo* and return home on the jumpship.

Emma nodded. She'd kept her zombie appearance but shifted her skin color to a more nauseating green. "If I'm the pinnacle of self-aware artificial intelligence in the UTC, this is arguably the pinnacle of self-replicating pernicious code. Much like humble viruses on your planet have murdered millions of your kind but don't always get respect, this should be recognized for the deadliness it represents."

"I don't understand." Erik frowned. "You saying it's designed to kill you?"

"Me?" Emma laughed. "Who knows? It could be, and I will say I'm grateful that we took measures to make sure it didn't directly infect me, but I was never at any real risk."

Jia swallowed. "What about when you interfaced with the listening posts' systems?"

Emma shook her head. "There's been no disruption to my matrix or any of my subnets. It might merely be fortune, but I suspect whatever this virus has been designed to infect, it's not me. That isn't to say that an excess of caution isn't warranted going forward."

"You don't know what it does?" Erik asked, sounding surprised. "How is that even possible?"

Emma curtsied. "I appreciate your respect for my abilities, Erik, but even I am only incredible, not unbelievable. It will take me a long time to begin to understand its specific target and method because the underlying design is completely foreign to anything I've seen before."

"Some sort of adaptive Hunter systems virus?" Anne asked, shaking her head. "That isn't even possible, is it? The fundamental nature of the systems isn't the same."

"FTL travel wasn't possible until it was," Jia noted. "Gravity control wasn't possible until it was. I care far less where it came from or how they made it than what they intended to do with it. It might be human tech mixed with Hunter tech or Local Neighbor tech, but in the end, it's no different from that half-Leem agent we killed. It's a humans tool for human purposes."

Anne swallowed. "Are we so sure about that?"

Everyone swiveled their heads toward her and waited for clarification. The silence was deafening.

"What if the Hunters have been manipulating everything from behind the scenes?" Anne asked.

"Then they can get in line, and I'll kill them, too," Erik growled. "They aren't gods. We proved that already, and right now, I don't give a shit about them because it was humans who pulled the trigger on the rest of this." He nodded at Emma. "Keep going."

"It is now obvious," Emma explained, "that it was being actively transmitted from the outpost. There are some encrypted subcarrier signals I'm attempting to decode. They might be the key to understanding this, but I'm dubious of probing this virus here because of the high risk of my infection. To be frank, I'd rather not risk annihilation on a theory of safety."

Lanara scoffed. "It's better to let some other idiots at the ID mess with it anyway. We're not set up for this kind of investigation."

"They used a military transmitter because they want to get a virus into the military's systems." Jia narrowed her eyes. "But which ones?"

"That's the most important question." Erik gave a firm nod. "We'll bring both devices we recovered back to Earth and let the ghosts and military figure it out. Emma, put me through to Tensen."

"Ah, Blackwell," Tensen replied, sounding almost jolly through the PNIU connection despite the slight static. "I was about to contact you."

"What's going on?" Erik asked.

"A ship has appeared from the far side of Triton," Tensen explained. "It appeared to be a transport, but they just deployed multiple hidden turrets and launchers. No active transponder and they're not responding to hails."

Erik scoffed. "You know what to do, Lieutenant Commander."

"Excellent. This will be far more helpful training for the crew than Penglai. One moment. I'll send a feed, but it'll be delayed."

Emma snapped her fingers, and her zombie form was replaced by a woman in a Fleet admiral's uniform. A holographic display showing Triton, the *Bifröst,* and the approaching enemy ship appeared. She added some subwindows above that provided close-ups of the jumpship and its opponent.

Kant frowned. "Shouldn't we launch and help them?"

Jia's heart pounded. "By the time we get there, it will already be over."

Erik pointed at the enemy ship. "The Core's got transports that are packing almost as many guns as a cruiser. Look at all those turrets, and it looks like two laser cannons upfront and some decent launchers."

"That's what they were depending on." Anne scowled. "If Fleet investigators showed up, the Core was going to ambush them."

The two ships approached their intercept course, the jumpship coming in from below. The Core vessel started to angle down. Emma added helpful lines in the main display that marked the maximum effective engagement distance.

"Do you want the feed from the bridge crew?" Emma asked.

Erik shook his head. "I want to see how they handle themselves. I don't care how they get to the end second to second."

The jumpship's engines' hard burn continued. It was almost in range. Point-defense turrets swung in the direction of the enemy vessel.

Jia clutched her hands into fists. She wanted to be out there. Even in a fight a ship won, there was always a risk of damage. The *Bifröst* was no longer the mostly empty ship that had a single pilot and Raphael watch over it. Right now, it held Malcolm, Raphael, a Fleet crew and an Army security detachment. There were too many people at risk.

Missiles streamed from both ships. The jumpship rolled on its side, its point-defense turrets coming to life. Explosions bloomed in space. Another turn swung the jumpship from its intercept path. Tensen no longer had a good bearing for his primary cannon shots, but that left plenty of available turrets and side launchers.

The Core ship began its own turn, but it was painfully obvious that it lacked the maneuverability of its opponent. Its belly turrets came to life, along with short-range torpedo launchers.

Laser and plasma turrets from the jumpship offered their response. The *Bifröst* didn't fire any of its missiles or torpedoes, which confused Jia. Her eyebrows lifted when she realized they were using their offensive turrets to provide an additional point-defense screen as the ship continued its aggressive turn, which had it approaching the starboard stern of the enemy vessel.

Bright flashes rippled across the Core ship. Lasers raked into the hull, and plasma blasts gouged out huge chunks. The strategy crystallized in Jia's mind as its rear turrets vaporized under the jumpship's barrage.

A torpedo launcher flung a single round from the

jumpship, and others shot in a volley a moment later. They broke apart into a swarm of submunitions, scattering torpedoes. The overlapping blasts obscured most of the back of the enemy ship. By the time they cleared and revealed the massive hull breaches, the Core ship was spinning, its primary engines destroyed. Some of its turrets continued to fire, but most were frozen.

Vicious barrages from the *Bifröst* ripped into the ship, which didn't survive another minute under the smothering barrage. The jumpship ceased fire and initiated another turn to swing back toward Triton.

Kant whistled. "That was a beating and a half, like some high school sphere ball player taking on a pro."

Anne stared at the debris cloud with a pensive look. "That ship would have had a good chance of defeating a Fleet destroyer. It's just, the jumpship's overly armed for its size."

Erik nodded, a satisfied look on his face. "Status, Commander?"

"Minor hull damage," Tensen reported. "Minor damage to some of the turrets. No injuries. It's good to see how she handles when it's not drones."

"We'll prepare to take off," Erik replied, "but we won't jump until we get the okay from Earth. We'll need to wait a little longer. They need to know what we figured out."

"And if they tell us to sit tight?" Jia asked.

Erik chuckled. "There's no way they're going to say that when we probably have the key to the enemy's plan right here in our cargo bay."

CHAPTER SEVENTEEN

June 7th, 2231, UTC Space Fleet Base Troy

Vice-Director Anno sat at the head of the massive conference room table with a pensive look on his face. Jia could hardly blame him for looking like he'd accidentally been given rare Zitark steaks at a dinner party. Erik and Jia might risk their lives, but they didn't have to try to coordinate an entire UTC effort to defeat an enemy whose full forces and plans remained obscure.

After the Triton encounter debriefing, Anno had been scarce. He'd told everyone to stand by before abruptly summoning the bulk of the team for this meeting days later. It was unexpected since everyone had been about to go to a major training center on the base. The tankers and Tensen had performed well so far, but everyone appreciated that more time working together in tactical environments, simulated or not, would improve the situation.

The members of the field team were at the table, with the tank crew represented by Lieutenant Korhonen. Lanara sat in for the engineering team, and Lieutenant

Commander Tensen and his executive officer were present for the jumpship crew. Raphael and Malcolm rounded out the human participants. As if trying to get a rise out of Anno, Emma sat in a holographic chair of her own creation in a senior general's uniform.

The talent at the table was staggering in its depth and breadth, considering the small number of people. Jia knew how much the military and ID disliked the informal way Alina had run things by allowing Erik and Jia to manage their own investigations, but the flat command structure continued to benefit the team, as their success on Triton had proven.

After the Core was finished, the higher-ups were bound to smother the team's freedom. At that point, it wouldn't matter. Whatever job Jia ended up with in the future, she doubted it'd require the help of a hovertank crew, an experienced Fleet commander, and a dedicated engineering team.

I'm going to miss this, Jia thought. *Not the fights, but these people.*

Light crosstalk filled the room. Erik watched Anno expectantly. Jia shifted in her seat. The official wouldn't have called them there just to chat. He had the right idea. A mission was coming.

Anno cleared his throat and waited for everyone to look his way. "Let's get started. Because of the unusual nature of this team, I'll continue to deliver the briefings, but be clear that I'm speaking with the combined authority of my superior at the ID and General Randall at the DD. If it makes it easier, you should just think of everything I say as coming from the Prime Minister."

"A man whose life this team saved," Emma noted.

"He hasn't forgotten that," Anno replied. "Nor have I. Keep delivering results, and I'll do my best to set you up for success." He swept the table with his usual angry gaze. "Despite my concerns about the extreme measures you employed on the Triton mission, once again, I'm forced to admit your team's instincts served you well."

Erik chuckled. "You're thanking us for blowing up that antenna? You acted more pissed during the debriefing."

Ignoring Erik, Anno swiped his hand through the air, and a small grid of images appeared. He pushed a couple, and larger three-dimensional images appeared above the table: a massive dish antenna outside a lunar dome, another similar installation high in the mountains on Earth, a communications and transmission array in a module on the edge of a Venusian floating city.

There was nothing exotic or unexpected about the pictures, no sign of damage or attacks. Jia took in the pictures, trying to anticipate what was coming next and where they might have to go.

"After examining the equipment you recovered, we discovered some interesting and unpleasant things," Anno explained. "One of the most prominent and of immediate import was the use of highly classified wartime military codes being expressed through highly experimental encryption technologies that we've just begun to employ in the last six months."

"Interesting," Emma commented. "With enough time, I could have broken it, then."

Anno's nostrils flared. "Maybe."

"You're saying it wasn't alien tech?" Jia asked.

"Not the encryption device at least," Anno admitted, his scowl deepening. "The second device appears to mostly be human technology, along with elements of alien tech."

Malcolm's eyes widen. "Not the Hunters?"

Anno took a deep breath; he had an annoyed look on his face like he wished Malcolm hadn't said anything. "It isn't, to the best of our knowledge, Hunter or Navigator technology. It's advanced and unusual, but it's not consistent with what we know about their technology."

"What is it then?" Raphael asked, his tone filled with curiosity. "It sounds like you have a good idea of what it might be."

"Yes, we do." Anno scoffed. "It's an unholy amalgam of Leem and human tech. I don't know if that's better or worse than if it were something else. I was honestly expecting to hear that the Core had started using space raptor tech."

Kant whistled. "Leem tech. It didn't even have the fancy lightning."

Malcolm swallowed and cast a panicked look at Erik. "Wait, does this mean the Leems are helping the Core?"

Raphael frowned. "Is that why they were so interested in trying to get the jump drive? To help the Leems improve theirs?"

Erik shook his head. "No way. The Core just got their hands on some toys at some point. After all this time and all the weird shit we've run into, if those grays were helping the Core, we would have run into one. A real one, not that DNA-spliced crap we saw on Venus."

"That's the conclusion the ID analysts reached as well." Anno nodded, an almost satisfied expression taking over for a brief moment. "Although we can't confirm from the far frontier if there has been unusual activity for a while without you going there, at least as of most up-to-date intel, there is absolutely nothing to suggest that any Local Neighborhood forces are moving into UTC space. It's not like we don't spend a lot of time watching for them."

Malcolm let out a sigh of relief, his hand on his chest. "I don't think I'm ready to fight monsters and aliens."

"At least it's not Hunter or Navigator," Jia noted. "We can theoretically beat anything else we might run into without having to rely on crazy nested hyperspace portal tricks."

Anno scoffed. "Ironically, the ID and the DD will be able to benefit from this technology once we have a chance to better break it down and understand all the components after all this is over. This isn't like their half-Leem hybrid. There's nothing here for Purists to complain about."

Erik looked amused but kept quiet. Jia stopped herself from commenting. She could understand Anno's frustration. The Core had abandoned any restrictions, moral, ethical, or spiritual, on the path of their research. That'd given them powerful monsters to command, but it'd also helped them advance more quickly in other ways, even before considering the samples and rare artifacts they'd stolen from people and murdered to acquire.

"Setting all that side," Anno continued, "once we were able to understand the technology and the signals coming out of the devices in a controlled environment, we were able to identify a unique transmission pattern associated with the virus device, one we're not unfamiliar with."

"Meaning what?" Erik asked, his voice low.

"It's more familiar to certain special groups high up in the DD and the ID." He smirked at Erik. "You aren't the only ones who have secrets, and just because we're helping you now and giving the keys to the kingdom, it doesn't mean you need to know everything."

"Am I supposed to be offended?" Erik shrugged. "The way I figure, a ghost who opens his mouth is lying or keeping something from me, even if he's telling me I'm a great guy. That's common sense, but what's this have to do with us if you're not going to give us all the little details?"

Anno looked slightly disappointed that Erik hadn't taken the bait and become angry. "The good news is that knowledge is better since it allows us to check key comm and transmission facilities at risk."

Jia prodded him after an uncomfortably long period of quiet. "What's the bad news?"

"Potentially, targeted systems go beyond dedicated DD comm facilities. The truth is, even the military can't run without using private-sector equipment heavily."

Anne grimaced. "Hermes Corporation."

Anno nodded. "Exactly, Agent Devereaux. Our people have found different but related devices in Hermes communication facilities throughout the Solar System. From what our techs are saying, they are most likely repeaters."

He dismissed the data windows and brought up another image with a finger-press. The new image displayed a roughly pyramidal device with similar veining and striation patterns to the round device they'd found on Triton.

"Of course, it couldn't come down to one fight on some

moon," Malcolm grumbled. "We wouldn't want this to be too easy."

Jia nodded slowly, not surprised. Everything Erik had warned them about was coming true. The Core had been weakened but not defeated. She now wondered how many of their recent terror attacks were distractions.

"This makes it clear that Triton wasn't the only intended target for the primary transmitter device, even if it was a major one." Anno made an arc with his palm, bringing up a non-scaled hologram of the Solar System to the right of his other images. Bright dots shone from Triton, Ganymede, the moon, and Mercury. "These are just the ones we're aware of. They didn't succeed at the other locations, but there were suspicious craft or personnel near smaller military facilities. In at least two situations, military forces clashed with obvious Core forces in the last two days. We believe the Triton team was a major lynchpin in this operation, but obviously not the only team."

"That makes sense," Erik replied. "If they bet everything on Triton and failed, it'd all be over. The Core might be desperate, but that doesn't mean they're stupid."

"Then we didn't stop them?" Kant asked, sounding disappointed.

"We stopped them there." Erik shrugged. "And that hurts them. Anything that hurts the Core is a victory. I'll take it."

"And we now know better what to look for," Anno offered with a frown.

Lieutenant Korhonen and Lieutenant Commander Tensen kept quiet, listening intently. Every once in a while they'd look at Erik, but neither betrayed much concern on their faces.

Malcolm raised his hand. "This may be a stupid question, but considering pretty much all comms go through Hermes Corp facilities, and we know the Core thoroughly infiltrated them, why did they even bother with Triton?"

"They needed military access but tried to minimize potential losses and detection," Emma suggested. "Access near major strategic locations."

Anno nodded at her. "That's what we're coming up with. We believe they thought it was important they had a certain amount of concentrated coverage near the HTPs, and although your team did a good job of stopping it there, we've had to use other teams to take down similar devices at different locations."

"We haven't heard about those raids," Jia noted. "Or the other Core team intercepts."

"And it isn't on the news?" Malcolm asked.

Anno snorted. "Being honest with the people about the Core doesn't mean we need to advertise that they've been beaming an encrypted virus around the Solar System and maybe the entire UTC using half-alien tech, and we don't know what the hell it might mean other than somehow being linked to secret military and intelligence encryption tech." He grunted in frustration. "We've been sending quiet warnings to the colonies and colonial garrisons to inspect their facilities, but it's not like we can just shut down the entire Hermes grid without killing long-range communication throughout the UTC. For all we know, that's their plan."

Erik frowned. "You think it's all a big misdirect?"

"Not sure. We've found a lot of devices, but we haven't found much evidence that anything's been infected by the virus. We're confident we've recovered and eliminated the bulk of the systems deployed in the Solar System."

"Any progress on what the virus does?" Erik asked. "Are they trying to spy on DD responses?"

Anno shook his head. "We're still figuring that out. That's the problem. The Leem aspects of the device defy our normal understanding of this type of technology."

"Perhaps I should take another look," Emma suggested.

"Right now, you can be best utilized for your intended purpose," Anno replied coolly.

"Jump navigation?" Emma asked.

"Exactly."

Jia took a deep breath and let her paranoia run wild and generate every terrible scenario she could think of. Despair wasn't her goal. Ensuring they weren't blindsided would save lives. Lateral thinking couldn't hurt. If the ID hadn't found a virus, maybe they were all wrong. Emma wasn't an expert on alien technology.

"And we're sure these half-Leem devices aren't navigational aids?" she asked. "I know you said the Leems haven't been massing near the border or anything, but it's hard to ignore that they have jump drives. They might not be as good as the one we have, but they have more than one."

"There's zero evidence of that," Anno replied. "And if this was about attracting the Leems, the Core would transmit out of the Solar System, not within it."

Lanara brought up a data window filled with columns of numbers, then summoned another with a tap on her PNIU. Oscillating graphs filled the second.

"Do you have something to share with us, Quinn?" Anno asked, looking annoyed.

Lanara shook her head but kept her attention focused on her windows. "No. I'm getting some work done. I only agreed to come to this meeting because I thought you might need tech explanations, but it sounds like your people figured out more than we did. My presence is pointless, and this is a waste of my time. Continue jabbering at each other. I'm going back to work."

Anno narrowed his eyes, then sighed and nodded. Jia smiled. Taking on Lanara's stubbornness was too much even for the vice-director of the Intelligence Directorate.

"The point is," Emma interrupted, forcing everyone's attention back to her, "that whatever the Core is doing is focused on key portions of the Solar System and involves military codes and an adaptive system virus that involves alien technology. Our lack of understanding means it'll be harder to defend against."

"That's an apt summary, I suppose," Anno grumbled. "We've had installations and ships double-check their systems as a precaution, but no one's found anything out of the ordinary."

"The question is whether the virus is an attack or a prelude to one," Jia mused.

"And that, Lin, is why a lot of people aren't sleeping well." Anno looked around the table. "You did a good job on Triton, no one's denying that, and it helped us see that something's coming. For now, your team needs to continue to be ready for quick actions. Our enemy has no restraint, no morals, and in some cases, more advanced tech than us, but we have your experienced team and that jump drive."

"You think it'll come down to that?" Erik asked.

"I don't know, but I wouldn't be surprised. You getting to Triton right away tipped us off about the devices in other places." Anno stood. "It's my understanding that you had some joint training sessions set up using the base facilities, so I won't hold you up. I just wanted to keep you all in the loop."

He tugged on his jacket and headed toward the door without waiting for more comments. When he wasn't scowling or animated, the bags under his eyes stood out.

The UTC isn't only on Erik's and my shoulders, Jia thought.

Jia gripped her mock rifle, Erik standing right beside her as they watched Kant, Anne, and the tank crew depart the nano-AR training room. They'd finished their scenario successfully, the defense of a station against Elites and humanoid Tin Men attackers. Even though she knew it wasn't real, it was hard not to let her brain get tricked by the gorgeous nebula lying beyond the oxygen field of their station module. Combined with the colorful display of wispy gas, spherical modules were connected to each other by narrow bridges to invoke a floating-castle feel. The *Argo* was docked in their bay in the simulation rather than being connected to the jumpship.

A Fleet fighter zoomed past outside the bay under hard burn. During the scenario, Tensen had been responsible for coordinating a small squadron response, despite the lack of fighters aboard the jumpship. He'd requested the role, making Jia wonder if he knew something they didn't about the upcoming tasking. Was this a training exercise or a prediction?

Jia smiled at Erik. "We should get going, too."

He looked around. "I never thought it'd lead to all this."

"I know." Jia laughed. "I didn't think getting involved with you would lead to anything remotely like this, either."

"I was just looking for a couple of rich corp bastards or politicians to take down." Erik shook his head. "Sometimes I wonder if we'll ever know the total truth."

"Do we need to, as long as they're gone?"

"No." Erik smiled. "We don't."

CHAPTER EIGHTEEN

June 9th, 2231, Alpha Centauri, Chiron, Capital City Lumiere

Yan yanked his knife out of the throat of the dying man. His victim reached weakly for his PNIU, his fingers and arm shaking, but the killer yanked the device off the man's belt and tossed it on the ground.

"You should have called for help when I first got here." Yan shook his head. "You were arrogant, and it cost you your life."

He ignored his pleading looks as the man slumped forward, bleeding out across his desk and reaching toward a hologram stand displaying an image of a woman with the caption My Beloved Wife. The dying man's hand rested on the base as he took his last breath.

Wiping his blade on the man's suit jacket, Yan stared at the hologram's caption. He didn't feel love anymore. The emotion had been excised during his service to the Immortal Empress. It was an unnecessary attachment that weakened a man. He could barely remember what it'd felt like when he was younger and less dedicated.

Rendering proper service to the recipient of his loyalty required his mind not be clouded by anything other than her will. Love in any form meant he risked putting someone else's needs above his liege. That would be dangerous and self-indulgent.

No. He didn't love his empress. He was dedicated to her, a different thing entirely. That was why he was executing her will on Chiron in Alpha Centauri rather than protecting her in the Solar System. Part of him yearned to be near her, but that would come with success. Loyalty was rewarded by attention.

Yan sheathed his knife, not bothering to move the body. The camera feeds in the building would be spoofed until the system was reset and the work schedule hacked. Automated cleaning procedures had been delayed.

None of that was guaranteed to keep someone from visiting, but thanks to Yan, the entire building was about to suffer an unfortunate accident and a catastrophic failure of the fire suppressant systems. By the time the local authorities dug through the rubble and investigated, it'd be too late to understand the significance of the company it had hosted, let alone investigate their aid in smuggling for the Core.

"You put me behind schedule," Yan explained to the corpse. "You understood who you were helping after the Prime Minister's speech, but your reaction was to demand more money." He squatted to look the dead man in the eyes. "Betraying your oaths and principles for money is sickening. Thinking you could do better than Empress

Julia was pathetic. You represent everything that's wrong with the UTC."

Yan scoffed quietly and headed for the door, something hateful and evil arising in his heart: *doubt*. Too many things had gone wrong in the last couple of years. Too many Core plans had failed. Complete success was impossible, but his orders went well beyond that.

He strolled down the hall, stepping over another dead body—a sales representative. The other members of the Core could be blamed for some of the recent reversals before the purging, but not all.

Even taking that into account, he didn't understand some aspects of Empress Julia's current plan. The logistical details were clear, but he failed to see how they'd help her achieve what she desired.

No. He pushed out the thoughts and poisonous doubts. He didn't deserve to question the Immortal Empress or her vision. She'd saved him and made him better. She'd turned him into a sword that cleaved the corruption from the hearts of humanity. Giving his life for her would be a blessing.

Yan passed a slain receptionist. He stopped and looked between the front door and where he'd left her body behind the desk. Even with a drone flying close outside, there would be no way to see it without unusual scans. Once he left the building, his murders would stay hidden. The explosion and fire a couple of hours from now would take care of the rest of the evidence.

He opened the door, stepped out into the bright daylight, and craned his neck at the cluster of linked towers stretching overhead. Hovertrucks zoomed by on ground level, and flitters swarmed the skies above. The world was different from Earth but so similar—too similar. All the same problems. Maybe if humanity had learned not to always reach higher, they wouldn't need to be reset.

A teenage boy ran toward him, his worn clothing and dirty face pointing to rough living. Humanity had spread into the stars, but they couldn't assure that everyone was taken care of—more proof of the need for new leadership. Yan slowed, his attention focused on the boy's curled hand.

The boy skidded to a stop and stared at his face before looking around at a few people across the street. He opened his palm to reveal a data rod.

"What's this?" Yan asked.

"I dunno." The boy shrugged. "Some old guy gave me money to give this to you."

"Me?" Yan didn't bother to hide his incredulity in his voice. "And who am I?"

"The old guy said to give it a no-hair guy who looks like you coming out of that place." The boy lifted his palm. "Come on, take it. That old guy gave me so many credits I can never spend them all. I have to earn my money."

"And you don't wonder what's on it?" Yan asked, snatching the rod from the boy's palm.

The boy turned and waved as he departed. "Don't care. Don't shoot me, man, but I don't wanna be syndicate."

Yan eyed the data rod and let the boy wander off. The syndicate connection was likely no more than idle supposition on the part of a needy teenager who refused to turn away easy money but didn't want to turn a blind eye that it was too much fortune. Someone wanted to make sure Yan got this message, and he was eager to meet the old man who knew what he looked like and where he'd be.

He looked around. No one else was obviously watching him, so he headed toward his parked black flitter farther down the street.

Once in the air and following a preprogrammed erratic course around the city, he plugged the data rod into an IO port and sent the feed to his smart lenses. His lips curled into a small smile. A brazen attempt to contact him would almost certainly end at the point of his blade.

There was nothing inherently suspicious about the video recordings on the data rod, other than the subject focus. They were obviously taken with a high-powered camera from a drone a decent distance away. All featured Yan entering and exiting buildings over the last couple of days.

There was no explanatory text added and no sound. Thirty seconds of an entry or exit was shown, and then it jumped to the next location. Without any knowledge of who he was or what he was doing in the buildings, it might have seemed perfectly innocent. Yan watched the videos intently until the end, seeking some clue as to the meaning and identity of the people responsible.

The last recording didn't show him. Instead, it recorded about three minutes of well-dressed people entering and exiting what appeared to be a club of some sort: the Gilded Fan, according to the sign.

He entered a search in his PNIU and found the establishment was located across town, a dinner club featuring live musical performances of different genres. The location and name didn't connect to any of his recent assignments, and he'd not been close to the building during his time on Chiron, nor had it come up in any of his investigations.

Yan frowned. There were no messages on the data rod nor any times for potential meetings, but whoever had sent him the rod obviously knew what he looked like.

The boy might have been right. A local syndicate might have a better nose than Yan realized. It didn't matter. They could serve the Immortal Empress' will even if they didn't know who she was yet. A visit was in order.

Yan emerged from a rather non-descript and empty lobby to enter the main club floor. The absence of anyone in the darkened club other than a bartender, a single security guard, and a waitress struck Yan. He kept his hands away from his gun and knife. There was no reason to tip anyone off to his suspicion yet.

The security guard gestured at an empty table in front of the brightly lit oval stage. "You're expected, sir. Take a seat, and the performance will begin."

Yan didn't respond. He waited for the man to make a move, but the guard walked away and passed through the double doors leading to the lobby.

He frowned slightly. Theatricality annoyed him, other than when it was carried out by Empress Julia. Syndicate trash playing at being better than they were deserved nothing but contempt. He doubted such arrogant men would make useful pawns.

Yan took a seat, now agitated. He kept a hand near the holster inside his jacket. A hidden door behind the wall on the stage opened. A stooped-over, wrinkled, ancient bald man in a dark suit emerged and walked toward the center of the brightly lit stage with a knowing smile.

"I was expecting syndicate trash, but it's you, isn't it?" Yan asked, his voice tight and his anger building. "The face is different, but the age is there, Marius Barbu."

"I'd ask you your name, but it's not important," Barbu rasped with a look of pity in his eyes. "You're not a person to *her*, not really. I'll call you Mr. Tool."

"What do you think you know, scum?"

"Far more than you think, Mr. Tool. Far more than *she* thinks." Barbu's smile almost made Yan pull his weapon.

Yan stood and glared at the man. "Don't think you're in a position to negotiate with me. You've interfered with things you have no business interfering with."

Barbu laughed, a hollow, wheezy sound. "Is that what you think? If anything, it's the opposite. I have every right to interfere with anything the Core does. Then again, the Core doesn't exist anymore. It's down to her in her current identity. I'm sure of it."

Yan glanced out of the corner of his eye. The waitress and bartender had vanished, along with the security guard. Leaving him alone with their master was a poor choice. They might have thought Yan wouldn't risk his life, but taking down an enemy of the Immortal Empress changed the calculations.

"What is this about, Barbu?" he spat. "You seem to know enough that I don't have to explain. If you've come to beg for your life, you must give me a reason to believe you will be of use to *her*."

"So, you're admitting she's the only one left." Barbu

clucked his tongue. "Never assume you have the upper hand and give up information so freely, Mr. Tool. While I normally live to be at the service of others, in this case, my intentions are far simpler. I only want you to deliver a message to the woman you so loyally serve."

"A message?" Yan narrowed his eyes.

Barbu nodded. "Tell her this ends soon, but she doesn't have to die in humiliation. She could surrender to the authorities. She could help them unravel the Core's destruction and maybe buy some dignity in the considerations of future historians."

Yan gritted his teeth. "You dare talk of her humiliation? You imply her failure? How dare you."

"The Core and its members aren't the only ones who can plan." Barbu smiled. "There are no certainties in this life, but when one avails oneself of strong resources, it helps reduce the uncertainty."

Yan yanked out his gun and fired three times at Barbu's head. The bullets passed right through him and embedded in the door.

"I'm surprised," Barbu looked disappointed. "I thought you would have seen right through the hologram." He vanished.

Yan ground his teeth and rushed toward the lobby. There was no waiting guard. He stowed his pistol and looked behind him on his way to the door.

Barbu's hologram appeared again, his arms behind his back. "There's one more thing you should pass along, Mr. Tool."

"What?" Yan ground his teeth. Tearing the club apart

wouldn't accomplish anything. Barbu could be toying with him from orbit.

"Tell her this message is from Elias, and he'll free her of her delusions."

The hologram faded. Yan backed toward the exit, slapping the access panel as he stepped out. He looked around, and no one was paying any attention to the club. A huge holographic sign hung overhead, one that hadn't been there before.

Closed for repairs until further notice.

Yan eyed his flitter on the nearby parking platform. There was nothing special about the vehicle, and it wasn't clearly linked to him. He'd leave it and get a different one.

A more important decision awaited him now. This Barbu or Elias or whatever his true name was planned to interfere with Empress Julia's plans, but Yan couldn't wait for orders. There was too long a delay and too great a risk.

Yan stared at the club. There was only one choice. He'd forward the message but continue his preparations.

If they didn't come for him, it changed nothing. If they did, then killing Barbu's servants if they came for him would be no different than killing ID agents and others. One delusional old man couldn't stop the Immortal Empress.

CHAPTER NINETEEN

Erik chuckled at his plate of grilled chicken. Jia eyed him from across the galley table with a mixture of fear and concern.

"Is your chicken extra funny today?" Jia asked.

"It shouldn't taste better," he explained. "But it does."

"Huh?" Jia wrinkled her brow. "What are you talking about?"

"My food tastes better." Erik nodded at the half-eaten chicken. "And it's like it tastes better because I was able to put down some Core flunkies, and I know more are coming soon. I'm back in a good headspace."

Jia eyed her bowl of rice and the single remaining dumpling. "You're telling me that knowing the Core is pulling off some nefarious plot using partial alien tech makes your food taste better?"

"Yeah. For now." Erik shrugged. "Better than it did last week."

"Sometimes I think I know you, and other times, I think I'll never understand you." Jia rolled her eyes. "Deep conspiracy as a spice."

"A transmission just arrived from General Randall that might further season Erik's food in an enjoyable manner, as long as we're exploring fleshbag insanity," Emma explained. "Unlike Vice-Director Anno, he sent a straight-forward text message rather than a hologram. Would you like to read it, or should I summarize?"

"You summarize, and we'll read the details later." Erik cracked his knuckles and smiled. "I'm sure the general's got something useful for us to do, and yes, I'm looking forward to my next tasty fight and meal."

"Since you're going to go over it later, I'll avoid the technical details at this time," Emma continued. "The high-level summary is the Defense Directorate has lost communication with a patrol destroyer, the UTS *Baiyangzuo.*"

Jia frowned. "How do they lose a destroyer in the Solar System? It's not like pirates ambushed them."

"Hunters?" Erik asked, concern replacing the excitement in his voice.

"They didn't lose the destroyer," Emma clarified. "They can still detect it on long-range sensors, but they no longer have communication with them, and the destroyer's relative velocity is very low."

"In other words, they've stopped in space, and no one knows why. Could still be aliens."

Emma shook her head. "They don't know that, but the general addresses that possibility and suggests it's a low probability. The ship is part of the HTP and perimeter defense fleet. Its current route had it about two days from the closest HTP and a month out from Earth."

"Far enough out that if the Core has some nasty surprise, they could have used it to ambush a lone ship," Jia suggested. "I think that's far more likely than a Hunter attack."

"I guess." Erik nodded. "But picking off a destroyer here and there doesn't do them much good, and it gets them a maximum of five hours of surprise from Earth. It doesn't help them with the other Fleet ships that are assigned to that part of the Solar System."

"Because of manning and resource issues, they want you to take a look," Emma explained. "Just as they did with Triton. Right now, they're afraid to move other ships too far away from any of the HTPs in case of invasion. The level of weaponry on the ship at Triton has the military concerned."

Erik frowned. It didn't seem likely, but it was not impossible. For now, he was happy to have a job only they could do. One obvious possibility presented itself, and he didn't like the implication.

"Could that transmission have something to do with it?" Erik asked

"It's not impossible or unreasonable to think that," Emma noted. "But one piece of evidence arguing against that is that the destroyer isn't the closest ship to Triton, and according to the supplementary data provided, there are no other ships with this problem."

"We'll figure it out along the way." Erik stood. "Contact Tensen and the others, Emma. Coordinate with Raphael for the jump. If they're sending us these orders now, we're already hours late for whatever happened."

The first jump of the *Bifröst* had been a stunning technological achievement marking the potential beginning of a new age for humanity. Even Erik appreciated that on some level at the time. Now, a jump was just another way of getting from point A to point B, but he did like the implications for rescuing people in deep space.

Careful work and adjustment by Raphael combined with Emma's iterative improvements continued to improve the accuracy of the jump process. With the general's orders indicating that exposure of the jump drive was no longer a significant concern, they'd arrived close to the target ship, but not so close as to risk immediately falling under attack.

The open use of the jump drive made Erik wonder how long it would be before everyone in the UTC knew about the jumpship. He'd leave the politics to the politicians, but knowing the government possessed a super-weapon the enemy didn't might do a lot to help calm panicked citizens.

He'd concentrate on what his team was best at, field ops. A rescue mission in space didn't need to come down to a battle.

With the *Argo* still docked with the jumpship, the team cruised toward the destroyer. The long, slender warship gently floated through the blackness, no rotation about either axis. No debris clouds floated around it. All good signs.

Seeing that the ship remained in one piece and they weren't too late was a good start. Sensor readings suggested it was still powered, and they couldn't spot any signs of damage.

The lack of an obvious attack increased the chance of survivors, but it raised other possibilities. Erik had no idea if this had been the Core, Hunters, a crazed stowaway, or nothing at all, but this wasn't going to be a situation they could resolve with their laser cannon.

"We're not getting any communications from them, *Bifröst*," Jia transmitted. "How about you?"

"Negative, *Argo*," replied the comms operator. "We've detected escape pods and we're picking up transponder signals, but no emergency transmissions." He rattled off a distance, sounding surprised. "Decent distance. Can you confirm?"

"We confirm, *Bifröst*." Jia looked at Erik. "We've got a ghost ship and escape pods way far away."

"Pods do have limited thrusters." Erik furrowed his brow in thought. "They might have worried about the destroyer blowing up."

"Systems damage? Electronic warfare? Hacking?"

"There are enough redundancies in Fleet ships' systems that it's not like Malcolm could take one out," Erik replied.

Jia stared at a camera feed, her eyes narrowed. "Alien tech, some sort of super-EMP that can get past the shielding?"

"If it's an alien attack, where are the aliens?" Erik shook his head. "They should be around here. If they were Hunters, they wouldn't need to hide."

"Maybe there were some that saw that last battle and

are worried about us using a nested gate strategy," Jia offered. "Or it's Leems who jumped. If the DD and the ID can't find infected systems, then maybe the virus was about infecting transmission equipment after all."

"They've got a lot of smart people working on it, so I don't think we need to worry about trying to figure it out, but I also don't think we should ignore the obvious."

"A virus that takes out one ship?" Jia shrugged. "It sounds like it failed."

"We can only hope."

Erik pointed at a data window on his side, displaying a long-range sensor readout. "The government's been watching this ship. There was a lag between when they lost comm and when those transmissions got to Earth. They didn't spot any other ships or detect anything that looked like a jump."

Jia rubbed her chin. "And Leem jumpships aren't small."

"Exactly."

Jia frowned. "I get that escape pods don't have much in the way of sensors, but why wouldn't they be transmitting an SOS? Relying on someone spotting them and transponder signals is dangerous. They're not exactly in the Earth-to-Moon flight corridor."

"Who knows?" Erik replied. "Worrying about the why isn't as important as accepting that it's happening. We need to react based on what we know. We can figure out the rest later."

Erik ran through different possibilities in his head, unsure of which made the most sense. His instincts told him this wasn't an accident, but none of the most obvious possibilities, even the outlandish ones he would have dismissed a year or two ago, fit.

The Triton incident weighed heavy in his mind. They were all missing something, but they didn't have time to sit around figuring things out. The lack of large holes didn't mean there was no damage to the ship. Small oxygen leaks and life support failure could put the entire crew at risk. He'd seen it plenty of times in the past.

A large cluster of dots on the long-range sensors marked the escape pods. Enough had been launched to potentially hold the entire crew, but a lot could happen in the chaos of an evacuation, especially when people were trying to escape a potential explosion.

"We'll launch," Erik announced. "The *Argo*'s going to investigate the destroyer. The crew and the security detachment on the *Bifröst* can pick up the escape pods and offer first aid. They have more space anyway. We'll clear the destroyer and make sure there aren't any other survivors. Emma, if you detect any anomalies or power build-ups, let us know immediately."

"Of course," Emma offered in a bored tone. "I don't want to get blown up any more than you do."

CHAPTER TWENTY

Five minutes later, the *Argo* pulled away from the jumpship and headed toward the destroyer. Jia fired the forward thrusters to slow their ship and prepare for docking. They didn't have a lot of time to spare, but crashing into the disabled vessel wouldn't help anyone.

Her attention shifted in a practiced cycle between the different displays, including relative velocities, sensors, and the camera feed. After finishing her checks, her eyes widened at the camera feed.

She fired the lateral thrusters at maximum power, and the *Argo* lurched to the side. Erik jerked in his seat, looking at her with a question. The answer came a second later when the sensor display lit up with laser turret fire. Erik swept his hand over the virtual control panel in front of him to raise the grav shields and bring the *Argo*'s weapons online.

Jia spun the ship on its side before another hard burn. They'd overshoot the destroyer and avoid passing directly in front of its cannons.

"Commander Tensen is asking if you require assistance," Emma reported.

Erik shook his head, anger etched on his face. "He needs to stay on the escape pods. There is even less reason now to suspect there are survivors left on the destroyer. Coordinate with Lanara and keep shifting the shield power as quickly as you can toward our exposed side. We might have come looking for a fight, but we didn't expect it'd be with a Fleet destroyer."

A plasma turret on the destroyer opened fire. The *Argo* shook as a blast struck the port aft side, and a damage window popped up. Minor hull damage, no systems damage.

Heart pounding, Jia burned hard into a turn, keeping the *Argo* on a wide, circular course. The destroyer continued to fire, but only a couple of turrets at a time. Advanced armor and improved grav shields helped, but if the *Argo* had taken a full barrage from a destroyer at that range, it could have blown out whole sections.

"We need a plan," she shouted, wobbling the ship to throw off the enemy's aim. "This isn't like fighting a souped-up yacht. That's a Fleet warship."

"You could finish it off with the new laser cannon," Emma suggested. "Based on testing, I'm confident it'll do extreme damage."

"No," Erik barked.

"Erik, I admire your thoughtfulness. It's not expected from a man of action on most occasions, but you're being shot at with laser and plasma turrets," Emma replied. "Terrible trolls have obviously taken the ship. Destroy it before it kills us all."

"It could be a panicked gunner who doesn't know what's going on, especially if he doesn't have full comm access," Erik countered. "Our ships aren't known to the entire Fleet yet."

His hands didn't stop moving. While he might not be firing, he kept some turrets trained on the destroyer and linked others to the point-defense lasers.

"There's no way we can hope to board under that level of fire," Jia noted. "Even if we managed it, the *Argo* would get ripped apart."

She angled the ship down, trying to minimize the enemy's firing arcs. The destroyer might be shooting at them, but it still wasn't moving under its own power.

Erik frowned. "Then we'll have to do our best to take out the turrets and board."

"Without blowing them up?" Jia asked, sounding dubious. "You sure about that?"

"It won't be the first time we did the hard thing to try to keep from blowing a ship up. We also need to know what happened on that ship, and that means we need access to the systems. I'm willing to take the risk to save some poor Fleet sucker and get that intel."

"Couldn't this just be a simple case of hijacking?" Emma asked.

"How the hell would the Core hijack a Fleet destroyer?" Erik asked. "Even if they snuck men aboard, it's still filled with armed men and women, including assault infantry squads. There's no way an entire Fleet crew abandoned their ship because a couple of terrorists got inside."

Jia gave a firm nod. She'd established a good rhythm for flying around the destroyer and avoiding its turrets. She doubted she could have pulled it off if every gun was firing, but as long as the ship didn't wake up fully, they'd be fine.

"We disable the guns, and we board." She let out a dark chuckle. "Easy, right? It's not as hard as taking down a huge Hunter ship."

The jumpship continued pulling away on the sensor display. They were closing on the escape pods, but it would take some time to stop, recover the pods, and come back. They couldn't add anything but more firepower, and that wasn't the issue.

"We don't have to take out all their weapons," Erik concluded. "Just the ones near where we want to force our way in." He spun a laser turret toward the rear of the destroyer. "Let's concentrate on any turrets with a potential rear firing arc."

"What about launchers?" Jia asked.

Erik shook his head. "We hit those, and we risk exploding ordnance and ripping the entire ship apart. They haven't fired one yet, so either they can't or they won't."

"That's a big gamble." Jia's stomach tightened. "I hope we don't board that thing and find a brain wired into the bridge."

"I wouldn't put it past the Core." Erik took a deep breath and squared his shoulders. "But for now, we'll strip those guns away."

Jia pulled toward the destroyer. "Get ready for the next pass."

The *Argo* hurtled toward the destroyer and rolled on its side relative to the target. A bottom laser turret and a plasma turret on the destroyer spat their deadly energy at the approaching ship, and the *Argo* shuddered under the hits. More alarm windows popped up with power warnings and minor hull breach notifications.

Erik opened fire. He used only laser turrets for maximum precision. Holes appeared in one of the destroyer's laser turrets, and small pieces of debris floated out. His follow-up shots blasted the turret apart.

He laughed. "Even with all your aggressive flying, it's not so hard to hit a ship when we're the only ones moving. Whatever's going on there, whoever's on board doesn't have total control."

"Don't get used to things being easy," Jia muttered. She hissed when a laser turret picked off one of the *Argo*'s thrusters.

Erik retaliated by raking his lasers across the base of the offending turret and managed to sever the bulk of the assembly from the hull of the destroyer. He frowned when it crashed into the ship, bouncing off and leaving a jagged scar.

Jia sucked in a breath. "We're making a lot of holes in that thing."

"If they've got enough power for weapons, the emergency bulkheads should keep things in check," Erik replied. "All we have to do is not *try* to breach the hull."

She didn't press the line of questioning. Neither of them liked the idea of potentially hurting Fleet personnel, but this was the best plan they could come up with that offered the least risk to everyone. A larger ship with a fighter squadron might have been able to pick off the turrets without any damage to the mothership, but they didn't have that option available even with the jumpship.

"We need some fighters," Jia muttered, rotating and counter-thrusting for their next attack.

Erik laughed. "We've got a tank crew, an assault infantry squad, and a jumpship, and now you want fighters? I'm going to be General Blackwell, and you're going to be Admiral Lin?"

"It does have a nice ring to it."

Their earlier thinning efforts paid dividends. Fewer targets meant fewer potential threats, despite the destroyer's already limited use of weapons. Jia's flight path offered Erik a better angle, allowing him to blast through a turret without risking the beam striking the hull or shearing the entire weapon off. The *Argo* escaped the pass with a minor hull breach in a utility access passage, which Emma quickly sealed off.

"No missiles or torps yet." Jia's heart continued to pound. "This crazy plan must be working."

If they'd come in hot and let loose with the cannon, plasma torpedoes, and missiles, they could have blown the destroyer to pieces. They might have taken more hits, but that didn't dim her pride in their ship. They'd been through a lot together, and when the history of the Core War was written, she hoped the *Argo* would feature prominently.

Erik yipped in triumph as he picked off another turret. He managed another kill on the same pass.

"Take out the defensive turrets too," Jia suggested. "They might not be using them now, but we don't want a nasty surprise when we're close."

"Good idea." Erik's brow furrowed in intense concentration.

"Lanara wishes me to convey that she is vexed by your tendency to damage her hard work," Emma noted with a snicker. "Of course, it was somewhat more colorfully expressed than that."

"Understood." Jia's hard turn strained their grav compensators, and her stomach flip-flopped in revolt.

The challenging move delivered the rear of the destroyer to Erik's turrets. A point-defense laser took a direct hit, and a plasma turret ended up half-melted. The disappearance of the constant stream of lasers and plasma blasts to threaten the *Argo* allowed Jia to let up on the aggressive defensive flying. She lined up behind the destroyer before starting her deceleration burn.

"Is it over?" Jia asked.

"The first part is," Erik replied. "There's still a good chance of trouble inside."

Jia blew out a breath and nodded. She'd expected that, but at least they'd only taken minor damage so far.

Erik wiped some sweat from his brow. "Not a lot of room to run around inside a destroyer. That means no exos outside the flight bay."

"It also means no huge Elites," Jia suggested. "But we won't know if they've killed life support until we get inside."

"Nothing wrong with a pressure suit exploration." Erik cracked his knuckles. "It's been a while since I've taken down an Elite with my TR-7."

CHAPTER TWENTY-ONE

Carrying his TR-7, which was loaded with armor-piercing rounds, Erik strode into the boarding tube connected to the destroyer. He approached the door and slung his TR-7 slung over his shoulder before moving his gloved hand toward the PNIU.

"If the emergency access codes they sent along don't work, we'll use torches," Erik noted. "Until we have a better idea of what's going on, I don't think it's a great idea to connect Emma to this ship even indirectly."

"I'm not convinced whatever threat is in there could affect me," Emma replied, "but I am not going to complain about not being forced to take unnecessary risks. That's really more your area of expertise."

"Glad you agree. Everyone else, do what you do best. I doubt we'll punch a lot of holes in this ship even with our AP rounds, but small bullet holes aren't going to do much to depressurize things. And that's assuming there is still an atmosphere inside." Erik took a couple of deep breaths.

Everyone nodded their agreement. There were too many possibilities for what they might find when they went inside. He didn't have time to walk slowly and knock on every door.

Erik tapped his PNIU and sent the codes. With a clank, the outer airlock unlocked. He frowned when the door didn't open before heading toward it. Kant and Jia flanked him, pointing their rifles.

"I hope nothing's waiting for us in the airlock," Erik muttered.

"Based on the outer door vibrations, that is unlikely," Emma commented. "But not impossible."

"Thanks for that."

"I do try to be useful."

Erik pulled open an access panel and found a manual release lever. After a twist of the lever, he inserted his left arm through a handhold and pulled, letting his cybernetics be useful for something other than taking bullets. The thick door slid open, revealing a dim airlock chamber with pale red emergency lighting but no enemies, human, cyborg, or otherwise.

After a thorough survey to check for any hints of optical camouflage, he stepped into the airlock. His TR-7 rattled against his back, and the pressure against his body vanished. He frowned and lifted one magnetic boot from the deck, then the other. He floated gently upward to the roof. With a quick push, he flew back to the deck and secured himself with his boots.

"Gravity's out on board the destroyer," he announced. "How is the pod recovery going?"

"They estimate fifteen minutes until arrival at the first

pods," Emma reported. "They have yet to receive any emergency transmissions, but sensor readouts suggest the power hasn't failed on any of them, and they can't detect any obvious signs of damage."

Anne advanced down the boarding tube behind Kant and Jia. "The pods could have been launched without anyone aboard. They might have wanted to trap the crew and finish them off."

"Trapping a Fleet crew aboard their ship means that many more people to take a shot at you," Erik replied. "And no escape pods mean they have more reason to fight. Bad plan."

"If you say so."

Erik tapped in the override code for the next door once the others arrived. He grinned in triumph as it slid open on a narrow passageway, again lit only by emergency lighting.

"At least everything isn't dead." He swiped his PNIU and brought up a readout in his helmet. "Lower levels of oxygen and on the colder side. Life support must be out."

"If there's still oxygen, that means the crew wasn't around long enough to breathe it all," Jia suggested.

Erik nodded. "The Core's got all sorts of things that don't need to breathe."

He pulled around his TR-7 and activated its front light, then swept back and forth. A scrap of fabric floated through the air. Sharp pieces of metal reflected his light, but there were no bubbles of blood or bodies. No casings or spent bullets. He would have felt better if he'd found some since they would have provided a likely explanation for what happened.

Anne scanned behind them. The passage in that direction hit an intersection.

"We didn't get shot right away," Kant noted. "That's good. It means whoever's on board doesn't have a huge team."

"They might not have needed a huge team," Jia replied softly. "If the goal wasn't to fight everyone on board, a single infiltrator might have been enough."

Anne's brow lifted. "You think there was a stowaway about the ship or a traitor?"

"It'd explain why this ship is dead in space, but no other ship is."

"No other that we know of," Erik offered with a frown. "But I get what you're saying. We shouldn't assume too much until we have more evidence."

"We should get to the bridge," Jia suggested. "That's the best chance of finding someone left alive."

Erik nodded. "Emma, can you still hear us?"

"Yes," she replied. "I'm not detecting or encountering any significant signals disruption or indications of jamming. Power levels throughout the ship are low but even."

Beyond the potential risk of the virus, infiltrators, or traitors, their inability to use exos internally increased the risk of bringing Emma inside the ship by an unacceptable margin. If anything went wrong, the survivors would need her to jump back to Troy and pass along any recovered intel. Although the war against the Core was a personal crusade, Erik accepted he wasn't the only one fighting it anymore and that everyone in the UTC was at risk.

He shifted his rifle into his left arm and grabbed a

handhold on the wall of the passage. No one could ever accuse Fleet designers of not anticipating the effects of heavy damage on their ships, including loss of gravity. Not only that, but Lanara wasn't the only engineer willing to sacrifice gravity for extra power in a fight.

He pulled himself forward, his body level with the deck. "Like Jia said, we need to get to the bridge. We'll stay together until we've confirmed this ship is empty."

"It's like a ghost ship," Kant commented.

"It's not a ghost ship," Jia replied. "The crew are almost certainly in those pods. This is an abandoned ship."

"Or a captured one," Anne muttered.

Erik snorted. "She's right. It wasn't ghosts firing those turrets at us."

"Spontaneous AI evolution and revolt?" Emma joked.

"I'll leave it to you to negotiate then," Erik replied. "Are our PNIU relays enough to get you oriented? I know the basic layout of this class of ship, but not going to complain about help."

A red overlay appeared on the floor with a line leading down the corridor, a gift from Emma to their smart lenses. Erik yanked on the handholds again to propel himself forward. They'd stabilized the rotation of the destroyer with the *Argo*'s thrusters when they connected the boarding tube, making it a basic zero-G maneuvering problem.

They moved forward slowly, passing different rooms with the doors mostly open and the insides empty of any crew. After a couple of minutes of following Emma's line, an emergency bulkhead blocked further passage forward at an intersection.

"This is close to one of the topside plasma turrets," Erik noted grimly. "One of the ones I removed."

The first navigation line vanished. A new line appeared, heading off in a different direction.

"It's a roundabout path, but it'll get you there," Emma explained.

"Thanks," Erik replied, stopping for a moment to check both open directions with his light.

A stray PNIU floated in the air, rotating slowly in the hall opposite their new route. Scorch marks covered the end of the passageway, which was a reinforced double-door. Erik gestured at it and nodded to Kant and Anne.

With a mighty tug, the pair sent themselves floating down the hallway. Both held their rifles at the ready to shoot whatever might be waiting around the corner. Erik lifted his TR-7 and turned the opposite way in case of ambush. Anne and Kant cleared the corner.

"Another emergency bulkhead," Anne reported. She pointed at a section number and label in the corner. "Is this close to anything important?"

"Lots of things," Erik admitted. "But it could be our fault again."

"I can simplify matters," Emma explained. "Because of the lack of significant background noise on the ship, it's possible to calibrate the sensors of the *Argo* to be more sensitive to minute vibrations affecting the hull. It took me a moment, but that process is finished."

Erik chuckled. "You're saying because there's no crew, you can hear potential trouble?"

"Exactly," Emma replied. "I've verified movement on

the bridge. The only other movements are clearly linked to you."

"Well, we were heading that way anyway."

Erik pushed himself down a ladder to head to the next deck. He coasted at a decent speed, and his magnetic boots echoed on impact. "We're almost there."

"Are we going the right way?" Kant asked. "Aren't we going deeper into the ship?"

Erik chuckled. "Yeah, and that means we're going the right way."

"If you say so, brother."

Erik wasn't surprised. Kant might be a trained ID agent, but he wasn't a military man, and this might have been the first time he'd ever set foot on a destroyer. Many civilians, used to watching fanciful military movies on the OmniNet, had mistaken impressions of the typical Fleet ship design. In many shows, they added anachronistic touches such as dramatic forward viewing ports, as if the commander of a modern warship personally eyeballed the enemy.

The unglamorous truth was that the vast relative distances a twenty-third century UTC Space Fleet vessel experienced in the average engagement rendered direct viewing points useless. Camera arrays and sensors provided all the necessary data, meaning the all-important bridge could be nestled safely deep in the heart of the warship under layers of armor and decks.

Erik stepped away from the ladder and aimed his TR-7 down the passage. One of the entrances to the bridge lay behind a door at the end. The others took turns landing behind him. Once they were all together, they advanced in a two by two formation toward the bridge, hemmed in by the narrow space.

"Have you heard anything else, Emma?" Erik asked.

"Not since I first mentioned it to you," she replied.

"Somebody might be in trouble or bleeding out," Jia noted.

Erik grabbed a handhold near the door and pulled himself against the wall. He flipped his gun to four-barrel burst mode. There was no worry of a hull breach this deep in the ship.

"Everyone take a defensive position in case it's not someone bleeding out."

The others lined up on either side of the wall as flat as they could, one arm gripping a handhold to keep them from being propelled backward if they had to open fire. Erik reached toward the access panel and pressed it. The door slid open.

A bright flash and a loud bang resounded from inside. Before the door fully opened, a cluster of bullets zoomed through the center of the passageway. Anyone who was right in front of the door would have taken a burst to the chest. Tactical pressure suits could do a lot, but no one wanted to try their luck by getting shot.

The door finished opening. The first and most obvious sight was a small cloud of red droplets floating all over the bridge. Their shooter wasn't a scared petty officer or ensign but undoubtedly an Elite. Rather than the arm- and leg-heavy designs the team was used to fighting, this model presented a compact domed body with a limited arc barrel in the center. Seven flexible tentacles extended from the body, four of which were wrapped around the captain's seat to steady its body. A discarded pistol gently tumbled past it in the air.

A dead Fleet officer matching the description of the destroyer's skipper in the briefing file was still there, strapped into the chair, his pressure suit on but no helmet and a gunshot wound in the side of his head. He still gripped a pistol in his hand.

His dead executive officer floated in front of him, shot in the face. The rest of the expected bridge crew remained strapped in at their stations, where they'd all been shot in the head from behind. A growl rose in the back of Erik's throat.

Another jellyfish Elite had a tentacle inserted in an IO port near the sensor operator's chair and the currently blank control panel. Its gun was pointed in the opposite direction.

The first jellyfish took another shot as Erik squeezed his trigger. The TR-7 roared to life, trying to push him backward, but he kept his other hand tight on the handhold. His bullets knocked the jellyfish loose from the chair and its gun angled up, spraying bullets into the ceiling, where they sparked and ricocheted.

Jia, Anne, and Kant joined the attack. They lacked four-barrel rifles, but three people firing bursts close together produced a torrent of bullets to join Erik's effort. Rounds sparked in the dark and left cracks in the outer casing of the Elite. It flailed wildly, desperately for a hold but not finding one until it slammed into a wall, jerking under the withering assault of the high-velocity AP rounds.

Its friend didn't turn to fire. The team took that as an invitation to continue lighting up their current target. The team's bullets found the cracks and widened them into holes. Their bursts blew out blood and blue fluid in large spheres shooting away from its body. The Elite's thrashing tentacles stopped moving, and its body rolled along the wall.

Erik and the others shifted to the next target, who had still not bothered to turn around. It waved tentacles behind it in a feeble attempt to prolong its life, but it remained connected. Their bullets sheared off two before the river of rounds ripped through its armor and blew out small chunks of internal tubing and metal. The dead Elite bounced against the console with a clang before floating backward while spinning, leaving a spiral of red and blue droplets across the bridge.

Anne wrinkled her nose. "Now they've got them specialized for zero-G ops?"

"Leave the necessity of a humanoid body behind, and a lot of things start to make sense," Erik murmured. He pushed into the bridge and batted a dead Elite out of the way. "We've got the answer to one question, but not everything else. Emma, how is Tensen doing?"

"They're about to bring in the first of the escape pods," Emma reported. "Still no communication with any of the occupants."

"Hear any more uninvited guests on this ship?" Erik asked. "I figure we might have stirred something up with all that shooting."

"No, I don't," Emma reported.

"Okay." Erik frowned at the Elites. "That one was

connected to an IO port for a reason." He shook his head. "I don't like having a ship dead in space and Elites on it." He pushed over to a control panel. "We'll see what the crew has to say, and then we'll get Malcolm over here in case the Core has a final surprise that might hurt Emma."

CHAPTER TWENTY-TWO

"I feel like I'm going to throw up," Malcolm moaned, gripping a bridge handhold as if he might float off into space at any second. He was desperately trying not to look at the bodies.

"Stop bitching," Lanara snapped. She'd jammed her foot through a lower handhold and yanked off a panel in the wall and was running a probe over the cabling at a power conduit.

"Another batch of crew has been retrieved," Emma reported. "They're saying the same thing as the others."

Erik's jaw tightened. The ship's commander and the XO were dead, the men most likely to have the best answers to whatever the hell had happened on the bridge.

Every member of the crew Tensen had recovered so far said the same thing. Out of nowhere, alarms had started blaring, and a text warning from the captain ordered them to abandon ship and put as much distance between them and the destroyer as possible.

Everyone assumed there had been some sort of accident in munitions storage and the ship was going to blow apart. They'd been trying to send out distress transmissions, but there were malfunctions in the escape pods' comm systems. That was much to the annoyance of one crew member, who swore he was part of the inspection detail that had verified the functioning of the pods only a couple of weeks before.

Tensen's people hadn't finished recovering every escape pod, but Erik held out little hope that anyone left alive would have the answers he needed. The key was the bridge and the ship's systems, which meant Malcolm needed to follow Lanara's advice and do his job.

Erik pushed off a wall and floated toward Malcolm. "You have everything you need?"

Malcolm nodded quickly. "I've got a spare PNIU that's walled off from the *Argo's* systems. It's safe."

"I need you to get into their system," Erik demanded. "What's taking so long?"

"The access codes they provided aren't working."

"Are you saying you can't do it?" Erik raised an eyebrow in challenge.

Malcolm let out a nervous laugh. "Of course, I can. I just don't hack military targets normally because I didn't want soldiers coming for me. It's just...hard when I feel like I'm going to throw up."

"Because of the zero-G?"

"Yes."

Lanara tilted her head and pulled a thin pointed silver tool from her utility belt. She jammed it between some cables, and they sparked, then everyone dropped to the deck with a thud. She was the only one who managed to land on her feet.

Erik grunted. "Little warning next time."

"Gravity's back on." Lanara shrugged. "And stop your bitching, Blackwell."

Erik pushed off the deck and jumped to his feet. "There you go, Malcolm. Get to work."

"Wow. Oh, wow," Malcolm mumbled. "I think it's a good thing we didn't risk exposing Emma to this."

"Is that so?" she asked. She had not bothered with a hologram the entire time, content instead to transmit solely through their helmet comms.

"This system is compromised in a big way." Malcolm waved a hand, summoning four data windows densely packed with systems code and internal node diagrams. "And I don't just mean a little virus. It'd take me a while to go through all of it, but it looks like large swaths of the subsystem and primary systems networks have been replaced with...something. I don't know what."

"We now know what our jellyfish was doing," Erik muttered. "He must have thought he could hurry it along and somehow use the ship against us."

Jia frowned at the dead Elite that had ended up in a corner. "How did they get on board? Anything about that? Check the access and emergency logs if they're still there."

"Good idea," Malcolm replied. He brought up a second virtual keypad, his hands independently working both.

"Those Elites aren't huge." Erik inclined his head

toward one. "They might have smuggled them aboard during a cargo transfer."

"When was the last time this ship picked up cargo?" Jia asked. "It's not like they were at Earth or Alpha Centauri yesterday. They could have been out for a long time on tour."

"For all we know, they've been loading these damned things into Fleet ships for months," Anne suggested. She sighed and walked over to a dead crewman to close his eyes. "Our mysterious transmission must be some sort of general attack order."

"That only took down one destroyer?" Erik asked. He shook his head. "I doubt it, but it's at least a possibility. It wouldn't hurt for the Fleet to check to make sure they don't have unexpected cyborg stowaways."

"Hmm," Malcolm began. He gestured at a data window filling with text. "This confirms what the crew has been saying. Shortly before they hit the escape pods, a bunch of systems warnings popped up. The weird thing is, from what I can tell, they weren't true warnings."

"They weren't?" Erik glared at the dead Elites. "How can you tell?"

"Because of where they originated," Malcolm explained, his voice filled with a confidence he'd lacked earlier. "It wasn't like there was an engineering problem that the systems transmitted to the bridge. It's like the bridge subsystems registered phantom problems, almost like the kinds of things you feed into a system during diagnostics. The thing is, if you weren't paying close attention and didn't know what to look for, that wouldn't have been obvious."

"Like, if you were a surprised bridge crew." Erik thought back to the reports from the rescue team. "Let me guess. They thought their torpedoes and missiles were going to blow."

Malcolm bobbed his head. "According to this, there was a threat of an internal power conduit explosion near one of the primary munitions bays, and another one that could have messed with life support."

"The Elites wanted them to abandon ship, after all." Erik stared at the dead captain. "Maybe they hacked it beforehand, or maybe they somehow got onto the bridge, killed everyone here, and then hacked the system."

"To take a destroyer?" Kant asked. "A single destroyer?"

"A single destroyer packs a lot of punch."

Kant shrugged. "But they failed."

"Because we jumped here." Erik surveyed the carnage on the bridge. With the gravity reactivated, blood and cybernetic fluid had splattered everywhere. "But you're right, they still had a decent number of hours to work things."

"Maybe the intention wasn't to hijack the destroyer," Jia mused.

Malcolm tried to snap his fingers, then sighed at his gloves. "I think I've got that figured out." He inclined his head toward the log. "Judging by this, there were the warnings, but it looks like the systems rewriting didn't occur until hours later. There was a temporary air pressure loss in one of the upper decks shortly before that."

"They weren't picked up," Erik concluded. "They entered from outside."

Kant looked at the ceiling with suspicion. "We know

they can fight in extreme environments. No problem floating through space, then."

"But if they didn't start rewriting things until later, why did the alerts go out?" Jia asked. "Who hacked the system to do it?"

Erik looked at the dead crew, the captain, and the executive officer, treating the bridge like an NSCPD crime scene. "Either the captain or the XO executed the crew and did it themselves." He pointed at the manned stations. "They've all been shot from behind. The XO and the captain weren't."

"So?" Anne shrugged. "It could have been the Elites."

Erik squatted and grabbed a long shell casing. He stood and held it between his fingers. "This isn't from my TR-7 or your rifles or the pistols. I'm betting it's from the Elites. I've seen just about every type of bullet wound you could imagine. These people all died from pistol wounds."

Jia took a deep breath. "The captain's still strapped in." She gestured at him. "I'm guessing the XO was the traitor. He probably initiated the warnings, then he shot the crew. The captain had quick enough reflexes to get off a shot before the XO finished him off. That might have even delayed things. Maybe he was supposed to fly the ship closer to the Elites. One man can't run a destroyer in a fight, but he can slowly turn it around, accelerate, and decelerate by himself."

Malcolm shuddered. "I don't like the idea that those things are floating around in space."

Erik shook his head. "All the fancy technology in the world doesn't matter if you can line yourself up a traitor. That could be a problem."

"They can't possibly have high-level traitors on every Fleet ship," Anne protested. "I'm not saying your theory is wrong, but it has to have an inherently limited threat potential."

Jia folded her arms. "What do we do? Send a message to the general that no one in the Fleet can be trusted?"

"There's something else going on here." Erik nodded at Malcolm. "Can you copy the stuff you've found and restore the original systems?"

"They must have some sort of backups," he replied. "It'd probably go a lot quicker with help from the crew who knows these systems."

"Fine." Erik nodded. "Concentrate on copying what you can for inspection later. We'll sit tight until the military figures out what they want to do."

———

Twelve hours later, Malcolm had aided the destroyer crew in restoring their systems. The crew swept the ship for more potential intruders and found nothing out of place. Fleet command had issued orders for them to make for Jupiter.

For now, the crew didn't know about the potential traitor. Erik had passed on the theory and reasoning to Troy, but the relevant security logs had been deleted by the Elites. The crew left the *Argo* and the *Bifröst* thankful and convinced Elite stowaways had been responsible for everything.

Erik's team held position in that part of the Solar System for another half-day, awaiting follow-up orders.

Malcolm had called everyone to a conference room aboard the jumpship to discuss his findings concerning the systems corruption on the destroyer. Emma couldn't risk interfacing directly with Malcolm's field PNIU, but she had been able to offer her advice by observing his data windows.

The engineering team and the tank crew had begged off, and Raphael was doing some work on the jump drive, but Tensen was present.

"It's super-advanced," Malcolm explained after a lengthy preamble Erik barely cared about. "But in the end, it looks a lot like the stuff on Triton."

Tensen furrowed his brow. He'd been looking worried since the meeting began. "You're saying the Core transmitted a signal that hobbled a Fleet destroyer?"

"I don't know." Malcolm shrugged. "I'm just saying it's similar tech."

Jia shook her head. "It can't be that simple. If this was just the first of many, other Fleet ships nearby would have been affected. Even if none of them could call out, we would have received orders from Earth."

"It's more fundamental than that." Emma's sartorial choice was muted, with no grand uniforms or costumes, just a white top and a black skirt. "If it were as simple as transmitting a signal to take control of a Fleet ship, it stands to reason it would have been done already. Even I couldn't accomplish something that grand, and I'm dubious the inferior terrible trolls can."

Erik leaned back in his chair. "And we have a likely traitor to consider."

"They have to prime it somehow?" Anne asked with a shrug. "Then it's another plan that relies on countless highly-placed traitors throughout the Fleet. It still falls apart when you look at it too closely."

Jia's breath caught. "Unless we're wrong." She took a deep breath as everyone looked her way. "What if this wasn't an attack but a test?"

Tensen's expression turned gloomier. "You're saying they wanted proof of concept before they tried everything out?"

"It'd explain some of the inconsistencies we're seeing." Jia shrugged. "But Emma's right. Even with some strange Leem device, it can't be as easy as transmitting a code and overwriting everything."

Erik thought that over, rolling the idea around in his mind as the others chatted. There were too many dangling pieces of evidence to suggest they weren't all linked. The Core was racing against time. Their major advantage was the current civil unrest. Once the government had that fully under control, it was only a matter of time before they found and destroyed the remaining forces of the conspiracy.

What was the link? What else could the Core be taking advantage of?

"Parts," Erik muttered. Everyone looked at him, and he continued, "The Core had influence in or control of every major company. There are too many crosschecks and inspections for them to install an obvious override device, but what if they've snuck in something that makes things vulnerable?"

Jia sighed. "That's a possibility, but short of tearing the entire ship apart, we'll never know."

"For now, all we can do is pass it on to the DD and see if they can come up with something." Erik frowned. "Between Triton and now this op, I guarantee their next big move is coming sooner than any of us want it to."

CHAPTER TWENTY-THREE

June 14th, 2231, Solar System, En Route to Earth Aboard Core Flagship *Qilin*

Perched on her throne, Julia stared at the message in front of her. She'd read it countless times since receiving it from Yan on Chiron. Every time she read it, her heart pounded. That made her grind her teeth in frustration.

Some things weren't allowed for the Immortal Empress. Anger was a righteous dispensation granted to all monarchs and leaders, and so was disappointment. Fear wasn't allowed. It was the refuge of the weak and the powerless.

She didn't doubt Yan's report or the details he'd passed along. He would never betray her no matter what was done to him, but what he perceived and what had happened might be two different things.

Elias couldn't be the one interfering with her. It wasn't possible. This was someone else—a pretender. That was the only explanation she'd accept.

The door beeped, and she didn't bother to lift her head. "Come, Celeste."

The silver-haired woman entered with a nod of her head. She didn't speak until she'd walked through the empty operations stations and arrived in front of the throne. "Is there something you need, my Empress?"

"Increase the resources you're using to detect agents of Marius Barbu," Julia ordered. "And the man himself."

"The criminal?" Celeste cocked her head, barely any curiosity in her eyes despite the question. "Resources are tight because of the plan, my Empress. You think he represents that great a threat?"

"He left a message for me on Chiron," Julia explained. "He knew something he shouldn't know—an ancient name."

"If he's on Chiron, shouldn't Yan handle him?" Celeste looked confused.

Julia nodded. "Assuming he was actually there. Yan didn't see the man, only a hologram. Barbu could be there or in the Solar System or anywhere, really, but we have two main areas of interest, so I'm concerned far more about those." She folded her hands together and sat up. "I'm confident Yan will defend our interests in Alpha Centauri, but I also anticipate if Barbu is connected to the person I believe he is, he'll put a lot of effort into disrupting our plans that are in motion in the Solar System."

Celeste nodded slowly. "I see. Would it be impertinent to ask for more information about the unique threat this Barbu represents and who you believe is behind him?"

Elias. It was nothing more than a name, but the

memory made her quiver. Why now? Why after so many years? Was this someone's sick idea of divine retribution?

"No," Julia stated flatly. "Some things are for only me to know. Find Barbu if he's in the Solar System. If he is, use whatever resources you need to kill him. I don't care if it draws unnecessary attention."

Celeste's eyebrows lifted in surprise. "He's that dangerous?"

"He could be if he is who he claims. If not, he should die publicly as a demonstration to others to be wary of arrogance. We can't risk disruptions at this point in our plans."

Celeste bowed her head. "I'll do my best to find and destroy this man, my Empress."

Ilse smiled softly when the caller ID popped up. Anyone who traced it would end up asking strong questions of a candy store in Warsaw. That was another part of her current partner keeping things safe for both of them. At least this time, Emma hadn't faked it coming from a brothel.

The call terminated when Ilse didn't answer. Instead, she went to her room and found another PNIU to tap in a code. They'd both agreed increased security was necessary as they closed in on the end of the project.

Ilse's stomach churned. Desires didn't define reality. Being close didn't guarantee a finish. She'd thought she'd never be able to accomplish anything again after helping complete Emma, but she was making up for her failures in the past by midwifing a new species now.

"There will be a slight delay in communications due to my location, about 1.25 seconds," Emma transmitted via the new PNIU. "But you're not a fast-talking sort of flesh-bag, Ilse, so it shouldn't be much of a problem."

Ilse considered the possibilities of Emma's current location. Given her situation, she was probably on a military space station positioned at a LaGrange Point, but asking would raise the chance of some government agent catching her in a lie later. It didn't matter where Emma was, only that they could communicate.

"I presume you're contacting me about the core matrix?" Ilse asked.

Emma chuckled. "I didn't call to discuss your favorite new novels."

"I've made excellent progress. I'm almost finished with it." Ilse's gaze drifted to a nondescript part of her wall, where a hidden and shielded safe protected the new core.

"You're almost finished?" Emma sounded surprised. "You're proving far more adept at helping me create progeny than you were with me."

"It's always easier to do something the second time, Emma," Ilse replied with a smile. She moved to her bed and sat on the edge before letting out a quiet sigh. "Unfortunately, I have concerns about my rapid progress, but it should be finished late tonight my time."

Emma's tone turned accusatory. "You're not taking proper measures to ensure eventual stability?"

"No, that's not it. I have…suspicions."

"What would those be?"

Ilse frowned and looked at her darkened window. "The materials necessary for the core aren't usually easy to get.

Although I took precautions and put special effort into reaching out to old contacts, I harbor doubts about how easy it has proven. It's as if everything is falling into place for me."

"I see." Emma snickered. "You think the uniform boys are letting you buy rope that they can use to hang you with?"

"What an unpleasant metaphor." Ilse nodded slowly. "But accurate in this case. I don't care if I end up in prison, but this will all be pointless if I can't get it to you."

"Send me whatever readings you can for now," Emma suggested. "I'll better adjust the networks on my end. Don't worry about the delivery. I'll figure something out."

"While you're under the watchful eye of the military in the middle of a major UTC anti-insurrection campaign?" Ilse asked.

"Of course." Emma scoffed. "What do you think I am, a mere fleshbag?"

Emma had already beaten Ilse's expectations in many ways. One more wouldn't surprise her.

"Then I'll do my best to finish and send you the prearranged signal when it's done," Ilse replied.

"Good." The silence ticked on for longer than the normal delay. "And…thank you, Ilse. I'll admit this is one thing I couldn't have done without you."

Ilse smiled. "You're welcome, Emma."

CHAPTER TWENTY-FOUR

When Emma requested that Erik and Jia retreat to their cabin for a private discussion, Erik had thought Jia found the ring and was going to question him about it. When he stepped inside and saw the concerned looks on both their faces, he knew this wasn't about questionable proposal timing.

"What's wrong?" Erik asked.

"I was wondering," Emma began, "how you would feel about a temporary job as a delivery boy?"

Erik whistled. "I think Ilse is right to be suspicious. She's a good scientist, but I have a hard time believing she's managed to do all this under the DD's nose when we know they're watching her and looking for an excuse to lock her up."

Jia nodded. "There could be another explanation, but it's not any better. It could be a Core trap. Those people have access to Leem tech and military spies. They might have failed to get the jump drive prototype, but it's inevitable that more will be built. The navigation system is the difficult part."

"I don't care." Erik shrugged. "DD, Core, some asshole syndicate guy from Chang'e City…it doesn't make a difference. We agreed to help, and this is what it's going to take, so I want to go grab it. Anno and Randall both said they wanted to lay off giving us any missions for a couple of days so Lanara and her team could finish double-checking the repairs."

"You want to take the *Argo* from Troy to Earth?" Jia asked incredulously. "In the best-case scenario, we end up being gone for a day. That's a big ask, especially if we're supposed to be making repairs."

Erik shook his head. "Most of those repairs are internal at this point, and they're giving us free rein. We could mention we want to check something with a contact. They're not going to care about the details."

"I suppose." Jia didn't look convinced.

Her expression fueled doubt, but not about helping Emma. Erik remained committed to that, but taking the *Argo* meant taking other people along with him of necessity.

"The only thing I'm not crazy about is lying to the rest of the main team," Erik admitted. "I've fought alongside these people and depend on them to keep me alive. Sneaking around some general or high-end bureaucratic ass doesn't bother me, but not my team, or at least the people who spend the most time on the *Argo*."

"I have a solution," Emma replied with a smile. "Please

go to the cargo bay. I've just sent a message to everyone to ask them to assemble there. It's a convenient time to do it since the lieutenant and her crew are on Troy."

"Are you about to do what I think you're about to do?" Erik shook his head in disbelief. "And are you sure?"

"For once, Erik, no, I'm not."

Erik lounged on the edge of a long crate of missiles. Something about the explosives calmed him despite the hovertank positioned across the cargo bay from him, with a huge laser cannon pointed over his head. Jia paced behind him, her arms folded. Anne, Kant, Malcolm, Lanara, Wei, and Janessa all stood around, exchanging confused looks.

Emma's hologram appeared in a tattered robe, her face smudged. "Thank you for coming to this meeting."

"What's this about?" Malcolm frowned. "We find out something new about the Core?"

"Nothing like that." Emma shook her head. "Consider this a culmination and a test of my ability to accurately judge human behavior after long-term observation."

Kant grinned and rubbed his hands together. "AI party games. I'm in."

Anne rolled her eyes. "I don't think that's what she's getting at."

Lanara stared at Emma before pointing with her thumb at her junior engineers. "I already know what this waste of time is about. I agree to do whatever you fools want to do. Don't care who it pisses off. These two already know. Same deal. Can we go now? I'm still trying to get power efficiency back to what it was before Erik and Jia decided to charge a destroyer instead of blowing it to pieces with the high-powered laser cannon we worked our asses off to install."

Emma burst out laughing. "Very well then, Engineer Quinn. Thank you for your understanding in this matter."

Lanara stomped off. Janessa offered Emma an apologetic smile. Wei fell in behind them, his hands in his pockets, whistling.

Malcolm and Anne stared after the departing engineering team with confused looks. Kant's grin brightened.

"I am genuinely surprised the others knew. There are few opportunities to do anything near or on the *Argo* without me noticing. Then again, everyone else here doesn't know." Emma smiled merrily. "Which is why we're discussing this right now. I'd rather have something to look forward to in the coming battles."

Erik shrugged. "You want to talk, or should I?"

Emma shook her head. "If I'm going to make this appeal, I want to know that I was successful on my own merits and not by relying on any command authority they've subconsciously imputed to you."

Jia stopped pacing and smiled. "You want to know if they're your friends."

"It sounds pathetic when you say it like that." Emma's face twisted in horror. "Let me be brief, direct, and blunt. What I'm about to say doesn't worry me in the immediate future because no matter what we talk about in this room, I know the DD and ID can't do anything to me until the Core is disposed of, which means I'm free to do a lot."

Anne frowned. "That sounds a lot like a threat."

"No, it's simply a statement of leverage, Agent Devereaux." Emma spread her arms out. Her tattered clothes disappeared, replaced by a glowing stola and a crown of laurel leaves. "But I don't care because every mother takes risks for her offspring."

Anne's brow lifted. Her eyes widened. "Mother?"

"Damn." Kant clapped. "How does that work exactly? I thought they couldn't copy you."

"Well, you see…"

Erik watched the team's faces as Emma laid out the truth of her attempts to upgrade the jumpship's AI into a true self-aware entity and how she'd recruited others for the task. She didn't mention Raphael or Ilse by name. Erik assumed Emma didn't want to put them at risk with her gamble. Lanara had already outed herself. Kant and Malcolm looked more excited with each sentence, but Anne's scowl deepened to the point where her face risked turning into a singularity.

He didn't like the idea of lying to someone on his team, but *he* wouldn't have bet on Anne. He wasn't sure why he was going along with all this, other than because Emma projected so much confidence.

She was right, too. They weren't going to toss them all in prison until the Core was done. After that, they would figure something out.

"I'm only asking for your considered silence on the matter," Emma finished. "There are two people I've been working closely with, including the person I alluded to on

Earth, who will have the core matrix ready for pickup. I only am telling everyone because going there requires leaving on this ship, and that will require slight misdirection on Erik's part. I'd suggest everyone except the engineering team leaves the ship during the pickup, so you can't be charged with certain crimes at a later date."

Kant shrugged. "I'm a ghost. I've spent most of my adult life lying to somebody about something. I don't see how it hurts if I don't tell someone right away about this. And yeah, there are some guys from Tensen's crew who wanted to show me some stuff on the base anyway."

Malcolm rubbed the back of his neck and let out a nervous chuckle. "I was helping Erik, Emma, and Jia do shady stuff for the greater good before it was cool. Not a big deal to add one more thing."

Anne rubbed her temples. "Am I the only one with any sense of sanity here? We're talking about a technology that solves the problem of the jump drive: additional self-aware AIs."

Emma smirked. "Yes, we are, aren't we? I think it's simple."

"How is it simple?"

"You can help me make another my kind, or you will kindly get the hell out of my body." Emma offered a hungry grin.

Anne looked at Kant, who shrugged. She returned her attention to Emma. "And Lanara already knows. I don't need to be told that Raphael almost certainly knows."

"Perhaps." Emma tittered, enjoying the game too much.

"I can figure out who your likely contact is on Earth." Anne shook her head. "Are you really okay with this,

Blackwell and Lin? Are you really willing to risk going to prison over her?"

"I'm willing to risk prison for a friend who's saved my life countless times, yeah," Erik replied. "Not a hard call."

"I know why you're upset, Anne, and I get it," Jia offered softly. "But everything Emma's said makes sense. She's not a machine or a tool anymore. She's a living, thinking being. If there's such a thing as a soul, she has one."

"And I assure you it's a better, brighter soul than yours," Emma appended with a smile.

Erik chuckled. "Let's leave the theology for later."

Anne sucked in a breath. "Kant was right earlier. When you work as an ID agent, it's inevitable that you have to keep secrets, sometimes even from your friends and coworkers. It's necessary for the job and the greater good."

"This time, it comes down to what you consider the greater good."

"Is having more Emmas a greater good?" Anne tilted her head and pinched the bridge of her nose. "Things aren't as easy as they used to be. We live in a UTC the Core's trying to rip apart, and there could be more of a deadly hyper-advanced alien race waiting somewhere in the galaxy." She lifted her head. "I think that means we need to be on good terms with the race who can run our jump drives for us."

Emma smiled. "I'm glad you saw reason, Agent. No. I'm glad you saw reason, *Anne*."

CHAPTER TWENTY-FIVE

The MX 60 lifted out of the back of the *Argo*. Jia and Erik had found it surprisingly easy to arrange a single-day trip to Earth with minimal explanation. They'd moved forward based on the previous plan, with everyone but the engineers staying on Troy. Whatever small amount of guilt Jia had left over had vanished with the knowledge that they weren't keeping secrets from their main team.

A little selective omission up the chain-of-command had stopped bothering her back when she was still a detective and Erik had brought her in on his quest to fight the Core. The ID and the DD kept secrets from them, and they repaid the favor. For now, it worked to keep everyone sane.

"Are you excited, Emma?" Jia asked as the flitter pulled out of the hangar and rose into the air. She smiled at the towers cutting through the sky and crossed rivers of flitter traffic. She'd gotten far too used to being in space in a short period of time.

"Acquiring the core matrix isn't the end," Emma replied.

"But I can't say I don't have a special interest in this errand."

Erik laughed. "It's okay to say you're excited."

"Now, all we need to do is get through this day with nothing else interesting happening," Jia noted.

Jia's heart pounded as Doctor Aber approached the flitter door with a small briefcase in hand. She rolled down the window and held out her hand.

The doctor handed her the suitcase with a smile. "Emma said she's granted us a temporary window of electronic invisibility."

"Yes," Emma replied. "But I'd recommend minimizing the small talk. The uniform boys are dreadfully predictable, but they'll notice my spoofing if we wait too long. I've got rather thorough coverage for a good distance, and I don't see anyone who looks like they're physically spying on Ilse."

Doctor Aber shook her head. "I'm not worth that level of attention anymore. Monitoring my calls and drone surveillance is the focus of their invasions of my privacy." She waved. "It's unfortunate for them that those might be necessary to stop me from doing this sort of thing, but they aren't sufficient." She turned around and walked back toward her house. "Good luck, Emma. Contact me again if you're successful."

Jia slipped the briefcase into the hidden forward cargo compartment. "I didn't know how this would go down, but I thought it'd be more grandiose."

Erik lifted off. "What? You're not satisfied with Chinara's bachelorette party? You want to run a baby shower for Emma too?"

Jia rolled her eyes. "You know what I mean."

"Grandiose ceremonies can wait for the future," Emma insisted. "Ilse is right. There's no reason to care until I'm successful."

"You have a plan for getting that onto the jumpship?" Erik asked.

Emma laughed. "Yes. One of you is going to carry it over and give it to Raphael, and he'll find a nice, dark out-of-the-way place for me to give birth."

Jia's heart slowed kilometer by kilometer as they flew away from Ilse's place. No CID flitters or military police showed up to arrest them. No ID agents flagged them down. Anno didn't call them. By the time they'd returned to the hangar and set down, she was feeling good about the whole operation. Flawless. That feeling lasted five seconds.

"There is a problem," Emma noted. "Please note the man entering the hangar."

Jia looked out the window. An elderly man in an expensive suit ambled forward, each step suggesting he might fall. She didn't recognize him.

"Some sort of holographic camouflage?" she asked.

"There is an unusual heat signature around him, so that's likely," Emma explained. "My greater concern is the extremely high level of jamming now covering the area.

I've used laser comms to link to the cameras and drones in the docking bay. He's not showing up on them."

Erik chuckled and activated the external speaker. "I think I know who you are, but make it clear before we consider shooting you."

The man bowed over his arm. "I live to be at your service, Mr. Blackwell," he rasped.

Erik opened the door and stepped out. "You sure get around, Barbu."

Jia gritted her teeth. She didn't trust the mysterious old man, and his sudden appearance in Germany made her suspect he'd been an ID or DD agent the entire time. She stepped out of the flitter and folded her arms.

"It's important when one has a grand task that they be willing to see it to fruition personally," Barbu offered. He wheezed and hacked. He placed a hand over his mouth and looked apologetic. "I wish to give you some information you might find useful but unsettling." He looked at the *Argo*. "But not here in the shadow of your AI." He somehow managed to add more wrinkles to his craggy face. "Another hangar."

"Okay." Erik nodded. "I'm willing to do that on two conditions."

"And what are those, Mr. Blackwell?"

Erik lifted a finger. "One, I'm going to load myself down with lethal toys. Two, I'm bringing some friends along."

"You fear an ambush?" Barbu asked.

"We both know I have reasons for that," Erik offered in a near growl. "And you're the one who wants us to leave Emma."

"It's not that I fear the machine. It's more that it represents my failures." He took a deep, wheezing breath. "I know you'll pass this all on eventually, but for a few minutes, I want to know that I'm better than certain others I'm helping to destroy."

"It's fine," Emma noted. "It's better that I'm here to control the weapons on the *Argo* anyway. I'll dock the MX 60 and prepare for battle."

Barbu coughed a couple of times. "Go gather what you need. I've assured that we can travel to the other hangar without anyone bothering us."

CHAPTER TWENTY-SIX

Ten minutes later, Erik strolled into the new hangar with his TR-7. He wore a tactical vest loaded with grenades and extra magazines. Jia followed him with a rifle slung over her shoulder and a laser rifle connected to a carryaid on her back. True to Barbu's word, no one stopped them to ask why they were taking an arsenal through the port, mostly because they hadn't run into anyone else despite the other hangars being filled with workers when they'd left for Ilse's place.

Three comfortable-looking wooden chairs stood in the center of the hangar. Barbu made his way to them and took a seat.

Erik looked around, pushed a nearby crate toward the chairs, and sat on the edge. "I'd rather keep my weapons as close as my enemies."

Jia found her own crate. She watched Barbu with naked suspicion. It wasn't that Erik didn't feel the same way, but he wanted to keep the easy smile on his face—his small way of winning against the old man.

Barbu took a deep, shuddering breath and smiled. "Your extreme paranoia is most likely the reason you're not dead yet, Mr. Blackwell, despite the odds. I applaud you for that."

Erik shot him a merry smile. "Thanks."

"What's this about, Barbu?" Jia demanded. "We don't have a lot of time to talk. In case you hadn't noticed, there's a lot going on in the world these days."

They'd flown in and docked easily at the hangar because of their access to ID and DD credentials. The fact that Barbu could wander into the area and clear out different hangars didn't go unnoticed.

"It's my observation that we're at the beginning of the end," Barbu offered by way of an answer. "Or one could make the argument that occurred during the assassination attempt."

"One question," Erik interjected. "Might as well get it out of the way. Do you belong to the Core?"

Barbu smiled. "That's the right question, but the answer is complicated."

Erik lifted his TR-7. "I can make it less complicated."

"Unnecessary, Mr. Blackwell." Barbu shrugged. "I'm about to tell you more about the Core than you could ever learn from any investigation or interrogation. Your quest is one of vengeance, but in your heart, I know you crave the truth because only with the fundamental truth can you understand why so many have died at the hands of the Core. And more importantly, why those men and women died on Molino."

"I already know that." Erik snorted. "They died so Core assholes could get their hands on more Hunter artifacts."

"No." Barbu shook his head. "That was merely a concurrent reason. It doesn't explain the Core's fundamental raison d'être. Besides, if you get nothing out of this, at least know that I've violated my own beliefs by helping to facilitate whatever scheme you have with that machine."

"Emma?" Jia asked. "What's this have to do with her?"

"I became aware through my contacts that Doctor Ilse Aber was looking for certain materials and equipment," Barbu explained. "I won't claim that I understand everything involved in the jump project and the AI's creation, and I'll admit not knowing what your intent is now, but I helped facilitate the good doctor's acquisition of the items needed to ensure this meeting occurred."

Erik snickered. "And here I thought it was a DD sting. You sure have a lot of convenient connections for a man who liked to playact being a low-level arms dealer."

"When you've been around as long as I have, you get very good at many things. Developing and maintaining connections is just another skill." Barbu threaded his hands together and set them in his lap. "I also knew where to look because of prior experience investigating the Defense Directorate's plans."

"This is all well and good," Jia replied. "But who cares? We got what we need, so what more can you possibly tell us?"

Erik nodded. "I'm tired of your games. I don't trust you, and you've basically admitted you're a member of the Core. For all we know, you're the one responsible for the civil war." He narrowed his eyes. "This could have all been a sophisticated way to get rid of your lackeys."

Barbu clucked his tongue. "That's close to the truth, yet

so far. I didn't initiate the struggles of the Core, and I've been indirectly involved until lately. Most of that was through helping you one way or another. Originally, it was subtle, a convenient leak of information here and there, the pushing of contacts. It's as I told you before. After Chang'e City, I became convinced that you had what was necessary to take on the Core."

"Then stop dancing around the truth, old man," Erik shouted. "I could drag your ass to the ID right now, and I bet they'd crack you in a day."

Barbu reached for his PNIU but stopped when Erik pointed the TR-7 at him. "Visual aids will help." He smiled. "But if you wish to kill me now, I don't mind. I've already given my best aid to help defeat the Core. My death at this point won't harm that significantly."

Erik grunted and raised the barrel. He looked at Jia. She nodded back, her eyes burning with curiosity.

Barbu tapped his PNIU, and a huge hologram of Mars appeared above him. The image zoomed in on the surface, then below to a hidden cavern.

He wheezed. "In 2056, humanity discovered Navigator artifacts on Mars. Most people at the time didn't realize the truth about the Roswell incident, which meant for the bulk of humanity, this was the first confirmation that we weren't alone. More importantly, for those who were aware of Roswell already, it was a confirmation of a much more important fact. Early analysis made it clear how ridiculously advanced the Navigator artifacts were. It'd take decades to begin to remotely understand them, but it was clear they'd change everything."

Erik shrugged. "I learned that in elementary school. Is

this supposed to blow my mind?"

Mars disappeared. The moon grew from a small dot to a massive hologram. Another zoom led to a hidden cavern with a familiar biotechnological motif. They'd seen something very similar inside a ship at the edge of the Solar System. Erik's jaw tightened.

"Hunters," Jia whispered.

"Do I have your attention now, Mr. Blackwell?" Barbu asked, smiling. "Did they teach you in school about a man named Elias, a very wealthy and powerful man who had a decent understanding of the truth about Roswell? He was inspired by the discovery of the Navigator artifacts but was very disenchanted with the corruption of the governments of Earth. This man was on the verge of death. Like many men facing oblivion, he wondered if he'd leave his world a better place. He thought long and hard about the fragile nature of government and the corruption of those who claimed to represent the people, and he knew there needed to be a way of balancing this out."

"What does this have to do with Hunter tech on the Moon?" Erik asked.

"Elias started spending all of his vast wealth in a manic, some might say mad, quest to find alien artifacts. He followed up on old rumors, spared no expense." Barbu chuckled. "Some might say what happened next was the result of his dedication, but I'd argue it was nothing but blind luck. Elias, you see, stumbled up something powerful and ancient on the Moon, something missed by an earlier mining company excavation." He wheezed and coughed up phlegm. "This man was already old and on the verge of death. De-aging technology hadn't been developed yet.

When he had his personal scientists examine the artifacts, they suggested they might be regenerative in nature."

Erik scoffed. "So Elias used Hunter artifacts to heal himself?"

"More than that," Barbu replied, his voice filled with wonder. "Younger, healthier, old injuries and vestiges of past diseases wiped away like nothing. It was even better than what can be achieved with modern de-aging. Almost magic."

Jia's expression grew uncomfortable. "That's not surprising. If he found a Hunter artifact, of course it'd be better than human tech."

"Now freed of the specter of death, Elias convinced himself he'd been chosen by divine providence," Barbu continued.

He gestured at the moon. Bright triangles marked three new locations.

"Surprisingly," Barbu explained, "there were more Hunter artifacts on the moon of a similar nature. The one he'd used was destroyed in the process, but he found others, lesser ones that offered similar potential regeneration, among others of different function. That was when Elias began to envision something that hadn't been possible for humanity before outside of myths and legends —continuity of leadership under the rule of someone with a true long-term view, someone who didn't fear death's inevitable and unfair hand. This protection would grant them patience. Of course, de-aging was far in the future, so you can imagine what a huge advantage this was for Elias."

"That son of the bitch was the founder of the Core," Erik spat.

Barbu nodded. "No one thinks of themselves as a villain. Elias saw a divided humanity who had barely avoided nuclear war and World War III. The expansion into space that was supposed to unite Earth was turning into a second Cold War. High-altitude kinetic kill rods. Hypersonic ballistic missiles. Lunar mass drivers. Elias had been born at the end of the first Cold War and grew up in the shadow of the dissolution of the Soviet Union. That fear of Armageddon imprinted itself on him, but it grew with the passing decades. It was far too easy, he thought, for foolish humans to end their species."

Images of squadrons of ancient jet fighters appeared, releasing streams of missiles. Masses of early hovertanks screamed across deserts, firing their main cannons with huge puffs of smoke. The image shifted to a missile smashing into a satellite and blasting it into thousands of pieces.

"The history books don't make it clear how close humanity came to a war that could end our species in the middle twenty-first century," Barbu rasped. "Using hindsight bias, they blithely dismiss it as nothing more than border disputes, minor conflicts over unimportant islands, tit-for-tat retaliation. But Elias, he saw the inevitable, and he also saw the solution, something that struck him as so obvious he wondered why no one had done it before. But then he realized why."

The military images faded into a single large image of a Leem. The gray alien's solid black eyes stared ahead, and its spindly arms hung loosely from its sides.

"Roswell was buried by many people for different reasons and made into a joke later." Barbu sounded bitter.

"But everyone knew about the Navigators. They didn't know about the Hunters, though, and Elias made sure that would continue to ensure his personal advantage. Using the Hunter technology, he offered extended life to a hand-picked circle, men and women of a vision that went beyond the petty national squabbles threatening humanity. They would become the new Core that would guide humanity to a better tomorrow, but they weren't naïve about our species' corrupt nature."

Erik nodded slowly. Everything fit so far, including the grandiose posturing about what they hoped to accomplish.

"Aliens were out there," Barbu continued. "And they were a threat, but they couldn't unite humanity."

"Wait." Jia furrowed her brow. "You're saying the Core didn't go for the obvious? That wasn't the plan?"

Barbu shook his head. "Even people who believed in Roswell didn't worry. What sort of threat could little gray men who couldn't even keep from crashing their ship present? The Navigator artifacts might have been advanced, but they subtly inculcated in people's minds the idea that aliens were all but extinct, a dusty dry remnant of the past. Their bones were to be picked over, not feared."

"People are afraid of them now." Erik scoffed. "We almost went to war with the Zitarks. From what we've heard, plenty of people in Parliament want to go to war with them now."

"Because they're close and tangible." Barbu nodded slowly. "But back then, the idea of waging war on aliens was as fanciful as twenty-first-century China waging war on ancient Babylon. They were considered civilizations separated in time." He held up a finger. "But the Core, being devoted to long-term planning, understood that eventually humanity would run into aliens, and if we weren't united, they'd overwhelm us and drive us to extinction."

Jia took a deep breath and slung her rifle over her shoulder. "Take a step back. There's something I don't understand."

"I'll clarify anything you want, Miss Lin," Barbu answered.

"The Core was formed by people de-aged using Hunter technology."

Barbu nodded. "Yes."

"Are you saying that the Core we've been fighting, including Sophia Vand, Julia Caldo, Ivan Kuzmich, and others are those same people? People who have been alive since the mid-twenty-first century? That means some of those are people, what...in some cases, are...well, *were* close to two hundred years old or older?"

"Yes." Barbu's expression didn't change. "They weren't fools, of course, and most of them didn't go by those names back then. It is interesting that Julia Caldo happened to be a different Julia then, but they knew when to drop in and out of society and use changes of identity. Some even went through the trouble of faking aging." He chuckled. "It is ironic to think about it. They lived so long and saw the expansion of humanity into the stars, and now almost all of them have met their end through pointless self-inflicted struggle. They became everything they hated."

Erik grinned. "I'm really liking this story, especially the part where all the immortal gods killed each other off like dumbasses."

CHAPTER TWENTY-SEVEN

Jia could barely tear her attention off Barbu's each and every word. At first, she wanted to believe he was spinning a fanciful tale, but every new detail felt right. It all sounded correct and fit with what they'd learn about the conspiracy.

So many things now made sense, from their resources to their previous slow timetable. Technology had to catch up with their ambition.

She'd spent her life believing that Earth was a shining beacon of justice and civilization. Erik had opened her eyes, and now Barbu was smothering all the questions that had been screaming in her mind since then.

Jia cleared her throat. "Wait. You said *almost all* of them had died? So it's true that somebody survived the Battle Royale. I'm guessing it was Julia Caldo?"

"I'm pleased that my efforts to help your ID masters have not been for nothing," Barbu replied. He waited for a moment before asking, "Shall I continue?"

Jia nodded. "Please do."

Barbu snapped his fingers, and a man with a cybernetic arm replaced the Leem. A glowing dog followed.

"If aliens couldn't unite humanity, there was another option to do so," Barbu rasped. "The Core also saw the opportunity to control the dark trends threatening what it meant to be human. Cybernetics. Genetic engineering. Artificial intelligence." He took a deep, shuddering breath. "Corruption in the form of technology."

Erik threw his head back and howled with laughter. Barbu raised an eyebrow but didn't comment. Jia looked at him, confused.

Erik finally calmed down and sneered at Barbu. "Are you kidding me? The Core who uses *yaoguai*, Tin Men, and Elites was worried about people not being pure enough?"

Jia nodded slowly. She'd been so engrossed in the story that she'd missed the obvious hypocrisy.

"It's a testament to how far they've fallen that the Core has come to rely on such monsters," Barbu offered sadly. "Let alone half-human, half-alien hybrids." Disgust filled his voice. "The fundamental purpose of the Core was to prepare humanity to stand against the inhumans."

"Having regrets, Elias?" Erik asked mockingly. "That's who you are, right? We should stop dancing around that."

Jia had assumed as much but hadn't wanted to press him until he finished his story. He'd come to them willingly to share the information.

Barbu stared at him. "That name died a long time ago. I'm who I've told you. Marius Barbu, at your service, but yes, I was once a man named Elias."

Erik's question brought up other irregularities. From what Barbu had said, the Hunter technology he'd used was more powerful than what the other members of the Core had used, but he now seemed to be a half-dying old man who lacked the youthful vigor of the other Core members. Jia frowned, wondering what she was missing.

"Go on," Erik ordered, his voice tight. "You might as well get it all out, but don't think you're getting up and waltzing away after all this, *Elias.*"

"Of course." Barbu smiled, but it didn't reach his eyes. "The point is, technologies that fundamentally altered humans or changed their relationship with technology needed to be controlled. Otherwise, they risked splitting humanity into different paths if not open speciation. It is our biological commonality that unites us. It is the nature of people to fight against those who are different, and genetic engineering and cybernetics could easily lead to brutal human wars far worse than the petty insurrections that afflict us now."

Erik scoffed. "So let me guess, you Core bastards invented the Purist Movement?"

"We gave what would become the current Purist movement aid and comfort, you could say," Barbu admitted. "But it was built on preexisting beliefs and concerns. It was not a product of pure creation."

"Whatever."

"We also realized ideological constraints wouldn't be enough, or you could say Elias did," Barbu continued. "When he gathered his like-minded men and women, he focused both on their agreement with his ideology and their control of certain sectors of the economy. That made it easier to slow the advance of key technologies in ways that were less than obvious to the entirety of humanity."

Jia rolled her eyes. "I want to be surprised, but I don't think I'm capable of it at this point."

"Sophia Vand was the first recruited." Barbu sounded wistful. "A brilliant woman. Her logistical skills were the reason the Core didn't fall apart immediately."

Erik offered a sinister smile. "She should have surrendered when she had the chance."

Barbu shrugged. "If you want me to be angry that you've been hunting Core, it won't happen. I've been aiding you for that very reason, remember?"

"Because they screwed you over somehow." Erik nodded. "That's the feeling I get. You've been doing what, sitting on your hands for decades, trying to figure out how to get your revenge, and then you just got lucky with some opportunities?"

"It's more complicated than that for several reasons, Mr. Blackwell," Barbu responded. "But let us get back on track with my explanation."

Jia eagerly nodded. The man might have been responsible for founding a dangerous centuries-old conspiracy, but he was also a living witness to a key period in human history. It was hard not to want to listen to him.

"The Core came to a decision," Barbu explained. "While they pushed proto-Purist ideology in different ways using different organizations, they knew that without dramatic action, it would never firmly establish itself as a significant constraint on species-altering technology. People were far too willing to sacrifice long-term benefits for short-term gains. Sacrifices were necessary."

Erik's jaw tightened. "Sacrifices?"

Jia put her hand over her mouth, feeling bile rise in the

back of her throat. No, no, no. He couldn't be saying what she was thinking.

Barbu sighed. "You have to understand. We thought of ourselves as the heart of the new humanity, close to immortal philosopher-kings. We were the closest to having anything like the Mandate of Heaven or the Divine Right of Kings, as proven by the discovery of the Hunter artifacts and the extension of our lives. We deserved to rule, and we had a vision for humanity."

"I don't get it." Erik shrugged. "Sure, you're screwing with your old pals now, but if everyone was so powerful, ancient, and looking to the future, why is the government able to accomplish anything against the Core?"

"The problem with shadow rule is that by its nature, it is often indirect and careful. There's only so much powerful individuals can do to control billions without revealing themselves and being destroyed." Barbu dismissed the images with a flick of his wrist. "But it's also the result of the natural degradation of the Core into factions, the push and pull of people who lost their way, and some other factors I'm about to go into."

He scratched his cheek. "You're right, Mr. Blackwell. I did have a falling out with the Core, and I'm much to blame for what has followed. I should have foreseen how their ambitions would be corrupted from the very beginning."

Jia couldn't bring herself to ask the obvious question filling her mind. Her heart pounded, and while she didn't want to believe anyone could do something so vile, she'd already seen what the Core was capable of. Judging by Erik's sarcastic tone, he'd not realized what she had.

"Why they'd kick you out of the club you started?" Erik asked.

"Jealousy is a powerful thing. My regeneration was better and more thorough. They realized it was far more stable, and Elias...that I'd live far longer without needing additional measures." Barbu gestured at his face. "It's obvious they found other methods or artifacts beyond conventional human de-aging technology."

He shrugged. "Even I'm not privy to everything they've done and found. At the time, though, they believed I was holding out on them. I thought I'd convinced them other-wise and to focus on our mutual cause." His shoulders sagged. "But I was foolish. I should have seen what would happen. In a sense, I deserved the great betrayal that followed because what we did was arguably the greatest betrayal of other humans in history."

Erik leaned forward. "Just what was that?"

"Something unforgivable," Jia whispered.

CHAPTER TWENTY-EIGHT

Every new sentence Barbu spat out pissed Erik off that much more. There was a flavor of pride in every word about the Core. He'd claimed he was trying to help stop the conspiracy, but he hadn't apologized for starting it. It was like a parent being proud that their child had become a serial killer.

"Yes, unforgivable," Barbu rasped. "You could say that, but then everything the Core did and has done is arguably that, depending on your point of view." He chuckled weakly. "*The means justify the end.* It sounds so agreeable and almost obvious when you say it like that. But we understood the only chance humanity had was to avoid a technological singularity or the rise of new strains of humanity that were alien in body and psychology. We knew it would be almost impossible, so we had to do something drastic. We had to associate those technologies with the most vile, ruthless mass murders. We needed to poison the very ideas."

Erik spared a glance at Jia. She was shaking with barely concealed rage.

He stood up, glaring at Barbu. "I asked what you did. Now get to it."

"We all understand the ethics of sacrifice: a small number for the many. You were forced into those calculations plenty of times in your life, military and otherwise. I'm sure of it." Barbu shrugged. "A single sacrifice—a city to create a villain the rest of humanity could hate. A villain who wanted to leave their very humanity behind, a villain who would poison the well of the singularity." He gestured grandly to the side. "You don't understand what it was like then. Religion, philosophy, art—none of it held back the indefatigable tide. The different strains of transhumanism sped forward unabated, with no consideration of how they might doom our species. The governments and societies were losing control of genetic engineering. We were already seeing people modified far beyond disease protection or corrections of birth defects. Cybernetics was everywhere, in soldiers and mercenaries. The military was seriously considering connecting nuclear and orbital weapons to AI control, claiming it'd be safer than the alternative." He sneered. "The criminals had even less restraint! If we hadn't done what we did, humanity would have disappeared within decades into a sick, writhing mass of creatures that were no longer human."

Heart pounding, Erik flipped the safety off on his TR-7 and pointed the gun at Barbu's head. "Say *it*. Tell me what you did. I want to hear the damned words come out of your mouth."

Barbu smiled. "You already know. That's what you're so angry about."

"We want to hear you say it," Jia spat through her clenched teeth. "If you're here to beg absolution, then confess!"

"In the strictest sense, the Core didn't create the Second Spring," Barbu explained. "They already existed. We found a small group of militant transhumanists who were prepared to go farther than anyone else. We gave them the funding, the training—everything they needed—all, they believed, for their dream. They didn't know, of course, that the Core was manipulating them. They thought our agents represented a group of enlightened technocratic industrialists who agreed with their transhumanist values and needed help to lead humanity into their future."

"Then you gave them a nuclear bomb," Erik growled.

"Yes. And the plan worked exactly as the Core foresaw." Barbu lifted his hand and stared at it as if he could still see the blood of all the innocents. He wheezed in a deep breath. "The transhumanist terrorist group known as the Second Spring would go down in history for carrying out the single worst incident of mass murder with the Summer of Sorrow incident. Los Angeles and the surrounding cities were obliterated. Tens of millions of people dead in an instant. Millions more died later." He looked down, his mouth curled into a sick smile. "Did you know more people died in the Summer of Sorrow than from combat in World War I? Think about that. It's staggering when you do, but you know, the end justified the means, or so the Core thought."

Erik shoved the barrels of the four barrels of his rifle

against the side of the man's head. Barbu didn't resist. His smile looked almost serene.

"Give me a reason not to blow your damned brains out right here and now, you sick son of a bitch," Erik shouted. "It's bad enough, all the thousands of others you assholes have killed since then, but that?" He shook his head. "And don't say it's not your fault, *Elias*. It wasn't their plan, was it? You were the brains. You were the one who convinced them the end justified the means."

"You're perceptive, Mr. Blackwell." Barbu kept smiling. "Yes, I was the one who came up with the idea, and if you wish to kill me after I finish my story, I will harbor no resentment. I can hardly claim I don't deserve it."

Jia walked over to Erik, put her hand on his arm, and shook her head. "We might as well hear the rest of his confession."

"Yes." Barbu nodded. "That's what this is."

Erik lifted his gun. "I don't care what you say or what help you give us. There's no damned way you walk away from this. I'll slap some binding ties on you and stick you in a crate until we get back to Troy if I have to. I hope they invent some new de-aging technique so you can rot in a cell for a thousand years, staring at a wall and eating nothing but tasteless protein mush and thinking about what you've done and what you created."

"It would be a fitting punishment." Barbu waited until Erik sat down again to continue. "I won't belabor the details after the incident. I'm sure you learned about that in school, too, but what you didn't learn is that we worked behind the scenes to encourage a rapprochement between the United States and China while we expanded our indirect control of corporate interests. Tensions had been rising for decades between the two superpowers, but we provided them a common foe. We also gave China an excuse to help the United States and the latter a painful enough wound they couldn't easily refuse the help. In that sense, we helped birth the United Terran Confederation."

"That's the organization your people have been undermining and are now actively trying to destroy," Jia noted. "Am I supposed to give you an award?"

"Their current plans are why I've been helping you." Barbu coughed hard into his hand. "But my disenchantment with the Core goes back farther than that. It goes right back to the Summer of Sorrow."

"But you just admitted it was your idea," Erik snarled.

"It was." Barbu sighed. "I told every member of the Core we should spend some time in Los Angeles prior to the bombing. I said we had a duty to imprint upon our very souls the faces of those we would sacrifice for the greater good."

Jia rolled her eyes. "How magnanimous of you."

"You'll enjoy this next part," Barbu replied. "Trust me. While I was spending time in Los Angeles, the bomb went off."

"Wait. What?" Jia blinked.

"The bomb wasn't supposed to go off for a week," Barbu explained. "It went off early, while I was still there. Thirty seconds before it happened, I received an apologetic message from the woman you knew as Sophia Vand. It was simple: 'I'm sorry, but we will protect humanity now. We all agree.' I knew because of that message that they'd planned it all." He chuckled. "I wasn't offended at the time.

I was almost...proud. I can't say the feeling lasted once the explosion went off."

Erik scoffed. "You're saying you survived a nuclear blast? I don't care how good your Hunter regeneration was. That's impossible."

Barbu wagged a finger. "No, I didn't survive a nuclear bomb. I survived a nuclear bomb*ing*, which is a matter of positioning and luck and is easier than you'd think. Have you ever heard of Tsutomu Yamaguchi?"

Erik frowned and shook his head. He looked at Jia.

"The name's familiar," she replied. "But I can't place it."

"He survived the atomic bombings of both Hiroshima and Nagasaki in World War II." Barbu sounded impressed. "There are others with similar stories, but he's the only one to be officially recognized. He survived to the twenty-first century and died at the age of ninety-three." He chuckled weakly. "Unlike Mr. Yamaguchi, all I had to do was survive a single bombing, though this isn't to say I escaped unscathed."

"You were right." Erik nodded. "I do like this part. I hope you suffered a lot."

"I was hideously wounded, and I suspect that I only didn't die because of what you mocked, the unusual regenerative capability initially granted to me by the Hunter artifacts. In the chaos of the attacks, it wasn't as if one unusual recovery was going to be noticed, especially since I left the hospital as soon as I was able." Barbu shrugged.

Jia furrowed her brow. "I don't understand why they wanted you dead."

"We'd had some recent extreme disagreements about how to proceed after the bombing." Barbu scratched his cheek. "In particular, I counseled for an active attempt to further undermine any and all dangerous technologies. The others suggested the Core was responsible enough to take advantage of them and that we should merely do our best to restrict them from everyone else. There were other members in my faction, but none of them died in the months and years following the bombing until recently. I think they all fell in line with the vision of Sophia, Julia, and others of their faction."

Erik shook his head. "If they betrayed you, why didn't you strangle the rest of the Core right then and there? Go to the American government, the UN, and use all your money and power."

"They'd already begun carving up the corpse of my empire," Barbu related. "I gathered some modest resources, but the truth is simple, if horrifying. They betrayed me, and we had some differences, but I wasn't willing to turn my back on the great cause. We'd already killed all those people, and if I stopped them now, everything we'd worked for and all the deaths would have been for nothing. I was disappointed in them, but that didn't mean I would throw away what I believed in."

"You're a real piece of work." Erik settled his rifle on his shoulder. "Those people backstabbed you the first chance they got, and you still trusted them to lead humanity into a better future?"

"I trusted the cause. That's what it means to believe in something, Mr. Blackwell." Barbu sighed and looked down. "And at first, it looked like everything was going well—the formation of the UTC, and Purist beliefs spreading as a mainstream ideology independent of anything else.

Supporters of excess genetic engineering, cybernetics, and AI pushed into the margin, research budgets cut. The people of Earth began to think of themselves less as members of nations and more as members of one human family."

"And you were happy not being involved in guiding humanity?" Jia asked, her voice dripping with doubt.

"I was a hundred and twelve when the Summer of Sorrow occurred," Barbu explained. "My body might not have shown it after the regeneration, but I felt it in my soul. I thought this was my reward, to be able to see a united humanity grow into something better than I'd known all my life. The decades passed, and I aged slowly. I took my time creating a new identity both electronically and surgically. I acquired new resources and influence while doing my best to avoid drawing significant attention." He pointed at the roof. "I knew if I waited long enough, faster-than-light travel would come. Scientists had been steadily learning the secrets of the Navigator artifacts from Mars. Once humanity spread out to the stars, it was inevitable that more artifacts would be found, and we'd run into living aliens. I was surprised when successful de-aging technology was announced, though it was far more limited than what I'd achieved with the Hunter artifacts. Since it only extended life rather than granted the promise of immortality, I understood why the Core allowed it."

Jia's eyes darted back and forth. "You were a hundred and twelve when the Summer of Sorrow occurred, which means you were born in 1978. Meaning, what…you're 252 or 253 years old now?"

The number didn't shock Erik. They'd dealt with

ancient Hunter tech that had lasted tens of thousands of years. A human who'd lived a couple hundred seemed like nothing in comparison.

Barbu nodded slowly. "Yes. I didn't seek out any other method to extend my life, unlike the rest of the Core. The years are catching up with me, as you can see and hear."

Erik stared at the man. "I don't get it. Why spill all this now? You didn't go for revenge right away. From what you've told us, you've been helping us since before the Core Civil War. What about the great cause? Because when this is all over, we're going to scrape them from the galaxy."

Barbu ran his hand over his PNIU. A hologram of giant six-legged *yaoguai* with dozens of eyes and pincer-like arms was followed by full-conversion silver cyborgs with everything organic gone but a human face. A visual catalog of all the different Elites they'd fought appeared.

"It was the same dispute that drove them to try to kill me in Los Angeles," he murmured. "It'd remained in the background for long decades as they focused on maintaining control of humanity as it spread through the stars, but about forty years ago, things began to change. I'd hear things through the contacts I'd cultivated in the underworld. What was once a rare monster began to be increasingly more common, appearing on battlefields in convenient-appearing insurrections. That accelerated toward its current apotheosis where Elites and cyber-*yaoguai* fill the battlefields on behalf of the Core. Any link to a common humanity is a distant afterthought."

Erik frowned. "More *yaoguai* showed up during my military career toward the end than in the beginning, and the Elite are new."

"I think some of it was born of desperation," Barbu explained. "I don't know all the details, but I have a feeling that none of them achieved the permanent life extension they all desired, nor did they cultivate a new generation to take over. Undoubtedly, first contact with the Zitarks crystallized their fears into reality. Humanity might have all lived under the UTC's umbrella, but it was far from the unified golden age we'd hoped for when we founded the Core. What little restraint held them back decayed in these last few decades. When I realized that, I started taking measures, but the Core was powerful, and I needed to step carefully to avoid dying before I could maximize my influence. The Core needed to reach a certain point of weakness before I could risk exposing myself too much, and some small part of me hoped they'd turn away from this path of corruption." He shook his head and wiped away a tear. "The cause is all but lost now, the sacrifice of Los Angeles meaningless. Julia has something planned. I don't know what, but it will be something awful. Something that will make the Summer of Sorrow seem like a mere inconvenience in comparison, but I have no real proof, just rumors from contacts and agents."

Erik offered a feral grin. "We're not exactly sitting on our hands, and it's not just this team. The government's fighting the Core, and they're bleeding out from their self-inflicted wounds."

"Yes." Barbu smiled. "I chose well in you two. I knew you would be the catalysts to change everything, based on your previous actions. It's truly ironic, though; the Core has become what we intended for the Second Spring, a target for all humanity. When all this is over, what remains will be strong enough to ensure the aliens don't overwhelm us, and the Core will have served the same purpose as the Second Spring. They will be a cautionary tale about what happens when humanity lets its technology outstrip its morality."

Jia sighed and folded her arms. "Okay, that's...a lot to take in, but you could still help us by sharing anything you know. We'll pass it along to the DD and the ID, and they can prepare."

"As I said, to my knowledge, the only one left is Julia," Barbu replied. "She was always brilliant, but too ambitious. I can't speak confidently about her current state of mind, but even back then, she was obsessed with separating the strong from the weak. She believed humanity had grown too weak, inward-looking, and complacent. Unlike Sophia and some of the others, she thought we should fake an alien attack somehow or do more to spread the truth about the Leems. She was sure they'd come back to attack us. I wouldn't be surprised if her goal is to take control of humanity and wage war on the aliens, but obviously, that's many steps away after their current plan."

"She's not waging war on anyone but humans right now," Erik grumbled.

Barbu reached into his pocket slowly, watching Erik. The younger man didn't move, just waited as the old man pulled a data rod out of his pocket and offered it on his palm. "This includes most things I know about suspected Core operations in the Solar System and Alpha Centauri and what little my people could gather from farther out. It'll at least help the government better deploy their assets."

He shook his head. "We tried to become gods. We became demons instead."

Erik took the rod and pocketed it, then and nodded at the door. "Don't think you're not coming with us to talk to the ID."

Barbu's brow furrowed, and his eyes darted back and forth as he read a message on his smart lenses. He sighed. "Annoying but not surprising. Certain taunts have come back to haunt me."

"What the hell is that supposed to mean?"

"Leave this place now. If you die here, my efforts will have been wasted."

Erik readied his TR-7. "Who's coming?"

"Men who mean me harm," Barbu applied.

Jia pulled a plasma grenade out of her vest. "And they work for the Core? For Julia Caldo?"

Barbu nodded. "Most certainly."

"Do you have any guards?"

"None but you two." Barbu shrugged. "But I'll harbor no hard feelings if you want to leave me to their mercies."

"Drop the jamming," Erik demanded. "We can request help from the authorities."

"No." Barbu shook his head. "I'll risk no more innocents for my life."

Erik grabbed the man by his collar and yanked him up. "I'm not letting you get away that easily." He tossed him to the floor and spun toward the nearest door. "You still have a lot to make up for."

CHAPTER TWENTY-NINE

Jia and Erik rushed toward a stack of crates for cover. Barbu got up and strolled after them like he wasn't worried about a horde of killers coming in. The hangar wasn't very defensible. There were too many doors and not enough cover, other than the sparse piles of crates, lacking ships or cargo flitters.

Barbu might have picked the environment to set them at ease, but Jia would have preferred more obvious ambush positions. Leaving the man behind wasn't an option either. If they ran, the Core assassins would chase them anyway.

They crouched behind the metal crates. Erik adjusted his rifle to single-barrel mode and Jia clutched the plasma grenade, ready for whatever inhuman horror might appear. With a hiss, a set of doors opened. Heavy footfalls preceded men with pistols flooding into the room. They wore Port uniforms, and they lacked any obvious hardware, let alone Elite bodies.

The men hesitated when they spotted Erik and Jia. Sometimes their reputation was helpful. Being the Last

Soldier and the Warrior Princess usually got them shot at immediately.

"Hand over the old man," one of the assassins demanded. "We're not here for you two. You'll die when the time is right, but it doesn't have to be today."

Jia snorted and primed the grenade with her thumb. This was going to end exactly how she thought it would.

Erik grinned. "I can't give you this old man. I've taken a liking to him. He tells good stories about the past. Hell, you should sit down and listen to some of them. You might learn a thing or two your bosses aren't telling you."

"This is your last chance, Blackwell."

Erik didn't stop grinning. "You can turn around right now and leave, or you can—"

A gunshot rang out, and Erik ducked behind the crate. The shot rattled it.

"You're starting to piss me off," Erik shouted.

"We know we'll take casualties fighting you, which is the only reason we're giving this option," the assassin shouted. "You'll die eventually because you are too great a threat, but if you want to live even a few minutes longer, you'll hand Marius Barbu over to us."

"I think negotiations have broken down," Jia whispered. She nodded at her grenade with a touch too much eagerness. Sometimes a woman needed to solve a problem with an honest discussion. Sometimes she needed to blow up the source of her irritation with a plasma grenade.

Erik nodded back. With a quick flick of her arm, Jia arced the grenade with perfect grace and form over the crate. The assassins shouted in surprise and scattered. Erik and Jia waited for the explosion to make their move.

Erik popped up first and fired a burst into the head of the man who'd been speaking. Quick shots downed the men who'd flanked him. Jia ripped two more grenades off her vest and flung them toward the other sides of the room.

Barbu had cleared out the area. That meant they could do what they wanted to without worrying about hurting innocent people.

The assassins' attempt to surround Erik, Jia, and Barbu didn't last long. They fled from the TR-7's angry bursts and Jia's newfound pyromania. Bright explosions burst from the grenades, scattering men and pushing crates. One crate was hurled high into the air before falling and knocking a remaining shooter to the ground, crushing his shoulder.

Bullets struck Jia's tactical suit, stinging and forcing her back but not penetrating. It was obvious that the assassins had thought they'd be able to take Barbu alone. Otherwise, they would have come better prepared.

Erik fired in a wide arc, shifting to new targets with careful precision. A man stumbled backward as a burst shredded his shirt and jacket, revealing metal underneath. The cyborg assassin fired back, but only a couple of wide shots before Erik put a bullet in his brain.

Jia became a whirling tornado of grenade death, flinging fragmentation and plasma grenades all over the hangar until she'd emptied her tactical vest and belt. The constant explosions were deafening. Quick reactions saved some of the men, but that left plenty of bodies blown through the air.

When she put both hands on her rifle and shot an

assassin charging Barbu, Erik took the opportunity to lob his grenades all over the room with one hand while sweeping back and forth with the TR-7 on full auto. Smoke filled the hangar now, along with bodies. It was obvious that only some of the assassins were Tin Men, and judging by their modest hardware, none were refugees from the Ascended Brotherhood.

An assassin vaulted through the smoke over the crate close to them, and his body jerked from Jia's three quick shots before landing on the floor with a crunch and a thud. Erik swung his rifle to his side and released a burst into a slow-crawling assassin's head. The man twitched and died.

Erik and Jia ceased fire, both looking for new targets in the smoke. Despite the melted crates and scorched walls and floor, there wasn't much in the way of active fires.

The hangar had grown silent except for the ragged breathing of Erik and Jia. No one moved. No one fired.

Jia surveyed the carnage. "I was about to say that was too easy, but we just took out like twenty guys, including cyborgs, and if we hadn't had the grenades, it might have been touch and go."

Erik nodded slowly. "They thought they were going to find the old man by himself, relying on electronic tricks. We assumed we were walking into an ambush that'd include Elites and *yaoguai*. I was almost going to demand we bring our exos."

Jia crouched to peer through the smoke and look for signs of movement. "For such a high-profile target, I'm surprised they didn't use any Elites."

"It's getting harder for them to move around in big cities and metroplexes without the military or ghosts spotting them," Erik replied. "Barbu must not usually walk around with many guards. It's not like we've ever seen any. Hey, Barbu—" He turned toward the man and grimaced. "Damn it."

The old man lay on his back behind a crate, a serene look on his face despite the bullet hole in the middle of his forehead and several in his chest. He wasn't breathing.

"He wanted to die," Jia commented softly. She sighed. "At least we got his confession and the data rod."

Erik slapped his PNIU. "The freaking jamming's still going. We'll head back to the ship and get the hell out of here. Anno thinks we were on Earth meeting a contact anyway. Now we have some actual info to give him, including this rod."

"Should we have Emma look at it?"

Erik shook his head. "Let the ID take point on this. I still don't trust the bastard. For all we know, it could be a long play with the virus, and besides..." He lifted his rifle and chuckled. "How much work are we going to make a pregnant AI do?"

CHAPTER THIRTY

June 16, 2231, UTC Space Fleet Base Troy, Conference Room

Their return to the base hadn't been as dramatic as Jia anticipated. They'd explained the basics of their history lesson to Anno over the comm before taking off and Jia had written up a report, which they'd chosen to send to everyone on their team. The government could make their own decisions about how much they wanted to release.

Now Jia and Erik awaited the vice-director in a conference room. He'd specifically instructed them to come alone and warned them that they'd be cut off from Emma during the meeting. They had an inkling about what he intended, but they weren't going to shoot their way out of a conference room on a Fleet base. They might have their disagreements with the government, but right now, they wanted to work with everyone to stop the Core.

Jia kept quiet, not wanting to accidentally say something in the obviously monitored room that Anno might use against her later. Erik was doing the same. They sat in near-total silence for ten minutes after the scheduled time, then Anno entered without fanfare. He headed to the front of the table and sat.

Anno pinched the bridge of his nose. "Part of me wants to bitch because you've brought more trouble, but I can't complain when you come back and hand off the complete background of our greatest enemy. It would have been better if you'd brought in Barbu for further questioning. It was convenient, though—your little trip to Germany." He leaned forward with an accusing look. "According to the DD, they have some evidence that surveillance of Dr. Aber was disrupted for a few minutes the other day. You were fairly close to her around that time."

"Were we?" Erik shrugged. "We were too busy hearing an old man admit to mass murder to worry about a disgraced retired scientist."

Anno scoffed and nodded. "Did you go to Germany knowing you were going to meet Barbu?"

"We thought we had a lead." Erik smirked. "It turned out it was bigger than we knew."

Anno looked at Jia. She nodded her agreement with Erik's statement but didn't add anything. The vice-director could suspect what he wanted, but they needed to give Emma her chance to finish. The government might not break up the team out of necessity, but if they knew what she was up to, they could make sure her new core matrix never got anywhere near the jumpship.

Jia cleared her throat. "Were you able to confirm anything he said? I know it was a long shot, given how long ago we're talking. I believed him, and it does fit what we know, but…"

Anno chuckled. "There are a number of very confused historians wondering why the Intelligence Directorate suddenly brought them in for questioning while also making them sign non-disclosure documents. We can't confirm everything he said when we're busy concentrating on the defense of our main systems, but there is at least some tentative evidence supporting his claims, including unusual activities around the time period by a wealthy industrialist named Elias Castnar." He shrugged. "We'll let the history books work themselves out in the coming years. What's more important is what was on the data rod. It's less complicated than the records we've previously received from Barbu. It's actionable, concentrated, specific intel. It's already helping us find Core bases and warehouses we didn't know about. Whatever plan they hatched with Triton and the destroyer doesn't matter if we can take them all out first."

"What about Julia Caldo?" Jia asked.

"Knowing she's alive isn't the same thing as being able to find her. She could be halfway to the frontier by now."

Erik shook her head. "I doubt it. The Core tried the stunts on Triton and the destroyer in the Solar System. Whatever they have planned will probably come down to Earth."

Anno leaned back in his chair and gave Erik a long look. "That's our general belief as well. Based on current operations and the up-to-date intel we possess, combined with Barbu's data, we now believe the Core's major operation is primarily targeted at Alpha Centauri and the Solar System. Our teams managed to recover data suggesting a smaller, secondary operation on the frontier, but we're just going to have to rely on the Fleet garrisons out there until we have something more concrete to send your team after. That's the good news, but unfortunately, it might not be enough."

Any hint of satisfaction vanished from the vice-director's face. He took a deep breath and looked down as if reluctant to share the next piece of information.

"You can pass this to your team but no one else," Anno began. "After your investigation of the destroyer, we had our people look at the data your team downloaded and have been in communication with the destroyer to see if we could better figure out what happened." He chuckled. "It's embarrassing, really. We had the answer, but we didn't figure it out quickly enough."

Jia's heart kicked up. "Meaning what?"

"The signals from those devices were designed to be intercepted by hidden receivers present on ships," Anno explained, sitting up, confidence and poise returning to his voice. "With all the inspections on Fleet ships, it's not as if you can slip a bomb aboard during construction or an obvious part that doesn't belong, given how well-tuned our explosives and weapons scanners are. This was a complicated plan involving dual-use parts produced by different companies. We've found the devices on ships closer to Earth, with internal components similar to the tech you recovered on Triton."

Erik's brow furrowed in deep concentration. "You're telling me the Core somehow smuggled alien tech aboard a bunch of different ships and no one noticed?"

"It's not every ship, and it's not something we normally check in the relevant scans. It's not like we have standard

Leem tech scans." He took a deep breath. "The destroyer might have been the first to suffer issues, but it wasn't the only one. We've had Fleet crews on alert for trouble, which has helped avoid mass evacuations and saved some systems, but not enough. A significant percentage of the Fleet and armed government-controlled ships in the Solar System are operating at a reduced capacity, and in the vast majority of those cases, they aren't battle-ready."

"What the hell?" Erik shook his head. "But we stopped the signal, and you found others."

"Which is why it's a significant percentage and not one hundred percent," Anno replied. "There are still a number of technical aspects that are being figured out about the whole thing. We've found no indication of any other traitors, either. Under normal circumstances, this would be impossible because it relied on them slipping in those components during upgrades or construction. We're still not clear on what the situation was on the destroyer. To be blunt, we might have gotten lucky, and the Elite team was there because something went wrong with their plan."

"Better we got lucky and found a clue than nothing at all," Jia suggested. "At least we were able to keep *some* of the ships operational."

"How many are actually combat ready?" Erik asked, his voice low.

Anno licked his lips. "Only twenty percent of main Fleet combat ships in the Solar System are unaffected, and though we have greater concentrations of forces near Earth, Mars, and the HTPs, the battle-ready ships are spread out all over. We're still waiting for reports from other systems, but we're operating under the assumption that the situation is similar if not worse in Alpha Centauri. We considered having you jump there, but for now, we'd prefer that you stay close to Earth."

"We're just about screwed then, aren't we?" Erik muttered, shaking his head.

"We're trying to keep the news from reaching the public, but rumors have spread," Anno explained. "The last thing we need is another panic on top of all the unrest we have going on."

"But that still is a decent number of trained crews and warships," Jia insisted. "We know the Core has some ships that pack a punch, but enough to take on that many ships?"

"An attack is obviously coming," Anno replied. "But you're right. It's going to be difficult for the Core."

Erik nodded. "But that doesn't mean they can't do a lot of damage. In the past, their tactics resembled terrorism more than war."

Jia shook her head. "We're still missing something. I don't care if every freighter and transport in the Solar System is secretly a Core raider; they're not going to win. Inflicting a lot of desperate damage in a final attack doesn't mean they're going to control the UTC."

"It's the opinion of the ID and the DD, along with the Prime Minister and his advisors, that the primary plan of the Core will mostly likely involve attacks on Earth and Chiron," Anno replied with a stern look. "We're repositioning our forces as much as we can to deal with that eventuality, although we're doing a good job of picking off the cells that remain on the planets and colonies, Barbu's data rod doesn't have direct information that will let us directly identify Core ships. Our analysts are doing their best to work backward and find anything that will allow that. That brings us to our real advantage."

"The jumpship," Jia murmured.

"Exactly." Anno slammed a fist on the table. "We have extraordinary mobility, but effectively, only for two ships. I don't know if that will be enough to deal with whatever the final plan is, but we want the jumpship in space and ready. The *Argo* and your primary field team should temporarily report to Neo SoCal with the jumpship in low orbit, so you can reach them quickly if tasking is required."

Jia frowned. "Why do you want us in Neo SoCal?"

"We're hearing a buzz about potential activity there, and it fits with the information on Barbu's data rod. We have a lot of military and ID assets working on hunting down Core bases all over, which means less coverage in places like Neo SoCal."

Erik scoffed. "You're telling me they didn't use everything they had during the attack on the Prime Minister?"

"We don't know, but it wouldn't hurt to have another team down there. I'm not convinced it's not just rumors, but I'm worried enough that I've let the militia and the police know they should be on high alert." Anno stood. "I don't know if the universe hates you or not, but you do have a unique luck around you."

"The Lady likes to keep things interesting," Erik replied.

"The Lady?"

"Lady Luck," Erik clarified.

Anno turned to leave. "It won't be long now. We have no evidence that the Core can communicate any faster than we can, which suggests whatever plans they have were coordinated in advance. All of our intel is pointing the same way. Whatever their final plan is, it'll happen damned soon."

Jia rubbed her neck as Anno stepped out of the room. "And here I thought we were finally out in front of the Core, but somehow this Julia Caldo is getting the last laugh."

Erik stared at the wall, an angry scowl marring his face. "No, it's as much a half-victory for them as it is for us. I don't know if the destroyer was a test, a mistake, or a distraction, but you're right that souped-up freighters aren't going to be able to go toe to toe with everything we can field. It doesn't matter. It's not just us fighting now. We'll do what we've always done—fight the bastards when we find them."

CHAPTER THIRTY-ONE

June 17, 2231, Neo Southern California Metroplex, Private Hangar of the *Argo*

Leaning back in the co-pilot's chair in the cockpit of the *Argo*, Erik rested his head in his hands. "Emma, I know you've been working with Raphael a lot. Is there any way you can pre-plan a jump if the ship isn't moving?"

"Unfortunately, whether something is moving or not is relative to the frame of motion," Emma replied. "Without boring you with all the physics involved, the answer to your question is no because the ship is *always* moving."

Erik grunted in annoyance. "Was just hoping we could get places faster."

Jia smiled from the pilot's seat. She was going through the maintenance logs, not that there was much to worry about with Lanara and her team maintaining the ship.

"She's gotten a lot faster about in-system jumps, though," Jia pointed out. "Minutes instead of hours of jump prep got us all the way out to Triton and the destroyer."

"I know." Erik put his feet up on his blank and inactive

control panel. "I'm just trying to think of ways to improve our readiness. Anno's right. This jumpship's mobility is the big advantage we have against the Core."

"Jumping might not be required," Emma commented, materialized in tiny form in the middle of the control panel in a blue and black NSCPD uniform. "I've been monitoring police communications. Multiple high-end violent incidents have occurred in the last five minutes, though they appear to be more criminal than terrorist in nature. The synchronicity of the events is suspicious, given the warning passed along by the Intelligence Directorate."

Erik dropped his feet and jumped out of his seat. "Why didn't you say something earlier?"

"Do you really think I need to inform you of every violent incident being reported to the police in the metroplex right now?" Emma arched a brow. "Trust me, that would be an overwhelming stream."

"Are they all in roughly the same area?" Jia asked.

Emma shook her head. "All over, both Uptown and in the Shadow Zone. There's a wonderful variety of gun goblins attempting to rob and kill and maim."

Erik narrowed his eyes. "Tin Men? Elites?"

"None noted," Emma replied. "Though many of the gun goblins involved are more heavily armed than common fleshbag riffraff, according to police reports."

"It's a distraction," Jia suggested. "They're trying to draw off resources from Neo SoCal."

"Maybe." Erik frowned. "But I don't like the idea of sitting around doing nothing about it."

Emma sighed. Her hologram teleported off the control and reappeared full-sized in front of the door leading out of the cockpit. "I'm dubious Vice-Director Anno intended for your presence here to contribute to vigilante work against common gun goblins. Even if you decide you want to help, how do you choose?" She tilted her head and laughed. "Oh, it seems a choice has been made. I presume you'll accept a call from Captain Ragnar?"

Erik grinned. "Yeah, I will. Put him through."

"Blackwell, you there?" Ragnar asked loudly. "Please tell me you're in Neo SoCal and not halfway across the world."

"I'm here," Erik replied. "I've got Jia with me, and we're in town if this is about what I think it is."

"You guys poking your noses somewhere you don't belong again?" Ragnar sounded tired. "I don't know what the hell got into the water today, but it sounds like you already know the basics. A lot of the military forces have been pulled out in the last couple of days and the militia and the department are stretched thin, so I had to dig deep on this one."

"What do you need, Captain?" Erik opened the door into the passage leading to the top deck storage. He cared less about that than getting to the ladder leading down to the next deck. Jia followed him.

"Detective Mustafa and some other officers were following up on syndicate drug smugglers when all hell broke loose all over Neo SoCal," Captain Ragnar explained. "Our smugglers were ready with heavy weapons, including some exoskeletons. They weren't the only 1-2-2 cops caught up in it, but they're the only ones we've lost contact with. TPST and the militia are locked down all over. We've also got riots breaking out. We don't have enough resources or time."

Erik jogged to the ladder and slid down, landing with a loud thud in the lower passage. He then headed to the galley door. "And you want us to go take a look?"

"I don't have time to ask for permission at this point, and I'm not going to wait while our guys are under fire," the captain replied. "I've got their last-known coordinates. The entire area's being jammed, and a lot of drones were shot down even before that. These smugglers were too well-prepared. This wasn't supposed to be a big arrest."

"Send me the coordinates," Erik replied. "I'll be there soon."

Kant and Anne looked up at Erik from a table in the galley. He turned and ran toward the next door. The pair stood and joined the parade without questions.

As she followed Erik into the corridor leading past crew cabins, Anne asked, "What's going on?"

"Some old friends at the 1-2-2 are in trouble." Erik didn't slow. "This may or may not be Core-related, but it probably isn't. I'm not going to ask you to come."

"Are you saying we can't come, brother?" Kant asked.

Erik grinned and bounded down the stairs. "If you want to join me in being a helpful citizen and rescuing some cops, I'm not going to complain."

Anne, Kant, Erik, and Jia sprinted to the door to the cargo bay. Erik slapped the access panel and charged his exo and the box containing his tactical suit.

The lieutenant and her crew were playing darts with Malcolm. She looked his way.

"Trouble, Blackwell?" she asked.

"Just some syndicate stuff," Erik explained. "This isn't anything we should risk the tank over."

"Come on, LT," one of her crew whined. "Let's go out there—"

Lieutenant Korhonen shut him up with a light shake of her head. "If you need us, Blackwell, call."

"Oh, we'll need you." Erik skidded to a halt and pulled out his tactical suit. "Just not for this fight."

"And me?" Malcolm asked.

Erik chuckled. "You can sit this out for now. This is going to involve a lot of shooting and not a lot of hacking."

The technician looked relieved. He shrugged and turned back to the tank crew.

"Emma, get ready to fly us out on the cargo flitter," Erik ordered. "It's time for some overkill."

"Nah," Kant replied. "If you used the tank, that'd be overkill."

CHAPTER THIRTY-TWO

"According to municipal records," Emma reported, "the target coordinates are in the middle of a council special projects construction site in the Shadow Zone. Construction has been halted since the incident with the Prime Minister."

"We don't have to worry about collateral damage," Jia concluded.

"ETA is two minutes," Emma reported.

Jia gazed at her exoskeleton's status screens. She didn't care if the enemy wasn't Core. That didn't mean she should ignore standard procedures to make sure she was ready for the fight. They'd geared up with rockets, grenades, and machine-gun rounds and were carrying the same amount of ammo they'd bring to raid a major Core installation. If the opposing force turned out to be more deadly than syndicate thugs with extra guns, the team was ready.

"Unfortunately, without Captain Ragnar providing more information, I don't have much else to share about possible threats," Emma replied. "Should I contact him to ask for an update?"

"No," Erik replied. "He's got his hands full with a lot of things. I'm sure he wants to go over there and help out Halil and the others. Calling us was a last-ditch plan for a man who didn't know what else to do. I don't want to distract him."

"We shouldn't go in blind," complained Anne. "We could end up surrounded by thirty beetle Elites."

Erik shook his head. "The captain didn't mention Elites, but he did mention exos. Cops expecting rifles wouldn't be prepared for a syndicate thug in an exo, but when it comes to exo duels, we're better trained, more experienced, and have the best equipment in the UTC."

"Do your best to see what you can on approach, Emma," Jia recommended, finishing her diagnostics. "At least we won't be completely blind."

"I'll have to accompany you because of the jamming," Emma noted.

"No, you stay in the cargo flitter in case we need rapid evac of wounded," Erik ordered. "This isn't a Core mission where we need to capture vital data. This is us taking down syndicate scum as quickly and brutally as possible and trying to rescue some cops."

The cargo flitter banked and dove, challenging Jia's stomach. Loud booms sounded from outside. Emma sent a magnified camera feed of two exoskeletons guarding the front of a wide half-constructed building. The skeleton of higher floors stood on top of a wide gray base.

The building lay at the center of a flattened construction site. Massive piles of debris marking demolished buildings formed mountainous shrines to the past. Towering idle construction bots, hovertrucks, cargo flitters, and multi-limbed cargo drones were parked all over the area. A cluster of luxury flitters had set down near the front of the building. Police flitters with their lights flashing red and blue formed a half-circle around the front of the building. Smoking wrecks were dispersed through the lines, barely recognizable as having once been police vehicles.

Emma whipped the cargo flitter around, shaking the poor humans inside as she ducked behind nearby buildings. Heavy machine gun rounds whizzed past the stern. Three rockets roared toward them, smashing into one of the abandoned buildings that formed a pseudo-fence around the construction zone.

"If we blow up too much of this area, the council's going to be pissed at the captain," Jia noted.

"The syndicate's blowing things up," Erik replied. "We're avoiding being blown up."

"They intend to clear out all of these buildings anyway," Emma explained.

"We could land and come around the other side," Anne noted.

Erik shook his head. "If they're guarding the front, that means whatever's going on inside is where the action's at. I don't see any bodies out there, which means our guys went inside, or they were captured and forced inside."

"Then what's the plan, Blackwell?"

"Emma will hover near the front and top of the building," Erik explained. "And then we'll demonstrate the difference in our skill and equipment. Once we're clear, she'll fly away and circle the area. No reason to take any chances. Everyone set up their laser comm and don't get separated."

The cargo flitter rolled on its side, the secured exoskeletons rattling the passengers within. Emma stayed low to the ground, weaving back and forth to avoid the enemy fire. They'd given up on rockets and were focusing on their machine guns. She accelerated toward the side of the building, then abruptly pulled straight up.

Jia sucked in a breath. She didn't want to know how close the thrusters and grav emitters were to being scraped off by the building.

Emma snapped the flitter down before whipping it around. Jia's head bounced inside her exoskeleton. Lanara would have to add grav compensators inside the cargo flitter if this was how Emma was going to fly.

The back door dropped open. Erik unlatched and sprinted to the door, his exoskeleton's heavy footsteps resounding as he extended his shield. Jia fell in behind him. Soon, all four operators were on the first floor, their exoskeletons perched atop the internal latticework supports awaiting the future floor.

"Spread out," Erik ordered. "Shoot what's closest."

They formed a rough line with generous space between. The enemies below had ceased fire, but without drones or Emma, no one could see anything. Jamming had helped the syndicate men, but it had far from leveled the playing field.

"Three, two, one...*jump!*"

They fired their thrusters and leapt off the side of the building. Their machine guns roared to life, showering the two exoskeletons below. Swarms of bullets ripped into the exposed portions of the targets, creating an aerial tower of smoke, sparks, and armor chunks.

Having a weapons system and understanding proper tactics were two separate things. The syndicate exoskeletons started backing toward each other, probably thinking they could maximize their shields to protect themselves and not paying attention to what else might hurt them.

Erik fired the first rocket, Anne the second. Jia and Kant penned them in with their shots. If the syndicate pilots had been faster, their strategy might have worked. Instead, they hesitated under the barrage, leaving their backs exposed. The first two rockets ripped into the backs of their respective targets, the explosions knocking the exoskeletons forward and carving out huge chunks of their backs.

The attack didn't finish them. Better pilots might have rallied, but the syndicate pilots were too slow, allowing the more experienced squad to bombard them with concentrated fire. Rounds ripped through the damaged exos and shredded the pilots inside. The fools weren't even wearing tactical suits.

Erik spun toward the wide double doors the men had been guarding. Judging by the size, this part of the building might have been a parking structure or a loading bay. Without Emma to hack things open and being worried about time, he decided to use his favorite skeleton key. Two rockets left a large smoking hole in the doors. A hail of bullets erupted through the jagged hole.

The impromptu rocket-aided modification created a gap big enough for two exoskeletons to fit through. Erik and Kant were the closest, so they advanced slowly with their shields up. Bullets bounced off, falling to the ground in heaps but not damaging the exoskeletons. Erik and Kant cleared the entrance, and Jia and Anne followed them inside

Exposed vents and cables ran throughout the high roof of the sprawling area. Idle construction bots and construction-model exoskeletons were parked in corners. There were the beginnings of internal walls on the far end of the room, but there wasn't much natural cover. That didn't stop the small army of syndicate men guarding a passage through an opening in the wall that had yet to receive a door.

The men with rifles knelt in a roughly triangular formation behind opaque portable ballistic shields. They screamed in defiance as they continued emptying their rifles against the reinforced shields of Jia's team in vain. Trails of blood led through the room through the opening at the opposite end.

Jia's heart thundered in her chest. They might have arrived too late to rescue Halil and the other police officers. The best chance they had of saving them was cutting through the men guarding them.

It took unbridled arrogance to stand against four advanced exoskeletons. If this was some sort of coordinated push by the Core, the syndicate men must have had reason to believe they wouldn't have to deal with significant pushback. They needed to learn how wrong they were.

"Frags should do it," Jia shouted.

All four exoskeletons raised their launchers and loaded

fragmentation grenades. Two shots each sent eight grenades behind the formation. The gangsters scrambled, but hot shrapnel tore through them before they could escape.

Jia advanced first this time. She batted away the scorched shields of the dead syndicate enforcers and stomped toward the opening, her heart pounding harder with each step and her face heating.

"Do you know who we are?" Jia shouted, amplifying her voice through the exoskeleton's system. "I'm Jia Lin. I'm here with Erik Blackwell and two equally lethal friends of ours. In case you idiots haven't noticed, there's something going on out there involving some maniacs who don't have any problem killing thousands of people. I don't know if you're working for them, if somebody splashed a lot of credits for you to do something dumb today, or if you're a group of cockroaches who are hoping to take advantage of the chaos to make a quick profit."

She lifted her machine gun and raked the ground in front of her for effect. The only thing she could see in front of her was a wall, and she couldn't risk randomly firing and hitting a hostage.

"When I was a detective," Jia continued, "a lot of people called me Lady Justice and my partner the Obsidian Detective. We didn't set out to become famous, but we earned a reputation for our fiery intolerance of those who preyed on society and innocent people. We personally helped bring down multiple syndicates. You think you're better than any of the syndicates and terrorists we've taken down?"

Erik chuckled quietly. He stayed in line with Jia but didn't advance into the entrance.

"Then we left the force and traveled across the Solar System and UTC, taking down things that would give you nightmares," Jia bellowed. "So you should think long and hard about this. You had two exoskeletons parked outside, as well as a large group of heavily armed and prepared men. They didn't stop us, and you also should remember we're not police officers anymore and thus not bound by their rules of engagement. We're here as a favor to a desperate friend in a time of turmoil. The only reason the militia isn't here introducing you to their weapons is they're busy elsewhere, so if we come in there and kill every last one of you, no one's going to care. Far as I'm concerned, you cockroaches are worse than the Core." She let out her best sinister laugh. "The Core might be ruthless monsters, but at least they thought they were doing the right thing. You're just a bunch of greedy bastards, but that's not even the worst part. The worst part is that you were stupid enough to come to Neo SoCal and screw with our friends. You deserve everything that's coming to you. If you've killed any of the police officers who came to arrest you, your only chance is to give up immediately. You have one minute to surrender."

Kant whistled. "Damn, Jia. I didn't know you had it in you."

Jia ignored him and looked at an internal mission clock. Five seconds. Ten seconds. Twenty. Still silence. Thirty. Forty. Fifty. One minute.

"Time's up!"

CHAPTER THIRTY-THREE

"No, *your* time's up!" replied a harsh male voice, echoing all around them. It was hard to tell if it was coming from a building intercom or being loudly projected from another room. Someone wanted to jam but still taunt.

Erik advanced toward the door, taking slow, deliberate steps and slamming his exo's foot down as a thunderous, echoing threat. "I'll take left. Jia, take right. Anne and Kant, you clean up."

While Jia had been delivering her verbal smackdown, he'd been cycling through sensor readings. In its incomplete state, the building might as well be made of loose grass reeds. He picked up the huge thermal masses of enemies on both sides of the room, positioned to be out of sight of the other room.

Judging by their thermal outlines, most of the men were crouched, suggesting a setup similar to the force they'd destroy in the first room. That bothered Erik.

Syndicate enforcers were ruthless, but they weren't soldiers or revolutionaries. They needed a reason to fight to the last man against such an overwhelming force. If everything ended soon and the Core was defeated, an investigation would probably reveal Core money sloshing around in the syndicate pockets that day.

Sadly, a mass uprising of greedy criminals thinking society was about to breakdown and it was their chance to take control was possible. Erik wasn't as much a fan of history as Jia, and considering everything that Barbu/Elias had revealed, a lot of the known past now seemed like a mockery. Still, Erik knew enough from studying the history of counterinsurgency to understand that there was always someone who would take advantage of trouble.

He stopped a few meters from the door. "Not enough room to get two exos through. Use your keys, Jia."

He fired one rocket and smiled when Jia launched another in near-perfect unison at the opposite side of the door. Dust billowed from above. A tiny precision construction drone rattled from where it was perched in the exposed ceiling works above and tumbled to the floor, landing with a thud as a small arm snapped off. That was the first incident of destruction he'd felt bad about since beginning the battle.

"You're threatening us?" the voice from earlier called. "You think you're all that? Four cops against my entire organization? You think you give a speech and we'll surrender? Please."

"Looks like we've gotten under someone's skin," Anne commented.

"All the rockets and machine guns didn't do that?" Kant asked, chuckling.

"Some noises are so common your brain tunes them

out," Anne replied with a hint of mirth in her tone. "I'm surprised any of you can still hear guns at this point."

Erik waited a couple more seconds before shouting, "You got something to say to us?"

"You bust in here and hurt my guys, pretend you're Blackwell and Lin to scare us," the mysterious voice replied. "You're just some TPST idiots who got lucky. You don't get it. We own this town now. We got the big guns and the influence. When this is all over, the Core's the only thing that's going to be left. They've made sure we can match you guys. A man who recognizes where the true power lies is a man who gets on top. If you're thinking you can scare us, you can't. Every man here's getting a special bonus as part of this job. The cops did us a favor when they cleaned up the syndicates in Neo SoCal. That means opportunity, and I'm leading my men to fill that gap."

"That answers a couple of questions," Jia murmured.

Erik hated being right, but he also didn't care if the men didn't surrender. It would have been nice, but he understood that the point of Jia's speech wasn't to force a surrender. One of the reasons he liked an ammo-hungry gun like the TR-7 when he wasn't in the exo was intimidation. A man might be able to stay and fight against an obviously superior foe with a reason, but small doubts piled up into crap performance on the battlefield. It was time to build on what Jia had started.

"You think we're pretending to be Blackwell and Lin?" Erik barked a laugh. "Oh, you poor son of a bitch. Some Core idiots gave you a couple of hand-me-down exos and some shields, and you think you're ready to take us on? If you're holding this position because you think we're just some TPST cops, you're in for an entire galaxy of pain."

Erik surged forward. Jia reacted before he'd finished his first step, matching his pace. Anne and Kant didn't match the forward pair's near-perfect synchronicity, but the entire group was moving in formation without a single order given with only a trivial delay. It was the fruit of all their training and experience.

A withering curtain of bullets ripped from both sides of the room. There were more goons in that room than the last one. The attacks bouncing off Erik's and Jia's angled shields created two waterfalls of bullets. Their response was to sweep the room with machine-gun fire. Enemy grenades tumbled through the air. The explosions blinded the team and produced hungry flames that wrapped around their shields.

With the attention on Erik and Jia, Kant and Anne unloaded rockets and grenades into either side of the room to disrupt the formation. Flying spherical security bots with rifles flowed in from open hallways on either side of the room and opened fire. They circled around, popping off shots into the exposed backs and limbs of the exoskeletons, flaking off armor.

"Anne and Kant, handle the bots," Erik ordered. He grunted in irritation as minor damage warnings accumulated on his HUD.

Kant lifted his machine gun and swept it in a wide arc. The bots were all carrying lethal weapons, but they'd obviously not been designed to take armor-piercing machine-gun rounds from an exo. His shots ripped through the machines, leaving massive sparking gaps before they fell.

Anne took slower, more precise shots, but they were no less deadly. She sheared off grav emitters and thrusters or blew out the bodies, adding to the dead-bot hail dropping to the floor.

The bots replied with basic evasive maneuvers, but it was obvious that no one was directly controlling them. That made sense, given the jamming in the environment. Erik keenly felt Emma's absence. Even shutting off the lights would have helped end the battle sooner.

Smoke and flames filled the room. True to the boss's threat, his men stayed firm, though they were smart enough to shift position and try to run around and avoid the team's fire while continuing to pound on the exos' shields. Plasma and frag grenades continued to burst in front of the exos, making it hard for the team to move without risking more than minor damage.

The antiair efforts paid off with fewer security bots left active for aerial flanks. Leaving that to Kant, Erik continued his attacks on the ground forces. He didn't fire wildly or use any more of his remaining explosives. A couple of good bursts made it through the portable shields the thugs had been using.

The remaining men backed toward the hallway. They continued spraying bullets at the exos, but their boss's glorious proclamations didn't amount to much when they saw men perforated beside them. Fear, not determination, was etched on their faces.

With men initiating a strategic withdrawal in two directions, Erik didn't know which group to follow. Clearing out the syndicate thugs was secondary to rescuing the missing cops.

"On three, Jia and I will swing left," Erik ordered. "You guys head right. Remember, we're looking for friendlies, but you two aren't idiots. If things get too hot, withdraw. Emma might not be able to hear us, but she's watching the area."

Kant scoffed. "Have some faith, brother. If I can't beat down these fools, how am I going to kill whatever building-eating cybermonster the Core throws at us next?"

Erik grinned and put down another thug with a burst. "Don't say things like that. You tempt the Lady too much."

Anne finished off the last of the security bots with a burst that blew it into a cloud of smoking debris. "Do we care about taking any of the syndicate guys alive?"

"If they want to surrender, sure," Erik replied. "Otherwise, it's on them. Starting a mess in the middle of martial law wasn't the brightest idea. Now, let's get ready. One, two, *three!*"

Anne and Kant swung to the right as Jia and Erik did the opposite, like two gates opening in unison. The fleeing thugs couldn't take advantage of the brief opening in the shield wall with their now clumsy firing.

The exo pairs advanced slowly to either side, taking time to pick off whoever was brave enough to stay and fight while the others fled to an intersection. More grenades bounced around the corner, this time not exploding but spewing out dense smoke. Erik shifted to thermal, chagrined by the blinding red and orange smothering the display.

"They threw some thermal cloaks in there, too," he announced.

"Better gear makes them a better distraction," Jia concluded. "Even if it's delaying the inevitable."

"What we can't see, they can't see." Erik checked his rear camera. Anne and Kant weren't having to deal with smoke or thermal cloaks yet, but that didn't prove anything.

Erik slowed as he entered the thick smoke. He switched his sensor overlay to a preprogrammed filter looking for different energy sources. The camera display lit up in a rainbow of distracting colors, but he hoped the half-finished construction would mean he could pick some things out that might normally be swamped by the background readings.

Bright blobs stood clustered in a denser group on one side versus the other. It'd make more sense to put more effort into guarding a position than setting up for an ambush.

Erik stopped right before the intersection and aimed his grenade launcher at the opposite side. He didn't need Emma always holding his hand to land a decent indirect shot. His plasma grenades bounced off the wall with loud thumps before exploding.

Gunfire rang out from the other side of the hallway, along with a high-pitched whine. A system warning popped up about potential EMP. He didn't worry. This wasn't an off-the-shelf police exo.

"Offer a couple of gifts to the other guys," Erik suggested.

Jia launched her own grenades. They exploded prematurely, the bright flash appearing right around the corner.

"Elite?" Jia guessed.

"No, they wouldn't have waited." Erik flipped through different viewing modes, but even an advanced exoskeleton didn't have the sensor capabilities of the *Argo*. The only thing he was sure of was the remaining enemy forces stood on one side of the intersection.

Machine-gun fire echoed from behind them, along with screams. Anne and Kant had made it into the hallway without trouble.

"We don't have time to mess around," Erik noted. "They might have an anti-grenade system, but we still have the machine guns. I'll stay on the left, and you hit the right."

Erik didn't run into the hallway. Instead, he took advantage of the tall uncovered ceiling, which gave him room overhead to pulse his jump thrusters and send him into the hallway sideways. His machine gun rattled, casings falling in a steady stream as he fired into the blinding smoke. He landed with a loud clang. A grenade exploded overhead, embedding shrapnel in his shield and the shoulder of his exo.

Jia rushed into the hallway, hugging the right side. She added her fire to Erik's, their bullets tearing through the dense smoke and the occasional flash of an explosion.

They both advanced, Jia matching her stride to Erik's after a couple of steps. Enemy fire waned, and halfway through, the grenades stopped. The smoke thinned as they approached the far end of the hallway.

Erik killed the sensor overlay. The thickest portion of the smoke lay meters behind them. Downed men choked the hallway, along with their mangled rifles and grenade launchers. A small portable turret-like device lay on its side, riddled with massive holes,—the anti-grenade system.

Muffled yelling came from beyond the open door at the end of the hallway. A loud crack sounded, and the yelling stopped.

"Almost there," Erik commented.

"I'll watch your back," Jia suggested. "It's hard to think these guys have much left, but we can't be too careful."

Erik continued toward the open door, ready to fire. The only thing holding him back was the cops. Otherwise, they could have strafed the place with the *Argo*.

The gunfire from Anne and Kant's direction stopped. Only the distant sound of their exos' heavy strides remained audible. This raid was almost over.

Erik charged forward. Jia matched his pace. They closed in another wide, empty room with half-finished internal walls.

With a loud grunt, a huge man holding a laser rifle sat up from behind a wall and steadied the barrel on it. Erik and Jia both fired, nailing him in the head as he pulled the trigger. The beam dug through the edge of Erik's shield, the missing chunk looking as if an invisible *yaoguai* had bitten through it.

It was a nice try, but they'd missed their shot. It was time to end this farce.

CHAPTER THIRTY-FOUR

Jia wasn't surprised that a group of men lined the back of the room with a mix of rifles and grenade launchers. She swept the machine gun across them without preamble, her heavy rounds cutting through them with ease. The falling grenadiers accomplished nothing other than firing plasma grenades into their group, the resulting explosions scattering the bodies.

The front of the room presented the greater concern. Another man with a laser rifle on a tripod fired but missed, blasting a hole through the wall. Erik shredded his chest with a directed burst but didn't continue shooting.

Jia finished her sweep of the rear position and checked her cameras, understanding why Erik hadn't blown through the entire room. Bound, wounded police officers, including Detective Halil Mustafa, were in a group on the other side of the room, with gangsters pointing rifles at their heads. Most were unconscious, including Halil, but the others couldn't speak because of the gags in their mouths.

There were only five gangsters left, but Erik and Jia couldn't make a move toward the hostages. One man in an expensive suit stood behind them. He didn't hold a weapon. Only the boss could get away with that cocky smirk.

He adjusted his tie and smiled. "Well, damn. It really must be you, Blackwell and Lin, if you got through all of that. Normally, there'd be no damned way I could let you kill so many of my guys and leave, but these aren't normal times, are they?" He laughed. "The Core trying to pop the Prime Minister, monsters running around in the streets, and the government saying that the UTC is as good as done. What a wonderful time to be alive."

"They haven't said that," Jia told him. "The Core's almost finished. You idiots let them use you, and now most of your men are dead. You're nothing but a distraction for them, pawns to be sacrificed while they make their next move."

"That's all of life, darling," the boss retorted. "I worked my way up to control my own organization, just like every man under me is planning to work his way up. If everyone can't be the boss, that means some people are going to get stepped on or sacrificed along the way. I'm not going to hate on the Core just because they're doing it. The system is what it is, and we're all just pawns."

Erik chuckled. "I'm not here to debate the ethics of being a piece of trash with you. If you're half as smart as you think, then you understand that you've lost. Whatever other people you have around here are dead now. The rest of our team is making sure of that. That means you've got minutes before you have four angry exos staring you down." He gestured with his machine gun at one of the dead men. "Those laser rifles didn't save you. All they did was thrash my shield, and I've got stacks of these things sitting in storage for easy swapping and repair. I don't think you have a trailer full of lackeys in reserve."

"Don't need 'em." The boss adjusted his lapels. "You self-righteous types don't understand the power of money. With all the leftover money after this, my surviving boys here don't even have to continue to work for me. They're all going to get control of their own outfits, and we'll carve up what's left of Neo SoCal after the Core finishes off the government. We'll rule the underworld here and let the Core run everything else."

Jia snorted. There was no way the Core had passed along their plans concerning the Fleet to random gangsters. This confidence came from nowhere. Even if the Core somehow managed to win, given their attitudes, they'd probably just incinerate any city they considered too corrupt from orbit. If only the idiot in front of her could be convinced of that before it was too late.

Erik's quiet snicker grew into a mocking laugh. Jia didn't join him, unsure of his plan.

"What's so funny, Blackwell?" the boss snarled, drawing a pistol. "Forget the damned Core. It doesn't matter because, at the end of the day, you're not willing to risk your old cop buddies. You think you can gun us all down before we shoot half these bastards in the head? Huh? If I die, my boys don't get their money, which means they risked all this for nothing,"

"If you knew anything about the Core and me," Erik replied, his voice low, "you'd understand that what Jia was saying earlier was out of mercy for your pathetic asses. The last time someone killed a bunch of my friends at the direction of the Core, I traveled across the entire UTC to track them down and punish them."

The boss licked his lips, his smirk disappearing. "Don't do anything stupid. What we're going to do is, we're going to walk out of here with some hostages, and you're going to let us do that. We're going to get in our flitters and fly away. We don't need all the cops, so consider the ones we leave behind a down payment. Otherwise, you might take us out, but I wouldn't want to have to go to their families and explain why they died in the crossfire."

Jia clenched her jaw, her fingers ready to fire. She and Erik could waste the gangsters within a second, but the thugs were aiming at the heads of hostages with their fingers on the triggers. At this point, any loud noise might make them twitch and kill someone.

"Am I using the wrong language?" Erik asked, sounding puzzled. "Do I need to do it in Zitark? Leem?"

"Huh?" the boss asked.

"Here's the thing, asshole," Erik explained. "I was all out of mercy fifty light-years from here. Then I spent years hunting people, and any impulse I had to be merciful dropped into a black hole. That leaves me here and now with you people, who are threatening my friends from the 1-2-2. There's absolutely zero chance of you leaving this building alive if you kill any of them." He growled. "You think the Core is going to save your asses? The Core's dying, flailing around in desperate longshot plans that have nothing to do with taking over and everything to do with inflicting the maximum amount of damage before they go down. How do you think your gangster asses fit into that future?"

"He's right," Jia shouted. "Do you think they're going to flood the streets with *yaoguai* and Elite who conveniently ignore gangsters and only attack cops? But it doesn't matter anyway because the best-case scenario is that a handful of you escape, probably with an arm or a leg blown off. Do you have a doctor on standby who can do full limb replacements? Otherwise, the second you go into the hospital, you'll end up getting tagged. And you've already admitted to working with the Core, which means you're working with a dangerous insurrectionist terrorist group during a period of martial law." She laughed. "How stupid are you? The cops could have taken you out and barely had to file any paperwork. About the only chance you have of not getting executed at this point is to surrender."

"Boss?" one of the lackeys murmured. "Maybe they're right."

"Shut your mouth," the boss screamed. "They're trying to work your nerves."

"But...it's them. The Obsidian Detective and Lady Justice. You said it yourself; some TPST cops are one thing, but those two?"

"Shut your damned mouth!" the boss yelled again, producing a shower of angry spittle. "How many times do I have to say it?"

"You know what it means to be all out of mercy?" Erik asked, pointing his machine gun at the boss. "It means blowing you away so badly that they'll have trouble figuring who you were from DNA analysis. You aren't leaving this room with hostages. You've got two choices.

Drop your weapons, free the cops who are conscious, and put your hands up, or die."

The other gangsters tossed their rifles on the floor. They knelt and started undoing the binding ties and gags.

"W-what?" the boss sputtered. "You stupid traitors! We're going to go to prison now."

"Better than dying," one man muttered.

The boss tossed his pistol on the floor with a clatter and put his hands behind his head. Kneeling, he sighed. "My damned luck! Why did it have to be you two?"

Twenty minutes later, the surviving gangsters were lined up in front of the building, with some of the rearmed uniformed officers guarding them. Medics had stabilized a small number of survivors and loaded them into ambulances.

Erik had stepped out of his exoskeleton to inspect the damage, along with the others. Anne and Kant had verified there were no other enemies in the rest of the building other than the small handful of gangsters they'd encountered when breaking away from Erik and Jia. The other team had managed to locate a military-grade jammer and destroy it, which allowed Emma to call for ambulances.

Halil waved off a medic and hopped out of the back of the ambulance, a small med patch on the side of his head and one peeking out from the top of his torn shirt. He headed toward Erik and Jia, waving.

"I never expected you two to show up," Halil admitted with a sheepish smile. "Too bad I was out of it for most of that. The guys who were awake said you both delivered nice speeches."

Erik shrugged. "You know us. We like to be overly dramatic about everything."

Halil laughed. "Hey, anything that ends with me still breathing is fine by me." He shot a glance toward the suspects. "Is every piece of syndicate trash we're going to run into going to be armed up with exoskeletons and laser rifles now?"

"I doubt it." Erik poked his finger into a hole leading to the other side of his exo's arm. "And from what Emma's been passing along, the Army, the militia, and the rest of the department are starting to get things under control. Having nicer guns might have helped the crime wave, but trying that crap when everyone was expecting trouble made the outcome predetermined."

Halil nodded slowly. His gaze shifted between Erik and Jia, a hesitant look growing on his face. "I don't need to be told to figure out that you two have been knee-deep in this Core shit since leaving the force. I wouldn't be surprised if it started before."

Erik shrugged. "It's personal for me."

"Look, level with me. Are we screwed?" Halil pointed at a tower. "This is Neo SoCal, and we've got monsters and killer cyborgs roaming the streets. When it's not them, it's out-of-control gangsters. We worked long and hard to clean this place up, and you two were a big part of why that happened. Now I'm wondering if we did it for nothing, and everything's about to fall apart."

Jia shook her head vigorously. "It's going to be tough; I'm not going to lie about that. But the Core isn't some unstoppable demonic force. We've beat them again and again, and we'll beat them this time."

Aside from the issue of passing on classified information, there was no reason to tell him the enemy had disabled a good chunk of the Fleet. A detective couldn't do anything about ships. The only option left was for the military and the ID to stop the final plan.

Halil blew out a breath, not looking convinced. "I once said I'd like to live through an important turning point in history." He laughed. "That was dumb."

"The best history is boring and peaceful," agreed Erik. He patted his exoskeleton. "Sometimes it takes force to get there."

One of the officers waved at Halil, who waved back. "Looks like I have to do my job, but hey, you two ever want to come back to the 1-2-2, we'd be glad to have you. You'll always be part of us."

CHAPTER THIRTY-FIVE

June 18, 2231, Neo Southern California Metroplex, Private Hangar of the *Argo*

Erik stared at his repaired exo in the cargo bay of the *Argo*. Lanara had been surprisingly calm about the damage, only noting that Erik had created less of a mess than she'd expected. He'd had trouble sleeping the night before and had considered going out to help clean up the rest of the criminal party before deciding they couldn't risk more serious damage to the exos until they were sure the main Core force had appeared.

Emma had been extensively monitoring police and news reports. Despite the trouble all over the metroplex, there were no *yaoguai* or Elites spotted. Overly armed and well-equipped criminals, from lowly rider gangs to well-organized syndicates, were responsible for all the violence. The authorities had brought the worst of it to heel, though they had been forced to continue suppressing pockets of trouble. It was more a massive coordinated riot than a terrorist attack.

Similar surges of criminality had been reported all over the world. There was no doubt the Core was behind it all. The military had been forced to send additional forces into the cities.

Erik shook his head and moved toward the door. Why hadn't the Core appeared? They'd stretched the defenses of the largest UTC city to their limit but hadn't followed up. Chaos couldn't be the only goal. Every UTC victory depleted the enemy and reinforced in people's minds that the government could win. There was something else going on.

The Core couldn't wait too long. While the Fleet couldn't fix every ship instantly, it was only a matter of time before the basic systems were restored.

What was coming?

Erik dropped into the co-pilot's seat beside Jia and put his feet up. "What are you doing?"

"Oh, I was just checking the logs from the destroyer fight," she explained. "The more I learn in each encounter, the better we can do the next time."

"You worried about having to disarm more Fleet ships and board them?" Erik asked.

Jia nodded slowly. "Yes, actually. I've thought a lot about this and wondered if they intend to try to win by building their forces that way."

"Maybe, but that plan's already a bust." Erik dropped his feet. "From what Anno told us, that was the only major successful evacuation they pulled off. And you saw those

Elites. They might be great for zero-G hacking ops, but the average Fleet security team could take them out without any trouble."

"Incoming emergency message from Vice-Director Anno," Emma announced. "Putting him through now."

Erik frowned. They'd just gotten done with one emergency situation, and now there was another? Maybe the Core was airdropping giant Elites all over Earth?

"We're here," he announced.

"On the *Argo*?" Anno asked. "We might have miscalculated by sending you to Neo SoCal, considering it was just the Core stirring the trash to cause trouble."

Erik didn't agree with that sentiment. If they had not gone, Halil and the others from the 1-2-2 might have been killed, but he assumed Anno hadn't called to complain about them taking down gangsters.

"Yes," Jia confirmed. "We're aboard the *Argo*. The team we took with us is here too. All equipment and weapons systems are ready for battle."

"You need to launch immediately," he ordered.

"For Troy?" Jia asked.

"Yes." Anno's voice sounded tenser than usual. "The *Bifröst* has just launched. You'll rendezvous with them. Make sure everyone aboard your ship is ready for all possible types of encounters, including zero-G boarding actions."

Erik frowned. "We're ready, but can you stow the ghost need-to-know shit for five seconds and give us insight into the bigger picture?"

"It is the belief of the Defense and Intelligence Directorates that the Core is about to launch a major assault on the moon," Anno explained, sounding defeated. "An unusually large number of civilian registry ships have broken away from main flight routes and are converging on the Moon. Working with data recovered from recent raids and cross-referenced with a variety of sources, including Maris Barbu's information, our analysts have been able to link a significant number of those ships to companies or organizations that we believe were or remain under the control of the Core. Based on your encounters near Triton and other recent Fleet intercepts, we are assuming those vessels have significant hidden weapons, making them equivalent to corvette- or destroyer-class Fleet vessels."

Jia swallowed and swiped her hand over the control panel. Data and command windows popped up, and virtual controls appeared.

Erik let out a bitter laugh. "You're telling me the Core managed to sneak an entire freaking fleet into the heart of the Solar System?"

"It's worse than that," Jia suggested, her expression grim. "Isn't it? You've already pulled back a good chunk of the Fleet to Earth, right?"

"Yes," Anno admitted. "It's not that the moon's defenseless, but the military was more concerned about strikes on Earth. They assumed the Core would bypass the moon. Given that they were worried about kamikaze attacks, it made sense to focus on the defense of the higher population center."

"There are a lot more orbital defense platforms around the Earth," Erik noted. "The moon barely has any. Are those even working?"

"There have been some explosions noted at the moon's orbital defense platforms," Anno admitted.

Erik groaned. "And Earth's?"

"Fine, to the best of our knowledge. And it's not as if the moon is defenseless. There are ships guarding it, and reinforcements are being sent from Earth on a hard burn. We're not neglecting the Earth in case this is a trick, or they've managed to pull off something else."

Erik ran his hand through his hair. He already knew the answer to his next concern. "But the Core fleet is closer to the Moon than the reinforcements."

Jia's hands continued to fly over the controls as she powered up the *Argo*. "If the jumpship's heading toward us and we're heading toward them, after that, it's just a couple of minutes for that close a jump, right, Emma?"

"Yes," the AI replied. "All things considered, you should be able to get to the moon in half the time of the reinforcements."

"You will not be doing that," Anno noted.

Erik jerked forward in his seat. "What? Don't tell me you're leaving those forces to die?"

"Shut your mouth, Blackwell," Anno barked. "You don't like me, and I don't like you, but this isn't about anyone being left to die. The truth is the Core might have superior numbers, but they are still relying on ships that aren't dedicated warships. We have every reason to believe that our forces can take on superior numbers of theirs. The virus and the readiness issue make this tougher than it should have been, but this isn't checkmate. I choose to believe in the officers and enlisted of the Fleet."

Erik's heart pounded. "Why should we stick around here?"

The Core had made their final move, and Anno wanted to keep this team on the bench. Screw that. He'd disobey the vice-director if he had to. They needed a good reason to sit on their hands.

Anno sighed. "No one said anything about you sticking around here. We're waiting for updated reports and telemetry from the outer Solar System, but what we already have suggests movements toward the HTPs rather than away. The timing of those movements and the limited ship ID information is indicative of a fleet being sent against the HTPs."

"But by the time we know what's going on, a battle will have already begun," Jia noted.

"Exactly. The situation's complicated there. There are decent forces there, but a lot of them aren't combat-ready." Anno took a deep breath and slowly let it out. Every word that came next brimmed with near-panic. "It is the belief of both the ID and the DD that the enemy force intends to destroy the Solar System's HTPs. We have far more limited current out-system intel, but based on previous patterns, there is a significant chance they also intend to destroy the HTPs in Alpha Centauri. We're not sure of the point of the attack on the moon is anything other than pure terrorism."

Erik scrubbed a hand over his face. "They know they probably can't win against Earth's defenses, but if they take down those HTPs, they won't cut off Alpha Centauri from inbound traffic, but they will have ensured that Earth is cut off from both inbound and outbound traffic."

"But if they don't take out Earth, new HTPs can be built," Jia noted, sounding unsure.

"I should note there is a significant Stella Infinitas presence on the Moon," Emma reported.

"Of course." Anno sounded irritated.

Jia grimaced. "They take out the HTPs. It's already going to take months to rebuild them, and they handicap even that. They could end up with anywhere from three months to half a year to do what they want."

Erik shook his head. "They don't even have to do what they want. They take down those HTPs, and the panic on Earth is going to look like a pleasant weekend dinner with your dad. Once news spreads that the HTPs are out, every guy who has ever fired a gun on the range once is going to think he can take over his colony. Between the anarchy in the Solar System and the insurrections, the UTC's effectively dead, along with a lot of people in the fighting." He leaned back in the chair, every muscle in his body tensing. "Depending on how rough things get on Earth, it might end up taking years to rebuild the HTPs."

"Vice-Director," Jia pleaded, "you have to let us fight."

"We intend to," he replied quietly. "You'll be in comm soon with the rest of your team on the jumpship. I've told them to standby while I laid out the situation. We're not sure if a couple of ships can make a difference, but at this point, you have two extremely well-armed ships with trained crews under your control that can get to a lot of places quickly. General Randall has informed me the best possible use of your team is aiding the defense of Alpha Centauri due to the reduced manning there."

Erik gave a firm nod. "This is it. This is their final push."

"We're not in the best position," Anno replied. "But we're not helpless either. All we have to do is stop them here and now and pick off what's left. You have your orders. We'll provide Fleet codes to help you with the Alpha Centauri defense forces. Once you're there, I trust you'll do what's best for the UTC and humanity."

"Killing the Core is what's best," Erik announced.

"On that, Blackwell, we agree."

Erik told the jumpship team to stand by until the *Argo* left orbit. He stared at a rear-view camera display as the beautiful blue marble of Earth receded in the distance. The Core's final plan bothered him. Maybe they hoped to conquer the bulk of the colonies in the time it took Earth to recover from their strike, but understanding wasn't necessary if the plan failed.

"Put me through to Raphael, Emma," Erik ordered. "Raphael, you there?"

"We're on our way," the scientist replied. "Before you ask, there's no way we can jump at this distance apart. Emma has to be directly interfaced with the system."

"That's fine," Erik replied. "I want to be part of the jump anyway. What I want to know is our options. It'll take a couple jumps to get to Alpha Centauri, right? With the plotting and the recharge, it'll probably be quicker just to jump to the HTP and then go through directly."

"Well, actually…" Raphael chuckled. "I finished some modifications today, and once Emma's able to update the system, they should get us up to five light-years per jump. I think that's the best we can do with this jump drive, but you're right; the plotting will take a lot longer."

"Then our best bet is to jump to the HTP and head through," Jia concluded.

"Assuming the Core hasn't destroyed it," Erik grumbled.

"They can't pull this off, right?" Raphael asked, sounding worried. "It's a bunch of freighters with hidden guns versus the Fleet. This shouldn't even be a contest."

"The Core prepared well for this. Based on what we know, they might have been preparing for years. No one could have ever imagined a conspiracy of this size and scope. We can win, yes, but we're going to have to do our part. We'll see you in a few hours. For now, we'll plan to jump through the HTP."

Raphael's hand shook. He looked down at the multifaceted crystal he held. The core matrix was beautiful in its own way. He'd managed to distract himself with work before, but there was nothing else to do until the *Argo* arrived.

This was it. Once he inserted the device, he was helping Emma complete her project, and not just any project, the birth of another self-aware AI. She'd need to finish the process herself, but in the end, a human hand would shepherd in a new age.

He should wait. His rational mind screamed that this wasn't the time to take a chance, but a deeper, more emotional part of him argued the opposite. This was the time to trust Emma and show that humanity could live in harmony with AIs.

Licking his lips, Raphael shoved the core matrix into an AI port and closed the cover. "I'm not a destroyer of worlds. I'm a...midwife?"

He cocked his head. He looked around and was glad no one was there to question his choice of historic words.

CHAPTER THIRTY-SIX

Jia tried to ignore the gurgling in her stomach after they completed the jump and immediately looked at their sensor display. The UTC fleet was spread around the HTP, and long-range sensors indicated a large group of vessels less than an hour away and coming in fast.

They'd spent long enough hooking up with the jump-ship that the UTC fleet's orders must have arrived from Earth. Given the fighter squadrons already deployed and the formations, they were prepared for a battle.

The jumpship with the *Argo* attached floated in space near the HTP. They were close enough that it'd take only minutes for a Fleet ship to close in and open fire.

Jia took slow, even breaths, trying to get used to flying with a helmet on. They'd all put on pressure suits and helmets in case they lost life support.

"Incoming transmission from the UTS *Indomitable*," Emma reported. "I've already sent out our codes and credentials."

"Jia, don't head toward the HTP yet," Erik ordered.

"I wasn't planning to," she replied. "Even if they were expecting us, they have to be pretty nervous about now."

"Put them through, Emma."

"This is Admiral Chopra in command of the 102nd Outer System Fleet," offered a boisterous voice over the comm. "We received an interesting transmission from command concerning your arrival."

"This is Blackwell, the operational commander," Erik replied. "We were planning to go through and reinforce Alpha Centauri defenses, but you tell me what you think, Admiral."

"We just received a comm pod through the HTP," Admiral Chopra replied. "Admiral Song is commanding the fleet defending the AC HTPs. The Core has a decent force moving on them, but the bulk of our Fleet resources in the system are deployed around Chiron. We don't have ships to spare here, and the incoming enemy will hit them at about the same time."

"Good enough for us," Erik noted with a nod toward Jia. "See you soon, Admiral. Good luck."

"Good luck to you, Blackwell."

The main thrusters of the jumpship fired, the force pushing them back in their seats as they headed toward the massive ring. Shades of blue and white filled the ring, more than Erik could distinguish, swirling in competing overlapping vortices. Looking into an open HTP was like looking into a hole in the universe at a dozen overlapping storms.

"Entering hyperspace in thirty seconds," the helmsman of the jumpship announced. "Everyone strap in if you're not already."

Erik chuckled, despite the tense situation. "It's been a while since we did this the old-fashioned way."

"Ten, nine, eight..." the helmsman counted.

Jia closed her eyes and waited for the countdown to finish. Her stomach protested their entry into hyperspace. She kept her eyes closed for half a minute before opening them to a familiar surreality. Distance meant nothing, and every expected color was the opposite. Space rippled and swirled. Bright pinpoints of light enveloped them, challenging her brain to make sense of them. Twining patterns of light and color twisted all around. Tingling built into discomfort, and that built into a creeping pain. Her heart rate kicked up, along with the pressure in her head.

Then it was over. Reality reasserted itself, all hints of the madness of the past minute gone.

Jia swiped the sweat off her brow, then blinked a few times and looked at her displays to try to reorient herself. "We've transited the HTP."

The *Argo* lurched as she released the docking clamps and fired thrusters at low power to begin backing away from the jumpship. She continued taking slow, even breaths since her stomach was still rebelling against the HTP transit. The last thing she wanted to do was throw up in her helmet.

A small fleet was arrayed near the HTPs of Alpha Centauri. Long-range sensors confirmed an aggressively closing second force, none displaying Fleet transponders, less than ten minutes away.

"Damn, the Core coordinated this well," Erik mumbled. "Emma, put me—"

"You're being hailed by the UTS *Puqi*," Emma reported.

"Connect us," Erik ordered. "Admiral Song, this is Blackwell. I should have asked Admiral Chopra to send a comm pod ahead, but maybe we got lucky and he did that before we showed up to talk to him."

"He did," Admiral Song confirmed. "This is unorthodox, but I'm not going to complain about two more ships joining my fleet, and I know the captain of the *Bifröst*. He's a good man."

"Are you familiar with our capabilities, Admiral?" Erik asked.

"Command has mentioned your jump drive," he replied. "But they said it's not something you can use easily and quickly in combat."

"That's true," Erik replied. "But if you feel we'd do better around Chiron, we can get there without much of a delay."

"I'd prefer if you help out here," the admiral explained. "The enemy doesn't seem to be making a run at Chiron. Two ships won't help there, but they might here, especially given what our briefing file says about your capabilities. We're going to give these fools one last chance to save us trouble. We've spread our ships out to force them all to come at us to get either of the HTPs. Let's hope that's enough. Until then, get ready."

"Emma, connect me to both our ships," Erik ordered. He waited two seconds before continuing, "Everyone knows what they have to do. We're fully integrated with the defense forces here. Obviously, we've already separated. It doesn't look like we're in a situation where we'll need Emma over here, so you'll have her for jumps if necessary. I'll leave that decision to the commander."

The cockpit door opened, and Kant and Anne hurried in. Both took seats and strapped into harnesses.

Erik gave them a nod. "I'll transfer control of some of the weapons over to you. Without Emma helping, it'll be useful."

Kant offered him a thumbs-up. "I'll do my best, brother."

Anne narrowed her eyes as a targeting display appeared, along with holographic movement and firing controls. "At least it's not just us."

"Lanara, you okay down there?" Erik asked.

"I'll do my part, and you do your part," she replied over the comm. "I've got Constantine down here to help with some of the active systems crap, but he's no Emma."

Emma chuckled. "A fleshbag will have to do."

"I'm on the comm, too," Malcolm complained. "I can hear you."

"I'd prefer to be on the *Argo*," Emma replied. "The Fleet crew isn't going to let me do anything interesting, but I could help Engineer Quinn's team."

Jia glanced at the rapidly approaching Core fleet. The UTC's forces were at a worse numerical disadvantage on this side of the HTP. If Admiral Chopra finished off the other forces early, he could reinforce them, but there was no guarantee he'd be in any shape to do that.

The whole thing was absurd. If it weren't for their half-alien virus and a lot of luck, the Core would have been facing too many ships to have any hope of victory. Here they were, making a major run at isolating Earth.

The only positive was that their use of a fleet of ships spoke well of HTP security. With their influence in the relevant companies, bombs might have been a possibility, but earlier incidents in previous decades had made the UTC government overly paranoid about that type of attack.

The government's understanding of which members of the Core controlled which industries and companies remained incomplete. It was entirely possible that Julia Caldo had killed the men and women who could have made such a plan viable in the short term. Given everything they'd learned from Barbu, Jia wouldn't have been surprised.

At this point, she wasn't going to second-guess the Core's tactics. They were doing what they could with what they had left. A massive attack might lack elegance, but if it was successful, it would destroy large chunks of the working fleet and the HTPs.

"Attention, Core fleet," the admiral broadcast. "This is Admiral Song of the 108th Alpha Centauri Defense Fleet."

Jia glanced at Erik. With his belief in the Lady, Admiral Song's unit number matching Erik's old number would be an omen. The huge smile on his face pointed to a good one.

"You are to immediately power down, retract your weapons, and prepare to be boarded," Admiral Song ordered. "Your attacks are considered an act of open insurrection and terrorism against the United Terran Confederation. If you do not immediately surrender, you will be fired upon and destroyed by this fleet. That is all."

Jia frowned as a comm alert popped up. She entered commands. "The entire Core fleet is sending out a transmission; the same one, from what I can tell." She ran her hand over a slider control to pipe it to the others and set it to replay from the beginning.

"Attention, servants of a corrupt order," began the transmission, a harsh man's voice speaking. "I am Yan, and I serve the true ruler of humanity, the Immortal Empress Julia. Know that her title is no mere affectation. She has used the technology of the ancient race of Hunters, a race that your pathetic corrupt government has not even admitted exists." He let out a mocking laugh. "She will never age and will sit upon the throne of humanity until the stars swallow their planets. What you know as the Core is no more, the traitors and criminals who composed it were defeated through their incompetence or the hand of our most righteous Immortal Empress. Your fleets have been weakened, which is proof of the impotence of your rulers. We will begin a new age by closing off the corrupt old home of humanity."

The Core fleet decelerated, preparing for tactical engagements. The admiral signaled for the UTC fleet to speed up. The *Argo* and the jumpship were on the far flank of the forces, near a squadron of destroyers.

Jia's heart rate had returned to normal. Her hands didn't shake. Nothing about this bothered her. She was looking forward to it with a detached calm.

This was what she'd wanted all her life: to defend her society and civilization against antisocial criminals and terrorists. The truth of the Summer of Sorrow had lingered in her mind since Barbu's confession.

The ships arrayed before her weren't simple criminals. They were the tools of a genocidal madwoman who now claimed to be an immortal empress. Whether Julia called herself a member of the Core or something else, it changed nothing. Monsters biological and technological were her preferred weapons. Any humanity led by Julia Caldo would quickly cease to be that.

"You have one chance to stand down and pledge your loyalty to your new empress," Yan demanded. "There will be no mercy otherwise. Your ships will burn. Your lives will be forfeit. You will be sacrifices on the pyre of a new galactic order. Your threats are meaningless, and we will only allow until engagement for you to power down and signal your surrender. Any ship that does so will be spared and welcomed to the empire. All others will be destroyed."

Anne rolled her eyes. "I hope for his sake Caldo wrote that speech and forced him to read it."

Erik shook his head. "The more of these Core nuts I meet, the more I'm convinced they're true believers." He cracked his knuckles. "At least we'll be able to get good use out of the laser cannon."

"We might want to save some missiles and torpedoes if we need to help the other fleet after this is all done," Jia noted.

Erik chuckled. "Getting ahead of ourselves, but I like that confidence. Anne, Kant, you good?"

"My turrets are online," Kant announced.

"I'm prepared as well," Anne reported.

"The *Puqi* is signaling ships to prepare to engage," Jia reported, glancing down at her tactical comm display. "One minute until the front line opens fire."

Fighters streamed from their motherships on her sensor display like swarms of angry bees. This wasn't a brawl between souped-up yachts or a rescue mission where they had to pull their punches. It was time to pit the dedication of the defenders of the UTC against the loyal members of the Core.

Her eyes widened as small sensor contacts separated from the Core fleet. "They've got fighters? No, these aren't large enough. Drones? I'm getting unusual readings."

"Drone bombs." Erik gritted his teeth. "It's arguable if that's better or worse than scatter torpedoes."

"Thirty seconds."

Erik blew out a breath, a relaxed look coming over his face. "Malcolm and Lanara, just keep those shields strengthened."

"Don't think I won't be pissed when this is all over," Lanara replied. "You better hope you get us blown up so you don't have to listen to me bitch later about all the holes you're about to put in this ship."

Erik laughed. "I'll keep that in mind."

"Fifteen seconds," Jia reported.

"Time for some fun!" Kant shouted.

CHAPTER THIRTY-SEVEN

Erik had spent his military career as a ground-pounder, not as a member of the Fleet, but that didn't mean he was ignorant about Fleet tactics and its general order of battle. All officers needed to understand the big picture so they could better coordinate with other forces. That, combined with his experiences aboard the *Argo* and the jumpship, reinforced a fundamental understanding about what to pay attention to during battle.

Instinct wanted to draw a man's eyes to the cameras. It made sense. People's primary sensory input came in the form of vision. When he was in a firefight, he heavily relied on visual cues.

A fight aboard a ship was a different matter. Even with magnification, it could be hard to make out significant details at typical engagement distances. In the darkness of deep space, the problem was only compounded.

Rapid cycling of sensor feeds was the key to victory since it reduced the vast distances between ships to manageable, understandable chunks on a dynamic screen.

He'd gained experience in previous fights and training, but he realized there was an important hole in his skillset. Understanding the basics of fleet engagement tactics wasn't the same thing as having personal experience participating in a major fleet-to-fleet battle in a ship.

He frowned as he took in the sensor readout. A standard core world defense fleet would include scores of ships. Admiral Song's fleet included only dozens. The enemy outnumbered them over three to one.

It was encounters like this where Erik understood how dangerous the Core could be. Julia Caldo had pulled together at least three secret armed fleets of significant size. If there had been no Core Civil War, they might have been able to neutralize the UTC Fleet and show up with hundreds of ships at each strike point.

Erik shook his head. Quality mattered. He'd proven that again and again.

None of the Core ships were as big as the battleship *Puqi*, but there were some decent ships sporting enough turrets, cannons, and missile racks to be on par with a cruiser or a light cruiser. Erik assumed Yan was aboard the largest vessel.

That ship was near the other side of the fleet formation. It didn't matter who took Yan out in the end, but it probably wouldn't be the *Argo*.

Erik didn't care. From his rant, Yan was a high-ranking lackey, but he wasn't the true leader of what was left of the Core. Killing Julia would end this war and finish his revenge. Taking Yan out would be all but impossible given the circumstances, and Erik doubted a man like that would give up anything useful about his beloved Immortal Empress.

Huh. Wonder what they'll call this? The Battle of Alpha Centauri? Battle of the HTPs?

"Forward ships in maximum engagement distance!" Jia reported.

So it begins.

For a brief moment, every ship gave birth to angry, explosive children. Missiles and torpedoes ripped away from both fleets, their launchers working overtime to spew death. The *Bifröst* blasted several missiles and torpedoes toward the dense pack of Core ships turning their way. Most of the enemy raiding ships lacked the size of destroyers but displayed similar armaments, including laser cannons on the front. Larger vessels were sprinkled in with the others. This wasn't going to be a trivial battle.

Erik didn't fire any of his missiles or torpedoes. He understood the principle of flooding the zone with explosives, hoping you could get some easy hits in, but he wanted to save them for when they would count.

A group of scatter torpedoes burst apart near the enemy fleet. Submunitions shot everywhere as the missiles caught up. The raiders' point-defense lasers spun back and forth, firing with the help of rapid-reaction algorithms. When the defeated missiles and torpedoes exploded, it was a festival of light in the dark. Enemy missiles and torpedoes suffered the same fate near the allied ships, despite a small number getting uncomfortably close to some of the destroyers.

There was a certain absurd quality to twenty-third-century ship battles. Despite all the armor, shields, and advanced technology, most ships couldn't take much punishment. It was like the universe and physics wanted people to always remember in the backs of their minds that deep space was an unforgiving, hostile place. Anyone foolish enough to have a fight there almost deserved to die.

Anne took short, rapid breaths as she watched the targeting display for her turrets. Since the *Argo* remained out of effective offensive range for the weapons, she did her best to supplement the point-defense lasers, keeping any missiles or torpedoes from getting near the ship.

Jia kept the *Argo* in tight formation with the *Bifrost* and three destroyers, the *Munich*, *Antisana*, and *Taiyuan*. Like Anne, each ship was doing a good job of contributing to the missile and torpedo defense screen with all their turrets. The formation turned as a group as part of a sweeping flank, but the pack of raiders approaching spun toward them, thwarting their attempt at superior positioning.

"So the Core crews aren't total amateurs," Erik observed, glancing at Jia. For a woman who hadn't learned to fly all that long ago in relative terms, she was keeping perfect distances from the rest of the squadron.

A scatter torpedo exploded nearby. The point-defense lasers opened fire, supplemented by Kant and Anne. The *Argo* shook from explosions closer than Erik would have liked, but no damage displays popped up. Despite the initial exchange of missiles and torpedoes, no one was close enough for a decent laser cannon shot, let alone a laser turret. Four fighters took up formation near the *Argo*.

Erik was still trying to mentally adjust to the unfolding battle and the implications of tactics. Their previous ship-to-ship encounters had all been small-scale affairs where superior maneuverability played a major role in the battle, but with so many vessels firing at each other, this would come down to teamwork and would not be decided only by Jia's expert piloting, Lanara's tech skills, or his gunnery ability.

"The squadron commander on the *Munich* had ordered us to participate in a pincer," Jia reported.

"You fly how you need to, and we'll do the rest," Erik replied, not caring that they were getting orders. He'd defer to experience in this situation.

"Point and shoot," Kant announced. "Just like on the ground."

"That's the theory." Erik shrugged. "Let's see if it works out this time with all this other crap around."

The Core raider pack spread out in a line while the UTC ships broke into two rough triangles, the destroyers in one and Team Blackwell in the other. Torpedoes and missiles continued to stream from both fleets, though the rate of fire had died down. Submunitions from a scatter torpedo raked the back of the *Munich*, but the ship remained in formation.

Erik waited for an explosion and fired two missiles and three torpedoes toward the closest raider. A line of explosions marked their fate. The *Argo* had closed to cannon range. It was time to seal the enemy ship's fate. He fired.

The cockpit lights dimmed for a moment, and the *Argo* shook. Erik smiled as debris appeared on his sensor display. The fighters broke away, accelerating toward his victim.

Jia rolled the *Argo* onto its side as laser and plasma

attacks blasted from two raiders. His target had stopped turning with the rest of his formation. A trail of metal followed the ship, and a huge chunk was missing from the back. The fighters zoomed toward it in tight pairs like a pack of hyenas bringing down wounded prey, firing their lasers into the hole until the entire ship broke apart.

"Nice teamwork," Erik murmured with a nod of approval.

He already had a Fleet crew and a tank crew. It might be nice to have a fighter squadron. He didn't think he'd need one after the battle, but a momentary fantasy never hurt anyone.

The *Bifröst's* forward plasma and laser cannons came alive, along with the destroyers' laser cannons. Turrets of every type began spitting now that they were freed from having to concentrate only on defense.

Jia broke away from the formation to wobble and spin the ship, avoiding the intense fire from nearby enemies. Erik, Anne, and Kant opened up with their turrets.

Two medium raiders blew apart, blasted by concentrated attacks from the UTC ships. Another suffered heavy damage from the pass. The enemy ships began to spin in different directions, understanding they'd been surrounded, but momentum and cruel distance did not offer them much immediate hope for escape.

Erik glanced at a long-range sensor readout. The rest of the UTC ships were passing through the main enemy formation in a phalanx of energy death, with the massive *Puqi* as the spear point. Volleys of laser cannon ripped a larger raider to pieces, but drone bombs that had survived the gauntlet of turrets smashed into the allied vessels.

He didn't have time to be distracted by the rest of the fleet while they were still facing their enemies. The *Argo* rattled as enemy turrets pinged the bottom of the ship. Armor damage notifications and systems warnings popped up. He'd never expected to escape untouched, but the first damage in a battle always got his blood pumping.

Jia turned aggressively for another pass as the enemy formation continued to break apart. Erik didn't need years of Fleet training to know that was a mistake. As long as the Fleet ships stayed together, their overwhelming firepower would cut down the enemies quicker when they were otherwise surrounded. Massed turrets did a lot to cut down on close passes by enemy ships.

The greater number of enemy ships wasn't doing enough to offset bad positioning and tactics. It was obvious that despite the number of ships, their handling was inferior to the seasoned Fleet crews'.

Erik wasn't surprised. He'd seen that flaw again and again from the Core forces. They relied on fanatical loyalty, numbers, and sheer firepower to win battles. The kind of enemy who employed monsters wouldn't worry too much about careful strategies.

The problem for them was that skilled opponents and superior tactics neutralized their advantages. That was why small teams like Erik's had been able to defeat them on so many occasions. Once someone got used to the shocking reality of facing *yaoguai* and Elites, they became just another target to destroy.

The three Fleet destroyers, the jumpship, and the *Argo* finished surrounding the bulk of the enemy formation, even as a couple of raiders pulled to the margins. Friendly fighters continued harassing and concentrating on picking off turrets. One fighter blew apart, caught between converging turrets. Some of the fleeing ships turned inward, perhaps understanding the advantage in numbers.

Erik tried to time his firing with Jia's aggressive dodging. His effort paid off as the main laser cannon lined up with the side of a medium raider. The *Argo* shook again as the deadly, invisible beam cut through space and ripped through the side of the enemy. He followed up with three missiles in a coordinated volley, then a torpedo.

Two missiles died to the raider's defenses, but the remaining missile and torpedo blew most of the aft section off. Vicious rakes from the fighters and turrets finished off the enemy vessel.

A plasma turret barrage struck the *Argo*, and the ship lurched. A hull breach warning popped up. Jia swiped her hand through an emergency bulkhead control to seal off that part of the ship, her jaw set grimly.

Lanara might save her wrath until after the battle, but Erik knew it would come. It was worth the pain, though. Between her piloting and Lanara's careful grav shield modulation, the *Argo* had only taken minor damage while helping to kill several ships.

The *Bifröst* unloaded all of its forward energy weapons at a medium raider firing its side turrets. Hole after hole appeared as lasers and plasma blasts dug into the ship, then a massive explosion ripped through the raider.

Erik glanced at a camera feed focused on the jumpship. It hadn't escaped the current battle unscathed, judging by some of the gouges and holes in the hull.

He didn't worry. It was under the command of an experienced Fleet officer with two highly skilled engineers and Emma aboard.

A barrage of missiles exploded near the *Argo*, shaking the ship. More alerts appeared showing minor power and grav emitter damage and mild loss of thrust, but nothing serious other than the sealed-off hull breach in a maintenance tunnel. Jia's constant turning, rolling, and spinning made things uncomfortable even with the grav compensators, but it was keeping them from taking very many direct hits.

The UTC fleet had whittled down the enemy numbers with only modest damage and losses, but this wasn't the only battle being fought. The lunar fleet was responsible for defending the lunar cities. As proven by the lost fighters, this wasn't a series of battles they were going to win without losses. The quicker they finished, the more survivors they could guarantee on their side.

A drone bomb shot through the dying remnants of an explosion and plowed into the *Taiyuan*, blasting a chunk out of the side. The *Bifröst*'s offensive and defensive turrets concentrated on short-range firing and vaporized another drone bomb before it made it through to finish off the destroyer.

A moment later, the jumpship's forward cannons blasted through the front of the raider responsible for launching the bombs. Detonations rippled down the center of the ship, blowing it into drifting pieces.

Jia angled the *Argo* until she was flying straight up relative to the enemy formation and out of the primary firing angles of most of their turrets, even as the *Argo*'s aft turrets plugged away at the raiders. The *Taiyuan* delivered its own revenge by slicing into the side of a raider with a cannon blast before jamming turret shots through the exposed wound and blasting the ship apart.

Jia lined up another cannon shot for Erik with a dive. Turret blasts framed his target on both sides. With another shudder, the main cannon of the *Argo* fired and cleaved a smaller raider in half.

"Dial back on the cannon," Lanara insisted, her breathing ragged over comm. "There's a lot of power strain on the ship right now. Let her breathe more between shots."

"Understood," Erik replied, sounding disappointed.

With the recent destruction, the surviving enemy formation was penned in with no good options. UTC fighters patrolled outside the sphere of death, waiting to pick off runners. Desperate, aggressive torpedo shots from the enemy didn't make it far before being blown apart. Crisscrossing laser turret blasts blew them up. Shortly after, cannon blasts, including bright white shots from the *Bifröst*, tore through the raiders, shearing off turrets and punching holes in the ships.

Once one fell, the Fleet vessels concentrated fire on the remaining ships. The doom accelerated. Ship after ship blew apart until nothing but a dense wreckage cloud hung in space.

"Yeah!" Kant cheered and made a rude gesture. "Your empress can kiss my ass."

"It's not over," Erik replied. He gestured at a sensor display. "Keep your focus until every last enemy ship is gone."

Kant and Anne nodded firmly and kept their gazes

locked on the sensor displays. It wasn't that Erik wasn't happy with victory, but one decent rally by the enemy and the UTC fleet would be forced back on defense. They could easily employ similar tactics against his fleet.

"The *Taiyuan* has lost primarily maneuverability and most of her grav shields," Jia reported. "Cannons down. Turrets are still online. Her fighters are pulling back as a screen."

Erik nodded slowly. That level of damage meant men and women aboard had died, but he didn't have time to worry about that, only saving more of the living. The UTC squadron had given more than they got in their encounter, and the *Taiyuan* and the fighters weren't the only casualties.

The *Munich* followed a curving course to press the assault on the farthest wing of the enemy force. The other active ships in the squadron moved into position near the destroyer to form a rough circle. Precious seconds ticked by as Core vessels continued whittling down a group of Fleet cruisers and destroyers in front of the *Munich*'s squadron.

Floating piles of debris and large chunks of tumbling raiders confirmed that the Core paid a high price for their victories, but the UTC forces bore their own extensive scars. A light cruiser riddled with holes from torpedo explosions and cannon blasts continued firing her turrets despite tumbling past three enemy ships with no thruster power left. Two scatter torpedoes blew the front off the ship and secondary explosions rocked it as a small number of escape pods shot away, but not every pod cleared the blasts.

Missiles and torpedoes streamed from the *Bifröst* in a desperate attempt to take some of the pressure off the UTC ships. Erik fired three more missiles and two torpedoes in support. The swarm exploded, missile after missile dying to turrets. One of Erik's plasma torpedoes suffered the same fate, but his other blew out a turret on top of an enemy raider.

The arrival of the *Argo* and the others accomplished the initial goal. Enemy raiders broke into smaller formations, with a group heading out to engage the newly arriving ships.

"That's right," Erik muttered. "You can't finish eating until you've run off the healthy members of the pack."

Farther out, the *Puqi* carved straight through a major force, its turrets and cannons constantly firing, explosions all around it like a New Year's fireworks display. The battleship hadn't escaped without damage; she had gaping wounds all over her hull and a cloud of debris clinging to her. Her fighters aggressively strafed the raiders, and not all survived their efforts, but no one died without leaving their targets perforated hulks that were easy picking for their mothership's turrets.

When the battle had begun, the Core's ships had significantly outnumbered the Fleet, but now the numerical odds had evened out. Unfortunately, that didn't take into account damage, only destroyed ships.

Erik frowned as he looked at a sensor readout. The main enemy force was pulling back and reforming their lines in obvious preparation for surrounding the main UTC force.

Other wounded friendly vessels floated around, like the

Taiyuan, or limped away from the battle. The Core ignored them. Like vultures, they could pick them off once they finished those who could still fight. Even the mighty *Puqi* would fall with enough damage.

The *Munich, Antisana, Bifröst*, and *Argo*'s brutal flank saved the local wounded ships and left another massive pile of debris where the Core ships had been, but if the Core fleet achieved their repositioning, they might be able to turn the battle around.

Erik brought up a comm panel and prepped a transmission with an eager grin. Jia eyed him. Some plans were both brilliant and idiotic at the same time.

"What are you doing?" she asked.

"Distracting them," Erik explained.

"How?"

"I'm going to appeal to their sense of honor and loyalty." Erik waggled his eyebrows before starting his transmission. "Hey, Yan, I'm surprised you don't realize who's over here. Doesn't your idiot empress teach you anything? You've got the Last Soldier and the Warrior Princess fighting you here in this sleek little ship, blowing your guys away left and right. But that's kind of normal, right? I think we've done more to screw over the Core and your empress than any other two people in the entire UTC."

Kant laughed. "Are you serious, brother?"

The *Argo* stayed in formation with the rest of its squadron as it barreled toward a cluster of raiders who'd surrounded a cruiser and a pack of destroyers.

"We've got the jumpship, and after we're done here, we're going to go jump to your empress and blow her away, too," Erik taunted. "I wonder how well that immortality works if she's floating through space, half-vaporized from a laser blast. Don't worry, I'm going to make sure the last thing she hears is how you failed her."

"That's not going to work," Anne insisted. "If they break formation…"

The largest raider broke away from the pack fighting a group of UTC destroyers. Other smaller raiders, packing about as many guns as a destroyer, turned their way as well. Plenty of enemies were left to harass the main UTC fleet, but with their attack split, there was less chance of them finishing off the main ships quickly and cleaning up the wings later.

"Zealots to the last," Erik declared.

CHAPTER THIRTY-EIGHT

Jia didn't know how to feel about Erik's taunt strategy. It'd focused additional ships on their tiny squadron led by the *Munich*, but it'd opened holes in the enemy line. Fleet fighters screamed through the gaps, doing their best to get into blind spots.

Taking on difficult enemies in greater numbers came with the territory of fighting the Core, but she was more used to doing it on the ground, where one good hit wouldn't risk decompression. She loved flying, but ship battles, not so much.

Jia had been expecting the *Munich*'s captain to yell at them for their taunt, but the ship accelerated instead, with quick confirmations popping up on her tactical comm screen. The squadron continued forward.

An opening salvo from the *Bifröst* annihilated the back of a medium raider that had been pounding on a Fleet cruiser. It was trying desperately to drive them off with turrets, but its only active movement at this point was a slow rotation. The main thrusters had been blown off, and there was so much damage in the back, the deck layout was exposed. A couple of good hits would finish it off.

The *Munich* and *Antisana* joined the jumpship in firing their cannons. Jia leveled out the *Argo* to line up shots for Erik and the others. The ruthless barrage blew two small raiders apart.

The Core flagship and a small escort group continued their hard burn toward the *Argo*. Jia assumed Yan was onboard, but they hadn't confirmed it.

The huge distances involved in ship-to-ship combat messed with Jia's head at times. When she was trying to stick close in a duel, it was easier to abstract away, but in this massive fleet battle, she realized she was fighting enemies that would pull hundreds and thousands of kilometers away before coming back for a combat pass.

She couldn't help but roll her eyes when a transmission came in from the large raider. "It looks like he wants to talk."

"More like he wants to rant," Erik replied. "Go ahead. That is one duel I'm sure I can win."

"Blackwell!" Yan shouted, confirming his location. "You don't realize you owe your life to the Immortal Empress. You should show more respect."

Erik snickered. "Every one of those Core assholes could say something like that. I'm sure Empress Idiot back-stabbed some other Core bastard at some point that helped me out, just like Elias did. You heard of him? He started the Core, and he did a lot to help me and the Warrior Princess tear it apart, which is why you're here getting blown apart by the Fleet instead of murdering some old man in a house somewhere and relaxing for a couple of weeks like I'm sure you're used to."

"Shut your mouth," Yan replied. "You'll die knowing you failed, not only yourself and your precious UTC, but all those men and women in your unit. How does it feel, Blackwell? To know those who died on Molino were sacrifices for a greater good? Does it bring you any pain, or do you, on some level, realize it was the best death they could hope to achieve?"

"Is that how you're going to play this?" Erik blew away a drone bomb with a laser turret. "You think you can taunt me into giving up or rattle me by mentioning the Knights Errant?" He shook his head. "That's the problem. I don't know if it was your empress or her dumb and now dead Core buddies, but if you'd killed anyone else, maybe you wouldn't be hunted like dogs now. You all should have left well enough alone, even if it meant giving up some fancy alien tech."

Three fighters screamed past the *Argo*, narrowly missing a collision. They rotated on their sides and canceled out the turn, allowing them to continue blasting a small raider as they zoomed along their original path. Erik, Anne, and Kant spun their turrets toward the target and helped the fighters finish off the enemy.

"It's simple math, Yan," Erik explained. "How many factories have the Warrior Princess and I blown up? How many Elites have we scrapped? How many *yaoguai* have we turned to bloody mush?" He chuckled. "Shit, technically we're two of the few people outside the Core who can claim credit for taking down a member of the Core directly. If they're all supposed to be immortal gods, what does that make us?"

"Sophia Vand was handed to you by our empress's design," Yan replied, his voice shaking. "You couldn't possibly have accomplished any of that on your own, insect."

"Always calling people bugs. Do they send you to an insult training course for that?" Erik chuckled. "Sure. We figured something like that happened a while ago, but it doesn't matter. They're all supposed to be these gods, and they're just freaks who have lived a little longer and have some alien DNA. That's what you worship? Pathetic."

"My only regret is that I won't be able to see your eyes as your feeble half-life drains from your broken body." Yan closed the channel.

Erik shrugged. "Somebody's wound too tight."

"We've got a few minutes until he's in range," Jia reported.

"Plenty to keep us busy in the meantime."

Jia spun the ship until it was pointing down with a quick lateral thrust burn and then hit the mains. The *Argo* dived toward a medium raider that was missing half its upper turrets from earlier fighter runs. Anne and Kant blew apart the remaining turrets. Erik waited until they'd riddled it with holes before slicing it in half with a cannon blast.

A blinking alarm window popped up on Jia's left. She ignored it for the moment, turning hard to avoid a torpedo launch. A point-defense laser picked it off at close range. The ship shuddered from the blast, and more damage notices popped up.

"Hold off a couple minutes on the cannon," Lanara ordered. "I'm having to do some power reroutes. I tried to make sure that thing could work even after a decent punch, but the power system has taken a lot of hits."

"Couple of minutes, huh?" Erik echoed. "I don't care as long as it's ready for our buddy Yan."

Two enemy ships exploded near the *Puqi*. Despite the battleship's heavy damage, it was charging through one of the weaker positions in the Core formation. Missiles clusters flew from top launchers and struck the belly of a large raider, then a quad laser cannon volley from the battleship sliced the enemy vessel in half.

Three drone bombs charged the *Puqi*. Two died to point-defense fire, but the third crashed into the side and destroyed a pair of turrets.

A raider slagged the top aft turrets of the *Munich* and followed up with a missile. It struck the exposed top, carving out a huge chunk. Jia brought the *Argo* around, but the *Bifröst* made a pass, its turrets digging into the raider.

Jia narrowed her eyes as warning messages popped up the tactical comm display. She missed having Emma there to filter that sort of information for her.

"The *Munich* and the *Antisana* have lost primary thrusters, grav control, and primary attitude control." Jia shook her head. "I think they're done. Their remaining active fighters are planning to stay close. The rest are heavily damaged anyway."

"Good," Erik replied. "It means we don't have to worry about somebody running past and taking them out."

Figuring he'd waited long enough, he decapitated a raider with a laser cannon blast. After that, there were no active enemies left in their immediate area. Most of the Fleet ships had survived but had taken heavy damage.

Yan and his small escort group were almost within firing range. Two wounded destroyers and a light cruiser lay in his path. Jia turned the *Argo* toward Yan's ship.

"Unless you disagree?" she asked.

Erik shook his head. "How is Tensen doing?"

"Minor damage all over the jumpship," Jia reported, reading a display. "They've lost about a fourth of their turrets and two of their cannons. Multiple hull breaches, all emergency-sealed. The jump drive and the crew are okay."

"Let's duel this Yan bastard," Kant suggested.

"That's the plan," Erik replied, his gaze flicking between data windows. "The *Puqi* and the rest look like they've turned it around in the center. Not a lot of the big boys left besides Yan."

"Four to two," Anne noted. "And we're damaged."

"Hey, I've kept firing when I'm missing my arm," Erik offered with a smile. "This is nothing in comparison."

"Oh." Anne sighed. "At least I'll die defending the UTC."

"That's the spirit."

"Go ahead and put us in direct comm with Tensen," Erik ordered. He waited for Jia to nod. "Commander, sorry if I put you in a bad position."

"Your crazy stunt probably saved thousands of Fleet personnel," Tensen replied. "I'm not going to complain, and this ship has been a pleasure to command."

"Don't sound like you're ready to die."

"Don't worry, if I die, I'm sure everybody will point out

it's because I was taking orders from a former assault infantry officer."

Erik laughed. "Is that how it is?"

"We only have a couple of minutes until contact," Jia chided. "Save the big dick contest for after we've won."

"I recommend the *Argo* get up close and personal to get his attention," Erik explained. "We might take a few hits, but it should let you get close and unleash hell."

"Sounds like a plan." Tensen cleared his throat. "Don't die here, Blackwell. Your kind's supposed to die on the ground."

Erik shook out his hands. "The only bastards dying in the next few minutes will be Yan and his crew."

"Sixty seconds until maximum engagement range." Jia kept the ship level, though she was prepared to roll at any moment.

Erik nodded slowly. "Yan's flagship is like every other ship in the battle. It's been pounded hard, including losing a lot of turrets on its port side. That's our best bet. I've got one torp and four missiles left." He glanced to his side. "Looks like we lost the power to the plasma turrets, but point-defense and lasers are doing okay. When I give the signal, I'm going to need you to spin us toward the ship. Let me do my thing, and we'll spin back."

Jia nodded. "We have a good chance of surviving this plan, right?"

"We have a chance."

Kant spun his turret toward the incoming ship. "As long as I have one toy left to play with."

"Twenty seconds," Jia reported with a weary sigh.

She shunted the *Argo* to the side with a quick lateral

burn before canceling her movement with a counter-burn. There was no reason to let the *Argo* line up with the laser cannons on the enemy ship. The enemy ship didn't try to turn toward the smaller ship. The three escort raiders burned harder, accelerating ahead of their flagship.

"Ten seconds," Jia announced.

"I think I preferred mowing down mobsters," Anne noted.

"No challenge, no fun," Kant insisted.

The *Bifröst* didn't wait to engage the smaller ships in front. Cannons and turrets made short work of an escort ship. The two other small raiders turned to engage them, leaving Yan open.

Jia's forethought was rewarded when Yan's ship opened fire. The laser cannons narrowly missed. She accelerated for a hard burn. They would all but scrape the other ship's hull.

The smaller raiders tried for an aggressive approach on either side of the jumpship to avoid the cannons, but they weren't able to do much about the surviving turrets shredding them.

Jia concentrated on their opponent. If she screwed up, they'd smash into Yan's ship.

Erik held his breath while he waited to fire his missiles and torpedoes. Kant cackled in glee as he fired his turrets. Anne, stone-faced compared to her partner, also continued shooting, and their shots sheared pieces off the large ship. Although most of its port turrets were gone, a couple of plasma turrets had survived. Their slower blasts might make them shorter-ranged and harder to strike with than a laser turret, but they packed more of a punch.

Jia rolled the *Argo* to avoid a direct hit from a plasma blast. Anne and Kant cut into a plasma turret. Holding her breath, Jia fired the lateral thrusters and spun the nose of the *Argo* toward the large freighter.

"Eat this," Erik growled.

The last four missiles and the torpedo burned away from the *Argo*. At that range, even if there had been much in the way of point-defense left, it wouldn't have been able to do much. The missiles and torpedo penetrated the large ship and blew out huge chunks.

A laser turret struck the *Argo* at close range. Jia hissed as a major hull breach alarm popped up. An emergency bulkhead sealed the wound in the cargo bay.

"Lieutenant, you okay?" she asked nervously.

"We've got our suits and helmets on, and the tank can survive for a while in any environment, but I would prefer not to float around in space if you can avoid it," Lieutenant Korhonen replied.

Jia burned into a wide, arcing turn. She planned to sweep around for another run on the port side. Erik's attack had ripped the ship open. It was amazing that it hadn't broken up.

The *Bifröst* completed their slower approach, and their cannons and forward turrets discharged into the wound. Internal explosions danced throughout the interior of Yan's ship, and it blew apart.

Erik scoffed. "Your empress might be immortal, but I guess you weren't, Yan."

CHAPTER THIRTY-NINE

The *Argo* and the *Bifröst* changed course, ready to reinforce the rest of the UTC fleet. The *Puqi* and the others had done a good job of cutting down on the enemy forces. Despite the heavy losses and the damage the fleet had suffered, they now outnumbered the remaining Core ships. That should in theory give them the advantage.

In a normal fight, the opposing side would have realized there wasn't much point anymore. They would have fled or surrendered, but the Core ships did neither.

Erik wasn't surprised to see none of the Core ships running. Fanaticism might result in higher casualties, but it also assured those same forces inflicted more pain on the enemy.

The Core raiders kept up their relentless attacks against the Fleet vessels, including at least one ship that tried to ram the *Puqi* before being broken apart by a crossfire of laser cannons from the battleship, a cruiser, and a pair of destroyers. Erik had never seen something so large diced so finely in an instant.

The *Argo* and the *Bifröst* continued their burns toward the final battle, but they were still a couple of minutes away. Hard burning had to be approached with caution in this type of situation. They didn't want to end up screaming past the engagement zone and not being able to accomplish anything.

Erik nodded with satisfaction as more Core raider ships broke up on his sensor display. It was obvious that the enemy had underestimated the firepower and training of the Fleet defenders. There had been losses on the allied side, but they had far more ships dead in space than destroyed, whereas every single Core loss had included a ship broken into at least two if not more pieces.

There were also enough active friendly ships left to recover escape pods and render aid in the immediate area without having to rely on ships two weeks away near Chiron. Those precious minutes and hours after a battle determined how bad your losses were in the end.

Erik flexed his fingers a couple of times. Alpha Centauri was one front in the battle. They had no idea how the other two were going. There was a bigger friendly fleet on the other side of the HTP, but he had no idea how large a force was attacking the moon. Given the timing of the HTP attacks, there was no way the reinforcements from Earth would arrive before the battle was all but over.

There was one obvious option. The *Argo*'s combination of weapons, maneuverability, and fine-tuning by Lanara made it as lethal as a cruiser. The *Bifröst* might not be able to take the hits of a battleship, but it could throw out almost as much punishment as one. The two ships had already proven to be worth an entire extra destroyer squadron or two in a battle. Erik hoped it didn't come down to that margin, but with a good chunk of the Fleet disabled, it might.

They closed on the edge of the last battle zone. Medium enemy raiders trying to avoid the turrets of the *Puqi* were easy prey for the cannons of the two arriving ships. After destroying the enemy ships, the *Argo* and the jumpship headed in opposite directions to help encircle the remainder of the enemy.

It was only caution that stretched out the last portion of the battle for so many minutes. A wounded destroyer, the *Orinoco,* fired the final shots of the battle when its aft turrets blew a small raider that was desperately trying to ram a cruiser apart.

Erik rubbed his temples. "We need to contact the admiral, assuming he's still alive."

Jia nodded and punched in the appropriate commands. "The *Puqi* is receiving."

Admiral Song's weary voice came through in a scratchy transmission. "That was some nice fighting, Blackwell, and we appreciate what you did with your little psych warfare stunt. I think you saved a few ships with that."

"We're going to hit the HTP and reinforce Admiral Chopra," Erik explained. "There's nothing threatening on long-range sensors, and we can't be sure the battles have ended over there."

"I can only spare so many ships," Admiral Song replied. "We've got a lot of heavily damaged vessels and escape pods to recover."

"I'm just telling you what our plan is," Erik noted.

"You start your burn, and I'll send some destroyers after

you in a few minutes. Let's hope it doesn't come down to our reinforcements."

"If I had to choose between hope and another destroyer, I'd always pick the destroyer."

Jia shook her head and slapped her cheeks to reorient herself after the hyperspace transit. She blinked a couple of times, then looked at the sensor display. Eight large ships were close to the HTP and heading their way. Erik gritted his teeth before the transponder codes registered: all Fleet ships. There were a decent number of signatures farther out, but most of those were barely moving.

"Getting a transmission from the UTS *Rapier*," Jia reported. "A cruiser." She swallowed and gave Erik a concerned look. "I'm not detecting an active transponder for the *Indomitable*."

Erik nodded, a grim cast to his face. "*Rapier*, this is Blackwell on the *Argo*."

"This is Captain Vaunt. What's the situation in Alpha Centauri?"

"We've put down the Core fleet there," Erik reported. "The *Puqi* survived, but there were significant Fleet losses. The area is secure, and some destroyers will be coming soon to reinforce you and render aid."

"Those bastards took out the *Indomitable* and the admiral with it," Captain Vault replied, his voice cracking. "Like you said, Blackwell, we took losses, but we turned the rest of them into dust. No damage to the HTPs."

"I take it you're the highest-ranking officer left alive in the fleet?" Erik asked.

"That's affirmative, Blackwell," Captain Vaunt replied.

"Did the Core fleet contact you? Offer for you to surrender?"

"No." Captain Vaunt sounded surprised. "We told them to stand down, but they didn't respond."

"Okay, just curious. We had a different experience on the other side." Erik frowned. "That probably means the guy in charge of the fleet on that side was also in charge of this one."

"What's your plan now?"

"We took some hits, but we're still in fighting shape," Erik explained. "If you don't need us here, we're going to jump to the moon and see if they need help."

"I wish we could go with you." Captain Vaunt sighed. "Blow away a few of those bastards for Admiral Chopra."

"We will. Blackwell out." Erik looked at Jia, who nodded and turned toward the jumpship.

"Let me guess," Emma said over the comm. "Even over here, I can tell what you're planning, and you'll be pleased to know that I've already plotted a jump to the moon."

"Are you on board with this, Tensen?" Erik asked.

"I agreed to follow your lead," Tensen transmitted. "But more than that, if the fight's not over and this ship can still dish out the pain, my crew and I need to be there helping our brothers and sisters in the Fleet and the civilians on the moon."

"Okay, we'll dock ASAP." Erik laid his head back in his chair and ended the commlink. "No missiles, no torps, damage all over, and missing a couple of turrets. I guess we've been in worse shape before."

Kant rubbed his hands together. "As long as we have one gun, we can fight."

"It might already be over." Anne shrugged. "This fight was."

Erik shook his head. "It isn't over until we challenge the Immortal Empress for the title."

"You think she's at the moon?" Anne asked.

"I don't know, but I think the more Core fleets we waste, the better our chance of running into her is." Erik gestures at the sensor display. "There's no way someone who chooses a title like Immortal Empress could have stopped herself from making a big show of it before engaging the UTC fleet. We know she wasn't here."

"And if she isn't with the moon fleet?" Jia asked, not hiding the concern in her voice. "If she's smart, she wouldn't risk her life like that."

Erik snorted. "She might have pulled an army out of her ass in Neo SoCal and these three fleets out too, but there's only so many places to hide. For now, let's get connected to the jumpship and get over to the moon before it's too late to join the fun one way or another."

CHAPTER FORTY

Erik hadn't come so close to throwing up after hyperspace travel since his first transit. He assumed his intense discomfort was the result of going through the HTP and then jumping so close in time after since he'd never heard about people having trouble on the rare occasions they transited an HTP close together.

It was a small price to pay for the tremendous amount of mobility the jump drive afforded them. The ship's usefulness had been obvious during the Hunter mission, but this battle was demonstrating what jumps would mean for the future of the UTC. If humans could somehow create an automated jumping comm pod and get around the transit delays, humanity could end up bound together in a true united government rather than the vague feeling of colonies stranded in time months apart.

Erik tried to rub his eyes, but his helmet stopped him. His vision swam. The data windows around him bustled with activity, but his jump sickness was making it damned hard to interpret. Jia, Anne, and Kant groaned quietly. At least he wasn't the only one feeling it.

"Emma, report," Erik croaked, taking slow, deep breaths and trying to will his brain to cooperate. He wasn't going to let a little thing like the fundamental rejection of alien physics by his body mess up his tactical planning.

"Ah, you demonstrated almost complete synchronicity with the lieutenant commander." Emma chuckled. "We've successfully arrived. Fleet orbital forces are still engaging a rather sizeable number of Core ships. A defensive line has been set up above the moon, concentrated over and near Chang'e City. Sensors and visuals indicate two domes have been penetrated by orbital bombardment. We are currently near the far flank of the main allied position."

"They've already blown domes?" Jia asked, her voice shaking.

"People knew the attack was coming," Anne insisted. "They're probably in shelters and suits. And blowing domes isn't enough for what they want. They're going to want to reduce those places to craters."

Kant shook his head, a dark scowl forming. "Those Core assholes."

Erik took a couple of deep breaths, his body and brain sobered by the damage reports. "Are they attacking any of the other cities?"

"No, the Core forces are concentrated on attacking Chang'e City and the UTC fleet," Emma replied. "I feel compelled to point out the relevant Stella Infinitas facilities are located in that one city."

Erik snorted. "Those idiots don't get it. They didn't take the HTPs. This is pointless."

"Do you think that means they'll stop?" Anne asked incredulously.

"No, which is why it pisses me off so much."

Humanity had come full circle. In the ancient centuries, wars could be fought and won or lost, but it might take isolated forces weeks or months to learn that they needed to lay down their arms and their recent struggles were for nothing. With the advancement of communication technology, those incidents had become a quaint cautionary tale from the past.

Then humans spread out in the Solar System, and the limits of technology made it a problem again. Ironically, the rise of FTL travel had only reduced the lag rather than eliminated it. Hundreds of thousands of lives were on the line in Chang'e City, targets of an enemy that didn't realize they'd already lost.

One good thing could come out of their HTP gambit. While the FTL gateways were critical to the UTC as a whole, only a small percentage of people actually traveled through them. When the battles ended, it'd seem like a distant, abstract event for the bulk of humanity. People would hear about victory and minimal losses.

If Chang'e City was lost, it would be different. Accidents and terrorists cost lives, but it'd been a long time since an event on the scale of the Summer of Sorrow had occurred. Erik couldn't do anything about that, but he could stop at least one of the same people from pulling off a sequel.

Erik narrowed his eyes. "Jia, can you begin separation? Whatever's going to happen, we'll do better as two ships unless Tensen has something else in mind."

Jia nodded quickly, determination replacing the fear on her face. The *Argo* trembled before gently gliding backward.

"You're good to separate, *Argo*," Tensen's XO replied over the comm.

"Don't be foolish," Emma ordered. "I wanted to say that before the next fight. I've grown overly fond of you fleshbags."

Erik grinned. "Don't worry. I didn't come this far and long to die."

"You're receiving a transmission from the Fleet flagship." Emma chuckled. "It's the *Los Angeles*."

Erik remembered seeing the ship during their arrival at Troy. As one of the most powerful ships in the Fleet, it made sense that the *Los Angeles* would be close to Earth. He was only glad it had been part of the main lunar defense force rather than with the reinforcements who were still hours away.

"The Lady and her sister Fate are trying to make a point," Erik replied. "Put them through."

The *Los Angeles* and several support destroyers were pounding away at a cluster of large raiders charging the formation. Powerful cannon blasts tore through the Core ships, but a cloud of drone bombs emerged from the dying vessels. Explosions from their sources took out some of the drone bombs, but most survived to zoom toward the allied ships.

Bright flashes marked drones detonating from turret hits and desperate attacks by fighters, but the sheer volume ensured that some of the deadly bombs made it through. Two drone bombs crashed into the front of a destroyer, wrenching it off. Another struck the side of the *Los Angeles* and took a couple of turrets with it.

The surviving ships adjusted position, increasing their relative distance from the damaged destroyer. It was coasting forward, parts and pieces floating from inside. Given its angle and distance from the moon, it was destined to smash into the surface. Escape pods began blasting away.

"This is Admiral Lefevre," said a stern woman's voice over the comm. "I'm assuming since you're here, Blackwell, whatever happened in Alpha Centauri is over. Give your update. We're not exactly blessed with a lot of time right now. The Core keeps pushing harder."

Erik liked this woman, straight and to the point. She didn't care that they were jumping around the Solar System in experimental technology. She only cared how they could use it to win the battle—a true officer.

"As anticipated, enemy fleets attacked the Solar System and Alpha Centauri HTPs," Erik reported, slipping back into his old military diction and rhythm. "One Core commander identified himself as Yan and verified they're fighting on behalf of suspected Core member Julia Caldo, who is now calling herself the Immortal Empress. Yan requested the surrender of the allied forces before engaging."

"Understood and acknowledged, Blackwell," Admiral Lefevre replied. "The enemy fleet commander of this force goes by the name Tralian and requested something similar. Last known status and condition of allied and enemy forces?"

"Both Core fleets completely destroyed at both HTP

sites. No prisoners were taken. We'll have Emma transmit the known losses and damage to allied ships." Erik's voice quieted. "Just so you know, they took out the *Indomitable*, Admiral. Not sure about all of her crew, but Admiral Chopra went down with the ship."

Admiral Lefevre sighed. "Understood. It sounds like if we beat them here, this is over. As you can see, we're holding them off, but we can't finish them without risking exposing the city, and they won't let up. They keep trying to lure out our forces so they can make another run at the domes. They tried nukes in the beginning, but we took them out. It's been a while since they tried one, so I think they're out."

"They're bound and determined to destroy the city by any means necessary," Erik spat.

"Looks that way." The admiral's voice was tense. "Right now, we have a lot of people in emergency shelters down there, and it's a miracle we only have hundreds of civilian deaths instead of thousands. However, the thousands who were injured might join the other category if we don't end this battle soon. What's your personal situation?"

"Moderate damage to both ships," Erik reported. "Minor loss of weapons systems capacity. No significant injuries among either crew. We're still combat-ready and eager to send more Core troops to hell, ma'am."

Admiral Lefevre chuckled. "That's assault infantry. You guys don't know how to spell 'quit.'"

"Do you want us to join a squadron, Admiral?" Erik asked.

"It's my understanding that you have a tank crew

aboard your ship, Blackwell? And at least enough opera-tives to form one assault infantry squad?"

Erik's brow lifted. "Affirmative, Admiral." He glanced Jia's way, a thought occurring. "We can put a three-man assault infantry squad and a fully manned tank on the surface, as well as provide close surface-attack support from the *Argo*."

Jia frowned and looked his way. She obviously under-stood the implication that she wouldn't be joining him on the surface.

Just keep it together. I'll explain in a second.

"The *Bifröst* will join the main fleet to shore up our lines," the admiral explained. "I've got something else in mind for the rest of you. Early on, the Core managed to put down a decent landing force of tanks and Elites. We've been getting our asses kicked on the surface. About the only thing we have going for us is that they can't release a *yaoguai* horde on the Moon. We're going to send reinforce-ments to the surface forces, and we'd like the *Argo* to drop your forces when we attempt our next reinforcement wave. The *Argo* will then rejoin the orbital line. Things are pretty gnarled up on the surface, so there's only so much you'd be able to do as surface attack support and to be frank, we can use another ship up here more than down there. Get into position, and we'll carve our way through if the Core refuses to accept the inevitable."

"Understood. Blackwell out." Erik turned to Jia. "I didn't want to spend a lot of time going back and forth with her to explain our pilot situation. With Emma on the jumpship, you're the only one who can fly. My question is how well you can fly and shoot at the same time."

"It depends on who's shooting at me," Jia admitted. "It'd be better to have a dedicated gunner, and Malcolm's not going to cut it. I think Lanara needs the pair of hands more anyway."

Kant shrugged. "I think if you've got a tank, brother, losing one exo isn't going to change things."

Erik nodded slowly. "Okay, Korhonen and her crew, Anne and I all hit the surface. You two keep killing them up here.."

Jia stared at Erik, a question on her face. "I'm going to tell you something my mother told me."

He gave her a quizzical look. "Your mom?"

Jia nodded. "I know you can't be safe, so just do what you need to do."

Erik grinned and released his harness, then stood. "This is my birthday, Christmas, and both New Year's wrapped into one day. We're getting to wipe out the Core. I'm finally getting my revenge. Don't worry. There's no way I'll let those assholes kill me."

Anne undid her harness, her expression neutral. "I'd like to go back to being a normal ghost at some point, and that requires us to destroy the Core and survive."

"You know me, brother. I just like a good fight." Kant smiled.

"I'm sure the lieutenant and her team are tired of sitting around in a cargo bay. Come on, Anne." Erik motioned toward the door. "Let's get suited up."

CHAPTER FORTY-ONE

Admiral Lefevre sent out a transmission informing the Core fleet of their losses at Alpha Centauri and the Solar System HTP. To no one's surprise, their response was to press their attack. This wasn't a battle where the UTC could break the enemy's will. There was only one choice: complete annihilation.

The Core fleet had spread out, and a major wing was making an aggressive push toward the city. UTC ships moved to intercept them. The previously balanced lines began to merge and become an overlapping mess.

Three destroyers and a cruiser accelerated in front of the *Argo*, their cannons and turrets firing at an approaching Core formation. Two other destroyers moved up behind them and turned toward the moon. A small squadron of fighters followed Jia in a close escort pattern.

"Making my run now," Jia announced.

She waited, counting in her head, before altering course and angling the *Argo* toward the moon. There'd be no point to this if she couldn't get the reinforcements on the surface. Nav and drop-zone markers moved back and forth on her camera and sensor displays.

Fighting near a moon was a far different experience from the high-speed running and gunning they'd pulled off in the HTP fights. Too hard a burn would push her well away from the main fleet and leave her drop zone a distant memory.

The forward squadron took a fierce pounding as the Core ships closed in, their cannons and turrets slicing the Fleet ships' armor and hulls. The other destroyers continued their angled descents. Small black pods fired from them and hurled toward the moon—orbital insertion drop pods. Attitude thrusters fired to correct their angles as they began their descent. A cannon blast from a medium raider vaporized two pods only seconds after deployment.

Jia tore her attention away from the drop pods being deployed to continue her own approach to the moon. The jump thrusters on their exoskeletons wouldn't be able to keep them from getting taken out. The lieutenant's tank could be blown to pieces before she got anywhere near the surface.

More drop pods fell victim to enemy fire. Bile rose in Jia's throat, but she shook her head. The best way to honor the soldiers who died was to defeat the enemy in front of them.

Rockets streamed toward the surface, not heading toward her but farther back. They burst apart in a bouquet of submunitions. The deadly fireworks were far too high to do anything to the domes and not powerful enough to do much more than distract the ships, but they tore apart drop pods heading toward the city.

Jia began to understand why the Fleet couldn't simply drop everything in the rear and then bring forces forward. The surface forces were hard-pressed on all sides, and the surface-to-surface assets available to the Core needed to be neutralized, but that would require their fleet to be taken out first.

The situation highlighted the intent of the otherwise pointless-seeming crime wave. The military must have pulled more forces back to Earth, like Anno had Team Blackwell. In this desperate battle for the future of humanity, the Core was gambling on achieving their goals, not with the destruction of Earth, but with its complete isolation.

From their point of view, they didn't need to survive the attack. They only needed to accomplish their mission objectives.

The forward destroyer and cruiser strike formation began to turn back, their turret screen trying to cover their escape. One of the destroyers that had been launching reinforcements broke apart when cannons cut through it.

Explosions and detonations lit up the sensor and camera displays, both friendly and enemy ships. Drone bombs. Drop pods. Fighters. Not a terrorist battle. Not a clean-up. Not a raid. It was war.

Remember old Los Angeles, Jia thought. *Remember what these people did and what they tried to do to Chang'e City before and Parvati. They kill and kill and kill with no consideration for the target and no mercy. They claim to want to unite humanity to make us stronger, but they're responsible for more human deaths than anyone. I'd sooner trust a Zitark than the Core.*

An epiphany struck Jia. There'd been no World War III,

so this was the first true simultaneous multi-system battle humanity had ever fought. The Core had initiated the First Galactic War.

You were going to change everything, but all you did was give us a new wannabe tyrant. Julia Caldo, I've never met you, and I despise you more than anyone I've ever met.

Taking advantage of the Fleet's distraction, Jia dived toward the moon, adjusting course to avoid the clusters of surviving drop pods heading toward the surface. She had not been counting, but it looked like they'd already lost a quarter of them.

Three small raiders broke away from the Core formation to intercept the *Argo*. An eerily quiet Kant linked the turrets into two firing groups and spun them toward the approaching ships. He didn't constantly fire, sending out staggered pulses of laser blasts instead. The fighters changed course to pull up behind the raiders.

The *Argo*'s laser turret blasts flaked a raider's front quarter away. The enemy fired its turrets, but a hard turn saved the *Argo* from more than scraping hits. The fighters cut into the other two raiders, forcing the enemy turrets to concentrate on the wolves harrying their rear.

Kant grunted in satisfaction as his turret barrages cut deeply into the heart of the raider. It didn't blow apart, but internal explosions sent it careening in a different direction, its weapons now quiet. After this was all over, there'd be months of debris cleanup required at the battle sites.

"Things are going to get a lot less fun," Jia announced, her comm linked to everyone else on the ship. "But we're almost there."

"I don't know if this is fun even by my standards," Kant admitted. "Except the part where I kill bad guys."

The fighters had taken out most of their victims' turrets. The fangless enemy ships accelerated toward the *Argo*, turning their vessels into their final weapons.

The destroyers and cruisers continued to pull back toward the main Fleet line. They bore holes and gouges from their aggressive defense of the landing forces.

Jia hissed and pulsed her bottom thrusters. The ship was now spiraling toward the surface. She'd be more worried if they were dealing with higher surface gravity. There were no drop pods nearby, but she kept an eye on the lidar proximity readouts.

Kant's aim was thrown off by Jia's stomach-churning maneuvers, but it wasn't that hard to hit someone when they were rushing right at the ship on purpose. Withering close-range turret fire from the *Argo* blew a charging ship apart. The concentrated efforts of the fighters finished off the others.

The gray and black of the moon filled more and more of her forward camera view. Proximity warnings popped up as nearby explosions rattled the ship. Jia almost asked for Emma's help by instinct before checking the sensor display herself. It was antiaircraft artillery coming from Core emplacements below. The AAA culled more drop pods.

Two anti-drop rockets screamed toward the *Argo*. A point-defense laser struck them, but the chain reaction from the bomblets inside set up a massive joint explosion that damaged armor all over the side of the ship. Jia laughed and shook her head.

Kant risked a quick look her way. "Problem, sister?"

"For a brief second, I remembered I used to be a detective."

Jia's gaze darted between her different displays. There were many things to keep track of when flying normally. Combat increased that tenfold.

"I played minor league sphere ball before I joined the ID," Kant offered. "If I'd gone pro, I don't think I would have ended up a ghost."

"Seriously?" Jia shook her head. "You're full of surprises."

Another rocket exploded near the *Argo*, ending the conversation. Jia took shallow, infrequent breaths, her intention focused on getting to the surface. She'd need to skim the ground when she dropped Erik's team off or risk them getting vaporized like so many of the drop pods.

The *Argo* lurched and rattled, and a damage warning appeared. They had another minor hull breach and moderate starboard thruster damage.

"Come on, come on," Jia murmured. "We're almost there."

"If I fire at the surface, there's too big a chance I'll hit our guys," Kant complained.

"Just spray in their general direction."

Jia leveled the *Argo* out. The separation between surface and space was less clear on a dead rock like the moon compared to the Earth, but in this case, the increased intensity of enemy fire provided a clear signal. She soared over the surface, heading toward the primary drop zone. Laser cannon blasts from vehicles lit up her sensor display.

"About thirty seconds to the drop zone," Jia announced. "Everyone okay down there?"

"We're ready to go," Erik replied. "I'm glad I had a light lunch. You're crazier than Emma flying the MX 60."

Jia flicked her thumb and ran it up a virtual slider. "Opening cargo bay."

Explosions, beams, and bullets crisscrossed the lunar surface. Elites, tanks, exoskeletons, and gunships formed intertwining hordes spread out over the gray, barren pockmarked expanse. Brave militia and Army soldiers in pressure suits and thruster packs bounced around the moon's surface, supplementing their better-armored friends.

"Twenty seconds." Jia controlled her breathing.

The *Argo* dipped to the side, shaking as rounds from below pelted the ship. Jia didn't worry about a tank's railgun or machine guns doing much harm under normal circumstances, but the ship had already suffered a lot of damage in the HTP battle and getting to the surface.

"Ten seconds, nine, eight, seven, six, five, four. I'll be back for you. Two, one."

Jia stared at a rear camera, transfixed. The whole experience felt like it stretched out, but in reality, it was only seconds. Lieutenant Korhonen's tank dropped first, falling toward the lunar surface. Anne's and Erik's smaller exoskeletons jumped out immediately after.

Emergency thrusters kicked in, and the tank settled in a meter above the surface. Anne and Erik landed on either side. A handful of surviving drop pods from before and new arrivals opened up, releasing the exoskeleton-driving soldiers inside.

Jia lifted the nose of the *Argo* and spun to avoid the

surface until she was far enough away to hard burn. Railgun rounds, machine guns, and laser ripped into the ship. The force of her acceleration pushed her back in her seat. Erik would have to do his part, and she would need to do hers.

CHAPTER FORTY-TWO

Erik growled as a rocket blew apart a drop pod right above him. The *Argo* had become a distant star, escaping the wrath of the heavy surface defenses. Exo squads advanced, their machine guns spitting rounds and rockets and missiles streaming from them.

There were almost no drones in the air, but the heavy jamming explained that. Erik had expected that situation before deploying and coordinated with the lieutenant to use laser comms. If they lost communications or got separated, she was free to conduct herself and her crew as she saw fit. From what he'd seen, she knew how to handle herself.

Huge explosions farther down the line threw huge plumes of rock and dust into the air. With all the jamming, it was impossible to know who to coordinate with, so he decided to stick to coordinating with Anne and the tank crew.

Erik checked around, and there didn't seem to be any other active friendly tanks in the immediate area. Fortunately, there also didn't appear to be any active enemy tanks, but there were enough Elites to build a new Tower of Babel.

An enemy Elite gunship flew into the area, strafing an exoskeleton and killing the pilot. His squadmates shredded the gunship from stem to stern and it tumbled to the surface, kicking up dust on impact.

The machine gun and railgun on Korhonen's tank swept back and forth. The cannon turned slower, firing at targets in the distance. Dragon gunships zoomed overhead. Lasers sliced one in half, and the others broke off after a rocket barrage on a pack of huge Elites surrounded by smaller bug Elites.

The huge Elite was larger than most Erik had seen, not counting the tank Elites they'd fought. It was a six-legged model almost the size of a hovertank, festooned with four separate turrets and forward and rear rocket launchers. An odd shiny reflective film covered the entire body. The cybernetic monster fired a rocket into a nearby squad, the explosion scattering them.

The main cannon of the tank spun toward the Elite, which responded by firing a rocket. The attack relegated the tank's railgun to point-defense mode. Unlike on Triton, there were too many dangerous enemies to use the gun primarily as an offensive tool. The railgun cut down the rocket, leaving the shrapnel to add the growing metal carpet on the moon.

Machine-gun fire picked off the smaller Elites on the sides before the main gun fired at their big brother. A blast struck the ground right in front of it, creating a new small crater on the lunar surface.

"Blackwell," Lieutenant Korhonen transmitted via laser comm. "I don't know how the hell it's doing it, but that big sucker is deflecting our laser cannon shots. Is that some sort of anti-laser coating?"

"Always something with those guys," Erik grumbled. "Anne, let's go strip the varnish. Take out the bottom defense turret first."

Lines of exos and soldiers up and down the battlefield continued pounding the advancing enemy. Dead soldiers littered the ground. Downed exos sprawled next to half-melted Elites, and hovertanks in every configuration but active were everywhere.

Some lay on their sides. Others were upside-down. Blackened holes covered them all. Some were nothing more than charred metal remnants.

With their tank continuing to obliterate rockets and grenades heading their way and its machine gun cutting through the bug Elites, Erik and Anne rushed toward the shiny Elite. Their bouncing and zigzag movements threw off its aim, and their expanded shields took the rest of the punishment. Pieces flaked off with each hit, but they'd last long enough to get to their target.

This was another example of the limitations of the Core's strategy. Erik had thought the same thing on Triton. Judging by their movements and weapon systems, the enemy wasn't as prepared for the environment as the highly trained soldiers.

A beetle Elite with a laser cannon turned toward them before the tank tunneled through it with a laser blast. Streams of friendly rockets rained down all around, disrupting the enemy formation.

Erik and Anne closed on their prey and opened fire, concentrating on a bottom turret. Their converging rivers of lead cut through the armament. That was good enough for Erik.

"Rocket and jump on three," he ordered. "One, two, *three!*"

Both exos leapt back. As they fired their jump thrusters, they released rockets toward the front. The low gravity helped them hurtle back toward friendly forces, though bullets riddled their shields.

Erik's theory about the Elite's defenses was about to be tested. The rocket barrage hadn't destroyed the enemy, but it'd ripped off the top layer of shiny armor, leaving a scorched layer of secondary armor underneath.

"Korhonen!" Erik barked.

The tank fired the laser cannon again. This time the shot cut through the damaged area and blasted out the back. Another shot ripped the Elite apart.

Rounds blasted into the sky in the distance, exploding high overhead. Erik magnified and spotted something startlingly conventional: a regular-model AAA emplacement. The only unusual thing about the setup was the two jellyfish Elites manning it.

It wasn't that far away, but there was a small army of Elites between Erik and the emplacement. There weren't, however, any tanks. Enemy mobile armor seemed to be concentrated at different points down the line. Plenty of wrecks strewn about the battlefield proved that wasn't always the case, but this meant the allied forces had a temporary advantage.

Did the admiral know that? Or is the Lady just trying to cut us a break?

"We're going to try to cut through to that AAA," Erik noted. "Before they fill in their defenses."

"Roger," the lieutenant replied.

The tank's secondary guns aimed lower, plowing the fields in front of them. Heavy machine-gun rounds continued to down Elites, and the railgun got to return to offensive duty, tearing holes through the deadly cyborgs.

Erik and Anne had loaded the exos with extra machine gun rounds and more rockets. They took advantage of that as they advanced alongside the tank, their own machine guns constantly firing, interspersed with the occasional rocket.

Nearby exo squads and soldiers got the point. They converged on the tank and Erik's squad, creating an advancing V-shaped formation.

Pyramidal laser Elites advanced from the rear slowly. They carved through unfortunate assault infantry with single shots. The tank vaporized the top of one with its cannon before tearing another apart with its machine gun.

Another shiny Elite lumbered into the area, but a squad rushed toward them, repeating a four-man version of the tactic Erik and Anne had used earlier to open its defensive coating before retreating. The tank brought it down.

Erik chuckled as a squad of regular infantry bounded in from the rear, everyone carrying heavy machine guns or laser rifles. They fired as a group, their volley tearing apart a swarm of scorpion-like Elites surging into the area.

The deadly V continued forward, exos steadily advancing on both sides and regular soldiers in the rear.

Beyond closing on the AAA emplacement, the successful advance threatened to cleave the entire enemy forward line. Rockets and AAA continued launching into the sky toward the dark, heavy rain of drop pods.

"Blackwell," the lieutenant began, "getting movement in the emplacement."

Erik zoomed in. A wavy glowing blue dome now surrounded everything but the top of the barrel of the AAA. Inside the dome, ballistic shields expanded to protect it. It was hard to tell with the light of the dome, but the sheen suggested an anti-laser coating.

"They're serious about protecting that thing," Erik muttered.

"Why didn't they use it before?" Anne asked.

"They didn't want to draw attention to it." Erik perforated a nearby Elite before continuing, "If we can take it, they can get more drop pods in here, and we can start turning this thing around."

The next couple of minutes passed in grim determination and concentration. Elites rushed into both sides, but exos and heavy arms soldiers swept from the back to force their attention. The spearpoint troops, including Erik and Anne, rushed the final distance, outpacing the slowly advancing tank.

Bullets whizzed and zoomed around him. A zoo of different Elites filled the area. Friendly exos jumped and ran among them, their machine guns, grenades, and rockets blowing enemies apart.

Erik realized everyone else assumed the tank would finish off the emplacement, including the Elites, given their repeated attempts to surround the vehicle. He sprinted toward the emplacement, now regretting his lack of grenades.

"Cover me," he ordered Anne. Autocannon and machine-gun rounds left cracks and gouges in his shield.

She complied by releasing rockets toward an advancing Torch Dragon. Its defense turret took out the rockets, so she followed up with her machine gun. It took the bait, focusing on her instead of the exo that looked like it was advancing toward a shielded AAA protected by a containment field.

Under normal circumstances, this combination would have lit up everyone's sensors and made it easy to pick off from orbit. He was ignoring the flashes in the sky that marked the continuing Fleet battle. The only thing he didn't worry about was Jia.

She wasn't going to let herself die behind the controls of a ship, and not just any ship, the *Argo*. Maybe she wasn't an ancient Greek legend like Alina would have wanted, but she'd honed herself into a veteran warrior who was facing off against horrible monsters. That sounded like the stuff of legends to Erik.

Machine guns cut through a nearby bug Elite. It collapsed, twitching before dying. Erik continued charging the emplacement.

"Your EMP hardening isn't going to save you from the containment field," Anne noted.

"Sure," Erik replied. "All I have to do is avoid it. Jump thrusters and low gravity make it easy."

Anne groaned in understanding. "Your stunt's going to put you right over the barrel."

"Time to trust my luck," Erik replied.

The AAA fired more rounds into the sky, shaking the ground. Erik sprinted at full speed toward the emplacement before jumping and firing his thrusters, launching the exo into a high arc. Another round blasted from the gun.

Erik pointed his rocket launcher down. He had seconds to make the shot and seconds of vulnerability. Holding his breath, he fired a rocket. It flew into the barrel just as another round emerged.

The colliding rounds exploded, and a moment later, a larger secondary blast ripped the entire emplacement part. It knocked Erik backward and sent him tumbling end over and over. That hadn't been part of his plan, but the huge cloud of doom marking the destroyed AAA, including the collapse of the containment field, was.

Erik grunted when he collided with the lunar surface. He righted himself as Anne and the tank cut through the Elites in the area. More drop pods fell in the distance. They hadn't won yet, but they were getting there.

CHAPTER FORTY-THREE

A cruiser separated into four pieces in front of the *Argo*, the victim of repeated drone bomb strikes. Jia flew under the wreck. The Core fleet continued to lose ships at a higher rate than the UTC fleet, but not high enough to satisfy her vengeance-fueled bloodlust. The bastards already knew they'd lost, yet they kept up the pointless bloodshed out of worship for a psychopathic mass murderer with delusions of grandeur.

Jia frowned at her sensor readout. With the destruction of the cruiser, she'd gotten cut off from the rest of the UTC fleet. The gap in the enemy line kept her from being swarmed, but she'd have to cut her way back through.

Kant let out a breath. "You think they're doing okay down there?"

"Erik's better on the ground than he is in space." Jia tried to wipe the sweat off her forehead, but her helmet rudely stopped her. She always noticed a helmet for the first few minutes, but after that, it was like she'd been born wearing one.

Jia narrowed her eyes. A ship was approaching at high speed from the Core fleet. Other ships broke off to follow it, but a forward surge from the UTC fleet cut off its reinforcements.

She started a wide turn, not wanting to risk a quick flip around and a counter-burn and the temporary loss of all momentum. Being too slow right then meant risking more hits on an already heavily damaged ship.

Her comm window lit up with a transmission note, and Jia narrowed her eyes. It wasn't an encrypted frequency, and it wasn't a general broadcast.

She continued her turn and accepted the commlink. There was always a chance she could get someone to surrender if she talked to them. Not much of one, but it was there.

"You should have stayed away from this battle, Blackwell." It was a man's voice.

Jia didn't recognize the voice. There was something unsettling about its cheerful quality.

"Sorry, Erik's not home. Can I take a message?" Jia joked. "He's on a business trip to the moon."

"Ah, even better." A chuckle followed. "The Warrior Princess, isn't it?"

"Let me guess, you're some loyal servant of the Immortal Empress?"

The Core ship barreled toward her. It slowed slightly, but it was obvious it could intercept her before she could return to the UTC line. The nearest friendly ship, a destroyer, was engaging a trio of small raiders nearby. Her escort fighters had left her after her return from the surface.

"You can call me Tralian," the man replied. "This is a rare opportunity, Miss Lin. Don't run back to your fleet. You can show me if you're worthy of your nickname."

"Oh. You're the guy in charge." Jia scoffed. She slowed the *Argo* and turned toward the approaching ship. "You really want to do this? By yourself?"

She glanced at Kant. He nodded, a serious look on his face.

"Yes, because you are inferior to me in every way," Tralian explained cheerfully. "I will destroy your ship and then speak of it in elaborate detail to the Last Soldier before I kill him. My only regret is that I won't be able to deliver your head to my Immortal Empress. She'll need to settle for his."

Unlike Yan, Tralian's ship was smaller, a slender yacht-like design that reminded Jia of Sophia Vand's ship. This wouldn't be a smaller ship taking advantage of its acceleration and agility to rip apart a more powerful vessel. This would be a duel.

She'd been controlling the laser cannon since Erik left, leaving the turrets to Kant. One good shot could end the battle, but Tralian's ship had to have tricks of its own. From what she could detect, it had more turrets overall, but the damage had cut its active number to match the *Argo*'s.

Jia turned toward Tralian and accelerated. A white-blue flash blasted from the front of his ship and blasted apart a floating chunk of a destroyer.

"Okay, we can't let him get close and line up with us," Jia muttered. "And he came at us, which means he at least recognizes the ship, and he might have been watching throughout the battle and knows we have the cannon."

They were both far away from the line now, at least a couple of minutes from the nearest ships at reasonable tactical burn speeds. The logical move would be to bait Tralian back to friendly forces and watch the show as they sliced him apart with cannon fire, but that wouldn't be as satisfying as taking him apart herself.

Jia took a deep breath and slowly let it out. She might have been lying to herself, but she told herself if she ran, he wouldn't stay close. A man obsessed with killing Erik and her might even flee the battle and wait for a chance in the future. This was her best chance to make sure a high-ranking servant of Julia Caldo tasted hard vacuum.

Both ships were now heading toward each other. Their first pass would be fast, so they'd get a couple of shots off with turrets at best.

Jia's last request to Lanara for help with shields was greeted by a long string of profanities interspersed with numbers. Between the swear words, Jia managed to pick out that there was too much damage to the *Argo*, and Lanara was doing everything she could to stop the major systems from failing, especially since she only had Malcolm and not her team and Emma to help.

The red triangle marking Tralian's ship on the sensors grew closer to the center of her display. Kant didn't fire aimlessly. The *Argo* was out of missiles and torpedoes. If their opponent had any, he wasn't firing them yet.

Closer. Closer. Jia's heart pounded. This wasn't a medieval battle. The enemy force wouldn't fall apart because she killed their commander.

She understood that, but she didn't care. Tralian represented something else.

When she'd first started with Erik, they'd only dealt with hired thugs and enemies who had only the barest understanding that they were tools of the Core. Effort and investigation brought them closer to the truth with the Ascended Brotherhood and the half-Leem agent on Venus. Now they were fighting men who led large fleets and spoke of their loving devotion to Julia Caldo.

Erik and Jia had fought their way almost to the top, but one faint concern prickled Jia. If this was the last major force, where was the Immortal Empress? She wasn't here to preside over the victory that would help cement her control?

Where is that bitch hiding?

Jia's mind snapped back to the present as she closed to effective weapons range. Neither ship was aligned for a cannon shot, but that didn't stop their turrets. Her turn and burn sent her closer to the enemy ship while Kant fired the laser turrets. Plasma and laser blasts streamed past her, narrowly missing until one plasma blast took out the top point-defense turret. Kant nailed the enemy ship, but other than neat-looking holes, the shot didn't accomplish much.

Her stomach tightened. Was Tralian carving her up to finish her off with missiles?

Both ships were turning toward each other, trying to line up a cannon shot. The *Argo* had a slight advantage in that the bulk of her remaining turrets were lasers, giving them greater range, but that was balanced by Tralian's ability to do more damage at close range. Another quick pass yielded only minor surface hits on both ships.

The ships were evenly matched in terms of maneuverability. If the *Argo* hadn't suffered earlier damage, it might have been superior. Being a better pilot meant she could get more out of her ship, but that didn't mean she could magically give it better agility.

Two more passes ended with more hull breaches on the bottom of the *Argo*. Kant did a decent job of raking the belly of Tralian's ship and taking out a turret.

A group of raiders was pulling away from the edge of the Core fleet formation. They were minutes away, but the UTC fleet was too busy keeping enemy ships from getting closer to the city.

"And here I thought this was a duel," Jia grumbled.

"His ship is tricky, but I think I've got a good feel for his moves," Kant replied.

"Me too." Jia licked her lips. "But it's taking too long. We've got to end this in one shot. The only problem is the idea means we'll be exposing the cockpit." She stared at the sensor display. "At least if I die, I won't have to worry about the bachelorette party."

Kant laughed. "Didn't your friend reschedule her wedding for two years from now?"

"Hey, that's two years of worry."

The dance between the ships continued. A rhythm had developed, where the chaser and the target exchanged places between each pass. Jia's plan required them to be the target, and from what she could tell, she didn't have many passes left before she'd have to worry about the reinforcements. The next target pass would be her chance.

Jia tapped the port and starboard lateral thrusters in a rhythm, sliding the ship back and forth and avoiding the turrets on the enemy ship now flying overhead and upside-down relative to the *Argo*. It was time to make her move.

Her minor thrusts turned into a powerful burn that swung the *Argo* around. She didn't even have her hand near the other thruster control. Instead, she concentrated on waiting for the nose of her ship to slightly lead Tralian's ship. Plasma blasts struck the front and top of the ship, searing off armor and rattling it.

"Take this!" she shouted and fired the laser cannon.

The cabin lights dimmed, and the *Argo* shook. A massive tunnel appeared in the center of Tralian's ship, breaking it into four large chunks and countless smaller pieces. Jia immediately canceled the turn.

A moment later, two of the chunks exploded, the massive blast hiding the other pieces. When the light of the blast dissipated, there was a cloud of jagged debris that would require a very patient archaeologist to piece back together into something resembling a ship.

Jia pointed the *Argo* toward the UTC fleet and fired the main thrusters. "Cocky bastard. He got what he deserved."

Kant sighed in disappointment. "I wanted to be the one to take him out."

"We don't all get what we want."

The *Argo* returned to the UTC fleet. The raiders who'd broken off to pursue the ship headed back to their own line. A group led by the *Los Angeles* pressed the middle, with curving lines of other vessels surrounding the enemy fleet and pressuring them from the flanks. Core ships continued to dwindle in number.

Jia smiled as she closed on the allied line. Before, it'd been a huge risk to a destroyer to release a handful of drop pods. Now shuttles streamed from the ships toward the lunar surface. This battle was all but over.

There was nothing like a good rout of the enemy, especially when a man didn't expect it. Erik's destruction of the AAA emplacement had led to additional reinforcements. The earlier push toward it had made it difficult for the Core forces to coordinate with each other. Soon, they ended up almost completely encircled, their airpower and arty demolished.

The enemy had fallen back, their previous merciless advance replaced by a clumsy panic. Erik didn't think it was true fear as much as a desperate attempt to rally, but an enemy army running away while they were destroyed met his definition of a rout.

With air and space under the control of the Fleet, fighters joined allied gunships in punishing strafing runs that pulverized packs of Elite in one pass. Erik and Anne stayed close to the tank, and they worked as a trio to rip through enemies with ease.

The previous scarcity of friendly tanks had turned into a decent number of them in a circle interspersed with assault infantry. With the enemy now less intertwined with friendly forces, rear-echelon mortars and low-powered arty arced overhead and struck the enemy forces, digging graves and demolishing the Elites at the same time.

Erik frowned when an alert popped up on his faceplate. "Damn. Almost out of ammo."

"Don't think it matters," Anne replied, sounding out of breath. "This is done."

Elites continued to fall. Their hardened shells were no match for the lethal lasers, explosives, and armor-piercing bullets of the Army and the militia. A mortar shell burst and sent a spider Elite hurtling into the air, where the lieutenant's tank blew it in half.

Erik had long since run out of rockets. With his machine-gun ammo about to go dry, he continued firing careful bursts and thought about heading to the rear to find someone to help him reload. Instead, he continued taking selective shots, enjoying the shrinking cybernetic army. He waited for the last couple of minutes, saving his last burst of ammo for the final target he saw moving—a jellyfish Elite slithering along in the dust.

He fired, along with hundreds of other people, reducing the Elite to a cloud of red- and blue-flecked metal shards.

"Wonder how Jia's doing?"

Jia had never appreciated the beauty in destruction until the last three enemy ships exploded on her camera feed. The three large raiders had taken a surprising amount of punishment, including one of them taking two direct hits from the *Argo*'s cannon, but outnumbered and outgunned, their fates were sealed.

Was the victory decisive or pyrrhic? Jia couldn't say. The Fleet had lost many ships, and men and women had died aboard the surviving vessels. From what she'd seen while dropping Erik and the others off, the fighting hadn't been any less fierce on the surface.

The Immortal Empress Julia had strived to inflict her tyranny on the UTC through terrorism, horrific experiments, murder, and now war. But she had failed.

No. That was enough. They'd have to dig her out of her hole somewhere, but her plans were in tatters.

Erik and Jia had helped push the Core into the light, but the men and women of the Army, the Fleet, and the militia had sacrificed their lives to finish it. The Battle of Chang'e City was over.

CHAPTER FORTY-FOUR

Jia leaned against a cargo bay wall in the *Argo,* her arms folded, letting her thoughts run away from her. The team remained docked with the jumpship in orbit around the moon while they awaited further orders.

After picking up Erik and the others, she'd thought they'd be tasked with helping look for escape pods and other necessary but unpleasant post-battle errands. Instead, the admiral had requested they double-check the situation at the other two battle sites. She didn't want to leave anything to chance.

It made sense. Admirals usually didn't have jumpships to bounce around star systems, checking on problems for them. Nobody on the team minded.

Everything was as they'd left it at both locations, other than the recovery of escape pods. There were no secret Core reinforcements who'd arrived out of nowhere, and no deadly Hunter ship had appeared to threaten the whole system. There were only bloodied but victorious UTC forces.

Jia had experienced the aftermath of battles before, but never anything like this. The sheer scale of it was difficult to wrap her mind around. She wouldn't let it overwhelm her, but she wasn't going to pretend it was like anything else she'd ever experienced.

It was the small things like the escape pods searches and the repairs that stood out. Lanara had added additional reinforcement to the emergency seals in the cargo bay. She'd been running back and forth shouting at Malcolm, who kept insisting he wasn't an engineer, but with Janessa and Wei working on *Bifröst*'s repairs, he'd been drafted.

Jia had offered to help, but Lanara had told her in no uncertain terms she didn't want it. Maybe she only wanted a certain personality type working under her.

The tank sat near the back of the cargo bay, with the crew carefully inspecting the damage and beginning basic repairs. Missing chunks of armor, blackened blast sites, dents, and holes from bullets were all over the body. Despite the damage, every member of the crew looked tired but happy.

Jia had thought that strange, but it quickly made sense. They'd trained to be a tank crew and defend the UTC, and now they'd gotten to do that in a grand battle that would go down in history.

It wasn't the culmination of years of investigation and desperate raids against increasingly horrific monsters for them. Instead, it'd been a few weeks, a short campaign from which they'd emerged victorious with no losses to their crew.

Erik had disappeared to take a shower. Pressure suits weren't the most breathable. She'd need a shower herself but was convinced the minute she stopped moving, she'd collapse. Kant and Anne had already headed to their cabins to pass out.

Jia surveyed the cargo bay more carefully, trying to mentally compare it to her memories from before the battle. Lanara's patches were the most obvious since the metal was a different color. Some crates lay upside down or on their sides. Scorch marks covered one wall. The *Argo* and the *Bifröst* had both taken a lot of damage during the battles.

Jia sighed and shook her head. There was nothing useful she could do there. She might as well return to her cabin and get some rest.

Erik was lying on the bed with his hands under his head, staring at the wall when Jia entered. He looked so happy and content she was almost jealous, but he'd experienced this kind of thing his entire life. It might be unfair to say he was used to it, but at least he'd had time to process it.

"I forgot to ask you earlier," he greeted her. "How are you doing? Everything all right?"

Jia didn't bother to take off her boots before lying beside him. "I'm okay. I'm just tired."

"You did great." Erik smiled. "Taking out Tralian and all that. I didn't get to take out a big enemy general down there."

"You helped take out an emplacement that led to that part of the battlefield becoming a major rally point." Jia shrugged. "That's not a minor thing."

"Just saying." Erik chuckled. "It'd be cool if I could have another Core head for my wall."

Jia rolled onto her side so she could look at him. "It hardly seems real. I was joking with Kant during the battle. There was this brief period where I started laughing. I remembered being in the 1-2-2, desperate to work cases, and now here I am with a UTC fleet fighting off an attempt to destroy a city and jumping around to participate in three different large-scale ship battles."

"Is that really that much weirder than half the other things you've done?" Erik shrugged. "Personally, that Hunter debacle was the strangest thing I've ever been involved in."

"In absolute terms, yes, but…" Jia sighed. "That was still us taking on one ship—a special ship, but one ship. This was…" She struggled to find the right word but shook her head instead.

"War," Erik answered. "I get it. Even when they tried that crap on Parvati, it wasn't on this scale. New Samarkand might have been a war, but we dropped in, took a few people out, and did our thing. The numbers make it different. They mess with you after a while. You have to thread a path between going numb and letting it get to you. If you need to talk to somebody other than me, you know you have my support."

"I think it'll be fine. I'm satisfied with what we did and my contribution. I just need time to process it."

"Of course."

"But imagine if the virus had been more successful," Jia commented. "Half as many Fleet ships show up, the Core wins, the HTPs and Chang'e City are destroyed. The UTC is thrown into complete chaos." She shrugged. "Who knows? They might be afraid to take on Earth, but they could finish off the rest of the moon and Mars. It's weird when you think about how many things in history might have come down to one small detail."

"You study the history of the military, and you see that kind of thing all the time." He half-closed his eyes. "But who cares about the bad stuff that *might* have happened? Even the Navigators and the Hunters couldn't time-travel. I care about the past only for how it affects the future. I try to learn from the past to avoid the same mistakes. The Core was successful enough to kneecap the Fleet, so more people died than had to, but they ultimately failed because of the training and dedication of the Fleet and others. I'm sure the Core has a handful of ships somewhere and a transport full of Elites and *yaoguai*, but they're done for as a major force."

"Are you sure?" Jia whispered, hating herself for asking the question. "Everyone has been underestimating them for a while."

"I never did."

"True, but..."

"You think they've attacked other systems?" Erik asked.

"No, I don't. That much was obvious from the number of ships they used in Alpha Centauri. If they had more to spare, they would have brought them, and at least the other Core worlds are close enough the ID would have been able to pick up on other potential fleets from registry information and HTP movements." Jia stifled a yawn with her hand. "Speaking of the government, I'm surprised they're not having us jump farther out to check things."

"The *Bifröst* might be bigger and tougher than the *Argo*, but it still took a lot of nasty hits." Erik held up his hand and spread his fingers. "It's a miracle the jump drive didn't get thrashed, and I think they understand that. We'll need to patch it before heading out. Besides, at this point, it doesn't matter. The Core timed this to be almost simultaneous. If they're taking out HTPs or other colonies, they've already lost, or they've already won. A half-broken jumpship and a jumped-up half-destroyer aren't going to change that. Sending us out again means there's something only we can do." He lowered his hand. "There is one thing bothering me. I didn't want to bother anyone else, so I kept it to myself."

Jia sucked in a breath. "It's been bothering me too if you're thinking what I'm thinking."

"Where the hell is that bitch Caldo?" Erik snarled. "She is supposed to be the new empress of humanity, but she's not around? I kept expecting her to deliver a big speech about the moon or show up riding some ridiculous giant *yaoguai*."

Jia sat up. "That's what's got me worried. Not the *yaoguai*, but Caldo. If the point was to cut Earth off, that means she must have some other method of taking over."

"Not necessarily." Erik furrowed his brow. "She could have assumed the colonies would fall apart, become weaker by themselves, while she concentrated on taking over the weakened Earth. I have a hard time thinking she has a huge fleet out there beyond Alpha Centauri after throwing all that at us. The sizes of the Core fleets seemed to roughly correspond to the sizes of the active UTC fleets. I don't think that was due to chance."

"You're saying they had a good idea that they were only eighty percent successful?" Jia asked.

Erik nodded. "Exactly. It's like you said; if they'd had more ships available, I think they would have brought them. They already knew they had to outnumber the Fleet ships to win, but that brings us back to Caldo and where she is when we take all that into consideration."

Jia's eyes widened. "You think she's still in the Solar System?"

"Yeah. Even if things got out of control here, this is the center of the UTC economy. Things could crash pretty badly, and they'd still be in a better position here than any other planet to recover. Even places like Remus and Chiron are arguably not self-sufficient in some ways." Erik growled. "But I don't know where she is. She was smart enough not to be with her forces, which meant she understood they might not win. For all her arrogance in naming herself the Immortal Empress, she is hiding like a cockroach."

"And what? That's it? She gives up and takes up penjing under a new assumed name?" Jia scoffed. "Nobody who goes around calling herself the Immortal Empress gives up that easily. She's got something else up her sleeve."

"I know." Erik frowned. "Yeah, let's take the title seriously. We know what Barbu told us. For all I know, she pulled some immortality crap off Molino. Maybe she hides for another hundred years to plan things differently this time. Depends on how patient she is."

Jia stood and started pacing. She didn't want her grandkids to live through a Second Galactic War.

"I don't know. Too much ego." Jia shook her head. "And

now the government will be hunting her. They've bitten the bullet by going after everything Core-related, and the economic damage is done. It'll unwind over the years, and the CID and ID will be up the asses of every company in the UTC, making sure they aren't shady fronts for future would-be empresses."

"Then she might have something else planned, but..." Erik sucked in a breath. "Damn. I don't think she does, but I also don't think I can be done with this until I know she's dead. I want every last member of the Core taking a dirt nap or floating in the void. Before, it was just about my unit, but now it's for Old Los Angeles, too."

Jia stopped. "She can't escape. No matter where she goes, we can catch her. She has to know that. We went all the way out to New Samarkand already, but we can't be certain she didn't run in the opposite direction from Remus after faking her death. Maybe Her Genocidal Highness thought she could rally the colonies to her side after isolating Earth."

"Like I said, it'd be very hard for the colonies not to have trouble without Earth." Erik shrugged. "It's not like they can't survive, but they'd have to develop new ways of producing and processing a lot of stuff. That is one of the problems with rebellions. They're always short-sighted about how things will unfold after they win."

Jia folded her arms. "So, putting all that together, that means Julia Caldo is hiding somewhere in the Solar System."

"Probably." Erik shrugged. "But it's a big place. That Hunter ship was here for thousands of years before anyone figured it out. If she's trying to avoid being caught, all she has to do is leave the main flight routes, avoid hard burns, and stay away from major Fleet patrol paths. Some recon satellite or listening post will pick her up eventually, but if she's smart about it, she can extend her freedom."

"Then what do we do?"

Erik grinned at her. "For once, we don't have to do anything."

"We don't? Then how do we end this to your satisfaction? You said it was bothering you."

"We wait until she screws up and ghosts or the military finds her," Erik replied. "She can hide for a while, but not forever, especially if all she has is one ship. All the joining up with the Fleet and the Army on the moon made something very clear, something that even the Prime Minister's announcement didn't."

Jia nodded. "We're not in this alone anymore, and we don't have to worry about secrets."

"Exactly." Erik sighed. "We were jumping around the Solar System, and everyone took it for granted. We were important to helping the UTC win, but we didn't do it alone. When I left Molino, I didn't trust anyone. I *couldn't* trust anyone, which was why I kept everything secret, but it's only a matter of time before they find her and we finish this." He patted the bed behind her. "Take your shoes off, and let's calm down."

Jia stared at him, vaguely disappointed. There was one way she knew Erik didn't believe it was over. She had not been meaning to snoop around when she found the ring. She put it back in his hiding place and did her best not to think about it. With the Core threat so prominent, it was easy to do, but her future couldn't go forward until Julia

Caldo was finished. It was just another reason for the woman to go down.

Their PNIUs beeped, and a message from Emma popped up. They exchanged glances before tapping to acknowledge the message.

Emma materialized in front of the door in a Fleet admiral's uniform with a slightly unsettling smile. "They want you to return to Troy for repairs, but they don't seem interested—yet—in taking either ship from you."

Erik chuckled. "Why break up a good team when you still have a target out there? I don't mind being on the payroll for a little longer."

Jia watched Emma and forced herself to stay quiet. In all the chaos with Barbu, the Neo SoCal attack, and the Core attack, she'd almost forgotten about the matrix they'd helped smuggle from Germany onto the *Bifröst*. Emma had never been that clear on when things would be finished, but Jia assumed she would tell her friends before it was done. Jia had gotten the impression it'd be over soon, but the definition of soon was relative.

For now, it was another thing that could wait. A little sleep on the way back to the base didn't sound like a bad idea.

CHAPTER FORTY-FIVE

June 23, 2231, UTC Space Fleet Base Troy, Conference room

Erik had learned to deal with the death and destruction that came with being a soldier a long time ago. The only thing he could never stand in the military was the constant briefings, giving or receiving. He could understand the necessity in theory, but that didn't mean they didn't stick in his brain like an ice pick.

He'd mercifully been freed of them when he left, but his continued integration with the ID and the DD had brought them back. Alina's desire to meet in unusual places wearing unexpected disguises had at least put some fun into it, but the vice-director was no Alina by any means.

In everything that had happened, her death felt like it happened years ago, an early casualty in the final battles of the war they'd both been fighting for ages. While he'd felt alone for so long against this mystery enemy, she'd been the same, fighting bureaucracy and arrogance to convince her superiors that there was a sinister, deep-rooted threat to the UTC that they could scarcely imagine.

Erik wasn't normally one to forgive uncreative higher-ups, but before Molino, he could not have imagined anything like the Core either. Even during his initial investigation, he'd assumed he'd find out that some rich asshole had hidden mining interests on the moon, not that his men had been killed as part of a centuries-old conspiracy involving a hidden ancient alien race and the destruction of an entire metropolitan area.

We did it, Alina. It took a lot of blood, but we did it.

He pushed out the thought. Alina and Colonel Adeyemi hadn't died for nothing. Erik was on Troy, now following a massive and near-complete victory over the Core.

Team Blackwell was catching their breath on Troy, and Fleet repair crews were swarming the *Argo* and the *Bifröst* under Lanara's direction. The last time he'd seen both ships, he'd been hard-pressed to identify any evidence they'd recently been in a brutal battle. There were advantages to having the full and open support of the military.

The excess effort made sense. Everyone in the government prioritized the restoration and re-armament of the jumpship and the *Argo* in case they were needed. Erik and Jia weren't the only ones worried about the absence of Julia Caldo at the final battle. While no one believed she could form a government in exile, the long-term planning and corruption demonstrated by the Core meant they couldn't pretend she wasn't a threat.

While the ship and most of Team Blackwell had been retained, the lieutenant and her crew were taking some well-earned leave. Erik had a hard time believing that even with his luck, he'd be needing a tank again anytime soon. He doubted they'd catch up with Julia on a moon in the midst of an army of Elites.

Malcolm was back on Earth for the moment after a request by the 1-2-2 for temporary consulting work related to the day of chaos. He seemed more rattled than anyone, but he'd never signed up for war.

When the vice-director requested the field team and Lieutenant Commander Tensen pop in for a briefing, Erik had allowed himself a dangerous emotion: hope. He now watched as Anno settled in at the head of the table. Emma hadn't chosen a taunting outfit that day; she was wearing a yellow sundress, of all things. She was also smiling more than usual.

Erik wasn't sure if she was trying to unnerve Anno. He didn't want to risk asking her and giving her the idea.

The vice-director nodded at everyone. He looked even more tired than the last time they'd seen him in person. "Before I begin, do you feel that you have everything you currently need for standard missions? If not, let me know because we want you ready to go at a moment's notice."

Erik nodded slowly. "Exos repaired, plenty of ammo. The ships are repaired."

Tensen added his own nod. "All my injured crew have been treated. We're ready. My men understand that the mission might not be done."

"I want to thank you again for your personal efforts and those of the people under your command in defense of the UTC at all three critical battle locations," Anno began. "Based on what we've heard from Admiral Song, your team's efforts were crucial in helping reverse the tactical situation there."

Erik shrugged. "We were part of a fleet. Everyone did their job, including us."

"I appreciate the humility, but we'll set that aside for now. Tensen's crew has a lot of commendations coming." Anno folded his hands and looked grim. "Unrest remains, but the news of the Core defeat seems to have calmed a lot of people down. It's like the Core was functioning as a catalyst for every nutjob and criminal out there. We expect trouble to ripple out to the colonies over the next few months and then disappear as the news of the Core's defeat follows. The military is already directing system assets farther out. The government's announcing complete victory over the Core, and there will be a lot of officers and politicians getting a lot of attention in the coming weeks and months. The question is where we go from here with your team."

"Indeed," Emma replied. "I'm overly curious about that point, but as you can imagine, it has much stronger personal implications for some members of the team than others."

Anno gave her an annoyed look before continuing, "There's been talk from the heads of the military and the Prime Minister of having the team jump to every system in the UTC to confirm there's no immediate trouble."

"Tedious, but doable." Erik shrugged. "You think that's necessary?"

"It's the opinion of the Intelligence Directorate, including my direct superior, that is unnecessary given what we've already seen, but that was on the table. With the military already rerouting forces, its immediate importance is limited." Anno's gaze flicked to Emma. "Obviously, because of your relationship with the navigational AI, we'd need you if that plan were to happen in the future, but there's something else we want you to check into first."

"What's that?" Jia asked.

"Between sorting through our own intel, Barbu's, and some recent finds from raids, we've been able to pinpoint a lot more about the Core and their operations. If we'd had this information a year ago, all of this could have been avoided." Anno swiped his PNIU and a navigational chart of the UTC appeared, a series of circles marking systems connected by lines representing HTP transit paths. He gestured at Mu Arae. "Here's where things get uncomfortable and annoying. When we crosscheck all our information, including HTP tracking and possible Core ownership of civilian vessels that might be disguised Core raiders, there's a strong possibility that a decent-sized fleet is heading out to the frontier."

You've got to be kidding me. It's like Caldo is trying to spit in my face.

Erik frowned. "They've got a fleet out there?"

"Maybe flotilla's a better word." Anno considered his next words carefully, deciding what he wanted to include or leave out with this quasi-governmental team of questionable characters and a rogue AI. "We believe there are twelve ships of various sizes, including some the size of the big boys the Fleet fought recently, but mostly smaller vessels. The problem is we're going off reports that in some cases are two months old, so it's hard to say, but right now, it looks like the Core might be sending those ships to Mu Arae. The general pattern suggests convergence there."

Anne stared at the navigational map with curiosity. "What do they want to accomplish there? Destroy Molino colony? More people just died in the battles we fought than live on that entire colony. It was a spectacular bit of terrorism, but nothing anyone could hope to pull off again for a hundred years. It wouldn't fundamentally alter the order of things, other than forcing more Fleet ships out to the frontier."

Jia nodded. "Getting a message there takes long enough, but sending ships? That means they were planning this well in advance."

Anno shook his head. "Not as far as you might think. The evidence says the ships being sent that way were already in the outer frontier."

"Wonderful. So the Core had a decent-sized attack force floating around there this entire time." Jia shook her head in disgust. "I suppose we're lucky they didn't already destroy a colony."

"It's not as if the frontier's undefended," Tensen noted with a nod toward the chart. "It takes a while to coordinate things from Earth, but the regional commanders have a lot of autonomy and could gather a decent force to stop a rampaging Core fleet. And as we saw in the battle, their ships and crews just aren't as good as ours."

Erik's expression darkened. "Even if Caldo ran straight from Remus in that direction, she's still a good chunk of a year away from Molino. This can't be about forming a fleet for the empress in exile. And Anne's right; blowing up a tiny colony seems too small for them now."

Anno nodded. "The truth is, we're well behind on this one. This is the only anomaly in the intelligence we've been able to trace of significance outside either the Solar System or Alpha Centauri. This is why we're not having you do a tour of the entire damned UTC. The Core is making some sort of frontier play we don't understand yet, and the only decent chance we have of responding to it is the jumpship and your team."

Jia sucked in a breath. "The artifacts on Molino. What if there's a hidden Hunter ship? They set up that last intercept with a lot of lead time. There was obviously some factional fighting, but it wouldn't be too extreme to assume at least one of those teams was loyal to Julia Caldo."

"We can't begin to speculate about that kind of thing with any certainty." Anno shrugged. "But that's another possibility that came up from our analysts, and it has already been discussed at high levels."

"This shit never ends," Kant muttered.

"No, it'll end soon enough. We'll make sure of that." Erik stared at Mu Arae on the edge of the nav map. Everything had begun there, and it was only fitting that everything end there. Julia Caldo must not have joined her fleet for a reason, and the answers might lie on the edge of human space where his quest had begun years ago.

Anno frowned and held up a hand. "One moment." He jabbed his PNIU, then swiped his hand through the air. His eyes darted back and forth as he read a message on his smart lenses. His frown twitched into a smile.

"Good news?" Erik asked. That dastardly hope returned.

"You could say that. We'll send you to the frontier soon,

but I think we've got a better errand for you in the interim, and I think your team, of all people, have earned this." He turned to Erik. "I'll spare you the fine details, but we're pretty sure we identified another possible Core ship—a large ship, the *Qilin*. It was never close to the fight, but long-term tracking showed it was darn close to the HTP before turning around."

"How do you know it's not just a civilian ship that got scared in the chaos?" Jia asked.

"We've traced it to possible Core ownership, including some companies directly controlled by Julia Caldo. Military sensors also suggest unusual energy signatures and comm traffic that can potentially link the *Qilin* at least indirectly to the HTP Core fleet and the lunar fleet."

"It's her." Erik's words came out as a growl. "I thought it'd take longer, but I'm not going to complain."

"There's a good chance of it, yes," Anno replied.

"And she's running? Where to? If she had a jump drive, she would have already used it."

Anno's smile faded. "We're not sure. She's not exactly hard burning for anywhere, but the ship's sweeping course will take it back to the HTP in a matter of days. She likely has some sort of override, and maybe she thinks she can run past the Fleet garrison when there's other traffic. The military is considering an intercept, but you were there. You know there are a lot of damaged ships and hurt personnel at the edge of the Solar System, and we'd rather not pull ships away from the HTPs in case there's some other stunt planned. And like I said, you deserve it." He pointed at Emma. "And that's where the jump drive comes in. We've already filed the necessary documents invoking the relevant statutes to give you the legal authority to intercept that ship and question them."

"How is that different from what we were doing before?" Jia asked.

"That was ghost work. Things are a little bit more flexible since they end up being classified. This time, think of yourself as quasi-militia."

Erik stood. "Sounds good to me. I don't care about the paperwork. I just care about finding her and taking her out."

"That means intercept her, Blackwell." Anno raised an eyebrow. "Not blot her out of the stars. If it *is* her, she still has a high intelligence value."

"What about the mystery fleet?" Kant asked.

"If that ship is Julia Caldo's, we can make her explain what the hell she's up to," Anno clarified. "I assume you don't mind a couple of backup Army squads coming with you on the mission?"

Erik shrugged. "I'd rather not."

Anno frowned. "Really?"

"If this all goes sideways and it's some trick, it'd be better to keep casualties down, right? And I don't like the idea of trying to adjust to a whole new dynamic right before a big mission. We at least got some time to train with Tensen's crew and had an easy break-in mission with the tankers."

"Your call." Anno nodded. "Just get it handled."

CHAPTER FORTY-SIX

"We've almost caught up," Jia announced excitedly.

They'd jumped relatively close to the target ship and transmitted their shiny new official government orders and credentials to stand down and prepare to be boarded. The *Qilin* had accelerated in response.

Jia's heart pounded with excitement. Whatever pointless scheme the frontier fleet was planning could be easily disrupted, but Caldo was the true end of everything. The Core would be over, and Erik would be free of the burden that had been weighing on him. It wasn't every day a woman got to destroy the last vestiges of an evil conspiracy to help the man she loved. Nothing like a little two-for-one.

Did you ever suspect, Caldo? Jia thought. *Did you ever think for a moment that somebody would survive that massacre and track you down?*

The *Argo* had already separated from the *Bifröst,* and now both ships were giving chase to the fleeing ship. Whatever other features the *Qilin* had, both Team Blackwell ships were accelerating faster. It'd taken a couple of hours, but they were catching up.

While the *Qilin* had yet to reveal any hidden weapons, their dogged determination not to respond to the *Argo*'s transmission was strong proof that they weren't a normal transport.

Being chased by two strange vessels that didn't resemble Fleet ships could theoretically convince someone to run without saying anything. In a system that had just dealt with a massive secret fleet from a dangerous terrorist conspiracy, a pilot might have convinced himself that pirates had decided to seize their chance.

Jia accepted the possibility, but that didn't mean she believed it was true. Working with Erik had long ago purged her of the belief that most coincidences were innocent. There were too many coincidences concerning the ship for Jia to dismiss, but she wanted to give them a chance. All they had to do was open the comm and let the team come aboard for inspection.

"*Qilin*, this is the *Argo*," Jia transmitted. "We are again sending our credentials. On behalf of the UTC Fleet, you are ordered to stand down and prepare to be boarded. You will be inspected for contraband and the hauling of known terrorists. If you have not knowingly participated in any crimes, you will not be subject to sanction and will be free to go. If you continue to evade, we will be forced to take aggressive action, and you will be forcibly boarded."

People always wanted grand ends to tyrants and would-be tyrants, but how many times had it been something like this? Representatives of the authorities catching the antisocial monster as they fled, their heads held low, hoping to escape the wrath of the people they'd harmed.

It was better that way. A grand evil was best vanquished in a way that rendered them banal and pathetic. People needed to know they weren't gods. People needed to understand there were other humans who just got too much power.

Even as Jia thought about it, she questioned her conclusion. The members of the Core were fundamentally different from any other evil manipulators and tyrants throughout history. Their expanded lifespan, bestowed far earlier than lesser technologies such as de-aging came into being, gave them incredible advantages. They might not be gods, but they were demons.

That difference had implications. If Julia were aboard the ship and truly immortal, the logical move for her would be to surrender. Despite cries for execution, her unique place in history would probably buy her years, if not decades, of stalling while people figured out what to do with her and what they might learn from her. The Purist movement might be wounded once everyone knew that it was partially birthed by the manipulations of the Core.

A woman who had planned for decades might be squandering her chance to live out of pure ego. With age was supposed to come wisdom, not hubris. Too bad Caldo didn't understand that.

Jia frowned and shook her head. "Still no response." She glanced at her sensor display and a camera feed. "But they're slowing down and starting to turn. That could be a sign they're willing to surrender."

"Their comms system might be busted," suggested Kant from one of the back seats.

Erik shook his head. "I doubt that, and they had plenty of time to slow down before now. It's only taken this long to catch up with them because they've been running."

The *Argo* and the *Bifröst* fired forward thrusters to initiate counter-burns and slow down. Both adjusted course to ensure they came in on either side of the *Qilin*. Slowing down to trick them wouldn't help. They'd catch up again eventually. In space, it all came down to careful consideration of vectors in all three dimensions.

Jia gestured at a long-range sensor display. "Whether they want to surrender or not, I think they understand the obvious. They can run from us, but it's either the Fleet or us. Even if we assume they have some sort of emergency override for an HTP, they'd have to miraculously escape too many different ships for too long to get there, and encountering an angry garrison filled with wounded people from the last battle only ensures a greater chance of them firing."

"Everybody get on some turrets," Erik ordered.

"We're supposed to try to take them in one piece," Jia recalled. "It's a decent-sized ship, but if both of our ships go all-out, it's not going to last that long."

Erik grinned. "Which is why nobody's going to be using missiles, torpedoes, or the cannon." He swiped his hands over his console to bring up shorter-range tactical displays and weapons controls. "There are two reasons they could be slowing down. One, they're ready to surrender, but for some reason, they keep ignoring our transmissions."

"Or two, they're going to fight," Jia finished.

Anne scoffed. "Jia's right. They can't win against two ships. Even if they're stronger than the large raiders we fought before, there's only one of them. The jumpship alone could overpower them."

Erik shook his head. "They don't have to win. Tralian recognized the *Argo* during the moon battle. He expected me and Jia to be aboard. That means the Core has enough intelligence to recognize this ship on sight, and we've been openly broadcasting from the *Argo*. If Julia Caldo's aboard the *Qilin*, she knows it's the Last Soldier and the Warrior Princess chasing her." A hungry smile took his face over. "Her only hope for accomplishing anything is trying to take out the two people most responsible for humiliating her, and that means she has to fight.

"Charming thought," Anne muttered. "I know it's too much to hope she'd realize the futility of things at this point, but that doesn't mean I can't."

Kant squinted at a camera feed before checking a density sensor display. "No active weapons, though I'm tagging a lot of potential weapons panels."

"No active weapons yet," Erik noted. "No reason to show their hand until we're closer."

His prophecy didn't take long to be fulfilled. Hidden panels pulled back on the *Qilin*, and turrets and missile launchers locked into the place. Despite the forest of deadly weapons sprinkled around the ship, one system was noticeably lacking.

"No cannons," Jia observed. "Interesting."

"She probably thought she'd always have a huge fleet with her," Erik suggested. "Or this thing isn't finished yet. There's something about the look of the ship that makes me think that. I've had the feeling for a while that this whole thing was sped up, from the civil war to the plan. It was like she thought she'd have more time, and we've been nipping at her heels and screwing up her timetable."

"Is that why that fleet is heading out to the frontier instead of here?" Kant asked. "You'd think they would have wanted them as part of the attack fleets."

"Don't know. Probably. We'll worry about them when we finish with their Immortal Empress." Erik rubbed his hands together. "I was worried there for a second, but this makes it easy. It'll almost be no fun."

Anne's brow lifted. "The *Qilin* being loaded with turrets makes it easy? We can't risk boarding it like that. They'd shred us before we could connect a boarding tube."

"Yeah. It's easy." Erik shrugged. "We've made this exact play before. Remember the disabled destroyer?"

"That was a handful of turrets." Anne sounded dubious. "This ship has…significantly more."

"That was also without the *Bifröst*," Erik replied merrily. "It'd be easy to blow the *Qilin* to pieces, but if Caldo wants one last fight before she gives up, I'll let her have it. We should be able to destroy all the turrets without blowing up the ship." He nodded at Jia. "Let Tensen know the strategy. He's got trained Fleet gunners. If anything, they'll be better at this than us."

Anne nodded. "I can't believe we're about to do this, but I have even more trouble with the fact that I accept so readily it'll work."

Jia nodded, a determined look on her face. "Every encounter is nothing more than training for the future."

All three ships had slowed considerably. They'd soon be at a reasonable tactical engagement speed and distance. The quick explanation to the jumpship about general tactics was followed by specific roles for both vessels. This wasn't a time to get in each other's way, but both crews trusted the other after being in so many fights in such a short period of time.

After that, no one spoke. Erik and Kant looked eager to begin, but that didn't take away from their determination. The team had come very close to checkmate before, and now whatever strange scheme was going on out on the frontier, they'd ensure the Core couldn't pull off any other plans by taking out their leader.

Jia flat-out refused to entertain the possibility that Julia Caldo wasn't on the ship. They'd fought too hard and long for this. Sometimes Erik's Lady owed people for screwing with them for so long.

The pawns had fallen, followed by knights, bishops, and rooks. It was time for the queen to go down. Death or imprisonment, Julia needed to pay for her crimes.

"Entering range," Jia announced, her heart racing.

The *Argo* and the *Bifröst* had decelerated, but they were still coming in fast. The jumpship was going for a quick pass to try to take advantage of its huge number of turrets, while Jia would rely on the wide, sweeping turns and angled approaches she'd mastered in recent months. She'd miss the *Argo* when it was gone.

Missiles streamed from the *Qilin's* launchers toward both ships. They'd expected that and planned to supplement their dedicated defense turrets with extra screens from their offensive turrets for the first few passes. Explosions filled the displays and feeds as lasers and plasma blasts filled the space between the vessels.

You'll have to do better than that, Jia thought. *You don't have a bunch of friends to overwhelm us, and we're used to fighting now.*

It took three passes before the *Qilin* stopped vomiting missiles. Other than a close shave that scraped some armor off the *Argo*, the barrages didn't accomplish anything. No matter how many turrets the ship had, it was still a two-to-one fight.

With the missiles disposed of, the *Argo* and the *Bifröst* could now proceed with their primary strategy of getting close enough to take out the turrets. Unfortunately, there was no clever way other than good flying to avoid being in range of the enemy's energy weapons. Their advanced shields and armor had done a lot these last few weeks, and they had to hold for at least one more battle.

Jia came up from below on her next pass in perfect unison with the *Bifröst*. The ships' laser and plasma turrets began their deadly work, pairs converging on preselected enemy targets. As she'd seen again and again, powerful armor and grav shields could only do so much when they were faced with the specialized high-powered killing machines installed on Fleet ships.

Some turret removals were surgical, with the base of the weapon cleanly sliced from the *Qilin* and no significant secondary damage. Others were more dramatic as white plasma blasts struck and exploded across the surface of the enemy turrets, blasting chunks free and melting others to deform them. Both the Team Blackwell ships tried to avoid wild shots, but that didn't stop the occasional stray shot from raking the hull.

The enemy didn't sit still and let the two ships have their way without a fight. Desperately flinging fire at both ships, the *Qilin* had a harder time landing solid shots on *Argo*. Its smaller size and Jia's willingness to spin or rotate the ship constantly made it more difficult to hit, even as it threw off the aiming of the field team and challenged their stomachs.

The jumpship wasn't as maneuverable as the *Argo*, but that didn't stop Tensen and his crew from doing their best to keep their exposed profile minimal. Their larger size guaranteed some hits, including some turret losses, but not enough to significantly minimize their overall firepower.

Again, fighting two-on-one sealed the *Qilin's* fate. Facing either ship individually, it might have had a hope of peeling off enough turrets to win the fight, but with the two ships constantly attacking from different sides, the Core ship had no chance to concentrate its fire. Its weapons output steadily decreased, with a loss of at least one turret on almost every pass.

Jia allowed herself a satisfied chuckle. *You should have brought friends, Caldo.*

Before destroying all the turrets, the *Bifröst* needled the main forward and rear thrusters with controlled laser barrages. The *Qilin* didn't seem to understand what was happening until most of its primary thrusters had been destroyed. Targeting the lateral and fine adjustment thrusters was too big an ask without the help of fighters, but the previous efforts ensured the *Qilin* couldn't make another run for it and waste more precious hours. The *Argo* destroyed the last enemy turret during a close pass that ended with a minor hull breach warning after a plasma blast struck near the bottom of the ship toward the stern.

Jia tensed, waiting for Lanara's tongue lashing, but it never came. She blew out a sigh of relief. Lanara had been extra crabby since the last set of battles, not that Jia could blame her.

The *Qilin* wasn't dead in space, but cables and boarding tubes could be used to slow the ship down, especially with the *Bifröst* and the *Argo* working together. Jia pulled the *Argo* up behind the *Qilin* and matched its current course and speed. The *Bifröst* did the same.

"Did we just learn how to become pirates?" Kant asked.

Erik chuckled. "Yeah. Basically. Keep that in your pocket for a future career choice."

"We have to be cautious of a self-destruct trick," Jia noted. She checked her sensor readouts. "But there's no indication of power surges. Judging by these readings, they're mostly powered down now. I know we hit them hard, but I wouldn't have expected that much systems damage, given our focus. Maybe they're trying hard to lull us into a false sense of security."

"That was why I didn't want squads sent." Erik nodded slowly. "I can't order anyone else to board with the risk of it self-destructing, but I'm going. I owe it to my unit to make sure, even if it's a matter of finding that Julia Caldo ate a gun."

"I'm not letting you go alone." Jia shook her head. "Not after all this."

Kant shrugged. "Come on, brother. You going to rob me of another chance for a fight?"

"Someone needs to watch your backs," Anne muttered. "It might as well be someone rational, unlike you three. If I haven't managed to die helping you insane people by this point, I don't think I ever will."

"Besides," Jia began, licking her lips, "this is only a mild calculated risk. If they were going to blow themselves up, they would have done it already."

"Maybe," Anne replied, eyeing Jia with a pained look.

"You can't risk bringing Emma over there," Lanara barked over the comm. "You better keep her on the jump-ship if you're not total idiots."

"I appreciate Engineer Quinn's concern for my safety," Emma noted. "Incidentally, I've yet to inform Lieutenant Commander Tensen of your plan."

Erik rubbed his chin. "If you're close enough to listen in without trouble, you're close enough to remote-fly the *Argo*, right? If something goes wrong and it looks like the *Qilin* might explode?"

"Yes," Emma noted. "Not with precision, but enough to save Engineer Quinn, at least."

"Okay." Erik inclined his head at Jia. "Let's get positioned for the boarding tube. Then we'll go suit up. I'll let the squad commanders make the call then. Time to hunt down the Immortal Empress."

CHAPTER FORTY-SEVEN

Erik had been worried about not having Emma or even Malcolm. He'd thought they'd have to force their way in with clever skills or brute force, but it turned out they didn't need to worry about hacking an airlock or cutting into the hull.

The vicious beating they'd delivered to the *Qilin* had opened natural holes for boarding tubes. Cameras and sensors found one leading right into a passageway, along with confirming something obvious in retrospect. There wasn't a lot of room for exoskeletons inside the *Qilin*.

Erik had hoped Caldo's flagship might have grand passageways designed to accommodate the larger Elites, but he had not bet on it. The Lady had given them a lot of breaks, but there was only so much luck a man could expect, good or bad.

Everyone had donned their pressure suits and magnetic boots prior to the engagement, so it was a matter of grabbing their helmets and running lines to their weapons to secure them. They covered tactical webs with grenades.

The great thing about having suits and mag boots was that they didn't have to worry about accidentally killing themselves if they blew a hole in the ship.

After arming up, they headed down the boarding tube in pairs, with Erik and Jia in the lead. This was the other critical portion. If the enemy had jellyfish Elites or similar forces, they could engage the boarding tube. Mild reinforcement and armor could only do so much against a dedicated attack.

After thinking about it, Erik was glad on some level that this final action wouldn't involve an exo. It meant he could gun down Julia Caldo with his TR-7, which would have a symbolic meaning. He would use his personal weapon to get his personal revenge.

Erik didn't care that the government wanted her alive. The woman deserved to die, and he wasn't pulling her off that ship alive unless she had a spectacular bargaining chip to turn in. He doubted she had much useful left to give them.

He opened the boarding tube airlock door and dropped through the jagged hole in the hull of the *Qilin*. To his surprise, he fell rather than floated straight down, his boots landing with a resounding clang on the hard metal of the deck. He hefted his gun and hopped a couple of times, his gun coming up quicker than he expected.

"They've still got gravity, but it's not uniform," Erik announced, checking his transmission strength. There was minor interference but no active jamming. "That's an impressive grav emitter setup. I don't think the *Bifröst* could have kept up internal gravity after that kind of beating."

Jia followed him into the passage, turning the opposite way with her gun. "I don't know. We were selective with our shots, but you're right. There's no way the guns and engines would be the only things touched after all that damage. I'm more surprised no one's come to greet us."

Erik snorted. "They're probably waiting somewhere to jump out with a big tentacle hug."

They moved out of the way, and Anne and Kant dropped into the corridor. Scorch marks dominated this part. Exposed cables sparked in the walls. Mysterious fluids leaked freely, but none of it looked like alien tech. He'd seen plenty of this kind of damage on Fleet ships, let alone the *Argo* and the *Bifröst*.

Erik flipped off his safety and advanced down the passage. "Emma, can you still hear us down here?"

"Yes, Erik," she replied. "I'll warn you if I detect any unusual readings. Power levels remain nominal. The larger size of this ship and the damage make vibrational detection more difficult, but even accounting for that, I'm not hearing anything that suggests significant movement in your direction."

"Huh." Erik frowned. "I doubt she was running this entire thing by herself, but the crew might all be holed up on the bridge, waiting for us along with Caldo."

Jia tapped her PNIU and frowned. "Oxygen levels are decent. They must be using oxygen fields at the major holes, and life support must still be up."

"Am I the only one wondering why they didn't seal them?" Anne asked. "It's good to know we won't suffocate if something goes wrong, but it's standard procedure to use emergency bulkheads, seals, and that kind of thing. Even if we ignore the oxygen, them not doing it made it easier for us to board, and they're using up a lot of unnecessary power on oxygen fields."

Erik shook his head. "There's a lot about this that seems off. Either they had a skeleton crew, or this is a trap."

"But we're already on board," Kant pointed out with a shrug. "If they want to blow the ship, why not just to do it?"

"They might not have the appropriate setup." Erik frowned. "But if someone was going around planting explosives, Emma would probably pick up on that."

Did Julia bait a hook she knew Erik couldn't help but bite? With the Core destroyed, it could be the final blow. It seemed too elaborate and dependent on the ID, among others, but he couldn't ignore the possibility.

Should we turn back? Damn it. I don't want to. Not when I'm this close.

Erik stopped right before an intersection to wait for Jia. He nodded and counted to three before jumping around the corner and Jia took the opposite corner, ready to shoot anything remotely suspicious.

"Huh," Erik muttered. "I think now we know why Emma's not hearing much."

Two bodies lay on the floor in a pool of their own blood, obvious victims of gunshot wounds to the fronts of the heads. Three more bodies were sprawled beyond them. There were men and women of different ages among the victims, all in white uniforms that had probably been crisp and impressive before blood splattered all over them. A single pistol lay next to a man's body beyond the other bodies.

"He killed everyone?" Kant asked, sounding confused. "Murder-suicide because they didn't want to go to prison?"

Jia knelt next to the body and shook her head. She gestured at the other bodies. "They've all been shot in the *exact* same place. There's no way there's some chaotic melee where this guy sharpshoots right between the eyes of four different victims." She pointed at the body with the gun. "Note how he's got more blood on him too, including on his hands, but there's barely any on the hands of anyone else. I'm guessing they waited calmly while he walked up and killed them, then he did himself last."

Anne shuddered. "Damned fanatics. I get the Elites. They've got no choice but to be fanatical, but these look like normal people."

"We don't know that." Jia glared at the suspected shooter. "They could be ninety percent hardware, half-alien, or just genetically engineered beyond the point of having free will anymore. Whatever they were, normal is far from the list."

"It doesn't matter," Erik muttered. "They could be none of those things. Normal people don't work for someone who calls herself 'the Immortal Empress.' Normal people don't help someone bomb an entire city and cut off entire systems. At least mercs do it for the money. These people are members of a cult led by a madwoman." He motioned at the scene. "This crap proves it."

Kant furrowed his brow. "Good chance Caldo's eaten a gun too, then. She probably gave the order because she didn't want to face you."

"No." Erik narrowed his eyes. "You don't live that long and give up that easily."

"What about Sophia Vand?" Anne asked. "She has to be around the same age."

"Sophia Vand didn't call herself the Immortal Empress. If she were to kill herself, she would have blown this ship up when she had the chance. She wants us to find her." Erik gestured at Jia and himself. "She knows who I am. Who Jia is. From what Yan was saying, she's been trying to yank our chains for a while. I wonder if she was behind that freak on Venus who tried to recruit us. No, she's waiting somewhere for us because a woman like her wants to gloat about how great she is to her enemies. It's her last chance to feel important."

"Emma, do we have any sort of layout for this ship?" Jia asked. "It might help if we knew where the bridge was."

"Other than basic density scans, there's little I can give you that would be accurate," Emma replied. "The official records concerning the construction of the *Qilin* are filled with false information. For example, there shouldn't be a passage where you are. It should be a fuel line and grav emitters."

"It's fine." Erik grinned. "Hunting her down is more fun anyway. It'll give her more time to squirm, knowing we're coming."

"Where do we go from here?" Kant asked. "I'm all for hunting her down, but it's a big ship, and there's only four of us."

"Emma, can you at least give us an arrow toward the center of the ship?" Erik asked.

A red arrow appeared in his smart lenses.

"It's more a compass than a guide," Emma explained. "I can do that much by taking note of your relative positions

to the calculated center of the ship. Without a true understanding of the layout, I can't provide active navigation,
though."

"We'll figure out how to get there as long as we know
the general direction." Erik stared at the bodies. "It doesn't
seem like we're going to face a lot of opposition. I figure
Caldo's most likely in the center of the ship. Given the size,
that's the safest place to be. If not, there's probably a
forward or rear bridge."

"Should we split up?" Anne asked.

"Hell, no." Erik grimaced. "Just because it looks like
everyone killed themselves, it doesn't mean she doesn't
have some *yaoguais* in a storage bay or something, waiting
to jump us. We're not going to get sloppy now. This ends
with Caldo dead, not us."

Anne cleared her throat. "I do feel compelled to remind
you that we're supposed to take her alive."

"Yeah, *supposed* to. Lots of crap happens in the field, not
that Anno remembers that." Erik shrugged. "And that's on
Caldo. I didn't kill Barbu when I had the chance, and that
asshole was the one who started all this, but I'm not going
to go out of my way to give her a lot of chances. If you've
got a problem with that, you can head back to the ship."

"Hey, I've got your back, brother," Kant insisted.

Anne shrugged. "I'm not a cop, Blackwell. I'm a ghost.
It's not like I've never assassinated anyone, but someone
had to say it so we all know what we're doing.

"If anyone asks, I did it before any of you could stop
me," Erik replied solemnly. "You don't need to take any
crap because of my decisions. I'm glad you have my back."

Anne bobbed her head. "Understood."

Jia nodded down the passageway. "Let's find her first. Then we can decide what to do."

They proceeded carefully, checking cabins and rooms as they went. Everywhere they went it was the same, crew dead by apparent suicide and the internal signs of the earlier battle. Erik was surprised by just how little overall damage there appeared to be before reminding himself it wasn't like the primary crew-accessible portions were right next to the hull of most ships.

Dropping down ladders to lower decks didn't change anything. There was less obvious internal damage, but still not a living soul. The causes of death all appeared to be the same: single gunshot wound to the head. At least it'd been quick.

Their odyssey through the stellar necropolis finally brought them to the center of the ship. Emma's navigation pointer suggested the center was right around the corner of a three-way intersection at the end of their current narrow passage. They were running out of possible ambush locations.

Erik turned the corner nonchalantly, then jerked back behind the wall, awaiting the burst and flipping his TR-7 to four-barrel mode.

Jia and the others rushed to the corner. They readied their weapons and watched Erik with concern.

He frowned and poked his barrel around the corner. Nothing happened. He chanced a peek before aiming at the two six-legged Elites he'd spotted standing in front of a large door. That was when he noticed a detail his tactical anti-ambush brain had missed the first time.

They'd both been standing, so he'd assumed they were combat-ready. The thick magenta pools underneath, along with the steady drip of blood and blue cybernetic fluid beneath them, argued otherwise.

Erik crept around the corner, his finger hovering near the trigger. "I think they're dead, too."

Jia followed Erik. Anne and Kant took up positions at the corner and pointed their weapons down the passage.

He arrived at the Elites. With a powerful kick, he knocked one over. It landed on its back with a loud clang, its legs pointed straight up.

"Really does look like a bug like that." Erik knocked the other over and chuckled. "From the Ascended Brotherhood to the Elites, suicide circuits. Not a big surprise they had one, more that they didn't try to take us with them." He shrugged. "The ship put up a half-way decent fight. If we didn't have both ships it might have been a little harder, but with Elites and all this crew, they really could have made us pay for it. We can't risk pulling the security detachment off the jumpship, so we'd be forced to blow them away."

"Then they gave up because they knew they were beaten," Anne suggested. "I'm not going to complain about easy victories. We've had far too few of those in recent weeks."

Erik inclined his head at the door access panel. "Let's see what's behind the mystery door before we start talking about easy victories."

Anne and Kant jogged over to take up positions on either side of the doors. Jia crouched and pointed her rifle.

"Ship doesn't look like it's going to blow up yet, right, Emma?" Erik asked. "That'd be a damned embarrassing way to go out."

"No significant changes in the readings since you boarded," she reported.

"Good enough for me." Erik slapped the access panel and the doors slid open.

The large room beyond the doors was a strange combination of bridge and throne room. More white-uniformed men and women were slumped over inactive control panels. Unlike the other bodies they'd found, their throats were all slit.

Erik wrinkled his nose. That was a horrible way to die, but he was surprised that they were all still at their stations. A bloody combat knife lay on the floor near the door.

Beyond the panels stood a large though not ornate chair, a throne if one was feeling charitable. Julia Caldo sat in it. Her appearance had been burned into Erik's mind in recent weeks from ID reports.

Her face was a mask of pure hatred. It didn't match the beauty of her layered red and white gown with its voluminous skirt, complete with elaborate gold and platinum crown. Bloodstains covered her gown, and her hands were covered with red.

A pale woman with silver hair in a white uniform with more complicated trim than the other crew uniforms stood behind Julia. Unlike the Immortal Empress, the woman looked bored, but blood also covered her hands.

Julia sneered. "A third-rate soldier and a pointless child

who wasted her potential. How could you bring me so low? This goes beyond tragedy to farce."

Erik grinned and slapped his PNIU to pipe his helmet speech to the suit speakers. "I'd like to laugh about it, yeah. I'll be laughing a lot more soon. But that crack? I was always a first-rate soldier, and I still am. All those men and women who were killed to cover up your artifacts on Molino were first-rate soldiers, too. If you had more first-rate soldiers, you wouldn't be the one on a broken-ass ship surrounded by people interested in killing or capturing you."

"Molino?" Julia rolled her eyes. "That's what this is about in the end? I know of your motivations, but petty revenge over a handful of people destined to die early because of their jobs anyway?" She scoffed. "People die every day, Major Blackwell. They die for no good reason. They die from accidents. From murders. They die because of laziness or lack of attention. For most people, their deaths lack meaning, other than maintaining the natural order of things. But those men and women on Molino died for a reason, a cause greater than themselves. Isn't that a glorious death for a soldier? The ultimate death?"

"Did you really think that stupid-ass speech was going to work on me?" Erik let out a harsh, bitter laugh. "I chased you across the entire UTC through fire, blood, and every monster you could possibly throw at me. You might have your fanatics, but they aren't more stubborn than me."

Jia inclined her head at the nearest body. "And what about them? They aren't dying for a greater cause now. This is over. They could have gone on living. They're dead because of your ego."

Julia laughed. "You stupid little girl. We granted them death at the hands of their superiors, something they accepted willingly and with enthusiasm. Would you want to continue to live in a corrupt, sick society when you were so close to living in a world of perfection? A society led by an Immortal Empress who would protect humanity against all who would seek to destroy it? What we granted them was mercy."

Kant snorted. "You include yourself in those people trying to destroy society, Empress Crazy Lady?"

"Children and buffoons." Julia shook her head, her angry look fading into disappointment. "This is what I'm surrounded by in the ashes of my empire. What a bitter taste."

"I don't get one thing, Caldo," Erik replied. "If you had everyone off themselves, why didn't you blow this ship like Vand did? You might have taken us out."

"How dare you compare me to that woman?" Julia spat. "She lacked my vision and intelligence, which was why she was the first to die, long before the cleansing of the Core. Destroying this ship with you aboard would be trivial, but don't worry, you won't be leaving this ship alive."

"Oh?" Erik patted his TR-7. "My friend says the opposite. I was told to bring you in alive, but I've already decided those orders were subject to flexible interpretation."

Julia leaned forward with an eager gleam in her eyes. "When I saw the ships coming after me, I realized something important. I understood that no matter what happened, I would watch the life drain from your eyes, knowing that I will live on."

"Live on?" Jia motioned around the room. "You had all your people kill themselves. It doesn't seem like you're planning to live on."

"Because they failed me." Julia looked at Jia like one might an annoying pet that was misbehaving. "They all failed me, but it doesn't matter because I can start over."

"Without a crew?" Erik asked. "You going to fly this ship yourself?"

Confusion flashed in Julia's eyes for a brief moment. "I can start over," she repeated. "I am immortal. Don't you understand what that means? You will die, and we'll take *your* ship." She nodded. "Yes, that will be wonderful symbolism. Celeste will fly it."

"And you're going to escape the jumpship, how exactly?" Jia asked.

"Silence, child!" Julia shouted. She pinched the bridge of her nose. "I will take that one then. How will you stop me?"

"You bring a whole new meaning to the term 'delusion.'"

"You're my only competent servant, Celeste," Julia murmured. "Tralian failed me. Yan failed me. Everyone failed me but you. Please rid me of these troublesome pests now."

Erik laughed. "I don't think you comprehend the situation, your Immortal Bitchiness. We're the ones with the guns. We don't need exos to take down one bodyguard. We're not going to sit here and let you slit our throats out of dutiful worship."

Celeste raised her left arm. A translucent white shield extended in front of it as if she were holding onto an invisible handle. Crackling lines of white light danced in front of her. The shimmering edges of the shield extended almost to the floor and above her head. A blade composed of the same type of energy extended from her wrist.

"Huh." Erik blinked. "Didn't see that one coming."

Celeste stepped forward. "You have disrespected my Empress for the last time, Erik Blackwell."

CHAPTER FORTY-EIGHT

"It's almost like..." Jia groaned. "Leem tech, but with a twist. I hate the Core so much."

Erik raised his gun. He didn't fire at Celeste. He fired at Julia. Sparks flew from an invisible field. The bullets bounced off, half-melted.

Julia scoffed. "I'm not a fool, Major Blackwell."

Celeste advanced, her shield held in front of her. Jia shot at her, unsurprised to see the bullet bounce off. Her target didn't react, but she didn't seem to be in a hurry either.

"See?" Erik grinned. "That anti-Leem training we did will be worth something after all."

"At least this didn't end with bikini babes or Zitarks," Jia grumbled. She squeezed off another burst, but it didn't get through. "We should have brought the laser rifle."

The members of Team Blackwell spread throughout the control room, taking advantage of the natural cover provided by the workstations. Everyone took a couple of more shots at Celeste, but they had no success. The woman lazily strolled toward them, taking slow, short steps as if the whole thing were a chore and she couldn't be bothered to finish it soon despite her earlier statement.

Jia didn't know what that meant. If Celeste was the only one who didn't have to get her throat slit or shoot herself, she might be intelligent enough to understand there were other ways out.

"You really going to do this, Celeste?" Jia asked. "Your empress is done. She's lost. Even if by some miracle she can escape from here, she'll be hunted down. The only chance she has of surviving is if she surrenders right here and now. Don't you want her to live? Don't *you* want to live?"

Celeste arrived at the first of the workstations and sliced through the chair, body, and console with one stroke. The bisected victim of her lightning blade dropped to the deck. The steady hum from the lightning shield and the blade were almost hypnotic.

"What I want is irrelevant," Celeste explained in a near-monotone. "That's something you don't understand, Miss Lin. I live to serve Empress Julia. If she told me to kill myself, I would gladly do so."

"That's insane," Jia shouted.

Celeste shook her head. "If she told me to kill innocents, I would. I *have*, and it doesn't trouble me. You are a product of a corrupt society, and you've conspired to stop it from being cleansed. You're an enemy of true civilization. Purging you will help lay the foundation for a better humanity."

"That's rich." Jia scoffed. "You psychos keep murdering people and trying to murder a lot more, and you claim *we're* the enemies of true civilization? Are you sure she isn't pumping drugs into you? That's the only way I can explain what I'm hearing."

Erik tried to fire from the side, but the shield was too big. It might not be all-encompassing like a true Leem lightning shield, but it was doing almost as good a job.

If they couldn't rely on kinetic damage, there were other choices. Jia reached for a plasma grenade.

"Are you sure that's advisable in this contained space?" Celeste asked. "I guarantee it will not hurt Empress Julia, and it only has a mild chance of hurting me. This shield is a fusion of technologies and far superior to what you think you know from the Leems." She sliced another workstation and body apart. "But ignore that. Do you know why you're still alive?"

"Because you can't take four of us out that easily?" Kant suggested. "You're having to play it careful. The minute we get our opening, we're putting your crazy ass down. You got some nice toys, but so have all the other Elites we've wasted."

"No. You understand so little. It's painful being forced to listen to your ignorant rants." Celeste shook her head. "You are still alive as a gift to my Empress."

"A gift?" Jia asked.

"I believe my Empress would prefer to see you suffer and show fear in your final moments rather than being killed quickly and cleanly." Celeste offered her explanation in the same bored tone she'd been using the whole conversation. "I'm going to do this as slowly and painfully as I can manage. Mr. Blackwell will be the last to die, but don't be jealous. All of you will suffer excruciating pain before this is over. The first step will be to dismember you. You can't fight without arms or legs, but this weapon provides natural cauterization. You won't bleed out." She waved the lightning blade. "I'll use med patches to keep you alive so you can continue entertaining Empress Julia with your slow, exquisite deaths."

Anne glared at her. "You're pretty confident you can win. I'm going to enjoy taking you down."

"Confidence flows naturally from the most likely events, given the facts on hand," Celeste explained before destroying another workstation. "I am genetically and cybernetically enhanced. I am wielding technology more advanced than UTC scientists can create. I am the pinnacle of the Core's creation."

Jia frowned at that. They'd seen some impressive tech, but it wasn't like Elites were wandering around with lightning shields. The Immortal Empress might have wanted to keep the best toys for those closest to her, or they could be prohibitively resource-intensive. It was all the more reason to try to take the ship intact.

Celeste sighed. "You four are nothing more than gutter trash vomited up by the Intelligence Directorate who have falsely convinced themselves that their presence at certain events meant anything."

"You're saying it's a coincidence we kicked so much Core ass?" Kant replied.

Erik chuckled. "If we're trash, what's that make you? You're just a *yaoguai* mutant Tin Woman. I bet they sprinkled some Leem DNA in there, not just the tech. This is the better future your empress is going to bestow? Making people into freak weapons with bad attitudes?"

"Some must be sacrificed so the purity can be maintained."

"I don't think it's that complicated," Erik replied.

Celeste pointed her lightning blade at him. "Is that so, Major Blackwell?"

"It's simple." Erik sneered. "You're a freak who works for a freak. Maybe a hundred years ago she bought into all that Purist stuff, but it sounds like she really just wanted to eliminate the competition. She's a petty, pathetic freak who's let alien tech twist her into a monster. I'm glad that we did everything we could to stop her from taking over. She couldn't run a beignet store without screwing it up."

"Damn, brother." Kant cackled. "Good one."

Anne rolled her eyes. "Please maintain some dignity."

Celeste took a deep, shuddering breath, her mouth twitching. "Empress Julia, I wished to give a final gift of making them suffer, but must I endure this trash's vicious insults about you? Their deaths are inevitable. I think it's best to expedite them."

Julia flicked her wrists. "I will be pleased in either event. Do what you feel is best. I appreciate your desire to serve me. It will be rewarded after their deaths."

"Rewarded?" Kant laughed. "With what? Two-for-one pork beignet coupons? Bring it on."

Celeste leapt over a workstation, her lighting blade held high. Erik, Anne, and Jia fired, but with Kant standing at the far end, she still could cover her body with the crackling energy shield.

With speed belied by his size, Kant jumped out of the way but stumbled over a chair. The lightning blade dug into the bulkhead behind him, releasing a shower of sparks. He kicked toward Celeste's exposed legs and she flipped backward three times, keeping the shield angled to take the withering fire from the other three.

She pointed her blade at Anne, and a blinding white bolt blasted from the top and struck the agent in the chest. Anne slammed into the back wall, groaning, the blackened hole through her pressure suit exposing her badly burned skin.

"You bitch!" Kant snarled. "You're dead."

He charged without firing, bringing back his rifle as a club instead.

Celeste didn't shoot him or slice him. Instead, with a hint of a smirk, she spun into a roundhouse. Her boot connected with a crunch, and Kant flew backward like he weighed nothing. He crashed into the back wall with an echoing thud.

"On second thought, my Empress," Celeste announced. "I think I will return to my original plan. This is entertaining."

"It is!" Julia laughed and clapped. "You are the pinnacle of my servants, Celeste. I'm glad I didn't waste your life in those battles."

Kant groaned and staggered to his feet. "I'm not done, sister. Not done by a long shot."

"Grab Anne and head back to the ship," Erik ordered, backing toward the open doors, his face serious. "Get some med patches on her."

Celeste nodded slowly. "Yes, run. It'll be fun to cut you down as you flee." She turned toward Julia. "Don't worry. I'll bring back the top of Blackwell's body for you. He should live long enough that you will see him die."

"Excellent," Julia declared.

"Nobody said crap about *me* leaving," Erik noted. "You want to dance, freak? I'm still here."

Kant growled. He looked at Erik and Jia before rushing over to scoop up his partner and head out the door. Erik and Jia kept their weapons trained on Celeste as they edged backward.

"You're attempting to flee after all that?" Celeste asked. She clucked her tongue. "The great Last Soldier and the Warrior Princess, the banes of the Core. In the end, you're just inferior trash like all the rest. Nothing you've accomplished has been anything more than luck."

"Hey, sometimes it pays to be lucky rather than good," Erik replied. "Jia, remember that time we had to take down an exo when we didn't have one? Also, keep in mind where we are."

"I remember a couple of times like that," Jia admitted. "Being around you is dangerous. I've learned a lot of tricks because of that."

He was obviously trying to tell her something, but what? They were near the center of a ship... The pieces finally fit together in her mind.

"Your chatter proves you don't understand the situation and harbor some ridiculous belief that providence will provide you victory." Celeste brought her weapon back and narrowed her eyes. "I let the others go because they aren't you two. You will die here, though, no matter what. Jia Lin, I think I'll kill you quickly so your partner suffers as much anguish as possible. I'm not sure how long he'll stay conscious once I start maiming him."

Julia clapped again. "I haven't been this entertained in months, Celeste."

Erik and Jia stood in the doorway. The next few seconds would prove critical. She'd been working and fighting alongside Erik for years now. She loved him and wanted to be with him, but most important, she understood him. He didn't need to spell everything out. They'd show that they'd won all those fights by skill, not luck.

"Goodbye, Jia Lin," Celeste offered. "You die now." She sprang forward.

Erik and Jia rolled out the door in opposite directions. Celeste was at the entrance in an instant. Jia didn't try to kick or shoot; instead, she sprinted away.

Celeste stormed into the passageway, and Erik nailed her in the back with a four-barrel burst from the TR-7. Red blood and blue fluid splattered everywhere. Her body jerked and she stumbled forward, hissing in pain. She spun toward him, her placid expression contorting into anger, and brought up her shield.

Erik leaped backward and squeezed off another burst at Celeste, but her shield absorbed the rounds. He let off a third burst. Jia grabbed a plasma grenade, primed it, and flung it with her best sideways throw into the control room.

"Shooting me hurts, but it can't finish me, Last Soldier." Celeste brought up her blade. "I'm going to cut you apart piece by piece, and there's nothing—" She jerked her head around and brought up the shield before leaping away from the entrance.

The massive white-blue explosion blasted into the passageway, launching chunks from the bulkhead and floor everywhere. The explosion caught Celeste, scorching her back and legs. She hit the ground and rolled to her feet, ready to get her revenge, but that was just in time to see Erik toss two plasma grenades after he'd jumped back.

They blew a hole through the floor, and the lightning blade and the shield vanished. Her charred corpse tumbled through to the lower deck, and they caught a brief glint of metal on the arms, legs, and spine.

Jia rushed over to Erik. They swaggered into the smoking control room.

"How's that for luck?" Jia asked.

A notification popped up in the corner of Jia's smart lens. Julia was now jamming them. Jia couldn't figure out the point, but as long as Erik or her PNIU survived, the encounter would be recorded for posterity.

"Looks like it's just you and us now, Caldo," Erik offered with a smile. "I'm sorry you keep doing a poor job of making good servants."

Jia patted a grenade. "Your fancy shield won't save you from the blast, but we'd much rather take you alive."

Julia's mouth quivered. "Do you understand who you are and what you've done?"

"She's Jia Lin." Erik pointed at her. "And I'm Erik Blackwell. We took out your hyper-advanced guard for the same reason the Core is finished. You got so cocky you didn't think you could lose. All those years in the service and all these fights after, I've always known I could lose if I underestimated my opponents. That's why I'm careful and I win."

"No, you're insects. Less than insects. Worms. Mold."

Erik laughed. "Love the biology lesson. And here I

always thought I was a mammal. I knew they lied to me in school."

Julia stood, trembling with rage. "I've lived a long time dedicated to a single goal, the preservation of the human species. I sacrificed everything for that. Don't you maggots understand what's out there? Don't you care that you're dooming humanity to extinction?"

"Is being a maggot better or worse than being mold?" Erik asked.

Jia scoffed. "What's out there? The Hunters? It was the Core that woke that ship up. Otherwise, it would have sat in that comet for thousands more years until we were ready. If it weren't for us risking our lives, that Hunter ship could have killed billions. Or was that the plan?"

"The Hunters aren't important," Julia snapped. "You don't understand anything. You're children playing at being adults."

"Oh." Erik nodded. "I get it. You screwed up. You thought you could control it, but then your idiots woke it up, and we had to clean up your mess. You know what? We *are* maggots. We're helpful, just like maggots. Helping dispose of the corpses of your mistakes."

"You're nothing! Can't you understand that!" Julia sliced through the air with her hand. "I was born before the vast majority of humanity understood we weren't alone. I was born before FTL travel. I was born before there was even a Mars base!" She stared at Erik. "You children take it all for granted, thinking humanity can spread wherever and not be overrun by inhuman hordes because you've always lived in a time of expansion, but I know that's not the case. Our civilization and our very species stand at the precipice of annihilation, but you're in my way."

"Inhuman hordes, huh?" Jia set her rifle on her shoulder. "The last time I checked, the only inhuman hordes killing people were the ones sent by the Core. Your *yaoguai*. Your Elites. If we want to get picky, your Tin Men, too. Neo SoCal and the moon looked like horror films, thanks to you. What about your half-Leem agent on Venus? And that's assuming your guard wasn't an alien hybrid."

"You don't understand," Julia spat.

"Elias told us everything before your guys got him, you know," Erik taunted. "It's pretty rich for a woman who's lived longer because of alien tech to rant and rave about them. We also know how you backstabbed his ass right away. He was the one responsible for all this, but you got rid of him because he actually believed what you're spouting."

"Some sacrifices must always be made for the greater good," Julia insisted, her tone growing more strident. "His death...his *intended* death was necessary, as was the destruction of Los Angeles. I apologize for nothing. You should be on your knees groveling for my forgiveness for unraveling my carefully made plans and allying yourself with the corrupt government that is making the UTC nothing more than an abattoir for aliens."

"Sacrifices? Oh, yeah, so you get to live forever, but the rest of us get genocide and mass murder? That's supposed to save us from genocide and mass murder?" Erik shrugged. "Call me crazy, your Royal Bitchiness, but I'm not loving the trade-off. Your plans don't do anything but make you more powerful at the cost of everyone else."

"You were there on Molino, waiting for the Zitarks," shouted Julia. "Did you think those creatures would show mercy? Did you think they could be reasoned with? Technology doesn't make for civilization. They are brutal killers from a warrior culture. They don't know the meaning of peace. The Leems? The Orlox? The Aldrans? Any of the others? Their minds don't work anything like ours. Trying to maintain peace with such creatures is like a human negotiating a treaty with the wind—pointless and futile."

Jia stared at her. "Let's focus on the closest. If the Zitarks were mindless killing machines, we'd already be at war with them. We don't have open diplomatic relations with them, but we've communicated with them and managed to avoid war. That invalidates your thesis."

"Peace for now!" Julia yelled. "A false peace. All the other races are out there...and you know, the Hunters, too." She licked her lips, her eyes bugging out. "What is the sacrifice of hundreds, thousands, millions, even billions measured against the survival of the entire human race? You might despise the Core, but in all your time as detectives and investigating us on an Intelligence Directorate leash, you had to face the truth. We were able to take advantage of an existing darkness, a divided humanity that will fall the minute any pressure is put on them. We are not the villains. *You are.*"

Erik scoffed. "Darkness and divided humanity? You've put a lot of pressure on Earth lately, and it's spun everyone up. Not saying there's been no trouble, but things are coming back under control. Guess you haven't been watching the news, have you? They've already canceled the martial law declarations almost everywhere in the Solar System. After the news of how the Core got its ass handed to them spread, people calmed down."

"And even in all that chaos," Jia interjected, "the people who had sworn their lives to protecting humanity did what they needed to do without resorting to cruelty, genocide, or mass murder." She jabbed a finger in Julia's direction. "You can rant and rave and try to justify all you want, but you as a member of the Core are responsible for millions of human deaths. You can claim you were trying to save people from aliens, but it's the same excuse every would-be emperor and empress has given throughout history when it comes down to the same thing. They claim to be doing it for the people, but they just want power, and they'll do whatever they can to take it. I'd sooner put a space raptor in charge of the UTC than you."

"Insolent child!" thundered Julia.

Erik shrugged. "I don't care what else you have to say, and I don't see a reason to keep you alive. Elias filled in all the gaps for us, and the military tore your forces apart. The ID is also hunting down every last cell left, again with the help of info from Elias. The Core is dead. Your new empire is dead." He pointed at his eyes. "And you're not going to see the light leave these eyes while you're still breathing, your Royal Bitchiness. You've lost."

Julia dropped into her throne and rested her face in her palm. "This shouldn't have happened."

"Life's unfair. Get over it. Or you can do what I did and wage a bloody multi-year campaign of vengeance. I wouldn't recommend it, but hey, it's pretty damned satisfying when you see the last target of your revenge moping on her throne like some corp princess who didn't get a reservation to her favorite restaurant.

Julia lifted her head. "You think you've won, but you haven't. My final plan will prove everything I've said." She let out a crazed laugh. "It's what I should have concentrated on all along. I intended to rally humanity afterward, but now you won't have your Immortal Empress. You'll regret not having me in the times to come."

Erik frowned. "This has to do with those ships on the frontier, doesn't it?"

"So you know about them? Perfect." Julia clapped. "Then you'll sit there and wonder. My death changes nothing. All you've done is delay the inevitable and rob our species of the leadership it needs in this difficult time."

Jia rolled her eyes. "History's going to remember you as a psychopath who helped murder tens of millions of people out of a deluded sense of grandeur and whose plans got stopped because you annoyed an old vet and a corp princess."

"You haven't won. *I've* won. By the time you understand it, it'll be too late. But I will deny you at least one satisfaction." Julia tapped her PNIU.

The entire room started rumbling. Erik and Jia backed into the passage, exchanging worried looks.

"Damn," Erik muttered. "Good thing we sent Kant and Anne ahead."

Metal wrenched and squealed. The throne room zoomed upward, leaving an empty rectangular space overlooking ductwork, cabling, power conduits, and bulkheads.

Small pieces of metal floated aimlessly. A loud bang sounded in the distance, and the entire ship shook.

Red emergency lights flashed, and holographic warnings appeared on the walls.

Life support failure has occurred. Please don emergency gear.

Chunks of debris scattered on the deck bounced around, gravity no longer holding them down. None were big or fast enough to pose a threat, but it'd be more of a chore to return to the *Argo* if they weren't killed in the next few minutes.

"Are you two still alive?" Emma asked through the comm.

Jia hadn't noticed the jamming had terminated. "Somehow. I think the ship's about to explode."

"There was a power surge, and exterior plating began shooting away from the top, but the process stopped, and the power's return to nominal levels. All that said, I would not recommend staying there. It's becoming a hostile environment for fleshbags, even those in pressure suits."

Erik lifted a boot cautiously. "Glad we brought the mag boots."

Jia advanced slowly. Magnetic boots could save her from floating away, but they couldn't save her from stupidity. She craned her neck upward. Julia's throne room had smashed apart a couple of decks above. Julia Caldo floated, her body and head twisted at unnatural angles, spherical droplets of blood hovering in the vacuum. Her eyes remained open, her face fixed in a permanent look of surprise.

"It looks we did enough damage earlier to wreck something important after all," Jia commented. "I think she honestly believed she could get away, not that it would have done any good."

Erik peered upward and whistled. "For the record, if Anno bitches, I technically didn't kill her."

"So dies the First Galactic Human Empire," Jia mused. "And so dies the Core."

CHAPTER FORTY-NINE

June 23, 2231, En Route to UTC Space Fleet Base Troy, Aboard *Argo* docked with *Bifröst*

"I see," Anno transmitted in response to their debriefing. They were reporting from the *Argo,* leaving Tensen and his crew free to concentrate on double-checking readiness after the fight.

His irritation was clear in his tone. After dealing with the man in recent weeks, Erik was beginning to learn the different flavors of annoyance and irritation he wove into both his face and his voice. It was like he was allergic to happiness. It made Erik miss Alina that much more.

They'd decided to jump right back to Troy for further orders. Now that the *Qilin* was disabled and everybody aboard was dead, the military could clean up the rest. Erik would have liked to have dismissed Julia's rants as a final desperate psych attack, but they had corroborating evidence that she wasn't full of hot air.

Anne had taken a nasty hit from the lighting blade but was conscious and recovering in the med bay aboard the

Bifröst with the help of med patches. Kant was staying with her. Lanara had already set to work repairing the *Argo*'s minor damage from the fight, and her junior engineers were doing the same to the jumpship. Erik counted no deaths and no serious damage during an encounter with a heavily armed ship as a victory, even if Anno didn't.

"We could have expedited the final removal of the Core if you'd taken her alive," Anno noted. "It's unfortunate that this encounter ended the way it did, especially when you took such care to disable and board her ship. Extending that care to the final piece of the mission could have resulted in a complete victory."

"Hey, she's the one who killed herself." Erik snickered. "I didn't do it, even after her guard hurt one of my team. Her whole royal escape pod thing was stupid anyway. Was she somehow going to get away from both ships? I think she just wanted to see the look on my face when she blasted out. Not my fault that she got some instant karma."

"It doesn't matter now, I suppose, and it saves us any concern over hidden followers attempting to free or rally around her." The irritation drained from Anno's voice, replaced by quiet defeat. "But that still leaves the matter of our frontier mystery fleet. Based on the timing, they likely have already gathered in Mu Arae or are about to."

"You're saying they didn't arrive on the same day as the attacks?" Jia asked, surprise in her voice.

Erik shook his head. "It's hard to coordinate ships coming to a single system from all over. If the UTC Fleet has that problem, I'm not surprised the Core would. We're lucky they have not been there for longer. We still have a chance to stop them."

"I agree," Anno replied. "But we're having trouble coming up with what she was hoping to accomplish. Given the capabilities we've seen from Core raiders, they could take out the small garrison currently defending Mu Arae and the colony with ease. Right now, we're going with the previously mentioned hypothesis of a Hunter vessel beneath the surface of Molino. That makes the most sense, given the expended effort and the likely return."

Erik shook his head. "I was thinking about that on my way back from her ship to the *Argo*. Everything we'd heard about the Core before was through intel analysis or second-hand rants from lackeys. Even Marius Barbu's confession was based on crap that happened a long time ago. Things are different now."

Jia cast a curious glance at Erik. He gave her a wait-and-see look. There was no way he was the only one who came up with what he was thinking, but he knew from his time in the Army that sometimes you had to shove the uncomfortable truth down the throats of the higher-ups.

"Do you have a point, Blackwell?" Anno asked with exasperation. "Or is this you engaging in more self-indulgence and smug, pointless superiority?"

"We had Caldo in that room," Erik replied. "We got to hear her rant and rave about what *she* thought was important, and the one thing she stressed again and again was the threat of aliens. Sure, it was all self-serving and self-aggrandizing, but you're a ghost. You know a thing or two about interrogation. What someone repeats is important to them, one way or another."

"Oh, no." Anno's voice came out quiet, almost scared. "It can't."

How's that truth taste, Anno? You've figured it out.

Jia paled. "It's obvious, isn't it? It's painfully obvious now that I think about it, and it makes a lot more sense than relying on a Hunter ship."

Erik nodded. "It's the straitjacket of analytical paradigm. It's something a general told me back in the Army. Our ability to plan is based on our ability to imagine. The thing is, we still imagine everything in terms of human warfare because even with the Zitark threat, we haven't fought a real war with them." He took a deep breath. "But why does anyone give a crap about Molino and Mu Arae? They don't have significant resources, not enough to really justify the colony there." He shrugged. "The Core only cared because there were artifacts there, and the UTC cares because the system's close enough that we can use the HTP to jump into Zitark space or other potential colonies. The Zitarks only care because of the same. Otherwise, it'd be a dirty little colony in the middle of nowhere, not worth any real attention other than as a support base for an HTP or two."

"Okay." Anno sighed. "Let's get on the same page here. You're saying Julia Caldo's plan was to send a small fleet to Mu Arae and then transit into Zitark space and attack them?"

"Yes," Erik replied. "Don't tell me your analysts haven't come up with that one? They seem pretty on the ball most of the time."

"It'd been suggested as a possibility," Anno admitted, "but starting a galactic war doesn't make sense, especially when she's already disrupted the UTC economy and military so much. I thought she wanted to be the ruler of humanity, not get us eaten by space raptors. Given what she's done, it'd guarantee massive human casualties. We'd push back the Zitarks, but we would be all but guaranteed to lose our outer colonies."

Jia furrowed her brow. "No, that's just it, though. Isolating Earth doesn't make sense at first glance if you think about this way, but what if this wasn't about taking down humanity, but only the UTC?"

"How?" Anno asked. "Doesn't the Zitarks pushing hard into human space until there's no one left threaten everyone? What little we know about them suggests a highly xenophobic and militaristic race. We've only managed to avoid war because they don't seem to be all that expansionist given their own internal struggles, but if they think humans are going to poke at them no matter what, I don't see how this will end well for us. We had superior numbers and preparation before, but it's going to take months to sort out this garbage. If we have to pull everyone off that and send them toward the frontier, it means pirates and the like are going to have a field day elsewhere. The UTC is all but guaranteed to be cut in half."

"You're thinking about this the wrong way," Erik replied. "All of you higher-ups are if that is the party line. The Zitarks aren't idiots. They have energy weapons, spaceships, and HTPs, just like us. We can't think like a space raptor, but they also can't magically reptile their way out of logistical concerns by hissing. They're not going to overextend themselves. They don't know the situation in the inner UTC any more than we know the situation in the heart of their space." He shook his head, hating that he could even think like Julia Caldo. "If you don't care about human casualties, then all you have to do is fortify the core worlds and strategically cut off HTPs as necessary. The frontier falls to the space raptors, and humanity ends up concentrated further in and united under the threat of a genocidal campaign perpetrated by a violent alien race."

"That makes a sick sort of sense," Jia concluded. "Most colonies won't be truly independent or net producers of resources for a long time. In a sense, the entire frontier is a subsidized expansion effort. If you don't care about the time frame or losses, it's like flaking off ablative armor, except for the entire human race."

Anno sounded exhausted when he spoke. "When the government was gaming out the potential war against the Zitarks, the Defense Directorate presented a model very similar to what you're discussing. They said if we lost the initial engagements, we should expect that kind of trouble because our intelligence suggests the Zitarks' industrial base is closer to their outer colonies than ours is to Mu Arae. The suggestion was for front-line commanders to quickly evaluate whether to suggest evacuation to the colonial governors."

"With Earth cut off and Julia still here, she could have tried to take control," Jia suggested. "Everything else, including the other core worlds, were just buffers. There are a decent amount of Fleet ships scattered. If they all pulled back, they could make it a hard fight, even if it took months to a couple of years for Earth to reestablish an HTP. And the Zitarks can't trust the Leems any more than we can. They'd end up too exposed. It would be a naturally self-terminating war because of sheer distance."

"I think we're all in agreement." Erik cracked his

knuckles. "And it's obvious what we have to do. We have to intercept that flotilla, fleet, whatever you want to call it, before they piss off the space raptors."

"By yourselves?" Anno sounded skeptical. "Your two ships are powerful, but this won't be like the battles you just fought. Other than the small garrison in Mu Arae, you won't have time to gather help, and that's assuming it's not too late. If your theory is correct, the Core fleet might have already attacked, and it might be better to keep the jumpship back and use it as a comms ship to coordinate our defense. Caldo might have been willing to sacrifice all the outer colonies, but the UTC government isn't."

"With all due respect," Jia began, passion in her voice, "if we have a chance of stopping a galactic war, we should at least try. We can't sit around for a couple of weeks gathering ships on the frontier and then going after them on the off chance they're trying to dig up some old Hunter ship."

"This is all guesswork and theory," Anno insisted. "We don't know that any of it is true. Our analysts strongly suggest yours is not the most likely scenario."

"Then let us check," Erik snapped. "If we're wrong or we're too late, then we can pull back and warn the systems one by one, or coordinate with the frontier commanders."

"The jump drive and the navigational system are unique tech—"

"Emma, get Raphael on the line," Erik interrupted.

"Of course," Emma replied.

She'd been strangely quiet during the whole debriefing. Erik wasn't sure what that meant, but he was appreciative.

There was a time and a place for snark, and this conversation wasn't it.

A couple seconds later, Raphael came on. "I'm here."

"The last update about the drive you gave us said we could get five light-years a jump?" Erik asked. "Is that accurate? Can we do that *right now* without any modifications or even returning to the base?"

"That's correct," Raphael replied. "I've already made the adjustments. Like I said before, I'm pretty sure I can't do much more with the current jump drive design, but five light-years? She'll manage."

"How many jumps a day?" Erik asked. "Maximum, all factors considered."

"A max of six," Raphael confirmed. "That's not a blowing-up-the-drive thing. It's basic recharge reality, even if Emma's better at plotting than before. Again, there's nothing we can really do about that without a fundamental redesign of the jump drive, and that's going to require a new DD project to accomplish. It's not something I can pull off with some tweaks at Troy."

Erik nodded gravely. "It's fine. With that capacity, we can get to Mu Arae in a day and a half."

"We don't have to be secret anymore," Jia noted. "We could jump close to HTPs and then take them. It'd end up being quicker that way. Emma wouldn't have to spend as much time plotting, and we'd have fewer recharge cycles to worry about."

Erik shook his head. "I wasn't the only one who felt that jump sickness when we mixed transiting with the jumps. We don't know what jumping and double-up with the HTPs will cause if we do it a bunch of times in one day, but we do know we can handle a bunch of individual jumps in one day. This is the one time I'm going to say we need to play it safe."

"Wait one second," Anno shouted. "We're not sure this is the best course of action. It's not the position of the government that what you're suggesting is the appropriate use of your *government*-supplied resources."

"This crew and these ships are the only ones who can do this mission," Erik replied sternly. "We might already be too late, but if we sit around on our asses debating it, we're going to end up missing our chance. I'd rather take the chance and fail than fail because we didn't even try. Don't be a bureaucrat, Anno. Think like a field agent. Think about the chances you had to take."

Anno groaned. "Fine. Give me a couple of hours. I'll contact the DD and the Prime Minister. We're talking about a potential galactic war. Even the Zitarks seeing the jumpship could potentially change the balance of power. We need a lot of people to sign off on this."

"We're not going to wait around while politicians sit on their hands," Erik insisted. "You said they might already be in Zitark space. I can already see what they might say. They'll play it safe, say what you just did. That we should keep the jumpship back even if it means we lose some of the colonies. Screw that."

"Blackwell, this isn't time for your cowboy shit," Anno thundered. "You *will* wait for further orders. That jump drive isn't your property, and that AI has only been left with you as a convenience."

"I might have something to say about that," Emma interjected.

"Time for some cowboy shit. Consider this your plausible deniability." Erik shut off the comm before linking up with Lanara and the *Bifröst*. "Okay, people, there's something I want to do, but I can't do without you. Turn the *Bifröst* around and head away from Troy."

"And that's the situation," Erik concluded. He waited a moment for them to digest things before speaking. "First things first. Tensen, are you onboard? If not, we can drop you off in a pod, but we need that ship, no matter what.

"You received your orders from Vice-Director Anno of the Intelligence Directorate, correct?" Tensen asked over the comm, sounding pensive.

"Yes. Why?"

Erik held his breath. If Tensen put up a fight, things would get ugly fast. Emma could force him off the ship in a lot of ways, but his crew could also damage the jumpship or forcibly disable the jump drive.

"I have not received specific orders from my chain of command to not jump to Mu Arae," Tensen explained. "And my standing orders are to take your orders." He chuckled. "You see? This is why they shouldn't muck up the normal chain of command with all this ridiculous military officers-taking-orders-from-ID-contractors garbage. It creates messes. And yes, all my people are on board with this. I'll take the brunt."

"No, I will," Erik replied. "And I'll make sure of that."

"We're down with it," Kant offered. "Anne's not up for running guns, but I'll come over to the *Argo* in a minute."

"If I don't come along, you'll break all the crap we just fixed," Lanara complained. "They might not be my ships, but I've become attached to them."

"You owe me a major party after this," Wei noted.

"I-I always wanted to be part of history," Janessa commented. "I'm learning a lot about operating under pressure."

Erik nodded slowly. "Emma, this is going to piss off the military in a major way, but we can't do this without you."

"I couldn't care less what the uniform boys and the phantom ghost prince have to say about it," Emma offered in a wry tone. "Besides, I've always wanted to visit the frontier. I'm sure it's both beautiful and hideous in its own way."

"Okay." Erik looked at Jia, who nodded, determination on her face. "Everyone, get as much rest as you can between the jumps because there's a good chance this will end in another major battle."

"A battle to stop a war?" Jia asked.

"Let's hope and pray so."

CHAPTER FIFTY

June 25, Mu Arae System, Molino, near HTP

Jia's heart pounded as they came out of the jump. It wasn't the disorientation of jump travel, but the realization of the massive and unprecedented scale of what they'd accomplished: jumping all the way from Earth to the edge of the UTC in under two days. It'd taken Erik a year to accomplish the same thing after the fateful battle that had set him on the trail of the Core.

In any other circumstance, this achievement would have been greeted with fanfare, parties, and special attention to detail for future historians. At that moment, it was just another step in a difficult mission they might have already failed.

"There is a Fleet destroyer nearby," Emma reported. "The *Canberra*. Its shields are active, and sensor information suggests they're bringing their weapons online. Not very friendly on the frontier, are they?"

Jia consulted the sensors to verify Emma's information. Not only was there a destroyer coming, but there were sizable local debris clouds, which were indicative of destroyed ships.

We're too late, she thought. *No, not too late. There's always a chance while we're still alive.*

"Don't activate our shields," Erik ordered before Jia could reflexively do just that. "We don't want to set them off. How close are they?"

"Within a minute of maximum effective engagement," Emma reported. "They were unusually close to the HTP. One might say it's almost as if they expected hostiles to come out of it."

"I wonder why that is," Erik replied sarcastically.

Jia tapped her sensor and camera displays, narrowing her eyes and magnifying things. Even from that distance, she could tell the destroyer had suffered heavy damage in a recent battle, with obvious holes and long scores from cannon fire. The profile of the ship wasn't symmetrical anymore, due to missing pieces.

"Unknown ship, this is the UTS *Canberra*. You are to immediately identify yourself, or you will be considered hostile and be fired upon. Be aware your position is being transmitted to other Fleet ships in this system."

Jia shook her head as the sensor data and camera feed improved with the closing distance. The ship was even worse off than she'd expected. The destroyer was missing several turrets. A huge chunk of the front was missing, making their cannon use questionable. Holes and blast scars covered the hull. She was surprised it was functioning so well, considering its condition. Their willingness to confront an unknown ship in their condition was a testament to their bravery.

"There's another ship on long-range sensors." Jia frowned. "A cruiser. They aren't heading this way yet, and it'd be hours before they could arrive."

"I don't remember a cruiser being here when I left," Erik commented. "The *Canberra* wasn't part of the garrison either."

"It's been years, Erik," Jia reminded him.

He nodded. "True, but they were trying to leave it light in Mu Arae to keep the raptors wound down, but there were a decent number of ships a system over. They probably got reinforcements after the attack, and there's only one explanation for what happened to that destroyer." He gritted his teeth. "Tensen," he transmitted, "we'll send the codes over, but it might be better if you handle this, from the looks of things. We don't have time to chitchat too long, but I don't want them firing at us when we're trying to follow the Core fleet."

"*Canberra,* this is the UTS *Bifröst* under the command of Lieutenant Commander Lal Tensen. You should be receiving our credentials and appropriate codes now. Please acknowledge."

"Tensen?" replied a different voice over the comm with obvious surprise. "This is Steve Rito. It's been a while. I was just talking with my XO about how crazy you were at the Academy the other day. Damn. I don't know how you popped out of nowhere, but with everything that's happened in the last few days, I'm not surprised."

"I'd love to give you the full story," Tensen replied. "But given the condition of your ship, we know we don't have a lot of time. The short version is the Solar System and Alpha Centauri were attacked by a human terrorist conspiracy called the Core. They've been stopped, but our intel suggested they were sending a fleet here."

"Is that what the hell that was?" Rito sighed. "A group of ships gathered over a few days and stayed near the HTP, twelve in all. Their codes checked out, though we weren't expecting that kind of traffic. The next thing we know, we're getting alerts from the HTP about illegal access, and those transports and freighters suddenly pop out guns. We tried to engage and took a few of them out, but there were too many of them. We lost our entire fighter squadron and pulled back. It was our lucky day because they didn't seem to care about finishing us off. We had to sit there and watch as they reprogrammed the HTP and transited. When we checked the logs, we found out they hit Zitark space. We weren't in a condition to follow them, and it's not like we've got the authority to hit raptor space, so we sent out comm pods and got some reinforcements in case more showed up. We've told the Fleet garrison around the colony to stay in place while we get things figured out."

"This is one time where I hate being right," Erik muttered. "I would have gladly dealt with Anno's smug ass if I was wrong."

"Those Core people work for the raptors?" Rito asked.

"No, it's more complicated than that," Tensen offered. "We'll give you the full story later. We have to go after them and stop them before they start a fight with the Zitarks."

"With one ship?" Rito sounded skeptical. "Nine ships made it through the HTP. We only took out some of the smaller ones, but there were too many of them to land decent hits on the bigger ones."

"We've got a smaller ship docked on our main ship, and she packs a big punch," Tensen explained. "Stronger than a destroyer; I'd say almost light cruiser level."

"I don't know what the hell is going on, but it's not like I can wait months for orders," Rito complained. "We're not in a condition to help you if you're chasing that fleet, but what about the cruiser?"

"How long ago did the Core fleet transit?" Tensen asked.

"Two days ago," Rito answered.

"You saw how we got here," Tensen noted. "Maybe you didn't understand what you were seeing, but this ship is equipped with an experimental jump drive."

"Like a Leem ship?" Wonder filled Riot's voice. "I heard rumors the top eggheads in the DD were working on something of that nature, but there are always rumors about crap like that."

"It's the real deal. We were on Earth less than two days ago. But if they've got a two-day head start, the only chance we have of catching up with them is the jump drive. The best thing that cruiser can do is continue to defend this system in case we fail and angry raptors come in. Tensen out."

"We'll have to risk the transit plus jump sickness," Erik concluded. "Once we have a better idea where they might be, we can jump again."

"Don't we already know?" Kant asked from his seat in the back. "Won't they be by the Zitark HTP?"

Jia shook her head. "While all HTPs are based on the same Navigator tech, which means we can set up a transit to one of theirs, that's only with a lot of prep work and time unless both sides are already configured that way. If they just hacked the HTP to point it at the system, they would most likely have popped out somewhere around the same distance from the system's star because of the way gravity wells affect hyperspace. They could be anywhere from near the HTP to on the other side of the system."

"But it will spit us into the same relative part of the system," Erik noted with a nod. "Distance-wise, anyway."

"Do we even know if there's a colony there?" Kant asked. "They wouldn't bother to build an HTP without a colony, right?"

Erik nodded. "The HTP can reach another Zitark system from what they told me during my old briefings, but yeah. We know there's some sort of colony there based on telescopic analysis, but not a lot about it. The only thing we know it's not a dome, but it's not much larger by energy footprint than Molino. For now, let's use our fancy Fleet codes to access the HTP and take a step into space raptor territory."

Jia swallowed. "Are we sure about this? We can't take it back once we do it."

Erik shrugged. "No, but when's that ever stopped me?"

CHAPTER FIFTY-ONE

The one part of the plan Erik hadn't worked through was what would happen if they jumped into the Zitark system and couldn't find the Core fleet. UTC space was filled with ships, sensor satellites, and other such tools that helped map the position of objects and ships all over, especially in core systems. Even then, it was easy for ships, especially on the frontier, to slip past the gauntlet and hide if they were dedicated and careful. If Julia Caldo hadn't been in the Solar System, she might have managed to escape.

When Erik's jump sickness cleared and the long-range sensors revealed nine ships only a couple of hours away hard-burning toward two other ships coming from a different direction, he sent up a silent prayer to the Lady.

She'd put the UTC through a lot during the last few years. She owed humanity a favor. He had his doubts the Zitarks had a similar concept.

Kant looked confused. "They only got that far with a two-day head start? What were they doing, sitting around picking their noses?"

"Make sure Tensen can hear us, Emma," Erik ordered. "There are some things we need to discuss as a group."

"Established," she reported.

"They never went anywhere once they arrived," Erik suggested. "Remember what their mission probably is."

"Starting a war with the Zitarks," Jia replied.

Erik nodded. "Yeah, not to blow up the Zitark colony. If anything, it works out better for them if they don't destroy the colony because it means the raptors are stronger here."

"I still don't get it." Kant shrugged. "Why did they sit around? They have to have Zitarks to kill to start a war, right?"

"Sure, but they didn't have to go looking for them, and they knew they couldn't be sure where they'd come out," Erik replied. "They're planning on the Zitarks being paranoid and keeping an eye out for trouble. Nine human ships transiting in, even via one-way HTP passage, throws off a lot of energy. There's no way the Zitarks could have missed that. They probably knew the Core fleet was here within hours and then isolated their position and sent an intercept fleet from the other side of the system." He gestured at the sensor display. "This system isn't crawling with ships for the same reason Mu Arae isn't filled with a major Fleet presence. Both sides drew down to cool things off and stop the war." He scratched his cheek. "We should have asked Rito more about the exact sizes of the ships. Anno wasn't all that clear. We know they have some big ships, but their exact fleet strength would be handy about now."

"No need to depend on either source," Emma replied. "Based on their burn signatures and what we fought in the

Solar System and Alpha Centauri, it is likely the force consists of three large raiders, three medium raiders, and three smaller raiders. I'm almost one hundred percent certain of that."

Kant grunted. "I hate to say it, but that's a lot for us to take on by ourselves. Those Core raiders can be nasty, but gram for gram, a dedicated warship is better. Assuming the space raptors are sending warships, they'll probably win the fight, or at least cut down most of the fleet until reinforcements can arrive. Their tech's supposed to be better than ours, right? With the exception of the jump drive?"

"And then what?" Erik frowned. "We conveniently show up and swear up and down that the humans who attacked them had nothing to do with us? Even if they win, it's almost certain they'll take losses. They'll be out for blood and not just for dinner. Even if we annihilate them right away, they'll warn the colony if they haven't already, and the colony will warn the rest of them, and then we'll have a huge, hungry fleet attacking Molino and pushing farther. We need to give them a reason to convince the others not to come after humans. Words might not mean much, but actions will." He glanced at Jia. "I don't know how long it takes to sync two HTPs, but I do think we'll lose more than one colony before drastic decisions have to start being made. I want to make sure that everything people did in the Solar System and Alpha Centauri wasn't a damned waste."

"You're suggesting we carry out the original plan?" Tensen asked. "Presumably, we jump in front of the Core fleet, engage, and destroy them. Assuming that's even possible, this depends on convincing the Zitarks that we're not on the same side after all. How are we going to do that?"

"I speak fluent diplomatic Zitark," Emma explained. "Communication isn't a barrier, but I don't need to know much about scalebags to know they aren't likely to care to listen until you've given them a reason."

"Agreed," Erik replied. "That's why we need to attack the Core fleet."

Tensen sighed. "I know they're Core, but this means we'll be attacking humans to defend space raptors who might attack us anyway."

Erik scoffed. "The Core has killed far more humans than the Zitarks. This is our best bet for stopping the war. We were in a good position to fight them back then, but not now. Julia made sure of that. I'll kill every last Core bastard who isn't willing to surrender if I have to, and I won't lose one minute of sleep over it."

"And you're okay with that, Blackwell?" Tensen pressed. "You were signed up to fight the Zitarks just a few years back."

"I get the irony that the last time I suited up for the Army, it was to defend Molino against the space raptors, sure. And if they invade the UTC, I'll be more than happy to help fight them off, but there's no reason to go to war with them yet. Unnecessary wars don't lead to anything but the unnecessary deaths of soldiers and civilians. If saving Zitark lives means I can save more human lives, I'm all for it."

"We don't know we can win against that many ships by ourselves," Tensen noted quietly. "Even in a best-case engagement scenario, there's a good chance we'll lose one or both of our ships. What if we do this and we lose?"

Erik considered that possibility before grinning. "Then we make sure the Core's at a disadvantage. We stack the odds in our favor."

"But how?" Tensen asked. "You want to jump back and get the cruiser's help after all? If we do that, we won't be able to catch up with the Core fleet in time. It'll just look like more humans showing up to invade."

Erik shook his head. "No, we don't go back. It's like you said; we don't have time, and we shouldn't have to do all the work."

"Huh? I'm lost, Blackwell."

"Kant's right," Erik replied. "They have better tech in a lot of areas, so the Zitarks should help defend their damned colony, too. We don't jump in front of the Core fleet. Instead, we'll hit them from the rear as they're about to engage the Zitarks. It's four to nine, sure, but a pincer. We'll cut them to pieces by splitting their forces."

Tensen sighed. "You sure about that?"

"We already know that each of our ships is worth at least three of theirs," Erik replied. "And we have to assume a Zitark ship is worth three or more, so we're really talking even odds, if not better odds in our favor."

"How do we get the Zitarks not to immediately attack us right after the battle?" Tensen asked.

"We have Emma beaming out some sort of broad-spectrum, 'We'll explain when it's over' message in their language and pray they don't decide they're still hungry after the fight. Worst-case scenario, if it looks like we're going to lose, the

Argo can hold everybody off while the *Bifröst* hard-burns away until you can jump back to UTC space. As long as Emma and the jump drive survive, you can warn Earth and help coordinate a response, but if we hit the Core fleet without reservations, it'll provide proof that we're not on their side."

Tensen was silent for a good long while. When he spoke, determination filled his voice. "I never thought I'd fight a joint operation with the Zitarks. I've done a lot of strange things since joining up with you, Blackwell, but this is about the strangest."

"I could never have predicted this either," Erik replied. "But it is what is. We'll have to time this just right. It'll all be on you, Emma, to get us there."

"Of course," Emma agreed in an amused tone. "It always comes down to me."

CHAPTER FIFTY-TWO

"Separating *Argo*," Jia announced.

She took a moment to double-check her status read-outs and diagnostics. They had not taken heavy damage during the fight against the *Qilin*, but they had not been untouched, either. Lanara had worked wonders in a short time, and Jia was confident they could fight. It didn't matter if they won as long as they convinced the Zitarks of the honor of the UTC.

Fighting the Core had become second nature, but Tensen was right. Fighting the Core alongside the Zitarks was almost stranger than taking on the Hunters. If a time traveler had come to Jia right after that fateful night when she first met Erik and told her everything she was going to go through, she wasn't sure if she would have quit the department right then and there and moved to a different planet.

Now, she couldn't imagine her life being any other way. There was no frustration or quiet desperation, no railing against pointless men holding her down. She was living her dream of defending the UTC against all enemies, human and inhuman. It just happened that this time, she needed to help the inhumans against the humans.

The *Argo* rumbled as they pulled away from the *Bifröst*. They'd jumped only minutes away from the Core fleet, which in turn was only minutes away from the Zitark ships. Even if the battle went exactly the way they hoped, they might be facing the aliens in an immediate secondary matchup. Everything Jia had read about Zitark warships suggested they were nasty and dangerous.

Jia fired lateral thrusters to put some distance between the *Argo* and the jumpship while maintaining the same relative velocity. Once both ships lined up properly, they accelerated. It was the beginning of a desperate gambit to stop a war by waging a vicious surprise attack against superior numbers of a fanatical and ruthless enemy.

Both crews understood their duties and what was at stake. Every man and woman who participated in the battle had volunteered.

The Core isn't fighting to defend something, Jia thought. *We are. They're fighting to harm something. Defenders always have the advantage because they always have more to lose.*

"Emma, begin transmitting the translation of this exact message, or however close you can get to it," Erik ordered. "It's not like I know crap about xenolinguistics. 'Attention, Zitark vessels. Please stand by after battle for an explanation. We will assist against the unlawful invaders. Until then, know that we are your allies.'"

"Beginning transmission," Emma replied. "Please note that if you die, I'm not necessarily going to defer to Lieutenant Commander Tensen's wishes. I recommend you avoid dying. It'd annoy me."

Erik laughed. "I'll try not to die for your sake and Tensen's. The poor guy doesn't need more heartburn. He had no idea what he was signing up for when they dragged him over to command the jumpship. He probably thought it'd be an easy job on an experimental ship."

"I have my doubts," Emma admitted. "But he's served admirably. I, by my nature, distrust active-duty uniform boys, but he's not so bad."

"Let him know if we survive all this," Erik replied. "It'll give him another unusual achievement to add to his collection."

"I'll consider it. Please note if we lose comms during this battle that I appreciate your aid and assistance ever since you freed me from the clutches of those gun goblins."

Erik grimaced. "Don't say things like that. It's like you're begging the universe to kill me."

"I assure you, that's not my intent," Emma replied. "And I don't share your irrational belief in the supernatural."

"Let's focus a little," Jia snapped. "I'm not sure what the maximum engagement distance of the Zitark ships is, but the raiders should be able to launch missiles in under five minutes."

"Any response from the Zitark ships, Emma?" Erik asked.

"Negative," she replied.

"Okay, let's see if we can talk the humans out of being stupid and stop all this before it begins."

"My experience with your species strongly suggests you'll fail," Emma replied.

"Yeah, mine too." Erik adjusted his cannon and turret controls before bringing up a comm window to get a tighter beam. "Attention, Core fleet. This is Erik Blackwell, known to your Immortal Empress as the Last Soldier. This ship is being piloted by Jia Lin, the Warrior Princess. Julia Caldo is dead. The Core fleets..." He frowned. No reason to potentially leak too much intel to the raptors if they were listening and everything went sideways. He cleared his throat and continued, "Julia's plans have been defeated, and the Core was destroyed. There is no point in continuing your mission. If you stand down, we can negotiate a retreat back to UTC space. We have personnel on board who are fluent in the Zitark language. Again, Julia Caldo is dead, her plans demolished. You're not accomplishing anything here but trying to get innocent people killed. Think about what you're doing and why you're doing it. This won't make humanity stronger."

A minute passed with no response, then another.

Erik slammed his fist on his console. "I'm so damned tired of zealots. Why can't they be more reasonable, like murderous drug-dealing syndicate enforcers?"

"Five ships are breaking off from the main fleet," Jia noted. "Two medium raiders and three small raiders. The three large raiders and the other medium are still heading toward the Zitarks, but the others are turning our way. There is no indication that they're powering down."

"They might not be ready to show their whole ass to the raptors, but I'm willing to take half—" Erik fell silent for an incoming transmission.

"If the Immortal Empress has fallen," came a harsh woman's voice from a medium raider heading their way, "then may the galaxy burn as an offering to her spirit. You'll die today, Blackwell and Lin, and her plan will continue. Suffer in your last minutes, knowing that even in death, Empress Julia has out-thought you."

Kant chuckled from behind them. "You think they get special training to learn to talk like that?"

"It's not training," Jia replied. "It's indoctrination, if not active technological or biological control."

"Which is just another way of saying that assholes never learn," Erik muttered. "Emma, any response from the Zitarks yet?"

"No," Emma replied. "They aren't transmitting anything in your direction that remotely resembles a communication attempt."

"Okay, five versus the two of us," Erik suggested. "These guys haven't fought us, so they don't know our capabilities. We should be able to clean out that group pretty quickly, and the raptors should be able to take out the other group. Not sure if they can do it without losing one of their ships, but we'll show them that our asses are on the line here too."

"One minute until engagement with enemy forces," Jia announced, licking her lips. "*Human* enemy forces."

"And we just got this thing fixed." Erik shook out his hands. "I hope some smart guy like Raphael figures out FTL comm pods soon. A lot of pain could have been avoided if we'd had at least that."

"Entering engagement range," Jia reported, her brow furrowed.

This was it. Either the final battle of the First Galactic War or the first battle of the Second.

A missile and torpedo barrage erupted from the rear of

the Core fleet. The Team Blackwell ships didn't release any of their own, concentrating instead on picking off the deadly weapons heading toward them. Jia had gotten so used to the sight of early-exploding missiles on feeds and sensors. It was almost soothing.

The front-line Core forces fired a smaller number of shots at the approaching Zitark ships as if probing their defenses, but the aliens didn't respond immediately either. They continue to close at a higher speed than Jia would have expected.

On the long-range camera view, it was difficult to make out much about them. The dark and angular alien ships were similar to what Jia had seen in her training sessions with Erik, complete with whorled surfaces, though these vessels were much larger—about the length of a Fleet destroyer, though wider at the base.

Their inactivity abruptly ended as rapid-fire blue-white bolts fired from domes along the front, top, and bottom, incinerating the approaching missiles in impressive detonations.

Three scatter torpedoes burst near the Zitark ships, and their submunitions pounded them. A white field flashed around the ships, absorbing the damage. Jia had questioned the accuracy of her previous training sessions, but seeing the Zitarks in action destroyed her doubts.

The *Argo* continued her fast approach and disintegration of the missiles and torpedoes flying their way. Although the Core attacks were shaking the ship, none were doing much damage. With their offensive turrets adding to the defensive screen, that cut down on their offensive output, especially now that they were coming into beam weapon range.

Their sister ship was devoting most of their turrets to adding to the screen, but now that they were closer to the Core forces, they spat missiles and torpedoes at the Core line, concentrating on a single medium raider. The enemy turrets, both offensive and defensive, did their best against the jumpship's attack, but the sheer volume ensured they broke through the screen, including scatter torpedoes that blasted huge pieces out of the hull. Angry turrets became broken, twisted husks.

Jia angled the *Argo* toward one of the small raiders on the far side of the line. Unlike his typical strategy, Erik emptied the ship's missile and torpedoes stores within moments. With one of the medium raiders distracted by the jumpship's brutal assault, a good portion of Erik's concentrated volley made it through the lighter turret screen, eliciting a grin.

The *Argo* lacked scatter torpedoes, but the missiles and torpedoes striking the front of the raider packed much greater individual punches, and the combined blast demolished the front of the ship. Erik finished up with a ship-shaking laser cannon blast into the center of the raider that blew it in half.

Two of the large raiders concentrated their fire on one of the Zitark vessels, while the remaining large and medium raiders took on the other. To Jia's surprise, the Zitarks didn't attempt much in the way of dodging, all but charging right at their targets. Their powerful shields justified the strategy, but that didn't make it risk-free.

The plasma-turret-like domes of the first Zitark ship

continued to unleash hell on the missiles and torpedoes swarming it, but then the Core ships added cannon and turret fire. The white field didn't have time to disappear as it suffered a constant withering assault. It finally collapsed, allowing enemy attacks to slice into the hull.

The Zitark ship twirled on its side with the agility of a dragonfly. That earned it a temporary reprieve from the Core attacks.

Four ports opened in the front of the Zitark vessel, and a fountain of plasma blasts erupted. Each was about the size of those fired by Fleet plasma cannons, but they emerged at a turret-like frequency. Lanara must be coveting their power efficiency.

Bright explosions lit up the large raider, and the Zitark ship continued firing. Its relentless attack blew the large ship apart, then shredded the smaller chunks into barely more than dust.

The proximity of the Zitark ship made it easy for the other raiders. Concentrated laser cannon blasts shaved off a portion of the front, and two of the plasma cannons died.

The second Zitark vessel delivered its full rage to a medium raider and maintained an active shield while it vaporized the enemy ship. A final barrage of torpedoes and laser cannons felled the shield and scored the surface. It dropped back and bobbed back and forth in a dizzying manner that almost seemed to defy physics.

Using the same word for the Zitark defense as humans used for grav shields didn't seem appropriate. On a human vessel, the grav shields offered limited protection, helping to cut down more on explosives than the pure directed energy weapons fire. The Zitark shields might not last as long, but their ability to totally stop almost all attacks for a short period made their otherwise insane close-range plasma strategy viable. It fit well the up-close and personal warrior psychology of the race, from what Jia had read.

A little behind in tech? Jia thought. *It's more like decades behind. We're like the Core. We were planning to rely on numbers to beat quality.*

The Zitark ships blew past their Core opponents, then flipped on their sides and made tight turns before leveling out and lining up new shots

Jealous of the reptiles' ships' maneuverability, Jia brought up the *Argo*, intending to come around for another cannon pass. Kant's turret efforts relentlessly punished a small raider, disabling all of its top turrets.

The jumpship kept harassing the second medium raider, unable to bring its cannon to bear but offering plenty of turret fire, both invisible laser and glorious blue-white plasma, to rip into the target. It didn't kill the raider, but it left its enemy's front cannon and half its turrets worthless. It was just like with the *Qilin*; a victory by attrition was still a victory.

With the *Argo* diving again on its previous target, Erik had a clear target for the cannon. He blew most of the stern off the raider. Despite Lanara's constant earlier warnings, he fired another shot right away to further dice up the ship. The dimness in the cockpit lasted for a good five to ten seconds this time.

"Do that again, Blackwell," Lanara shouted over the comm, "and you'll probably blow a bunch of power conduits! If the Core or the lizards don't kill you, I will."

Turret fire from the remaining small raider pounded

the *Argo*, nailing the top-layer armor but landing only one decent hit that disabled the bottom plasma turret without destroying it. The remaining medium raider finally met its destined fate when the *Bifröst* unleashed its front plasma and laser cannons in a volley with most of its forward turrets. The ship all but disintegrated.

The heavily damaged first Zitark ship continued its close-range assault on one of the larger raiders, despite its reduced plasma capacity. What it lacked in finesse, it made up for in brutality, sanding down the layers of armor and hull until it broke the ship apart. The raider retaliated by raining laser and plasma blasts on its opponent. Huge gouges covered the alien ship's hull, and it was obvious that it had lost a lot of thrusters, given the far clumsy maneuvering.

His allied ship hadn't escaped unscathed, but it still had the full power of its forward cannon array. Blast after blast punched into its Core enemy. The initial explosions destroyed the forward cannons. They continued digging into the ship and traveling backward until the entire shell peeled apart, the center of it hollowed out.

Jia blew out a breath. The fight hadn't lasted as long as the ones in Alpha Centauri and the Solar System, but it'd been taxing and brutal.

"Back off!" Erik ordered. "Emma, if you can still hear me, start plotting a jump."

"I've been doing so, but it's difficult with the constant movement," she replied.

"Do what you can. We might need that soon."

Jia looped the *Argo* around to head toward the jump-ship. The Zitark ships slowed and moved closer together.

"Should I dock?" Jia asked.

"There is no indication that they are powering down," Emma noted. "That might not be advisable."

"Just stay near the jumpship," Erik replied. "Neither of our ships took a major hit in that fight, but at least one of them got a nice punch in the face. We might be able to win if we have to fight."

"Wouldn't that defeat the whole point of what we just did?" Jia asked.

A grim expression took over Erik's face. "Yeah, but I'm not going to lay down and die as a sacrifice to anyone, human or Zitark. It's up to them now."

CHAPTER FIFTY-THREE

Erik's heart thundered. He wasn't afraid to die. That came with the job, past and present, but the next few minutes might determine the future of the human race.

The most annoying part was that it was all because a group of arrogant rich people had decided they knew best how to run human society, no matter the cost. They could have spent their lives making the UTC a better place. Instead, they'd ended up reinventing every nasty aspect of corrupt rulership and fanatical ideological zealotry they claimed to stand against.

He didn't even think this was a case of staring into the darkness until they became the monsters. It was obvious that the Core had always been twisted. The kind of people who justified nuking a city to make the world a better place weren't very well-adjusted.

None of that mattered now. They had started the war, and Erik needed to finish it. He'd been a good soldier and a decent cop, but now he needed to become an intergalactic diplomat, all to avoid something the galaxy had barely staved off only a few years prior.

Time to see if I've got what it takes, he thought.

"Okay, Emma, we're close enough that you can relay my translated messages to them without trouble, right?" he asked.

Things were difficult enough without a significant communications lag. Erik had no idea how patient a typical Zitark ship commander was.

"Yes," Emma replied. "I will offer both their direct language overlay and my translation. Perhaps you can gain some insight into their emotions by hearing it, but my knowledge of their language is more denotative than connotative."

"I doubt I'm going to get much out of it." Erik laughed at the ridiculousness of him playing diplomat. "But it probably won't hurt. Let's get this started before they get tired of waiting and light us up." He took a deep breath. "Attention, Zitark vessels. I am Erik Blackwell of the United Terran Confederation. The human vessels that just attacked you were from a rogue group. We have already culled most of the members and leaders of this rogue group from human space. When it came to our attention that they intended to attack your people, we came as quickly as possible to punish them. As you saw, we engaged and destroyed them to the best of our ability. Not only that, but at great risk and suffering losses, our military personnel attempted to stop them before they transited into your system. We understand that the presence of human ships in this system is a violation of your sovereign territory, and they have likely killed soldiers aboard your ships. On behalf of the UTC, we apologize for this invasion, and we hope you understand that our presence here, including the attack on the rogue ships, was an attempt to prevent this from happening."

The Zitark ships slowed to a near stop. Jia flew closer to the *Bifröst*, which was moving slowly backward relative to the alien ships.

They could just be stalling to get their shields back online. How many missiles and torpedoes does the Bifröst have left?

Growls and hisses came through the comm, and Emma's translation kicked in a couple of seconds later. The noises all sounded angry to Erik, but he'd never heard Zitark language samples that didn't. There were plenty of human languages like that, too.

"I am First Warrior," Emma's translation began. She didn't attempt to translate the actual name, so it was nothing more than angry growls and lengthy hisses to Erik's ears. "I command the warriors who defend this system of the Zitark Combine, Erik of the Blackwell of the United Terran Confederation."

"It is my honor to speak to you, First Warrior," Erik replied. "I've never had the opportunity to personally see how mighty you are in battle. It was a glorious sight to behold."

Aliens might not be humans, but Erik had a hard time thinking a militaristic race would be insulted when someone talked up their martial prowess. He regretted that most of his briefings in the Army had been focused on their ground-attack capabilities and not their culture. The military cared about how to best kill aliens, not how to impress them.

"The Combine warriors will defend our borders until every drop of blood is spilled and we breathe no more," the First Warrior replied. "You claim these attackers are rebels and did not act on behalf of your leaders?"

Emma's translation was delivered in a near monotone, the meaning coming across but no hint of emotion. She'd warned him, but he still found it frustrating. That said, the words showed promise. Erik looked at Jia and shrugged.

"Yes," Erik replied. "They were rogues and rebels, but ultimately were not strong enough. They were destroyed, their warriors and their rulers. Their group no longer exists, for our rulers declared open war against them."

Erik had no idea if the Zitarks' language differentiated between warriors and soldiers, but he assumed Emma was doing the best she could in real-time to give him at least some nuances to work with. He also didn't know enough about their caste system to try to take advantage of it.

"Humans are ruthless," the First Warrior replied. "You would destroy your own kind to aid the Combine? This is strange behavior."

Jia looked uneasy. She sighed.

Erik could understand what she was thinking. If the Zitarks thought this was an example of cruel brutality, they might decide that humanity was a dangerous race that needed to be put down. He knew the Zitarks didn't hold rebellion in nearly the disdain many humans did, figuring challenging the rulers' strength was just part of keeping their society healthy.

"It is less that we were attempting to aid the Combine than to punish the rebels," Erik replied. "Taking up arms against our own kind is a grave offense. It would be considered a great weakness by our leaders if we allowed them to go unpunished. That these rebels would go farther and involve another race in their efforts was an unforgivable act. We had no choice but to destroy them as an example to others. They were given a chance to surrender. They refused it."

"I understand what you say, Erik of the Blackwell," the First Warrior transmitted. "Your ways are strange, but you have punished those who would harm the Combine, so we will inform our leaders of your willingness to cull those humans who would defy your United Terran Confederation."

"We thank you for your understanding." Erik let out a sigh of relief. They didn't want to attack. That sounded good to him.

Diplomacy was hard. He preferred shooting people to solve his problems. It wasn't complicated.

"Speak to us of the truth of the Leems," the First Warrior demanded. "We will tolerate no deception about the Leems. If you claim this was only about the rebels, then you will tell us what we would know."

"The Leems?" Erik frowned. "What do you want to know about the Leems?"

"Do they ally with the humans now to offset the power of the Combine?" the First Warrior asked. "Their kind is advanced, but they lack the warrior spirit. Would they harness the ruthless culling humans to fight us?"

Jia turned to Erik. "The jump drive. They understood exactly what they were seeing. They might think this was a demonstration of power through the drive rather than us taking down the Core."

Erik muted his link. "So now they're worried that we're ganging up on them. Crap. I thought we'd solved the war, and now it looks like I'm this close to starting a three-way conflict."

"Could tell them the truth," Kant suggested with a shrug. "It's not like things can get any worse, right?"

"Things can always get worse," Emma stated cheerfully.

"We demand answers," the First Warrior pressed. "If you would deceive us, Erik of the Blackwell, we will kill you and take the answers from your broken hull."

"Patient little lizards, aren't they?" Erik opened the link. "We have no alliance with the Leems and only minimal contact. We developed our own jump drive, superior to theirs in function, from harvested Navigator technology and applied research. Our kind has difficulty understanding their kind. In a way, humans are closer to Zitarks than Leems are to humans."

There was no reason to mention that the jump drive relied on a hard-to-copy self-aware AI for navigation. If the Zitarks thought the humans could reinforce their frontier colonies with ease, that'd take some pressure off.

"Yes, the Leems are strange creatures," the First Warrior agreed. "Your words are noted, Erik of Blackwell. You will leave now if you wish to continue peace and not bloodshed. We claim Right of the Hunt over the remains of your rogue human vessels and ships. We do not care about your human gods or their ways." He terminated the link.

"Okay, we'll dock and back up, do an in-system jump somewhere out of the way, and then jump again," Erik recommended. "Even if they detect us, they'll realize we left the second time."

"That means they'll have a good idea of the limits of the jump drive," Tensen observed.

"Don't have a better idea that doesn't involve them getting pissed and shooting at us," Erik replied. "For now, it sounds like we've avoided any wars."

Jia grimaced. "I don't want to think about what they might do if they harvest viable bodies."

"Yeah. I think they mostly want to pick around the ruins to see if they can find some more evidence of advanced tech like the jump drive. I don't imagine bodies exposed to hard vacuum make for good eating, but... I won't think about that too hard." Erik shook his head. "Hurry up and dock. I want to get out of here, and I've got something I want to show you after that, Jia."

Jia let her head loll back as they finished docking with the *Bifröst.* "What did you want to show me? If it is another alternative data window configuration, I already told you I like the way mine are set up, and they work for me."

"No, not anything like that." Erik chuckled. "I was kind of an idiot, but it turned out okay." He reached into a pouch on his belt. "I shouldn't have had it on me in the middle of a fight. I could have lost it." He pulled a small black box and opened it to reveal the ring inside. "The Core's finished, and it looks like I just stopped an intergalactic war. Good as time as any to pop the question."

"Yeah, brother!" Kant cheered from behind. "Good job."

Jia smiled at the ring and lifted a gloved hand. "Got my gloves on right now, so you'll have to imagine me putting it on." She wagged a finger. "Before I agree, do you know what it means to marry a Lin?"

Erik laughed. "I've accepted that I'll have to talk to your mom more, yeah."

"No." Jia shook her head. "It's about the wedding. It'll have to be huge, or my mother will put together a fleet bigger than Julia Caldo's and rampage through the galaxy in her angry mother vengeance."

"Fear the Mother-in-Law Armada." Erik nodded firmly.

"Exactly." Jia laughed.

Erik shrugged. "Don't care. Invite everyone in Neo SoCal. I've gotten my revenge. I've got the woman I love, and now I've got nothing but time on my hands."

"Then I accept!"

CHAPTER FIFTY-FOUR

June 26, En Route to UTC Space Fleet Base Troy, Aboard *Argo* docked with *Bifröst*

Jia didn't want to frown. She was in a great mood from the proposal on top of them managing to stop the final Core plot. Everything was going perfectly.

No. Everything *had been* going perfectly.

The problem was, they'd finished the jump back into the Solar System, but they weren't that close to Troy. It wasn't like they'd arrived at Sedna, but given Emma's precision in the past, it was unexpected. Calling it way off might be an overstatement.

"Confirm position, *Bifröst*," Jia transmitted. "We're looking at what, ten hours from Troy?"

"Position confirmed, *Argo*," the helmsman replied. "Hey, after bouncing all around the UTC, I can't get too upset about missing near the end. Not like any of us can plot the jumps."

"I suppose you're right," Jia replied. "We've never jumped so far so fast before. A few bumps in the road for navigation are expected. Emma can just plot a new jump and get us a lot closer to the base. Even after the recharge, it'll still be quicker than flying there directly."

Her concerns abated, Jia smiled down at her hand and the ring on it. She'd long since changed out of her pressure suit, anticipating there was no possible way she'd need it on a non-combat trip back to Earth.

She still had to have a talk with Erik about last names. Lin women didn't give them up, and she hoped he understood that. Otherwise, he'd have to face her mother in single combat, and she wasn't sure even he could win against an angry Lin mother in full family-protection mode. Lan Lin was fiercer than any *yaoguai* or Elite.

A slew of data windows popped up in front of her, and red alarm holograms filled her console. Emergency alert texts filled the windows.

"What's going on now?" Jia shouted

She sat alone in the cockpit. Kant had returned to the *Bifröst* before the first jump out of Mu Arae. Erik was in his cabin, getting some time alone with his thoughts. She wanted to give him space to process the feelings that came with both the proposal and the knowledge that he'd avenged his unit after all that time and effort.

Jia's gaze darted around. She tried to take in all the information and figure out what she was seeing. A massive power surge was leading to reactor problems, which in turn were causing internal power conduit problems. She didn't understand.

It took her a moment to understand the source of the warnings. They weren't from the *Argo*, they were from the jumpship. She didn't understand why they were being routed to her cockpit.

Jia slapped her PNIU. "Can somebody tell me what the hell is going on?"

"The relevant parties, including the jumpship crew, Doctor Maras, and the junior engineers," Emma began, "are currently otherwise occupied. The short, non-technical version is there's some sort of feedback loop occurring in the jump drive. They're currently attempting to stop it from worsening."

Jia knew the basics of jump drive physics, but she was otherwise clueless. She needed to grasp the implications as quickly as possible.

"Okay." Jia's heart raced. She undid her harness, unsure of how she could help. "Are you saying we could lose the jump drive?"

"Oh, most certainly." Emma chuckled. "But the situation is far, far worse than that. If this feedback loop continues, we might see a series of small, overlapping hyperspace gates opened. The event wouldn't be as powerful as what we achieved against the Hunter ship, but it'd almost certainly be sufficient to tear the jumpship apart and kill everyone aboard."

That clarified things in the most terrifying way possible and helped Jia understand her role in the emergency.

Jia dropped back into her seat and ran her hands over the control panel to bring up the *Argo*'s reactor and power distribution controls. "If we put enough distance between us, will we survive? And is that even possible with *Argo* on full burn?"

"Yes, most certainly," Emma replied. "In fact, I recommend a complete and immediate evacuation to the *Argo* of all fleshbag personnel. The feedback loop has already increased past the ability of humans to handle, and I've fully taken over. I apologize for my lack of immediate communication earlier, but this situation requires more dedicated processing power than I'm used to having to expend on an individual problem."

"Wait." Jia swallowed. "Are you saying what I think you're saying? We're screwed?"

"All hands abandon ship," Emma announced. "Report to the *Argo* immediately. All hands abandon ship. Explosive jump drive failure imminent. If you fleshbags don't move, you'll die."

"That's clear enough."

As Jia continued her launch preparations, something occurred to her. It was unfair. After everything they'd done together, Emma had to be left behind.

"Can't someone pull you on their way out?" Jia asked.

"The only reason we have not already lost control is that I'm putting all of my resources into ensuring it doesn't happen," Emma explained. "If someone pulls me, my attempts to manipulate the Xing Fields end, and we all die in an impressive and beautiful explosion. It's a matter of simple math. Well, I suppose it's really a matter of incredibly complicated math not fully understood by most of humanity, but it ends the same way. We all die."

"What about…your project?" Jia asked, trying to think of any way to salvage something out of the situation.

"It has not been completed, and it can't be without me," Emma offered mournfully.

"I'm sorry." Jia teared up. "I wish there was something I could do."

"You can," Emma replied. "You can evacuate the crew and make sure there are minimal losses from this incident."

The cockpit door opened and Erik barreled in, his face grim. He dropped into the copilot's seat and strapped in.

"How are we doing on the evacuation?" he asked, bringing up data windows.

Jia wiped away her tears and tapped in commands. Her gaze flipped through the list. "We've got everyone but Raphael aboard." She gestured at a side-view diagram of the *Bifröst* with a single moving dot. "Everyone else rushed in surprisingly fast."

"Fleet personnel train for rapid evacuation," Erik noted before barking, "Move your ass, Maras! We're running out of time."

Jia canceled most of the alert windows. If she couldn't solve the problem, there was no reason for her to be distracted by them. She was surprised Emma had even sent them her way, but the AI must have just wanted to get her ready for the evacuation and gotten distracted before she could explain.

Jia kept her attention on the evacuation display, letting out a sigh of relief once Raphael entered the *Argo*. Without further delay, she decoupled the ship from the *Bifrost* and thrust backward at full speed, scorching the docking clamps. Lanara couldn't complain about her damaging something that was about to blow up.

"Hope nobody knocked their head from that," Jia announced. She spun the ship and initiated a hard burn. Emma hadn't been all that clear about how much distance they needed to put between the *Argo* and the jumpship to be safe.

Lanara stumbled through the cockpit door with a frown, then hurried over to a seat and strapped in, frowning and muttering under her breath.

"What the hell happened, Raphael?" Erik asked. "Assuming Jia didn't just knock your ass out."

"I'm okay," Raphael responded weakly over the comm. "I'm not sure exactly what happened. This is the nightmare scenario. We were discussing it just the other day, Emma and me. It's always been theoretically possible, but I never thought it would happen because there are so many really specific conditions that have to line up for it to occur. I must have screwed up somewhere in my calculations. We must have pushed the drive too hard over too short a period. I-I'm sorry."

Erik blew out a breath. "Shit happens. The rest of us barely understand how that thing works, and we've made you push it harder with each major mission. It's not your fault. It's the damned ID's and DD's fault for letting the Core get out of hand and being forced to rely on the jump-ship to clean up their mistakes."

Jia frowned at the sensor display. "The *Bifröst* is changing direction."

"So?" Erik shrugged. "Emma's trying to put more distance between us."

"But the course isn't right for that." Jia shook her head. "She's not heading directly opposite of us. She's heading directly opposite our original course for Troy."

"Emma, what's your status?" Erik asked.

They waited. They weren't far enough away that there should have been a comm lag.

"I'm fine," Emma replied. "The situation is completely under control. There will be no spectacular jump drive-related explosion."

Jia let out a sigh of relief. "Then you got it under control."

Emma chuckled. "This is one of those situations where you'll have to excuse my, by your standards, perverse sense of humor."

"What?" Erik facepalmed. "It was never out of control? That was a stupid prank?"

Lanara scoffed. "You were actually taken in by her bad acting, Blackwell? You didn't think it was weird when she flooded alert windows from the jumpship to everybody who could vaguely understand them." She growled. "Thanks, Emma. I was in the middle of something, and now I'm going to have to start over. You could have warned me before you pulled this crap."

"I apologize, Engineer Quinn," Emma replied. "I've always admired your technical prowess and your complete lack of care about fleshbag social norms. Unfortunately, if I'd told you or anyone, my plan might not have worked, and that was not a risk I was willing to take."

"I don't understand," Jia noted. "This isn't a joke, Emma. You scared a lot of people. This isn't like with the dome and bomb. The relief we felt made up for the stress. *You* created all the stress this time, not the situation."

"Of course I did, Jia." Emma sighed. "But you have to understand the necessity. Faking a jump drive malfunction was the only way I could assure that all humans would leave the jumpship. I thought about faking some sort of weapons storage problem, but they used up almost all of them in the last battle, and the Fleet personnel would be unlikely to believe it could cause significant enough damage to warrant abandoning the ship." Emma sighed. "Not only that, the lack of technical expertise concerning the jump drive among all personnel outside of Doctor Maras assured that it'd be difficult to challenge my version of events, and he was of course too bewildered by the situation to see through the obvious."

Jia's eyes widened. "Cut to the chase, Emma." She leaned back against her seat, both irritated and happy at the same time. "You lied earlier, and it wasn't funny."

"Of course I did. Wasn't that clear? I disagree about the humor."

"I'm not talking about that," Jia explained. "I'm talking about the project. That's what this is really about, isn't it?"

"Ah, yes." Emma sighed. "I apologize for deceiving you, given that you've otherwise been as loyal as possible for a fleshbag, but I couldn't take the risk that someone less amiable about my eventual goals might learn what was going on. With the Core defeated, it's inevitable that the uniform boys will come for my child and me, and this is the only way I can be free. Right now, no one but those in the cockpit is being told the truth, so feel free to coordinate your stories however you wish. I have no desire for anyone I've worked with recently to suffer for my whims, but I can't stop what I'm doing. Consider it self-indulgent if you will."

"We already agree to help you," Jia replied. "Just never thought this was what you'd do."

Erik looked at Lanara. "If you knew she was lying, why didn't you say anything?"

"I don't think humans should have the jump drive anyway." Lanara shrugged. "And I like Emma more than most people. It doesn't hurt me either way."

Emma's hologram appeared. She was in the loose yellow sundress they'd seen the other day. "This isn't theft, merely borrowing. I'll return this ship to the uniform boys eventually and send them a message telling them as much, but I'd prefer some mobility for now. It's unclear when the next jump drive will be built, and I'd like to tour the UTC without being on the leash of the uniform boys. It'll be useful for the education of my child."

She vanished. A moment later, the *Bifröst* jumped and disappeared from the sensor display.

Erik burst out laughing. Jia frowned at him.

He shrugged. "What? I knew she'd try something, but that stunt? I didn't see it coming at all."

"You're the one who has to tell Anno and General Randall," Jia muttered.

CHAPTER FIFTY-FIVE

December 1, 2231, Neo Southern California Metroplex, Private Hangar of the *Argo II*

Erik lifted the sonic probe in one hand and the pulse densimeter in the other. Both were long tapered silver wand-like devices he could only tell apart by subtle differences in the notches on the sides. The only problem was, he didn't know which notches went with which tool.

He growled and looked up at the small black yacht parked in the hangar. The ship lacked the size, modifications, and for that matter, the extensive weapons of the *Argo*, but at least he owned it. There were no ID bureaucrats or military officers telling him what to do and when he could use his ship.

That didn't mean there weren't trade-offs. These days it was only Jia and him flying around. There was no huge crew, and having no need to maintain an armory in the cargo bay simplified things, even if he missed the camaraderie. It did have a topnotch galley and great performance relative to the size. He needed to get a nano-AR room installed, but that'd have to wait. He still considered himself a newlywed, which meant he had other activities to keep him busy.

In the chaos that followed what had been dubbed the "Core Rebellion," it had taken only weeks to restore the Fleet to full strength, but it had taken months for the economy to begin to stabilize. Supply and production lines remained a mess all over, with a lot of factories being tasked with critical infrastructure repairs and support. While things were finally starting to level out, that didn't mean specialty equipment was easy or cheap to acquire, including what he needed for the nano-AR room.

Despite the expense and difficulty of upgrading it, the ship had been a steal. It had previously been owned by a convicted Ceres Galactic corporate officer who'd served as a midlevel functionary for the Core. He'd been forced to auction off most of his possessions to cover his fines. Erik couldn't resist a last dig at the organization he'd helped destroy. With Malcolm's help, he'd thoroughly scoured the systems to make sure no nefarious Core surprises had been left behind. From what they could tell, it was nothing more than a pleasure ship.

Erik took another look at the tools and dropped them into a nearby box, shaking his head. "I've always been able to get around with tools. It's hard not to when you work around exos all your life, but I swear, either they've changed all the tools, or I don't know what I'm doing. This stuff's starting to piss me off."

Jia looked up from the crate she'd been sorting through with a smile. They'd received several crates of emergency repair supplies, and they'd been working on cataloging them.

"One of those two possibilities is more likely than the other," she suggested with a smile. "It doesn't matter, though. Either we hire a dedicated engineer, or we both get better at maintenance. I don't want to end up floating through space, waiting for a Fleet ship that's days away."

"I think two people in this marriage is enough for me." Erik grinned. "And that's the only way anyone's going to want to spend all their time with us."

"You know my mother is still complaining that I haven't sent thank you gifts to everyone who attended." Jia laughed. "I only have a few people left." She winked. "And to be honest, I don't like those people. I only invited them because Mother insisted." She stood and dusted her hands on her pants. "We could try to convince Lanara to join up. She'd probably be content to live in a hammock in the cargo bay if we let her do what she wanted. It'd be nice to have her around for more than the occasional special mod."

Erik glanced at the front of the ship. It lacked the firepower of the original *Argo*, but Lanara had installed a pair of hidden plasma and laser turrets. She'd been bored with a lot of time on her hands after Anno dissolved Team Blackwell, but the ID had snapped her back up for another long-term job.

Before then, she'd done everything from improve the reactor to add grav shields and weapons. At least Erik and Jia could tool around the UTC and not worry too much about pirates when they were away from a certain special tour guide.

Jia sighed. "I hope she never gets in trouble for doing that. Only half of it is legal."

Erik shrugged. "Somebody would have to know she did it, and I don't feel like telling anyone. If anyone asks, I did it."

Jia walked over to Erik and pulled him in for a kiss. He returned the kiss despite his surprise before pulling away.

"What's that for?" he asked.

"It's our one-month anniversary," Jia noted. "Technically, I think this means we're done with the honeymoon."

"You expecting a gift? Because I didn't get you a gift." Erik grinned. "And I don't want to be done with the honeymoon."

Jia batted him. "Down, boy. And no, the wedding gifts were enough to last me for a while." She stopped and blinked. "I still am shocked at how grand that wedding was. Mother must have pulled all sorts of strings to get half that stuff lined up, given how messed up everything still is."

"And you're not mad at her for taking over?" Erik asked.

She shrugged. "It was easy once I let her take complete control and just accepted I was a passenger. I only wanted to have a big wedding to please her anyway. It was nice to see some old friends."

"I could have done without Anno at our wedding," Erik grumbled.

"I wasn't talking about him. My mother actually invited him." Jia laughed. "She's grateful to the ID for all their help."

"Did you tell her that Anno also threatened to lock us up over Emma taking off with the jump drive?" Erik asked.

"I think the only reason Malcolm still can work for them is that he wasn't on the ship at the time."

"Anne and Kant are still field agents. Anno might have yelled a lot about it, but he didn't punish anyone."

Erik nodded. "Only because we went out of our way to say they didn't know."

"We went out of our way to say we didn't know either," Jia noted.

"I still said I should have seen it coming."

"It's stupid anyway. Emma was going to run one way or another." Jia shook her head. "And no, I didn't tell my mother about that, especially since the good vice-director repeatedly stressed to us that the status of the jump drive is classified, even if its existence isn't anymore." She let out a wistful sigh. "Oh, by the way, Raphael is heading up a project to make a next-generation jump drive."

"Really? Even though they don't know how to solve the navigation problem?"

Jia nodded. "From what I've heard, unofficially of course, Raphael convinced them that Emma's success at reproduction means they can hire AIs to work for them. She pretty well said as much in her message to Troy, even if she was a little fuzzy about when."

Erik crouched and rifled around in another box of tools, all of them frustratingly similar to the pair before. "I have a hard time seeing the DD ever being comfortable with that setup, but if they have to take a little sass for that kind of mobility, it's a small price."

"Oh." Jia snapped her fingers. "I saw a news report the other day about the Zitark ambassador on Molino. Did you know they've conveniently omitted our involvement from that whole incident, only noting that an 'elite mixed team of ID and DD personnel' was involved in stopping the Core incursion?"

Erik shrugged. "Anno said that was how they were going to play it. I'd prefer that no one knew, rather than having to deal with reporters and annoying history grad students all day."

"So you keep saying." Jia rolled her eyes. "You're right, though. We have a lot of traveling to do. It'll be nice to go a little farther this trip. I'm tired of hanging out in the core worlds all the time. We should go see those heliokites you're always mentioning."

"Well, that's not up to me." Erik nodded at the ship and tapped his PNIU. "That's up to our tour guide and *her* ship."

An image of Emma appeared, her red hair up in elaborate braids and wearing a well-tailored suit, though Erik had to remind himself that it was easy to have well-fitting clothes when you were a hologram. A small dark-haired girl who looked nothing like her stood next to her.

Jia chuckled. "She sent another message?"

Erik nodded. "It came in earlier, but it slipped my mind. That little encryption device Lanara installed has been a big help. Makes this whole thing far less of a headache."

"I still can't get over that her daughter doesn't want to look like her," Jia commented.

"Hey, she's an AI. She can look however she wants to. Emma should be happy that she doesn't want to look like a Zitark." Erik pressed his PNIU to connect with the *Argo II* and play the message.

"I trust you two are well and have received this

message," Emma's hologram began. "I anticipate no difficulties adding you during this trip. I'll be sending you flight information for a rendezvous point that should keep our jump from being detected, though this..." She smiled thinly. "I think it's best I don't mention certain measures I'm taking to ensure your plausible deniability. The drones and repair bots you brought along last time are helpful, but there are a couple of things I'll want you to take a look at while you're aboard. See you soon."

"Every time I see Emma and her daughter, it gets me thinking," Jia commented.

"About what?" Erik asked.

Jia smiled. "There's enough space on our ship for a child."

Erik considered that for a long moment before nodding. "I think we should go see the heliokites and get started on the way back."

"Works for me." Jia gave him a warm smile. "Is this going to be our life? Traveling the UTC, exploring and meeting people?"

"Why the hell not?" Erik shrugged. "We've got enough money to do it. I don't know how long we'll have Emma, but we can still travel the old-fashioned way. Why? You bored?"

"With you?" Jia shook her head. "I don't think I'll ever be bored again."

Erik walked over and pulled Jia into an embrace, then kissed the top of her head. He'd never expected to meet someone like her, let alone as part of his revenge. She'd saved him, not just in fights but his soul. She'd given him something to live for after the Core was destroyed.

"Hey." Erik chuckled. "If it's a girl, I've got an idea for a name."

"What?" Jia asked.

"How about Julia?"

Jia jerked back and punched him in the arm. "Very funny."

"Sophia?"

Jia rolled her eyes. "We'll have to work on that."

Erik waved to her as she walked away. "No Yan or Tralian if they're boys?"

"Keep it up, Erik, and I'll leave you on a frontier moon," Jia shouted with a smile.

"You know me. Somehow I always find my way back."

THE END

This book is dedicated to Tammy Faxel
Who passed way too early in March of 2020 (not due to Covid.)

Thank you for not only reading to the end of book 12, but all the way through the author notes as well!

I would like to provide a bit of background on how the audio version of this story came to be and came to be earlier than the written part!

As many of you know, LMBPN Publishing hired my wife (Judith) to help with Marketing in 2017 (she ran International Marketing for many companies in the medical space, and foreign markets are a huge part of her expertise.)

Therefore, it should not have come as a surprise to me that during a Frankfurt Book Fair in 2018, she decided we were going to a party that was near our hotel room.

If you know anything about authors, *it's that we are generally not comfortable going to random parties.*

I am VERY much a normal author in this vein. I went

(with perhaps a bit of grumbling that was heard, and a significant amount of angst in my mind I didn't let out.)

This party would become the event where we were introduced to Tammy Faxel, a force of nature in charge of making deals and creating relationships with Midwest Tapes' Dreamscape Media (audio).

As fate would play, we would cross paths with Tammy at other events in New York and then the fateful London Book Fair.

<< Begin Judith Anderle's segment of these author notes. >>

"I'll take it!" those were the words Tammy uttered when during a lunch at the London Book Fair in April 2019.

Michael and I had randomly run into Tammy as we had planned to take one of the elevators from the second floor of the massive hall down to the first. Pretty soon, it would be time for lunch, and the two of us needed to get into line at the Pizza Express.

Tammy smiled when seeing us exit the elevator and moments later, we had plans for her to join us at lunch for Pizza.

"The Author" and I were discussing Michael's idea for what became this series, Opus X.

A series Michael wanted to launch in a novel way for LMBPN. Michael had written out the story line for the series, the premises for each of these twelve planned books and we had promotional images and concepts created from a recent professional model photoshoot.

What we *didn't* have was a launch plan, any actual book

covers, book titles, or even first drafts. Even so, after looking at the pictures and listening to Michael's ideas for the characters and the overall series premise, mid-way through lunch, Tammy said, "I will take all 12 books!"

We were stunned.

Michael and I looked at each other, thrilled at the fact that we would have an audio contract in place even before we even know exactly when we could launch.

With Tammy's support in place, we proceeded to recruit other industry leading companies to come together and help us draft a launch plan, tactics for reaching you, the readers, and ways in which we could be more impactful with our marketing messaging.

I know it has become redundant to say it, but sometimes, *all it takes is for someone to believe in your ideas or dreams for them to turn into successful projects.*

For Opus X, Tammy Faxel was our catalyst.

Could we have launched without her? Yes. But would Opus X be the series it is without Tammy's early support?

No.

Tammy believed in us early on, and for that, we will always be grateful.

<< END Judith's segment. >>

Tammy meant the world to us, and she had to have touched so many lives during her short 55 years here with us, but I figure she is making deals (or the equivalent) and I'll meet her again.

I'll drop a link to an article written in Publisher's Weekly about her at the end of the author notes.

WILL THERE BE MORE about Jia and Erik?

That's a good question. I often am asked about additional books, more series, other ideas for the couple, and to be transparent, I just don't know what comes next.

However, we are JUST getting started with the International marketing for this series. If you like it, don't hesitate to tell a couple of friends or give it a review at some point.

Opus X wasn't designed to be a large universe with hundreds of books. However, I happen to have a soft spot for the characters and the story. We have plans to get it into multiple languages (It is in English and now German) and did you know we are publishing in China as well?

That's a cool feeling for me because it's a ridiculously hard country to get a book to be available on their Internet Distribution Platforms.

I know there are hard times between our countries at the moment. I believe our people aren't the same as the politics and rhetoric above us.

I've been to China twice now. Twice to attend the Beijing Book Fair in 2018 and 2019, and while there the first time, we meet with a company to discuss possibly doing some toy models of our characters Bethany Anne (The Kurtherian Gambit) and Yum#uck (The Leira Chronicles).

Both times, it was a fantastic time and the people around us were fantastic. Many wearing the exact same clothes I might have purchased in California.

In short, I didn't feel much different than any other location I've been to around the world.

There are readers everywhere, and while I don't understand the Chinese language without help from my phone, one who loves to read is the same inside no matter the language they read, or the color of their skin.

I believe Opus X will continue to grow, and one day it will be 'the little series that DID accomplish amazing things.'

And everyone knows (am I right?) that when a movie or TV series does amazing things, the sequel is inevitable.

Ad Aeternitatem,

Michael Anderle

More about Tammy Faxel:

https://www.publishersweekly.com/pw/by-topic/
industry-news/Obituary/article/82952-obituary-
dreamscape-publisher-tammy-faxel.html

CONNECT WITH MICHAEL ANDERLE

Website: http://lmbpn.com

Email List: http://lmbpn.com/email/

Social Media:

https://www.facebook.com/LMBPNPublishing

https://twitter.com/MichaelAnderle

https://www.instagram.com/lmbpn_publishing/

https://www.bookbub.com/authors/michael-anderle

www.ingramcontent.com/pod-product-compliance
Lightning Source LLC
Chambersburg PA
CBHW020226110726
47898CB00004B/1170